Also by Stephanie McAfee

Diary of a Mad Fat Girl
Happily Ever Madder

DOWN AND OUT
IN BUGTUSSLE

◇◇◇

The Mad Fat Road to Happiness

Stephanie McAfee

 NEW AMERICAN LIBRARY

New American Library
Published by the Penguin Group
Penguin Group (USA) Inc., 375 Hudson Street,
New York, New York 10014, USA

USA | Canada | UK | Ireland | Australia | New Zealand | India | South Africa | China

Penguin Books Ltd., Registered Offices: 80 Strand, London WC2R 0RL, England
For more information about the Penguin Group visit penguin.com.

First published by New American Library,
a division of Penguin Group (USA) Inc.

First Printing, July 2013

REGISTERED TRADEMARK—MARCA REGISTRADA

LIBRARY OF CONGRESS CATALOGING-IN-PUBLICATION DATA:

McAfee, Stephanie.
Down and out in Bugtussle: the mad fat road to happiness/Stephanie McAfee.
p. cm
ISBN 978-0-451-23990-7
1. Female friendship—Fiction. 2. Family secrets—Fiction. 3. Grandmothers—Fiction.
4. Man-woman relationships—Fiction. 5. Mississippi—Fiction. I. Title.
PS3613.C2635D59 2013
813'6.—dc23   2013003874

Printed in the United States of America
10 9 8 7 6 5 4 3 2 1

Set in Carre Noir STD
Designed by Alissa Amell

PUBLISHER'S NOTE
This is a work of fiction. Names, characters, places, and incidents either are the product of
the author's imagination or are used fictitiously, and any resemblance to actual persons,
living or dead, business establishments, events, or locales is entirely coincidental.
The publisher does not have any control over and does not assume any responsibility for
author or third-party Web sites or their content.

To Mandi,
who entertained the character of Gloria Peacock
long before she had a story.
Thank you for always being there when I'm Down and Out.

DOWN AND OUT IN BUGTUSSLE

1

◇◇◇

From a distance, it looks better than it actually is: the starched white tablecloth, a carafe of red wine, the glass goblet candle-holder glowing amber against a terra-cotta wall. The ambiance is enchanting, the pesto is amazing, and sitting on the other side of that luscious chunk of rosemary bread is a fairly decent-looking fellow with neatly trimmed hair, light brown eyes, and a perfectly manicured goatee. He smiles. I smile. Dinner arrives. And then he launches into yet another idiotic spiel. "Have you ever envisioned the materialization of your most fantastical dreams?" he asks, smoothing the napkin on his lap with both hands. I have no desire to discuss my dreams—or my lack thereof—with a perfect stranger, but I welcome the odd turn of conversation, seeing as how he spent the past twenty minutes blathering about his mother. His eyes are locked on mine as he swirls linguine onto his fork.

"I'm sorry—have I what?" I say, looking down as I cut into my lasagna. I would attempt to change the subject, but I've gathered that whatever Mr. I Love Mommy wants to talk about, by golly, he's gonna talk about.

"Have you ever thought about how magnificent your life would be if your wildest dreams somehow came true?" He's peering at me like a Peeping Tom, no doubt trying to catch a glimpse of my bare-naked soul.

"Of course," I say. "Hasn't everyone?" I take a bite of lasagna while he continues to work those noodles and stare at me.

"So you have dreams?" he asks. I don't answer, and he continues. "Then you've imagined a marvelous existence with that man or that job and that house?" He's still moving the fork. Around and around. "Tell me your dreams, Graciela." His eyes are ripe with anticipation as they bore into mine.

"Again," I say, careful to hold his gaze, "please call me Ace."

"Tell me your dreams, Ace," he says without missing a beat. His fork is still twirling those damned noodles and his eyes are still locked on mine. I don't say anything, so he continues. "The verbalization of dreams makes our souls flourish with hope." He raises the perfectly wound ball of linguine to his lips, then stops. I think about reaching across the table and helping him get that fork into his mouth. "Share yours with me," he says quickly, and then finally takes a bite.

"You want to hear about my dreams?" I say with as little enthusiasm as possible. His eyes dance as he nods, and the way he's chewing his pasta is pissing me off. I think for a second about what to say and how to say it. And then, with great flourish, I begin.

"Once upon a time, I had a dream," I say, opening my eyes extra wide, "and what a spectacular dream it was. I imagined a splendid life with a handsome gent, a fanciful career, and a not-so-humble abode overlooking blue-green ocean water." I pause, and his pretty brown eyes are glimmering with expectation. He's swirling linguine again. "Then one day, the unthinkable happened!" And with all the dramatic intonation I can muster up, I say, "My dream came true."

"No!" he whispers, and I can't tell if he's shocked or disappointed. He keeps twirling noodles.

"Yes!" I whisper, and then return to my usual tone. "And that crap didn't turn out anything like I thought it would, so I packed up and moved back to reality." My date looks startled and a wee bit troubled. The linguine falls from his fork. He says nothing, so I continue. "I left the snow-white beaches of Pelican Cove, Florida, which was the actual physical location of this failed attempt to live my dream, on New Year's Day, and it was not the first, but rather the third, time I moved out of the ocean-view home belonging to Mason McKenzie, the love-of-what-turned-out-to-be-only-half-of-my-life." He crams a forkful of tangled noodles into his mouth and I keep going because I'm on a roll. "The first time, I stayed for six weeks, and when I left, it was my fault. The second time, I stayed for six months, and when I left, I had a better understanding of the legal term 'irreconcilable differences.' As a matter of fact, I had a better understanding of about a hundred thousand legal terms because when Mason wasn't at work, he was talking about work and, to be perfectly honest, it was exhausting."

"So your dream man was a lawyer?" Mr. Conversation Hog snaps before cramming another massive wad of pasta into his mouth.

"Is," I tell him, picking up a piece of bread and sopping it in olive oil. "He *is* a lawyer. And would you like to know something else?" He makes an awful face and I realize that I don't even re-member his name. "Mason McKenzie is a good guy," I tell whoever-he-is-over-there, "which is why I went back that third and final time to spend the holidays with him. I wanted to be sure we couldn't work things out, but sadly, those irreconcilable differences proved to be unresolvable, so we parted ways one last time and now I have no dream."

"You must have been chasing the wrong dream," he begins, and then, in an obvious attempt to recover his domination of the dia-logue, says, "One time I thought—"

"Oh, no," I say quickly, effectively blocking his shot at turning the conversational spotlight back his way. "My whole life, Mason was all I ever wanted. And I had him! I had him and I had my very own art gallery—which was a lovely building with a stunning view of the bay—and we lived in a khaki-and-cream-colored three-story stucco house one block from the Gulf of Mexico." I look across the table and see my date is cramming noodles into his mouth again. "I had it all," I say. He's looking at me now like he's in actual physical pain. "And little by little, bit by bit, my dream life let me down." I look down at my lasagna. "But there is some good news."

"What's that?" He's hustling more pasta onto his fork.

"Mason and I are still friends and I'm sure we always will be, but whoever came up with that line about the third time being a charm is full of shit." Several minutes pass during which the awkward si-lence swells. I take that opportunity to stare him down like he's been doing to me since we met at the door of this way-too-romantic-for-a-blind-date restaurant. He just sits there, chewing like a squirrel, look-ing back at me. Finally, I break the silence. "Yep," I say, and decide to entertain myself for a minute more. "The don't-mistake-me-for-a-model-citizen is back, and I'm sure the wanna-be-highbrows-with-overplucked-eyebrows couldn't be more pleased. You know what I mean?" He shakes his head and stares at me. His fork is still. "Neither do I," I say with a smile. I love the look on his face now. *Go tell this story to your damned mama,* I think as I continue. "But, hey! A few bad apples won't ruin the whole basket as long as they keep their rotten asses at a distance, right?" I smile at my date. I bet his mother has overplucked eyebrows.

"Uh, okay." He pushes his plate to the side and looks around for our waiter. "Check, please!" When the bill arrives, I consider giving him a twenty but decide against it. I think I earned my meal by sitting quietly through that series of painfully dull stories about his idyllic childhood and flawless mother. On the way out, he holds the door for me and says, "I'll call you," like men do when they think that's what you want to hear.

"Please don't," I say. "But thank you for dinner."

"Right," he says, and starts speed walking in the opposite direction.

"How'd the date go?" my pal Chloe asks when I call her on the way home.

"It was downright therapeutic," I tell her.

"So, not good?"

"Chloe!" I say. "This guy will never meet a woman he loves more than his mother."

"His mother is very nice."

"I think his mother might be the reason he's still single at thirty-seven!"

She sighs. "Well, I tried."

"And I appreciate that, Chloe. I really do. It was very thoughtful of you to fix me up on a blind date with this slightly good-looking yet somewhat dysfunctional guy." I pull onto the highway. "Just please believe me when I tell you that I'm not interested in dating right now."

"I can't help it!" Chloe cries. "I don't want you to spend the rest of your life alone."

"I moved home in January," I tell her. "It's the middle of March. Don't declare me a spinster just yet. What I need more than anything is some time to myself so I can think and sort things out inside my feeble brain."

"Okay," she says with a sigh.

"No more blind dates or I'll start adopting cats."

"See?" she whines. "That's what I'm worried about."

"Chloe Stacks! You know good and damned well that I would never get a cat!" I say, laughing. "Need I remind you that Buster Loo, superchiweenie, is and always will be the undisputed king of my castle? And I promise that the two of us are doing just fine."

"Ten or twelve cats wouldn't go over well with Buster Loo," Chloe says in her I'm-trying-so-hard-to-joke-but-I'm-really-serious voice.

"Right," I say, feigning earnestness. "And that's what I would do, too. I wouldn't start with one cat or even two. If I decide to become a cat lady, you can bet I'll be the cattiest cat lady around." I pause. "I'll go adopt fifteen or twenty. At least."

Finally, a giggle. "Okay, so I'll see you on Monday morning, then?"

"I'll be there with bells on."

"Let's hope not."

2

◇◇◇

Monday morning, I pound on the alarm clock with my fist until it falls behind the nightstand. The racket upsets Buster Loo, who pokes his snout out from under the covers at the foot of the bed and growls. "Sorry to disturb you, Buster Loo," I say as he nestles back into his warm spot. I roll out of bed and tell myself that everything is going to be just fine. I can do this.

After a steamy shower, a hot cup of coffee, and a rather ineffective self–pep talk, I decide it's time to get dressed. I walk into the guest room and pick up the pants I ironed last night. When I put them on, I discover that they won't zip. *Great,* I think. *Should've tried those on first.* I head back to my closet and dig through my "teacher clothes" for the hundredth time. After several minutes of pure, unadulterated frustration, I locate a pair of black pants that I think will work. It's the "big" pair reserved only for "fat" days. I take a deep breath and slip them on. It takes some huffing and puffing, but I finally get the bastards zipped. Who knew that two and a half months of wearing nothing but sweatpants would put such a strain on the ol' buttonholes?

I walk back to the guest room and iron the fat pants. Thank goodness the shirt I picked out is a pullover made of loose, flowing fabric. I kick my shoes around to where I can slip them on because God knows I don't need to bend over and pop that button off my pants. Along with my nerves, it's in enough of a strain already.

"Wish me luck, Buster Loo!" I say to my chiweenie who is still buried under the covers. A muffled "ruff" is his reply.

I go in the kitchen, get a Diet Mountain Dew out of the fridge, and stick a bottle of water in my purse. I pick up my keys and walk out the door. Pissed off and ridiculously uncomfortable in my tight-ass pants, I drive to Bugtussle High School for my first official day on the job as a permanent substitute teacher.

It feels strange turning into the parking lot, because the last time I was here, I'd just quit my job after being fired by my former principal, Catherine Hilliard, who was having an affair she thought no one knew about. But I knew all about it, and when she became privy to that information, she no longer wanted me out of there, but out that door I went anyway. She ended up resigning in order to keep her gross and disgusting affair with former superintendent Ardie Griffith a secret and, although leaving town with him in the middle of the night might not have been the best way to keep that under wraps, I'm glad that they're both gone. As I'm pulling into my old parking space, I remember it's not mine anymore and go park at the other end of the lot. I get out of my car, depressed by the fact that I didn't even last a year away from this place. I walk in the side door next to the cafeteria and report to the conference room where

Chloe Stacks, Bugtussle High School academic counselor, is wait-ing for me with a nice, neat stack of folders.

"Hey, what are you doing in here? I thought Mrs. Moore han-dled all this business." I take a seat and pray that my zipper has the strength to hold it together for the rest of the day.

"She does, but Mr. Byer asked me to help her with this particu-lar task because we've had some issues this year."

"What kind of issues?" I ask, not sure I even want to know. I tug at the band of my pants, wishing they would give a little and ease the squeeze on my waistline.

"Very frustrating and time-consuming issues," she says.

"Alrighty then." I take a shallow breath and tell myself to stay positive. "So how's the house coming along?" Chloe recently pur-chased a very nice lake home for herself all by herself, and even though I thought it was the most beautiful thing I'd ever seen in-side and out, Chloe saw much room for improvement. Maybe she just wanted to make it hers because the last deed that bore her name also bore that of Richard Stacks, her abusive, controlling, and unbelievably unfaithful ex-husband, whom Lilly and I eventually managed to run out of town, divorce papers in hand. It wasn't an easy thing to do and we had to pull a few shenanigans, but we got the job done.

Chloe's chattering away about the renovations when she stops talking and lowers her voice to a whisper. "Oh my goodness. Have I told you the latest Jackson family news?"

"Don't think so."

"Tate got transferred back to Tupelo."

"J.J.'s older brother?" I ask, and she nods. "I haven't seen him in years. How is he?"

"He's awful. Just awful. You know, I met him at Christmas and I didn't exactly love him, but I was like, *Okay, it's the holidays—he's probably just had too much eggnog, so just be nice.* Well, it wasn't the eggnog!"

"No?" I try not to smile. When Chloe finds someone she doesn't like, it's a rare moment and I want it to last.

"No," she says, whispering. "He came by my house Saturday morning and J.J. wasn't even there! My doorbell rang and I opened the door and there was Tate Jackson. Said he was just stopping by to see how the renovations were going. Like he's my contractor or something!"

"So was it a promotion or a demotion that brought him back this way?"

"Oh, it's a promotion. He's like the sales manager for the whole southeastern United States now, so he basically gets to pick where he wants to live. Fortunately, his job will require a lot of travel. He told me all of this while he was inspecting my new gutters."

"So is he married?"

Chloe stares at me. "Of course not. He has the maturity level of a sixteen-year-old."

"Sounds like my kind of guy," I say, and I'm only partly joking. Tate Jackson was a hottie back in the day.

"Right," she says. "Because you'd love to date a man who owns a stuffed fox and two dozen mounted deer head?" She shivers with disgust. "And don't even get me started on those disgusting fish that are, as we speak, sitting in J.J.'s garage along with all the rest of his junk. All except for the fox. It had to be kept inside, so it's in J.J.'s living room."

"Really?"

"Yes, really! He's staying with J.J. until he finds a house."

I can't help myself. That makes me laugh out loud. "Why don't you and J.J. just move in with each other already? I mean, y'all practically live together as it is."

"You know we have to be married first."

"You're so old-fashioned."

"I am not!" she snaps. "That's the way it's supposed to be! If you and Mason had just gotten married instead of shacking up down there, you might still be there."

"And I would be miserable," I remind her. "Can we just leave that in the past where it belongs? Please. Do you have any idea how relieved I was when I pulled back into the driveway of Gramma Jones's house and put my stuff back in my old bedroom? I never want to leave there again. I don't even want to go on vacation. Right or wrong, I'm happy to be home, okay?"

"I'm sorry, Ace. I shouldn't have said that."

"It's okay," I tell her. "You're all fired up about Tate and his taxidermy collection."

"You know, I don't understand why he couldn't stay with his parents or with their sister. Okay, his sister has a family, so I do understand that, but I don't know why he couldn't just stay with their parents."

"Maybe they're allergic to deceased animals," I say. Chloe ignores me.

"Why didn't he just stay in Birmingham? J.J. says he has a nice house on a golf course. Now he has to sell it. This just upsets the balance of my life."

"He's a golfer?"

"Oh, yeah, he's a regular outdoorsman," she says with more than a hint of contempt.

"You really don't like this guy, do you?"

"I really don't. And you know, I try really hard to like people, but he just rubs me the wrong way."

"If he's as good-looking as he used to be, he could rub me the right way," I say, grinning.

"He's not. Now stop saying stuff like that before I vomit."

"Just keep in mind what you always tell me," I say. "Things are never as bad as they seem."

"Well, that was before Tate moved home," she says. She looks at the folders again. "I wish you wouldn't do this, Ace. I wish you would just go to summer school and get certified to teach another subject."

"Like what?" I ask. "P.E.?" Maybe I could wear my sweatpants every day.

"Or psychology. Mrs. Webster is retiring and we're adding another block of classes in the fall, so there will be two openings in that department." She looks at me with those big brown eyes. "Subbing is such a big step down for someone who used to teach here."

"Don't snub the sub," I say, and she rolls her eyes.

"I'm concerned," Chloe says.

"About what?"

"That doing this might not be the best way to get your job back from Cameron Becker."

"Chloe," I say, "not only have I weaseled my way back into the good graces of the school board by taking a position that no one in her right mind would accept, but I could also use the cash.

You might have noticed we're having a bit of a cold spell and running the heat is not cheap. Besides, no one knows why I'm really here."

"Your motive will be crystal clear to anyone with half a brain."

"No, it won't," I tell her. "Just tell me who I'm working with and what hallway I'm in and I'll be on my merry little way."

"You'll be working with Stacey Dewberry."

"Who is Stacey Dewberry?"

"She's your rotation partner for the rest of the year."

"Yeah, I got that part, but who is she?"

"Oh," Chloe says, and I can tell by the look on her face that there's something she doesn't want to tell me. "You'll just have to meet her."

"What's that supposed to mean?"

"Nothing." Chloe lowers her voice to a whisper. "She's very, uh, unique, and she's had some trouble adjusting, I guess you might say, to the high school environment."

"Are you kidding me, Chloe? Is she a fruitcake? You better not stick me with a freakin' fruitcake." Chloe smiles that sweet, pitiful smile of hers. "Chloe?"

"She could really use a friend like you, Ace," she says. "And since you're dead set on being here anyway, you might as well take this small opportunity to do something good for someone who desperately needs a break. The kids make fun of her and she tries too hard and even I think she's too serious about her job. She's had a rough time, Ace, but she still shows up every morning with a smile on her face, and it would be so nice if you could ease a little of her pain and help her fit in." She smiles at me. "Please."

"Why can't you just put me with Mrs. Jennings?" I moan.

"First of all, you know she's in your—I mean, Ms. Becker's hallway."

"Can you not call it that? Call it Coach Hatter's hallway if you must assign it to someone."

"Mrs. Jennings and Mrs. Sable are in C Hall and D Hall like they have been since before we started working here. I'm just helping out with A Hall and B Hall. That's it. I don't have anything to do with what goes on in all the other hallways, and even if I did, it would be horribly tacky to suggest a change like that with only nine weeks left in the school year."

"Fine," I say. "Sorry."

"Thank you," Chloe says. "You will be covering A Hall and B Hall with Ms. Dewberry and, just so you know, Cameron Becker has a very good friend in A Hall, so don't say anything around him that you don't want getting back to her." She looks at me. "And don't use that to your advantage."

"Anyone I know?"

"Probably not," she says slowly. "His name is Freddie Dublin and, like Ms. Becker, this is his first year teaching."

"What does he teach?"

"Drama," she says.

"Okay," I say, making a mental note to try to buddy up with him the first chance I get. "So, what happened to the person who had this job before me?"

"I mentioned some issues . . . ," she says.

"And?"

"Well, the first person we hired asked to be transferred to another hallway because he claimed Stacey Dewberry was sexually harassing him. When I told him he'd have to file a report and we'd have to have a hearing before the school board, he told me he didn't want to do that and then he quit. The second person asked to be transferred to another school, but that was because of Mr. Dublin, and the most recent, a girl who started in January, well, she just stopped showing up after a few weeks." Chloe sighs. "And we've had a string of temporary subs in and out since mid-February, and it's been a mess because, as you know from experience, everything works better when we have the same people on rotation all the time."

"Well, you can depend on me to see this job through until the bitter end," I tell her. "And I promise not to start any trouble. I'll stay away from Freddie Dublin or be so disgustingly nice to him that it'll make us all sick." I smile and so does Chloe. "So, please, bring in my new partner in crime. I'm sorry, what I meant to say was education."

Chloe shakes her head and walks over to the intercom where she presses a button and pages Ms. Stacey Dewberry. Five minutes later, there's a knock on the conference room door. I sit up straight in my chair, curious about my new coworker.

"Be nice, Ace," Chloe whispers as she walks to the door. "And don't judge her until you get to know her."

"Oh come on, Chloe," I whisper. "She can't be that bad."

Chloe opens the door. "How are you today, Ms. Dewberry?" she asks sweetly.

"Oh, I'm fine as frog hair, Mrs. Stacks," Stacey Dewberry says with a big lopsided smile.

"Won't you join us?" Chloe asks, returning to her seat at the table.

"Sure thing!" Stacey says with a bit too much gusto. I sit and stare, unable to say a word. I take in the outfit, piece by piece, as my new partner crosses the conference room and takes a seat at the table. She has on floral stirrup pants with a green V-neck sweater that's layered over a hot pink turtleneck. There appear to be shoulder pads involved somewhere, probably in the sweater, which aren't working for her unless she got up this morning wanting to look like a linebacker for the New Orleans Saints. She's definitely more of a Fatty Patty than a Skinny Minnie, and her hair, which I have to force myself to stop staring at, is hot rolled and teased to the max. As she approaches the table, I fully expect her to whip out a boom box and ask me if I'm down with O.P.P. I'm slightly disappointed when she doesn't. After she takes the seat across from me, I notice that she has very nice features, but I can't really focus on the sea green eyes and Barbie doll nose because I'm so thoroughly distracted by that hair.

"You must be Ms. Jones," she says, jabbing a hand my way. I notice she has rings on every finger and one thumb.

"Nice to meet you," I say, smiling way more than I should.

Chloe immediately starts going over the schedule, after which Stacey informs me that she will be happy to show me around the teachers' lounge. When Chloe mentions that I taught at Bugtussle High for almost six years, poor Stacey turns bright red and my heart aches over her embarrassment.

"What did you teach?" she asks, not looking up.

"Art," I say.

"Oh, so you want your old job back?" she says, making a full recovery.

Chloe gives me a not-so-subtle I-told-you-so look while I say, "Oh, no, I'm just trying to make a little money on the side while I put in applications elsewhere. And I'm thinking about going to summer school and getting certified to teach psychology." Chloe rolls her eyes.

"I'm thinking about going to summer school, too," Stacey Dewberry tells me, still smiling.

"Ms. Dewberry is only one semester away from earning her bachelor's degree," Chloe gushes.

"Oh really?" I say. "When did you start working on it?"

"In 1993," she replies. "But I dropped out in 'ninety-seven, halfway through my senior year." She looks at the floor. "Bad experience with student teaching."

"Oh," I say. I glance over at Chloe who is looking at Stacey Dewberry like she wants to give her a big, sappy hug. "Student teaching is tough," I say, and Chloe nods.

"Did you do it?" Stacey asks me.

"No. I went for a bachelor's in art history, then took a test to get my license," I say. "Maybe you could do that instead of student teaching." I look at Chloe, who frowns at me.

"I tried that," she says. "Took the test three times."

"Oh, I'm sorry," I say. Chloe is shaking her head at me now.

"Ain't no thing but a chicken wing," Stacey says, only "thing" and "wing" come out "thang" and "wang." Chloe grimaces and I hold my breath for a second so I don't giggle. Stacey continues. "I have to finish my degree first anyway, so I just consider the tests I already took to be some really expensive practice." Chloe is smiling again. At Stacey. Not at me. "My transcript is under review right now by the University of Alabama because I don't know if they'll let me use the credits I earned back then or not."

"Well, they should," Chloe says.

"Yes," I say. "They certainly should."

"If I don't have to start all over from scratch, I'm moving to Tuscaloosa this summer and finishing that bad boy up. Finally gonna be a college graduate." She grins. "Roll Tide!"

"Roll Tide! Go Bama!" I say with a fist pump that draws another sharp look from Chloe. I decide to tone it down. "So, what do you want to teach?"

"My certification will be in music, and I'd really like to work with the band."

"That sounds like a great plan," I say, and then the bell rings to begin first period. I look at Chloe. "Man, I haven't heard that sound in a while."

"I know," Stacey says with a snort. "It totally took some getting used to for me, too."

I look at Chloe. She smiles and tells us both to have a good day. Stacey Dewberry and I leave the conference room and make our way through the crowded lobby to the double doors of A Hall.

3

<><><><><><><><><><><><><><><><><><><><><><><><><><><><><><><><><><><><><><>

Several students speak to me as I make my way down the hall-way. Some teachers smile and wave; others pretend not to see me.

"Who are you covering for today?" Stacey asks.

"Mrs. Davis."

"She has pretty good classes, except fifth period is a little rowdy and—" She presses her lips together and looks at me, clearly uncertain about finishing her sentence. I raise my eyebrows and nod, inviting her to continue, and so she does. "I'll tell you the truth, Ace—uh, Ms. Jones. Her third-period class is awful. Just awful. It's all eleventh and twelfth graders, and the last time I was in there, they all started acting crazy! Plumb crazy, I tell ya! They were tripping and falling all over the place. It was terrible. They knocked over a bunch of desks and I had to call Mr. Byer on the intercom. He put a bunch of them in detention, so they all got mad at me.

Like it was my fault they started acting like loony zoo animals." She looks around, I assume, to make sure no one is eavesdropping on our conversation, and, sure enough, not a soul appears to be concerned about what the substitute teachers might be discussing. "And that first period is a first-class pain in the bamboozle," she whispers.

"Bamboozle?" She doesn't answer, just points to her floral-clad rump. "Oh," I say, nodding. I glance at her, careful to keep my eyes off that hair. "Whose room are you in?"

"Mr. Tad's," she says with a smile. "He has small classes, so I'll have an easy day."

We part ways at Mr. Tad's door and I head down to Mrs. Davis's room. When I walk in, the students get quiet, which is seriously not normal. In the silence, I start to feel apprehensive about my decision to come back here and do this. Some of the kids recognize me, a few speak, and there is a lot of whispering going on. Just as the tardy bell rings, five students hustle into the room. Four rush to sit down and one stops to glare at me.

"Who are you and where is Mrs. Davis?" she demands.

"I'm Ms. Jones and Mrs. Davis is out today," I say with a smile.

"Where is she?" the girl asks. She props her hand up on her hip and scowls at me.

"I'm sorry, what's your name?" I ask.

"Brittany Franks," she announces with no small amount of pageantry. "Who are you again?"

"I'm Ms. Jones." I make a show of looking through the sub folder. "Well, Ms. Franks, I'm sorry, but Mrs. Davis didn't leave you a personal message explaining her whereabouts." I give her my best

I'm-so-not-impressed-with-your-attitude glare. "So why don't you take a seat?"

Her fellow classmates snigger as Brittany Franks rolls her eyes and goes to the back of the room. Another student yells that Brittany isn't sitting in her assigned seat, so I go through the folder until I find the seating chart. When I pull that out and hold it up for them to see, I don't have to say a word. They automatically rearrange themselves. Except Brittany Franks, whom I have to threaten with detention before she moves to her assigned seat.

Second period is Mrs. Davis's planning time, so, thank the good Lord in heaven, I'm off for forty-five minutes. I piddle around online for a little while, trying to distract myself from how tight these pants are, then text my pal Lilly Lane and ask her when she has lunch. Like me, Lilly graduated from Bugtussle High School back in 19-and-let's-not-say-when. Then we moved to Starkville and enrolled in Mississippi State University, and that's where we met Chloe. After Lilly graduated from college, she took off to pursue the magic of her dreams and spent a few very profitable years on the modeling circuit. When she got tired of the hustle and bustle, she moved back to Bugtussle and immediately landed a job teaching French, which isn't the most difficult thing to do because foreign language teachers tend to be in short supply in northeast Mississippi.

Lilly Lane hails from a wonderful and beautiful family, all of whom make living life look splendid and easy. Her handsome and distinguished father is a big shot at a furniture company in Tupelo, her lovely and petite mother runs the only investment firm in town, and her sexy older brother is halfway through a highly decorated army career. They're just a perfect freakin' success story whose only dysfunction is how normal they are. I've often wondered how her parents got everything so right and how they have such a seemingly trouble-free existence. They must make a lot of good decisions. Like hundreds and hundreds of consecutively good decisions.

Sometimes I wonder what my life would be like if my parents were still around. If it would be different or if I would be different. I wonder what it would've been like had we stayed in my mother's hometown of Nashville, Tennessee, rather than moving to my father's hometown of Bugtussle, Mississippi. Certainly my mom would've been much happier during that last year of her life. She didn't like Bugtussle. She didn't fit in. And she didn't want to, either. Perhaps they would still be around, because if we'd just stayed in Nashville, they wouldn't have been on the road coming back from there like they were the day the accident happened. I stare at the digital clock on Mrs. Davis's desk, fully aware that mulling over the "what-ifs" and "maybes" is a colossal waste of time, but sometimes I just can't help myself.

I remember standing in that funeral home where so many strange people kept hugging me and saying things like, "Everything happens for a reason" and "When it's your time to go, it's your time to go." I didn't believe that crap then and, to this very day, I think those comments were creepy and sadistic. I mean, I don't think God orchestrated a series of unfortunate events because the angels up in heaven desired the company of Jake and Isabella Jones. Likewise, I don't believe the Lord grabbed the steering wheel and jerked a truck into the front of my parents' car. The poor guy driving the truck was just trying not to run over a little old lady standing on the side of the road whose car had broken down. The whole thing was just bad luck and wretched timing. I fail to see any strokes of divinity or rationale in what happened, but whatever. People believe what suits them best and cling to whatever makes them feel the most comfortable while failing to consider that everyone doesn't experience life on planet Earth the same way they do. At least when it happened, I already had a year in down here, so when I had to pack up my room and move in with Gramma Jones, it wasn't that far of a ride. And at least I already had a few friends in place. One of those friends was Lilly Lane, who dutifully stood beside me while all of those people imparted what they mistook for words of comfort.

I pick up my phone and see that Lilly has texted back "3L," which I interpret to mean third lunch, which sucks because I have first. My phone buzzes again with abbreviated instructions to call her after school because she can't wait to hear all about my first day on the job as a permanent substitute teacher. Then she sends me one final message, which says, "Avoid Freddie D." I would like for her to elaborate on that, but the bell rings to end second period and I have to go stand in the hallway next to Mrs. Davis's door.

Much to my relief, I don't have any trouble with third period because more than half the class have been students of mine at some point in the past. Since most of them liked me and my class, I take that opportunity to put in a good word for my new friend, Stacey Dewberry. I'm not sure anyone takes it to heart, but at least I can tell Chloe I tried.

Fourth period is a long and drawn-out affair because as soon as I take attendance, I have to escort my class of twenty-six freshmen to the cafeteria. I join Stacey Dewberry at a teacher table off to the side and, after a quick recap of her day thus far, she proceeds to tell me about her alphabetized collection of vintage cassette tapes, which are, as we speak, in a special crush-proof carrying case tucked safely into the trunk of her 1989 Iroc-Z28. I'm very intrigued by this tidbit of information and start quizzing her about her favorite types of music. I'm not surprised when she rolls off the token big hair bands of the 1980s—Poison, Guns N' Roses, Def Leppard, and Mötley Crüe—but I am somewhat surprised when she tells me how many concerts she's been to and then proceeds to rank the shows according to venue, band visibility, and sound quality. She surprises me again when she tells me that she worked in the ticket office of the Rock and Roll Hall of Fame for three years.

"Is that in Ohio?" I ask her.

"Cleveland," she says. "Right on the shore of Lake Erie. Beautiful place."

"So did you meet any famous people while you were there?"

"No, but I did have my picture taken with every single figure in Madame Tussauds Wax Museum."

What? I think, struggling to make the connection. "In New York?"

"Yes. I lived there for a couple months after I left Cleveland. Just got a wild hair up the crapper one day." She looks like she's thinking hard about something. "Don't remember what year that was, but I do remember that I got my income tax check in the mail and then just decided to pick up and move to the Big Apple." She looks at me. "I didn't know a soul, but I met a lot of really interesting people. Living in the city was exciting, but not always in a good way, if you know what I mean." I don't know what she means, but I try to imagine. She's focusing on her corn chips now. "Anyway, it wasn't for me. Lots to do, but I couldn't take the crowds. Plus I was paying three arms and a leg to rent a place smaller than a porta potty." She looks at me again. "And, as you can see, I only have two arms, which means I couldn't afford it, so I ended up leaving after a few weeks."

"So, where all have you lived?" I ask, and can't help but wonder whether she's making this stuff up.

"Where all have I not lived?" she says with a chortle. "My parents were hippies, so I lived all up and down the West Coast when I was little." Okay, so now I'm really starting to think she's spinning a yarn, but I do my best to maintain a look of genuine interest as she continues. "Then when I was seven, my mom OD'd and my dad sent me to live with my grandparents in Alabama." She shakes her head and looks out the window while I sit there and hope that maybe she did make that part up. "I hadn't been to school, so I had to start a year behind. Never heard from my dad again. Don't know if he's dead or alive. Went to college on a Pell grant and did a pretty good job up until my senior year and that god-awful student-teaching experience." The thought crosses my mind that everything happens for a reason. I start wondering if maybe I had lost my parents so I could be more empathetic to this poor old girl with purple eyeliner and hot-rolled hair who didn't have her mom for as long as I did and doesn't even know what happened to her dad. Bullshit! Maybe we were destined to be friends. More bullshit! She's still talking. "Then I took the money I had left over from the grant and what little I'd saved working part-time at Papaw's feed store, and I took off."

I watch as Stacey Dewberry digs the last few corn chips out of a Ziploc bag. There's so much I want to say to her, so much I want to ask, but the bell rings to end first lunch and we have to get up and get going.

"Wait a minute," I say as we walk toward the gigantic garbage cans next to the cafeteria dish window. "How in the world did you end up in Bugtussle, Mississippi?"

"Well, I was on a pilgrimage of sorts," she says, tossing her lunch trash. "I'd moved back home to Centreville again—that's south and a little bit east of Tuscaloosa—and was staying with my grandmother, just trying to figure out what my next move should be. Then one day I saw something on TV about an Elvis festival in Tupelo and I knew that was where I was going next. I went and pawned an engagement ring I'd been hanging on to for a couple of months and off I went. Had to sleep in my car, but I didn't care." She glances at me as we make our way through the crowd of students. "I have a very nice body pillow that I keep in the car and my backseats lie down, so it's nice and flat back there. Anyway, after the festival, I was really feeling the Elvis vibe, so I decided to go on to Memphis and see Graceland while I was at it. I'd stopped to get some gas at the Pack-a-Poke and had just walked into the beer cooler when I met what I thought was my soul mate and anyway, to make a long story short, I ended up moving here." She looks at me. "I wasn't buying beer. I don't drink beer. I just went in there to stand for a minute 'cause it was hotter than Hades outside and the AC had gone bonkers in my car and I had to have some cool air." She shakes her head. "T-tops can do only so much in a triple-digit heat wave."

"So you have a boyfriend?" I ask.

"Oh, no, that didn't even last a month," she says. "Turned out he was the kind of guy who expected a lot out of his girlfriend. Like he wanted them to have a job or two, cook all the time, stock the fridge with beer, and keep his trailer clean. All while he sat on the couch all day every day watching *Cops* with a can in his hand."

"So he didn't have a job?"

"He was drawing disability, but I'll tell you right now that he's a heck of lot more lazy than he is crazy. But he did a fine job of making me crazy, which is why I had to ditch that fool." We pause to let a group of students come out of A Hall. I see a handsome fellow, tall and lean, lagging behind the group. I imagine it must be the notorious Freddie Dublin. I tune Stacey out as I watch him walk by. His dark hair looks like it was styled by a professional and he's wearing a striped button-up neatly rolled above the elbows with dark gray pants. He catches me looking, raises one eyebrow, and turns his head. Slightly embarrassed, I turn my attention back to Stacey, who is still yapping away.

"So by then I already had this job and thought I'd better keep it because, as I mentioned this morning, I'd like to finish my degree and maybe get a job as a real teacher, and I think this would be good experience and look good on my resume." She glances at me. "It's been hard, but I've stuck it out and learned a lot."

"That's good," I tell her. "Being a sub is definitely one of the best ways to get a teaching job." Or to get one back, I hope. She keeps rambling as we walk under the giant A and into our hallway.

"Yeah, so I found a little house to rent and took out a quick cash loan on my car so I'd have the money to pay all the deposits and first two months' rent. About a week after I moved in, Joe Red somehow found out where I was staying and came over. He wanted to kiss and make up and then asked me if I'd buy us front-row tickets to a monster truck show that was coming to town. Can you believe that?" I tell her I can't. She continues. "I told him I didn't think I would and that was our last fight. Haven't seen him since." She sighs and her shoulders slump a little, pads and all. "I should've known better than to get involved with a guy buying a case of Old Milwaukee at ten a.m. on a Monday." She shakes her head. "But I ignored that rip-roaring red flag and now here I am and that's how I got to Bugtussle."

"Well, that is quite a story," I say, stopping at Mrs. Davis's door. I realize that we've walked right past Mr. Tad's classroom.

"Yeah, you can tell me your story next time," she says, and I can see that sharing hers has taken some of the wind out of her sails. Or maybe she's just exhausted from all that nonstop talking.

"Oh, you don't want to hear mine. It'd be dull and boring compared to yours," I say in an exaggerated tone that makes her smile. "Have a good rest of the day."

"You do the same," she says with a little wave. She turns to walk back to her assigned classroom and I reluctantly step into mine. I stand behind the podium and watch the students file in, thinking that I'd rather have my face hot-glued to the dry erase board than be in this classroom with these pants on for the next three and a half hours.

Fourth period creeps by at a snail's pace, fifth turns out to be another class of rowdy freshmen, and sixth is a class of somewhat-less-rambunctious sophomores. Seventh is freshmen again, and they are buck wild and crazy from start to finish. I wonder why Stacey didn't mention this group to me, because they are, by far, the rowdiest and most noncompliant of the day. When the bell finally rings at 3:05, I'm seriously questioning my decision to be a permanent substitute teacher. Sitting in my car waiting for the buses to leave, I text Lilly and tell her I'll have to call her tomorrow. Today I have to go home, get these damned pants off, take a long nap and then drink lots of cold beer.

When the buses finally pull out, I bark a tire out of there and don't care who sees me. I drive home like a bat out of hell and turn into my driveway on two wheels. I hop out of the car and unbutton my pants on the way to the door. When I get inside, I go straight to the laundry room and dig a pair of cutoff sweatpants out of the dryer. I take off my bra, which had also started to squeeze me in all the wrong places, and put on a tank top and a sweatshirt. I go to the kitchen, get two beers out of the fridge, and retire to the living room where I plop down on the sofa. After turning on the television, I realize I can't stand the racket, so I hit the mute button and close my eyes for a second. I prop my feet up on the couch and drink my beer in silence. Buster Loo creeps out from behind the love seat and joins me on the couch. He nudges my hand with his snout. I put the beer on the end table, pick him up, and give him a good hug.

"Oh, I love him," I say, and he gets excited. "Oh, I love him so much. He's a good dog." Buster Loo gives me a quick lick on the cheek, then leaps off my lap and starts running in circles around the living room while I tell him what a good boy he is. That makes me laugh, which makes me feel better. Buster Loo is good at that. After three beers and a few rounds of indoor speedy-dog fetch, I feel like I might be able to get up and go back to work tomorrow.

I walk into the kitchen and think about what I want for dinner. What I need more than anything is some of Gramma Jones's creamy chicken noodle soup. I dig through the pantry until I find her cookbook, which is a small binder filled with recipes written on note cards. I flip to the soup section, and the recipe I'm looking for is the second card on the page. I reach under the cabinet and get the pot she always used. I wonder what she would think of my using canned chicken instead of boiling a fresh breast like she always did. She'd probably think my soup wasn't quite as good as hers. And she would be right.

Sometimes I think I should box up all of these old pots and pans and dishes and go buy myself some new ones, but then I remember how happy it makes me to be in this kitchen with all her stuff: plates I've eaten on since I was a child; a cast-iron skillet that belonged to her grandmother; the old wooden spoon she always used to stir the sugar into the tea. It all gives me a sense of security that I don't think belongs in a box in the attic. Not to mention that when I donated her old living room furniture to Goodwill several years ago, it took me almost two weeks to get over it. I line the ingredients up on the counter and smile, thinking I'll just hang on to my old-fashioned kitchen goods. I flip the pot over and look at the bottom. *Revere Ware Clinton, Illinois.* A stamp like that might be hard to find these days.

4

◇◇

Tuesday is a repeat of Monday, too-tight pants, smart-ass Brittany and all, and the only thing keeping my spirits from going into a nosedive is that the weather has warmed ever so slightly.

I drive home with the windows down and find my faithful companion, Buster Loo, snoozing in the backyard. When I open the gate, he spins onto his paws in one swift motion and then runs across the yard to greet me. I scoop him up and take him inside where he wiggles out of my arms and runs to the front door.

"Buster Loo wanna go for a walk?" I ask him, and he starts jumping up at his leash. "Just a minute, little buddy." I run back to the bedroom and put on some fleece pants and a long-sleeve Bugtussle Rockets T-shirt. When I get back to the foyer, Buster Loo is still bouncing like a basketball. I grab his leash and we head out the door to the park.

I call Lilly and tell her about my two terrible days, and then we get off on the subject of Stacey Dewberry.

"And, boy, she can chatter," I say. "Ask one simple question, and she'll tell you all kinds of crazy stuff."

"Poor thing," Lilly says. "I've overheard other teachers making fun of her. I feel sorry for her."

"I do, too," I say. "Today she told me an awful story about a kitten she had when she was little. She said it followed her inside one day, but she didn't know it was behind her until she slammed its tail in the door and then her grandma had to take it to the vet and get its tail amputated." Lilly starts sniggering. "What are you laughing about? That was not a funny story!"

"I know. I'm sorry. I was just imagining you sitting there listening to that," she says.

"I know," I say. "It's nuts. She's kind of pitiful, but then she's kind of not because she's so freakin' cool in her own outrageously weird way."

"That ball of hair on her head is not cool," Lilly says. "God bless it."

"Well, I didn't mean her hair. I meant her," I say, and then tell Lilly about the alphabetized cassette tapes. She doesn't believe me until I ask her if she's seen the black Iroc-Z28 with what has to be illegal tint on the windows parked in the teachers' parking lot. "That's her car!"

"You have got to be kidding me," Lilly says. "Did she get it when she graduated from high school?"

"No, she got it ten years after she graduated when the car was fourteen years old, and she's been driving it ever since. She said it was her dream car."

"That's hilarious," she says. "But it is a pretty badass car."

"I want to ride around in it sometime. With the T-tops out, listening to a Whitesnake CD—oops, I mean tape."

"Ace! Don't you start making fun of her, too."

"I'm not making fun," I say. "I'm dead serious. I think Stacey Dewberry knows how to have a good time. During afternoon break today, she was telling me that she goes honky-tonking all the time. Then she invited me to come along this weekend. I hated to say no, but I just don't think I'm ready for that kind of excitement right now."

"If you go out honky-tonkin' with Stacey Dewberry, you better invite me, because that's a trip I don't wanna miss!" Lilly says. "So have you had the displeasure of running into Freddie D. yet?"

"Only in passing," I tell her.

"You should probably stay away from him," she says.

"Why are you and Chloe so concerned about me having a conversation with him? Is he really that wicked?"

"It's not that he's wicked. It's that he's buddy-buddy with Cameron Becker, and you don't need to make any waves there or you'll never get your job back. Plus he's a bit of an instigator, and we all know how you get around people like that. Just try not to get tangled up in a conversation with him, because he'll manipulate you into saying something and then twist it around and start a bunch of crap. He's established quite a reputation for himself as a troublemaker, and we both know you don't need any trouble right now."

"We might like each other."

"Yeah, I'm sure you wouldn't," she says, sarcastically. "Chloe said that Stacey Dewberry nailed you first thing, and if she can figure out you're trying to get your job back, then, yeah, I'm pretty sure it won't go unnoticed by Freddie Dublin. He's sharp as a tack. I don't see y'all being friends at all."

"Are you saying I'm not sharp as a tack?" I ask, teasing.

"I'm not joking, Ace. He'll be onto you in a heartbeat if you try to pull something."

"What would I try to pull?" I ask, wondering what I could pull on Freddie Dublin to make him like me better than Cameron Becker.

"Can you hear me rolling my eyes at that question?"

"Fine," I say, smiling. "So how did he and Ms. Becker get to be such big buddies in the first place?"

"I don't know. Both first-year teachers, I guess. Or maybe they bond over their excessive fabulousness."

"Are you being serious right now?"

"Yes. He is fabulous to excess and so is she. You can't tell me you didn't notice how stylish he is."

"Yes, I did notice. He's dashing."

"Just do us all a favor and stay away from him."

"Whatever. Got it," I lie.

"Oh and there's something I need to tell you, but you can't say that I told." The tone of her voice makes me anxious.

"I get really nervous when you say stuff like that."

"Chloe has come up with another blind date."

"What?" I moan. "Why? Why would she do that? The guy she fixed me up with this past weekend was the pits! Who is it this time?"

"I don't know," she says.

"So why are you telling me this now?" I sense a conspiracy.

"Just wanted to warn you. That's all."

"Lilly, I'm not going on another blind date."

"C'mon, Ace, you don't want to hurt Chloe's feelings." She pauses. "Besides, what can it hurt?" Yep, this is a conspiracy for sure.

"It can hurt my feelings, that's what! I'd rather straighten my pubes with a flat iron than go on another blind date," I say, and she starts giggling.

"What are you going to tell Chloe?"

"I'm going to tell her that I have to straighten my pubes," I say, and Lilly cracks up. "Where does she find these poor, unlucky saps?"

"Who knows?" Lilly says. "And you never know, Ace. She might find you a good one."

"I don't see that happening," I say sarcastically.

"You never know."

"Whose side are you on here, Lilly?"

"Yours, of course! But I'm sympathetic to Chloe's efforts, too. She means well."

"Lilly, please," I say, and feel Buster Loo tugging on the leash. "Hey, I've got to let you go. Buster Loo is trying to tree a squirrel."

"Okay," she says cheerfully. "Maybe I'll see you at school tomorrow!"

"Maybe," I say, and then slip the phone into my pocket. "Can't wait for school tomorrow," I mumble, wondering what kind of substitute hell is lying in wait for me then. I jiggle the leash, but Buster Loo refuses to budge. "C'mon, Buster Loo!" I say to my stubborn little dog. "Let that squirrel enjoy his nuts in peace!"

5

<svg>〈〉〈〉〈〉〈〉〈〉〈〉〈〉〈〉〈〉〈〉〈〉〈〉〈〉〈〉〈〉〈〉〈〉〈〉</svg>

On Wednesday, Stacey Dewberry is wearing banana-colored pants with zippers all the way up both legs, an oversized button-up technetronic print top, and royal blue flats matching one of the less-prominent zigzag patterns in her shirt. She's wearing either panty hose or knee-highs, I can't tell which, and just like it has been for the past two days, her hair is hot rolled, teased to the max, and thoroughly coated with hair spray. "Good morning, Ms. Dewberry," I say as she joins me at the conference room table. I make a conscious effort not to stare at her eye makeup, which is bright blue and heavy on the liner. I see that her complexion is just as smooth as her silk shirt, and that makes me wonder if she's blessed with great skin or if all that foundation offers supreme coverage.

"I was almost late because this airhead lady in my neighborhood had to stop me and tell me about—" She stops talking when Chloe comes in. "Good morning, Mrs. Stacks."

"Good morning, ladies," Chloe says, sitting down.

"Ms. Dewberry, you're splitting the day today. First through third, you'll be in Mr. Harrison's room. You're off fourth and fifth, and then sixth and seventh, you'll be in Ms. Gale's class."

"Totally groovy, Mrs. Stacks, thank you," she says, taking the folders from Chloe.

"Ms. Jones," Chloe says, "you're back in Mrs. Davis's room today."

"Oh good word," I say. "What's going on with her?" I'm secretly jealous that Stacey is getting the lax schedule for the third day in a row.

"Her daughter has the flu," Chloe says evenly. "She'll probably be out the rest of the week."

Oh great stinkin' balls of monkey shit! No! "Okay then," I say, not wanting to make a scene.

"Hey, since I'm off all three lunches, I'll just come and eat with you again today!" Stacey says.

"Thanks, Ms. Dewberry," I say. "That's very nice of you."

I pick up my folders and get up to follow Stacey Dewberry out the door.

"Ms. Jones," Chloe says as I'm about to step out the door.

I turn around. "Yes, Mrs. Stacks?"

"What period are you off again?"

"Second," I say. "You need me to do something?" I ask, hoping she might send me to D Hall so I can spy on Cameron Becker.

"Could you come to my office, please?" She smiles and winks.

Dammit! I think, remembering the conversation with Lilly a minute too late. Stepped right into that one! "Sure," I say, turning to go. "See you then." *Wonderful. Just wonderful.*

First period, Brittany Franks acts like a fool for the entire first fifteen minutes of class. About the tenth time she starts talking out loud to her friend three rows over, I slide a detention sheet out of my sub folder and, while she continues to run her mouth, I scribble her name at the top. Without a word, I walk over and put her pink copy of the slip on her desk.

"I can't have detention," she says in a panic. "I have cheerleading practice and we're getting ready for tryouts!"

"Take it up with Mr. Byer," I say. "I can buzz his office and tell him you're on the way."

She takes a deep breath and looks at me like she wants to rip my face off. "Not necessary," she hisses, then slams her books around until, low and behold, she's working on today's assignment.

When the bell rings, I somehow refrain from screaming, *Oh thank you, Jesus!* at the top of my voice. I turn out the lights, lock the door, and then make my way through the students, none of whom seem to be in any hurry to get to their next class. Since I'm not exactly in a rush, either, I move along at their pace without saying a word.

By the time I get to Chloe's office, I have a laundry list of excuses and/or plans for the entire weekend. While I'm waiting for her to get off the phone, I text Lilly and tell her to pretend to go to the restroom and come up to Chloe's office and help me get out of this. She shows up a few minutes later, but we are unsuccessful in our attempts to dissuade Chloe from the topic. Not that Lilly tried that hard.

"Okay, well, if I'm going on another blind date for you, then you have to do something for me."

"The date is not for me, Ace. It's for you," Chloe says.

"No, sister, it's for you. Trust me."

"What then?"

"You have to make sure I get my job back."

"Ace, I don't have time to discuss this right now." She looks at Lilly. "Is this your planning period?"

"Uh, no," Lilly says. "And I was just about to head back to class."

Chloe picks up a stack of papers. "Okay, I'll see y'all later. I've got to get busy helping Mr. Byer finish evaluations so we can get his recommendations to the county office by the deadline this Friday."

"That's it!" I say. "Have y'all evaluated Becker yet?"

"You know I can't discuss that," Chloe says.

"You haven't, have you?" Lilly asks. "Because yesterday, y'all stopped with Mrs. Callon and Mr. Wendell, right?"

"How do you know that?" Chloe snaps.

"Teachers' lounge. Duh."

"Please don't use that word."

"Sorry."

"Chloe, you could talk to Mr. Byer and very nicely suggest that the current art teacher not be recommended for renewal," I say, glancing at Lilly who jumps onboard.

"That would be too easy," Lilly says. "Mr. Byer will do anything you suggest and he kind of owes you one because you've been saving his ass this whole entire year."

"Mr. Byer doesn't owe me anything."

"Chloe, please," I say. "I'm dying here. If I don't get my job back, I'm gonna be screwed."

"But, Ace," Chloe protests, "that would be nothing short of a blatant show of favoritism, and you despise small-town political shams, remember?"

"You know, I really don't so much anymore," I say.

"Ace Jones!"

"C'mon, Chloe," Lilly says quietly. "None of the students like Ms. Becker, and even the other teachers say she's terrible. Sometimes I hear her yelling all the way down in my room. You would be doing the school a huge favor, and all you have to do is make a subtle suggestion. Then, bingo! Ace gets her job back." Lilly winks at me. "You know she's the better teacher."

"Be that as it may," Chloe says, "maybe Ace shouldn't have quit her job to begin with if it was so important to her."

"What?" I say, shocked by her snide tone. Lilly looks at me, eyes wide.

Chloe shoves several files in her satchel and doesn't look up. "Ace, I fixed you up with a very nice guy this past weekend and you weren't interested. Nor do you seem very interested in meeting the perfectly nice guy I just mentioned. I told you about the job openings in psychology and you weren't interested. Now you want me to blackball a first-year teacher and I'm not interested." She looks at Lilly and then at me. "Good day, ladies," she says smartly, then walks out the door.

I look at Lilly, who appears to be as shocked as I am by Chloe's outburst.

"What the hell was that?" I ask.

"Who the hell was that?" Lilly says. "Maybe the stress of that massive renovation project is starting to get to her."

"She hired a decorator and a construction crew!" I say.

"Well, she still has to make a lot of decisions and she said last week that her cabinets had to be refinished because the glaze was all wrong. Maybe that's why she's in such a bad mood."

"Maybe so," I say. "And J.J.'s brother moving back has really gotten on her nerves."

"Tate?"

"Yes. Tate, with a stuffed fox and a collection of mounted fish and deer."

Lilly giggles at that. "I haven't seen him in years. How is he?"

"She said he was awful," I say, laughing. "He and his stuffed fox are staying with J.J. right now and apparently the fox is on display in J.J.'s living room."

"Wow," Lilly says. "I hate to say it, but that's kind of funny."

"She doesn't think so at all," I say, getting up. "So I guess I'm going out with Dweeb Numero Dos this weekend."

"I don't think that's such a bad idea," Lilly says. "I mean, it's a free meal and—"

"Don't say it, Lilly."

"What?" she says with a sly smile. "Don't say he might be your future husband?" She giggles and I give her the evil eye. "Just go out with him," she says. "Then call and tell Chloe how great he was and how much you appreciate her setting you up."

"Right," I say, getting up. "Because that'll surely put an end to this blind date madness. Thank you."

She glances at her watch. "Aw, man. I've got to get back to class!"

"Talk to you later," I tell her.

"Hope your day is better today."

"Thank you."

During afternoon break, I'm sitting in the teachers' lounge listening to Stacey Dewberry mourn the passing of Axl Rose's singing voice, when the door flies open and a gorgeous chick dressed to the nines bursts into the room. Hot on her four-inch-high heels is a very dapper Freddie Dublin.

"Oh my stars," Stacey whispers. "It's your nemesis from D Hall."

"What?" I whisper to Stacey. Then it hits me. "Is that—" I behold the face of my replacement.

"Cameron Becker," she replies.

"What is her problem?" Cameron Becker asks as she jiggles ass and titties across the room to the fridge without bothering to acknowledge Stacey or me. "Who the hell does she think she is?"

"Cameron, you should hire a lawyer and demand that evaluation be dismissed. You could lose your job over this."

"How dare she?" Cameron Becker fumes as she jerks the refrigerator door open. "Where are your Vitaminwaters, Freddie?"

"Uh, that would be the only Vitaminwater in there, sweetie," he says. "And you can't just let this go. You need to go up there and talk to her face-to-face and let her know what's up."

"I just did, Freddie, and she made a fool of me in front of Mr. Byer and Mrs. Marshall!" Cameron Becker takes a swig of purple Vitaminwater. "She's the one who should be fired. She thinks she's such hot shit sitting up there in her counselor's office with all of her pretty plaques on the wall. Well, I've got news for her."

"Hold on a minute!" I say, standing up.

"Ace, uh, Ms. Jones, I d-don't think you should—," Stacey Dewberry stammers.

"If you're talking about Chloe Stacks, you better stop right there." I look at Cameron and then at Freddie.

"Excuse me, Ms. Substitute Teacher," Freddie snaps. "This is an A and B conversation, and you need to C your way out of it."

"Are you serious?" I ask Freddie. "Did you really just say that?"

"Why, yes, I did," he says, giving me a wry look. "And I may have even meant it, too."

"Who are you?" Cameron Becker asks, scowling.

"This is Ms. Jones, former art teacher turned permanent substitute," Freddie says with a smirk.

She narrows her eyes and looks at me. "Oh, so you're the one that I was hired to replace?"

"Yes," I say.

"Yes," Freddie Dublin says. "And she's Mrs. Stacks's BFF." He looks at Cameron. "I told you to get a lawyer."

She stares me down for a minute. "So you're the reason she gave me a bad evaluation?"

"Or maybe it was because of your not-so-great teaching abilities," Stacey says.

"Or maybe it was because of your not-so-great teaching abilities," Freddie says, mocking her. "What do you know about any of this, Dewberry?"

"I know Mrs. Stacks is a fair and honest person and I know that Ms. Jones asked her to give you a bad evaluation this morning and Mrs. Stacks flat-out refused."

Now I'm the one scowling—at Stacey. "What?" I practically shout at her. "What are you talking about?"

"I was standing outside her office this morning while you were talking to her," she says to me. "Second period turned out to be Mr. Harrison's planning period, so I was going to ask her if there was anything else she needed me to do during that time because I heard her ask you to come up there, so I was going to see if maybe she needed me, too." She shrugs and looks back at Cameron Becker. "Ace wants her job back. Who wouldn't? She was just looking out for herself, and I heard Mrs. Stacks swear on a stack of Bibles she would give you an evenhanded evaluation." She looks over at Freddie. "So there. That's what I know about this."

"She didn't say she would swear on a stack of Bibles," I say, then stop short. "And I didn't ask her to do that."

"Yes, you did," Stacey says. "I was standing right outside the door and heard—"

"Not helping!" I yell at Stacey.

"Well, she had no right to jump all over me like she did when I went to speak to her about it," Cameron says, eyeballing me.

"She jumped all over you?" I ask, thinking Chloe must be having the worst day ever.

"Uh, yes."

"That is so not like her," I say. "If it makes you feel any better, she jumped all over me this morning, too."

"It doesn't." She smirks, then looks at Freddie. "Something smells here, don't you think?" Freddie nods in agreement.

"Don't blame me. I sprayed the restroom down double-time," Stacey says. Despite my best effort to keep a straight face, I laugh a little at that.

Cameron Becker stares at Stacey with disgust and says, "I think you're right, Freddie. I do need a lawyer."

"Well, a girl like you shouldn't have much trouble finding a lawyer who accepts sexual favors as payment," Stacey says, and we all turn to look at her.

"What?" Cameron Becker snaps as Freddie Dublin's eyes bug out of his head.

"What do you mean what?" Stacey replies, mirroring Cameron's glare of annoyance. "This is your first year teaching and we all know what you make and we all know it's not enough to afford a bad lawyer, let alone a good one, and personally, I don't think you have a leg to stand on, which means you're gonna need a really good one, so I'm just saying you're attractive and pretty and everyone says you like pecker, so I just thought I'd throw that out there." She shrugs and picks up her Dr Pepper. "You could say thanks."

The bell rings, so we all have to disperse, but not before I text Lilly and give her a quick summary of what just happened along with the quote, "Cameron Becker loves Pecker."

She sends back, "LOL" followed immediately by "WTEH = W w/C?" I interpret that to mean "What the effin' hell is wrong with Chloe?" Or something to that effect.

6

◇◇

The week finally drags to a close and I go home Friday and fall out on the couch. Buster Loo wants to go for a walk, but I tell him that I can't because I'm dying. He jumps up onto my chest and starts sniffing my face, no doubt checking my story.

I get a text from a mystery number that turns out to be my blind date for the evening and even though I promised Chloe I would go, I just can't. I'm sure she'll run me over with her newfound crazy train when she finds out, but I'll deal with that on Monday. I'm staying home tonight. I very cordially postpone what would certainly be another terribly awkward evening, then dial the delivery number for Pier Six Pizza.

Saturday, my effort to sleep late is thwarted by Buster Loo, who wakes me up by using his front paws to mine for gold in my hair. I roll out of bed, have a cup of coffee, then take him out for what turns out to be a very pleasant stroll. I take a deep breath, happy the air no longer freezes my lungs. Upon returning to our house, Buster Loo takes off to his secret hiding place behind the love seat. I have another cup of coffee and a few Oreos and then head over to Ethan Allen's bar where I find my pal Jalena Flores looking through a fabric catalog.

Jalena is a fellow fat girl from sunny Florida with a heart as big as her behind and she's just as proud of one as she is the other. When I met Jalena, she had a horde of online dating accounts and a romantic history jam-packed with Mr. Wrongs. She said she'd never leave that beautiful swampland she called home—an area known as Frog Bayou located on the north side of Pelican Cove, where she held the prestigious and enviable title of Frog Giggin' Queen of Escambia County—but I brought her up to Bugtussle one weekend and one weekend was all it took to change her mind. She met my pal Ethan Allen Harwood, who has always had the worst luck with the ladies and, well, everyone pretty much agrees that they're a match made in frog-giggin', tractor-drivin' heaven. They aren't engaged yet, but we all know it's only a matter of time.

Jalena waltzed into the life she'd always wanted here in Bugtussle just as I was leaving mine in a heaping pile of smoke and ash in Pelican Cove. We packed up our vehicles on the same day and convoyed up Highway 45. She moved into her dream home, which just so happens to be a farmhouse, with her dream man, who just so happens to be a farmer who also owns a bar right next door to where she plans to open the diner she's always wanted. It's currently under construction, which is why I show up on Saturdays and do whatever needs to be done to help her.

"Gotta pick out some curtains," she says cheerfully when I join her at the bar, which looks so different during daylight hours.

"Have you decided what color to paint the walls?" I ask because I really want to make some suggestions but don't want to be over-bearing.

"I want to pick out my curtains first because they need to have just the right personality, and then I'll pick a shade from those."

"What if you change the curtains?"

"Then I'll repaint the walls," she says without looking up.

"Okay, then," I say, thinking that sounds good to me.

We look through the catalog and she shows me several different styles and colors of curtains, all of which I like, and then she stands up and stretches.

"Lordy, I need to get back to work," she says, rubbing her back. "I just got that in the mail today and had to sit down a minute to take a look."

"Nothing wrong with that."

"C'mon, let me show you what we got done this week," she says. I follow her down the hallway and through a door that used to go outside but now opens into her mini-restaurant. "I can't wait for opening day!" she says, walking around in the wide-open space. She points out a few things, rolls off what's left on the to-do list, and then starts telling me about the new kitchen appliances. "We're finished in here," she says. "Just needs to be stocked!"

"Well, put me to work," I tell her. "I'm ready!"

"You're gonna have to start taking some money from me, Ace," Jalena says. "This ain't easy work."

"All I want is a year's supply of fried gator," I tell her. She laughs and hands me a broom. We pick up and clean up for a couple of hours and then walk over to Pier Six Pizza for an early lunch.

"I remember you used to complain about the pizza down in

Pelican Cove, and I thought you were crazy until I moved up here and got addicted to this fine stuff," she says with a grin.

"Pier Six deserves some kind of global award for excellence. That's for sure," I tell her as I serve us both another slice.

After lunch, we hit the fabric shops around town and she eventually finds just what she's looking for. She tells me that Ethan Allen's grandmother has volunteered to sew the curtains. All Mrs. Harwood needs is the fabric and a picture big enough for her to see without having to squint.

"Now we can pick out the paint!" she says as we leave the store, each of us toting large sacks of fabric. I'm so happy for Jalena, but her enthusiasm is starting to get me down. I look at the bags I'm carrying and feel a pang of misery when I think about my art gallery. I poured my soul into that place before I found myself horribly disappointed by the reality of my dream. Part of me still can't believe that I packed up and left it empty except for a For Sale sign in the window. In an effort to cheer myself up, I remind myself that I have made a small amount of progress in coming to terms with the dissolution of my dreams. I've stopped wishing things had turned out different and I'm trying to stop wishing that I could have been different, but I do wish it wasn't so tough to see Jalena hopeful and excited while I'm scraping the bottom of the emotional barrel. I want so badly to be as happy and carefree as she is, but a lot is going to have to change before that happens.

The worst part of my situation is having to work so hard to reassemble the life that I so casually walked away from. I never imagined I would be back in Bugtussle—not even a year after I left—working as a substitute teacher and hoping against hope to recoup my old job, my old life, my old sense of comfort and stability. I look at Jalena who is humming as she carefully arranges the bags in her trunk, and I certainly hope she has better luck with her dreams than I did. I wouldn't wish how I feel right now on anyone. Not even on Cameron Becker.

We go to the paint store and I'm delighted that Jalena asks for my input. When she finally decides on a color, even the man helping us agrees it perfectly matches her swatch of fabric. Or maybe he is just ready to get us to the register and out of what little hair he has clinging to the outskirts of his head. Who knows? Jalena buys five gallons of paint, along with paintbrushes, long handles, and a stack of sturdy paint pans. She signs the receipt, and we head back to the diner and get busy.

No matter what kind of mood I'm in, I love to paint—anything; it doesn't matter what—so I enjoy the next few hours chatting with Jalena as we roll bright yellow paint onto pale gray Sheetrock, slowly transforming the walls of her diner into something radiant and beautiful. *This is just what I needed today,* I think as I dip my brush into the paint again and again, fantasizing about rolling it over my soul, covering the dull gray with vibrant strokes of sunshine. If only it were that easy to fix.

By the time we finish the large rectangular room, I'm covered with paint splatter, thoroughly exhausted, but in a much better mood. Gramma Jones used to say that hard work was the best way to cure a troubled mind. While that may be true, I think I'm going to require some heavy-duty ibuprofen for my aching back. But I don't care. This has been the most enjoyable afternoon I've had since moving back home.

"You should let me paint a mural right there." I point to the long wall that backs up to Ethan Allen's bar.

"Of what?"

"Whatever you want," I say, walking over to the windowless wall. "Maybe something to remind you of home." I can see that she's considering it, so I continue. "I could do some marshy-looking grass along the bottom half, or I could fade in a bay scene and then glaze it. You picked a really great color, very versatile. I could do a lot of things with that, and I promise it would look very cool." I look at her. "If you want, I can paint Ethan Allen in the nude standing beside his big green tractor." I raise my eyebrows. "I think that'd be a real crowd pleaser. Especially on the days when you serve those Italian sausage dogs that I'm convinced are going to make you famous for miles around."

"You know, Ace, I'm gonna go out on a limb here and say that having a penis painted on the wall of my family diner might be bad for business," she says with a smile. "Especially on Italian sausage day." She starts gathering paint cans, so I start picking up trays. "Let me think about it," she says. "Not my future husband's sausage dog, but the marsh grass." She gives me a wary look. "It's gonna take a heck of a lot of pictures to cover that area, and it probably wouldn't hurt to have the lower part of the wall a shade or two darker."

"I could add a lot of texture with the marsh grass," I say, "and I assure you that it would add an ambiance that would blend nicely with the personality of the curtains." I reach down to pick up a paintbrush.

"Ace, you have no idea how much I appreciate you. Not just for this, but for everything," she says, and I pray she won't start talking about how happy she is again. "I can't believe how happy I am, and it's all because you talked me into coming up here last year for an impromptu visit." I look over and she's got a tear in her eye. I think about crying, too, but not tears of joy. I think I just pulled something out of whack when I bent over to get that last paintbrush.

"I couldn't be happier for you, Jalena," I tell her, rubbing my lower back. We say good-bye, and I give her a stiff hug and then hobble out to my car. On the way home, my phone starts buzzing and it's Lilly Lane. Her boyfriend, Dax, is on patrol tonight, so she wants to hang out at the bar and catch me up on the latest gossip. I tell her I'll be there just as soon as I go home, soak in a hot bath, take a nap, spend some quality time with Buster Loo, take another hot bath and possibly another nap. She tells me we don't have that kind of time, so I tell her I'll forgo the second nap and see her in a few hours.

At nine o'clock, Lilly and I squeeze in at the bar at Ethan Allen's. We order an appetizer and a round of drinks, and I can see that Lilly is ready to start talking.

"Okay," she says after we get our drinks. "So I told you Cameron Becker started sleeping with Coach Wills as soon as she got here, right?"

"Yeah, but she flirts shamelessly with anyone else with a twig and berries."

"Uh, yeah," she says, giving me a look that tells me she didn't think that was as funny as I did, "and she's always hanging out in the athletic department, which makes Wills's day because he's dumb as a stick and the only thought in his head when she's around is 'I'm hittin' that,' so it doesn't even register with him that she's throwing herself at the other coaches."

"Poor Wills."

"Poor Wills nothing! He couldn't have been any happier until she dumped him two days ago!"

"See? He's poor Wills after all." I look at her. "How did you come by this information?"

"How do you think? Hatter told me at lunch yesterday," Lilly says with a sly smile, and my spirits drop because I want to be back on third lunch with the two of them so bad I can't stand it. My old classroom is right across the hallway from Coach Hatter, and we've been friends—occasionally with benefits—since he moved to Bugtussle from the Delta nearly ten years ago. "He said Wills called him Thursday night, bawling and squalling!"

"Please tell me you're lying." I look at her. "About the crying. Not the breakup."

"No," she says, glancing around to make sure no one is eavesdropping even though it's so loud in the bar I don't see how anybody could. "According to Hatter, Wills is pussy-whipped beyond belief and he mistakenly assumed Cameron to be equally smitten, so he bought her a ring, invited her over for a candlelit dinner, and then got down on one knee in the dining room."

"What? Are you serious?"

"Yes," she says. "And according to Hatt, when Wills got down on one knee, he couldn't get the ring box out of his pocket, and she just stood there and looked at him like he was stupid."

"What a bitch!"

"When he finally pried the box out of his pocket, he flipped it open and she just kept standing there, looking at him. Didn't say a word, not even after he popped the question."

"Now that's just cruel."

"Yes, it is," Lilly says. "Then Hatt said Wills told him she walked into the kitchen and got a bottle of his vodka out of his liquor cabinet, hollered and told him it was over, and then walked out the door." She shakes her head. "All while he was in the dining room down on one knee."

"Class act, that girl."

"Oh, but that's not all," Lilly says. "Yesterday morning, she pranced into the coaches' lounge like she always does, completely ignoring Wills, and started flirting with Coach Spears right there in front of him. Hatter said it was awful and that Wills was crushed."

"So Coach Spears didn't know what had happened?" I ask, and she shakes her head. "What did he do?"

"Just sat there and ate it up like all men do when she shakes those big fake melons their way. Hatt said he was flirting like crazy and Wills was just sitting there looking at the floor."

"He wouldn't have done that if he knew what she'd done to Wills. Coach Spears isn't like that."

"No, he's not and I'm sure when it all comes out, he'll feel bad, but Cameron Becker stays in that coaches' lounge all the time, so I'm sure he just assumed it was business as usual. According to Hatter, everyone in the athletic department starts thinking with the wrong head the minute she wiggles into the room," Lilly says, then adds, "Which, of course, she loves. Skank. Slingin' that cooter around like it pays her bills."

"Maybe it does," I say.

"Ew!" Lilly exclaims.

"So poor ol' dumb Wills just sat there?"

"Hatter said if anybody had bothered to look over at him, they would've known something was wrong. Wills just got up and left.

Hatter followed him to his office and tried to talk to him. He's heartbroken. Poor thing." She takes a sip of her drink. "And that's all the story that I got because Chloe came and sat down at the lunch table with us and we had to stop talking about it." Dang it! I need my seat back at that table!

"Do you think Hatter would sleep with Cameron Becker?"

"Oh hell yeah!" she says, laughing. "In a minute! He is such a horny toad. It's like his brain hasn't evolved since he turned fourteen."

"You're right about that," I say, and wonder if I need to start sleeping with Logan Hatter again just to entertain myself while simultaneously saving him from the wiles of Cameron Becker. Or maybe I should give Coach Wills a little rebound action just for the heck of it. After all, it doesn't take much attention to the ding-a-ling to get a man's mind off his worries, and it would surely piss Cameron Becker off if I started having an affair with her ex. Or maybe it wouldn't. It's fairly obvious from what Lilly just said that Cameron doesn't care too much about Wills, so maybe I'll just pass on that because every girl in the world knows that the worst sex of all is with a guy who's just been dumped. Ugh. All Cameron Becker seems to care about is being the center of attention, so that's what I need to try to take away from her. Maybe I could steal some of her thunder if I started hanging out in the athletic office every morning and telling dirty jokes. That might work, but, dammit, she's got a lot of thunder packed into those D-cups.

We keep drinking and Jalena joins us a little later, then Ethan Allen appears behind the bar and chats for a minute. Logan Hatter and Drew Wills come in an hour before closing time and it's obvious they're not just getting started. Lilly and I make a fuss over

Drew Wills to the point that Logan Hatter starts getting jealous, so I turn my attention toward him so he doesn't feel so left out. Wills eats up the attention from Lilly and is sorely disappointed when Dax shows up in his uniform at midnight. Never the jealous kind, Dax joins us at the bar, orders a Coke, and strikes up a conversation with Hatter and Wills about baseball.

Lilly leaves with Dax an hour later, and I think long and hard about going home with Logan Hatter. He keeps draping his arm around me and dropping not-so-subtle hints about needing some company tonight. I haven't slept with him in who-knows-how-many years, but I'm sure he's still the same old-reliable good-time roll-in-the-hay he always has been. I've almost made up my mind to take him up on his offer, when Ethan Allen announces he'll be driving us all home tonight instead of Jalena. That causes me to balk on Hatter because if I start sleeping with him again, I really don't want Ethan Allen to know about it. Not that I care if he knows so much; I just don't want him to tell his best friend and my ex-fiancé, Mason McKenzie, that I'm backtracking.

Probably best, I think to myself as I continue to put some distance between my shoulders and Hatter's arm. Jalena would tell Ethan Allen anyway, and then Mason would still find out my life is moving backward instead of forward. Shit. I climb up in the front of Ethan Allen's truck while Hatter, Wills, and Pete the tire man climb into the back.

7

Sunday, I skip church and lazy around the house because my head is aching from the booze, my back is aching from the painting, and my nose is all stopped up, most likely from sweeping up Sheetrock dust in Jalena's diner. I fix myself a Sprite with six cherries, pop four ibuprofen and a sinus pill, and then grab a sleeve of crackers. I head to the living room and while I'm looking for the remote, I remember that I almost went home with Logan Hatter last night.

"Thank goodness I didn't do that," I tell Buster Loo. I stretch out on the sofa and he snuggles up next to me. I turn on the television and start flipping through channels. My mind drifts off, and I find myself wondering where I might find that elusive little bastard known as happiness. And I wonder how everyone around me seems to know right where it is all the time; yet for me, it seems to be eternally buried someplace I'll never find. Lilly and Dax are happy, wearing their contentment like comfortable underwear. They never flaunt it, just let it be what it is. Then there's Chloe with her big white house by the lake, which, according to her, is everything she's always wanted in a home, and the love of her life, Sheriff J. J. Jackson, who, according to her, is everything she's ever wanted in a man. Chloe took a bumpier path than Lilly, but they've both arrived at a place where they have a calm, quiet, and very grown-up kind of contentment. And then Jalena, whose happiness shines from her soul like a beacon in the night; and Ethan Allen, whose good-ol'-boy heart does the same. Each one of them seems to be with the person they were meant to be with. I take a sip of Sprite and wonder if there is someone out there for me and I just haven't found him yet or if maybe I was just put here to walk alone. Well, not alone. I have Buster Loo.

I'm well aware that I need to cease and desist with the pity party, pull myself up by the bootstraps, and get kickin' again, but I just don't feel like it yet. The truth is that I still love Mason McKenzie and I always will, but I know that it's finally over between us and that hurts so bad every time I think about it. Maybe I just need to be sad—just feel it—and take my time mourning the death of a relationship that I held up in my mind and in my heart as the Holy Grail of Happiness since we were kids. I can't believe how wrong I was about that. I also can't believe that I got all liquored up and almost went home with Logan Hatter last night. That's just what I need to do. Strike up an old flame that fizzled out years ago from lack of a spark. What a great plan. Jeez. Logan Hatter has to stay in the friend zone. I literally and figuratively do not need to screw that up. Relief will have to come from somewhere else and, in the meantime, I guess I have no choice but to tough it out and suffer through the consequences of my decisions. Dammit! I hate that. Consequences suck! I don't like living with them, but what else can I do? Maybe I should never leave the house again except to go to work and walk Buster Loo. Or maybe I should've gone to church this morning, because I always leave feeling better than I did when I got there.

I look down at Buster Loo, who is snoozing with his snout stuck straight up in the air. How I wish I could be so satisfied. I look out the window and see the buttercups have started to blossom. Early bloomers, as my grandma used to say. Gramma Jones sure seemed to have had life figured out. And she lived it so simply. She was never rich. Not even close. She never had a big fancy car or went on ritzy vacations. She had a cozy little home, a beautiful yard, her garden club, her ladies' Sunday school class, and me. Gramma Jones was the most peaceful soul on the planet, even after suffering so much. She lost her husband to prostate cancer and later buried her only son; yet she wasn't bitter or miserable or envious of anyone. She just lived her life and took care of her home and took care of me and seemed to be perfectly happy passing along tidbits of wisdom when the occasions presented themselves to do so.

Maybe I'm looking in all the wrong places. Maybe it's not, as that noodle-balling weirdo at the Italian restaurant said, about that house and that job and that man. Maybe it's just about me. Wow. That's some pretty scary shit right there. I've always banked on external things to float my boatload of happiness. Like having my own art gallery and living with Mason McKenzie in his ocean-side home in Florida. I thought that was it for me and, looking back now, it's hard to believe how bad I wanted it, how much faith I'd invested in it, and how much power I had given to the idea of the dream. It's even more shocking how desperate I was to escape it at the very end. I need to get back in touch with my soul, whatever that means, but I'm afraid I've spent so much time giving myself over to an illusion that my soul has become the ghost that just shows up now and then to haunt me.

A commercial comes on for a local furniture store advertising a zero-percent-interest-twelve-month-same-as-cash deal, and I start thinking that maybe a new couch and love seat might help my feelings. I'm wondering what time that place opens up on Sunday when it dawns on me I'm reverting to external fixes. Didn't I just figure that out? I stare at the television and try to ignore the uncomfortable notion that I have to go inside my own wacky head and misguided heart if I really want to fix what's bugging me. Which is me. I'm bugging myself. I don't like to think about my own problems. I like to solve other people's problems, preferably with crazy shenanigans and wild stunts that further distract me from my own. It's so much easier that way because all the consequences get to move in with them and not with me.

I don't want to analyze myself too much because if I do, I'm afraid I'll discover things that might make me unhappier than I already am. Like the fact that I seem to live my life backward. I spent my twenties, when most people travel the world and chase their big fancy dreams, working at a job I didn't love but that now I'd give anything to have back. My dreams have shriveled up. All I want is what I had this time last year because I'm sure I'd be more careful with it this time around. Don't mistake me for someone with ambition. I'm not. Not anymore.

I look out at the buttercups in the yard and think about Gramma

Jones. Maybe I should try to follow her model for living. Simple, with flowers blooming year-round. If she could see me now, she would surely tell me to get off my rump and stop thinking my life to death. I wonder where she got all of her crazy old sayings. From her grandmother maybe? I wonder if her grandmother was a gardener. If she passed along flower bulbs and secrets about happiness. I look back at the buttercups. Maybe they could make me happy, too. Perhaps I'll find my soul buried out there in that dirt.

For the first time in a long time, I feel a sliver of interest, a tad bit of intrigue. Could I make that garden grow? Could I restore it to its former glory? Could I get the weeds out? Could I keep the weeds out? Could I make flowers bloom year-round?

I sit up, startling Buster Loo out of his slumber, and he goose honks and rolls over. My curiosity sprouts a twig of hope, and I jump up, run into the hallway, and look up at the attic door. Buster Loo, totally over being drowsy, bounds off the couch and follows me. He starts running in circles around my feet, barking like crazy. I reach up and grab the string, then slowly pull the door, easing the steps down until they're resting on the carpet in the hallway. When I start to climb, Buster Loo stops barking and starts whimpering. I don't know if he's afraid that I'll try to take him with me or if he's more concerned about those rickety steps giving way and sending me to the floor in a hefty lump. Either way, he's backing away as he would from a dog catcher.

"Don't worry, Buster Loo," I tell him. "Mama will be right back."

The single bulb at the top of the steps is coated with dust and grime. I reach up and tug on the cord, surprised and delighted when dim light floods the attic. I shiver against the cool, stagnant air and then work my way up to where I can stand, careful to keep my feet on the wide boards. Even though I haven't been up here in a while, I know what I'm looking for. I'm looking for a box.

After my grandmother passed away, I had to pack up all of her personal stuff. I couldn't bear to part with any of it, so I put it all in the attic of this house that she'd shared with my grandpa since before my dad was born. I make my way to the boxes in the far right corner and soon find the one I'm looking for.

"Books!" I say, and cough at the dust. I drag it away from the slightly larger box right next to it. I haven't looked at this stuff since the day I packed it and hauled it up here.

I pull the book box to the attic door, thinking I must've been in a little better shape when I carted it up here nearly ten years ago. Of course I was! I was in my early twenties! When I push it to the edge of the opening, I see Buster Loo sitting at the bottom of the steps. When he sees the box, he takes off as fast as his little legs will carry him. I don't see him again until I've wrestled the box down the flimsy steps and hauled it into the living room.

"Probably should've checked the weight limit on those stairs before I did that," I tell Buster Loo, who creeps out from behind the love seat to sniff the box. "But I made it."

I open the box and see Gramma Jones's small collection of books. *Wide Sargasso Sea*, *The Sun Also Rises*, a few James Bond books. Finally, at the very bottom, I find what I'm looking for: *A Guide to Beautiful Gardens in the South*.

"Maybe this is just what I need right now," I tell my little dog as I run my hand over the worn cover. "A guide."

I get up and move to the couch. Buster Loo hops up beside me, sniffing the book in my hand. I flip through the first few chapters, all of which are dedicated to flowers. Flowers, flowers, and more flowers. I read until I fall asleep on the sofa, not from a lack of interest, but probably from a heavy dose of meds. I wake up late in the afternoon with the book on my face. I place it on the coffee table and stand up.

I take Buster Loo for a walk just before dark, then come home and start ironing my clothes for the next week. Pants too tight in the ass with a button barely hanging on? Check. Baggy shirt formerly reserved for "fat" days? Check. These days, every day is a fat day. Funny how that happens. I dig around in my sock drawer until I find a matching pair of polka-dot socks, and unless I wear a plus-sized pair of paisley panties, those socks will be the only item in my wardrobe with a trace of personality.

Now that I'm thoroughly depressed, I walk back into the living room and pick up Gramma Jones's garden book. I stare at the words on the cover and wonder if this book could somehow offer some relief from the hopeless misery sucking the life out of me. Damn those tight-ass "fat" pants. Damn them! I won't buy a size up. I won't. I put the book down and wonder if instead I should be reading a book called *How Not to Be a Fatass*. No, that wouldn't be right. I would need a book titled *How Not to Be a Fatass When You've Read Every Damned Book in Print About How Not to Be a Fatass but You're Still a Fatass and Here's Why!* Yeah, I'll go to the bookstore tomorrow and ask about that one. Just as soon as I get out of school. School. F me in the A. I'd rather have eyelashes burned off with a flamethrower.

8

<><><><><><><><><><><><><><><><><><><><><><><><><><><><><><><><><><><><>

Monday, I dread getting to work partly because I'm already burned-out after only one week and partly because I don't want Chloe to go apeshit crazy on me when she finds out I ditched the date Friday night. Lucky for me, Stacey Dewberry is already in the conference room when I arrive, but despite that, Chloe has no kind words for me as she goes over the day's assignments. On the way to our hallway, Stacey remarks that Chloe seemed a little irked with me.

"Oh, it's nothing," I say, thinking I better dream up a king-sized lie to tell Chloe later. I expect to be called to her office at some point during the day, but I'm not.

On Tuesday, Chloe is still giving me the cold shoulder, and I just let her do her thing and don't say a word. I leave the conference room and head straight for the teachers' lounge where I run into Freddie Dublin who is so nice to me it makes me nervous. I think about what Lilly said and try to keep my mind sharp as we exchange unusually polite banter. Lilly was right; I am blinded by his fabulousness. He's beautiful and his cologne is intoxicating. After speaking with him for five minutes, I don't even care if he's trying to manipulate me; I love this guy. He's downright enchanting and I want to be his friend.

Later in the day, I catch a bunch of freshmen making fun of Stacey Dewberry, so I give them a lecture, which they ignore, so I threaten to call some of their parents if I hear them talking about her again. That's much more effective, and I pat myself on the back for perhaps eliminating some small part of the grief Stacey has to put up with at school.

Wednesday, Stacey and I are off sixth and seventh, the latter of which turns out to be Freddie Dublin's planning period. Stacey takes it upon herself to tell us her whole entire life story, after which Freddie appears to be on the verge of tears. I watch him closely, looking for signs of insincerity. He turns the charm on full blast and starts counseling Stacey about her life, love, and otherwise. I say nothing during the entire conversation. I just watch and listen. His voice is smooth and mellow, and Stacey is eating it up.

"Do you moonlight as a therapist?" I ask when Stacey goes to the restroom because she drank too much Dr Pepper.

"No, I watch a lot of Oprah and Ellen," he says, smiling at me.

"So are we cool now?" I ask. "Because we had that little altercation last week and you were kind of snappy with Stacey then, too. But this week, it's like we're all pals."

"Oh, we are so cool," he says. "Cameron was just really upset and she had my feathers ruffled, but we're going to work on her teaching techniques before her final evaluation at the end of the year, so everything should be fine." He looks at me and I hold his gaze, searching his eyes for ill intent. "I've never heard of a school district doing evaluations the way they do here, but whatever. At least she has a chance to redeem herself."

"Okay," I say, but I'm thinking, This is your first year teaching. How would you know? We sit there and look at each other for a minute. I get the distinct feeling he expects me to say something. I don't.

"Mrs. Stacks seems to have turned on us these past few weeks," Freddie says. "Wonder what's going on with her?"

"Who knows?" I say in an effort to be elusive even though I've been wondering the exact same thing.

"Love life troubles?" Freddie says. "Has the handsome sheriff been cuffing and stuffing some other ladies?"

"I don't think so," I say, trying not to smile. "He's not that type at all."

"Too bad," Freddie says, and flashes a naughty grin.

I laugh out loud despite my best effort not to and don't give any indication of how startled I am by Freddie's forthrightness. I'm almost relieved to hear Stacey opening the restroom door because I'm keenly aware that I'm falling into exactly the same kind of conversational entanglement with Freddie D. that Lilly warned me about. Stacey takes two steps out of the restroom, shoots me a panicked look, then goes back in without closing the door. A second later, I hear the air freshener.

"No dukes. Just poots," she says matter-of-factly, backing out of the restroom as she sprays. "Can't be stinkin' up the place."

"I regret to inform you that's exactly what you're doing with that spray," Freddie says, waving a hand over his face. "Let's get out of here," he says. "The bell is about to ring anyway."

Thursday, Chloe calls me to her office and asks me, very nicely, if I plan on going on my date this weekend. Since she's being nice and I don't wish to rock the boat, I assure her that I will.

"Ace, I'm sorry I've been so edgy this week," she says. "I don't know what's wrong with me. I mean, my cabinets were all wrong and they had to rip them all out and redo them and that was quite a frustrating experience. They've finally got everything back in place and like it needs to be, so I'm going to be able to put all of my groceries in there over the weekend. Maybe that's what's been making me so crabby. I don't know."

"Cans stacked in weird places will do that, I guess."

"What?" she asks.

"Nothing," I say quickly, and then remember what Freddie Dublin said in the lounge earlier in the week. "So is everything okay with you and J.J.?"

"Of course it is!" she says defensively. "Why do you ask?"

"No reason," I say, backing off fast. "It's just that you haven't mentioned him in a while."

"We're great," she says, then looks alarmed. "At least I think we are."

Dammit! Why did I even open my mouth?

"Well, that means you are then," I say. I get up because I'm anxious to get away from her while things are still pleasant.

"So you're going out with Gaylen tomorrow night?"

"Gaylen!?" I say, turning around. "I thought his name was Blake!"

"That's his last name."

"No wonder he used that while we were texting," I say. "I can't believe you've fixed me up with a guy named Gaylen!"

"What's wrong with the name Gaylen?" she asks, and I hear that edge creeping back into her voice.

"Nothing," I say, turning to go. "Nothing at all." Because I'm sure it's going to be a freakin' disaster date anyway, so why bother.

"Let me know how it goes," she calls as I walk out the door.

"Will do! Thanks!" For nothing!

Standing in front of the mirror, I wonder if Gaylen would prefer my hair up or down. Then I laugh out loud because I couldn't possibly care less. I wonder what would happen if I shaved my head bald and showed up at the door wrapped in a toga sheet. That cracks me up again.

Thirty minutes later, the doorbell rings and Buster Loo goes nuts. I spend a minute calming him down before placing him in my bedroom and pulling the door closed, apologizing the whole time. I go into the kitchen where I take two quick shots of Crown, and then I go open the front door.

Oh my, I think. *What have we here?* Gaylen is standing on my porch in light wash denim jeans about two inches too short and he's running a big, beefy hand over his shiny, bald head. His shirt appears to be sprayed on, and I think his pants might cover his ankles if he pulled them down off his waist a little bit. I wish I had my phone so I could snap a picture of this hot mess and send it to Lilly along with a single word: "Why?"

At first, he doesn't notice the door is open because he's too busy admiring his reflection in the glass of my storm door. So I just stand there, looking. Then I get the feeling that he knows the inside door is open but continues to primp because that affords him the opportunity to flex his rather large biceps. Thank goodness I'm wearing this dress with fifty yards of slimming fabric, because I'm going out with a stud-muffin tonight! I giggle to myself as he stands there, flexing. I resist a strong and sudden urge to push the door open and "accidentally" pop him on the end of his oily, pointy nose. But then I think about Chloe and know that my only option is to politely tap on the door. So I do that.

"Hello," I say, then carefully push the door open. "You must be Gaylen."

"Garlen," he says indignantly. "Is Ace Jones here?"

"I'm Ace Jones," I say.

"Oh, I thought you might be the sister"—he looks me up and down—"or something."

Yes, you barrel-chested fool, I'm the sister who answers the door in a fucking strapless dress on a Friday night.

"So if you're Garlen, then where is Gaylen?" I ask, just to be contentious. I can come across like a real bitch if it's absolutely necessary and I feel that it is. "I have a date with Gaylen."

"I don't know a Gaylen," he says arrogantly, and I think again about hitting him in the nose with the door.

"Oh," I say, sighing in disappointment, and he immediately looks more interested. "So it's Garlen, then?" I look at him like he's already boring me to death. He smiles.

"Did I hear a dog barking in there?" he asks, peering into my house.

"No," I say. I step out onto the porch and close the door behind me. "That was my cat." Then I look him right in the eye and say, "That pussy is ferocious." I smile, thinking that will surely send him screaming off my steps and then I can call Chloe and blame this failed romantic interlude on him. Instead, he bellows with laughter and slaps me on the back.

"That's a good one," he says. He lets his hand brush my butt and then, in a most unexpected gentlemanly maneuver, extends his arm toward the sidewalk. Disappointed that my plan to send him running didn't work, I walk down the steps. When I get to his truck, which appears to be a foreign-made two-wheel-drive model decked out with mud tires for some odd reason, he surprises me again by opening the passenger side door. *Nice,* I think. Maybe I could get used to that waxed dome and light-wash denim after all. Ha-ha! Never!

"So where would you like to go?" he asks when we're on the road.

Somewhere I don't know a soul and can get shit-faced drunk. "Wherever you like," I say, deciding to act like a full-fledged crazy bitch whore all night so I can at least enjoy that part of the evening. "I'm easy."

He looks at me and smiles, and I can tell by the look in his eye that he thinks he's going to get laid tonight. I smile back at him because Cupid will shit a golden egg filled with tequila worms before that happens. As we debate going to Memphis or Tupelo, I try to decide which would be worse: a longer ride with him or the risk of seeing someone I might know.

"I like Buffalo Wild Wings," he says.

"You know what? Me, too!" I tell him, thinking, *Please don't let me see anyone I know*. I look at him and he looks at me and I can see that I'm moving up his I'd-hit-that list with speed and finesse.

"So, where are you from?" I ask.

"Everywhere," he says.

"How do you know Chloe?"

"Who?"

"Chloe."

"Is that the sheriff's piece?"

"Piece of wha—," I begin, then stop and cringe. I look at Garlen and, seeing I've figured it out, he starts sniggering. Really, Chloe. Really? I think. She would die if she knew she'd just been referred to as a "piece."

"Met her at a cookout. When she found out I was single, she said she'd fix me up with a fireball."

"Did she really say that?"

"Well, no, but I assumed that was what she meant."

"Right." Thank goodness I opted for the shorter ride.

I glance over at him and he's grinning, looking all smug and shit. I imagine he thinks he can startle and shock me all night long with his scuzzball words and phrases, but he doesn't know what he's up against if he thinks he can out-shock me. He hears a song he likes on the radio and turns up the volume, and I spend the rest of the ride thinking up outrageous things to say to Gaylen or Garlen or whatever the hell his name is.

When we walk into Buffalo Wild Wings, I scan the area looking for familiar faces. I'm thankful that I don't recognize a soul. The waitress tries to seat us right in the center of the restaurant, but I insist on a booth in the corner, claiming I want to be closer to the television. This impresses my waitin'-for-the-flood date even more. I smile as I allow him to take the seat with the best view of the TV, which allows me to face the restaurant, just like I wanted. Maybe if I am seen, whoever sees me won't be able to see this moron who is staring at his roll of silverware like he's not sure what it is. Goofy bastard. "You like sports?" he asks.

"I like watching men in tight pants."

"Really?"

"Yes, football is my favorite because I love seeing all of those hot, sexy men wallowing all over one another." Apparently, my date doesn't know what to say to that. "Baseball is okay, too. All of those long, hard bats."

"So you won't think I'm a pervert if I say I watch women's tennis just to see all of those tight asses under those short little skirts," he says, his voice almost a growl. I realize that I've made a terrible mistake by opening up this can of worms. He keeps talking about watching women's sports, and I curse myself for being such an idiot. The waitress finally shows up with our drinks and, after she takes our order, I excuse myself and go to the restroom. The way he's looking at me now is disgusting, but I have no one to blame for this but myself. Epic fail!

I hurry into the restroom, lock myself in a stall, and call Lilly. She doesn't answer, so I send her a text with a full description of my date. I wait a second and when I don't hear back from her, decide to go back out there and get this over as quickly as possible. I devise a plan. I'll sit down and immediately start talking about Buster Loo, continue to pretend he's a cat, and rattle on nonstop about my cat/dog until our food arrives. Then maybe he'll think I'm weird and be in a hurry to get me back home. I step out of the stall, look in the mirror, and desperately wish I hadn't worn a strapless dress. I take a deep breath.

"Just get it done," I tell my reflection. "It's just another hour. Two at the most." A lady whom I didn't know was in the restroom comes out of the last stall and looks at me.

"Bad date?" she asks.

"Blind date."

"Oh, I'm so sorry," she says as she washes her hands. "Those are the worst. Makes me glad I'm married."

"Right." Thanks!

"Well, you look lovely," she says with a kind smile. "Good luck."

"Thank you." I put on fresh lip gloss, not to be sexy but to make myself feel better. At least there's no one here I know. I walk out of the restroom and run right into Drew Wills.

"Woo hoo, girl," he says. "You look good!" Behind him, I see Logan Hatter.

"Dang, Ace," Logan says, eyeballing my boobs. "You get all dressed up like this to come to Buffalo Wild Wings?" My face burns with embarrassment and humiliation. I don't know what to say. I'm seriously considering making up some kind of wild story when Logan says, "You're on a date." It isn't a question. "Chloe was saying at lunch today how excited she was about fixing you up with some guy she thought was perfect for you." I can't read the expression on his face and if I didn't know better, I'd think he was a little jealous. No way! My brain is just shutting down because of this unbearable humiliation. Why can't I just disappear right now? They just stand there, looking at me.

"I'm so embarrassed," I say finally. "This guy is such a douche bag. It's horrible."

"You want us to invite ourselves to sit with you?" Logan asks.

"Might make things a little more bearable for you." Wills gives him an odd look.

"No, that's okay," I say. "I just—" I think about trying to explain the mess I got myself into by trying to out-shock my date, but then I decide against it. I mean, a person can only withstand so much shame in a thirty-second time frame. "I'll just tough it out."

"Well, we'll be at the bar if you need us," Logan says.

"Is he a big guy?" Wills asks.

"He's buff," I say. "In all the wrong ways."

Wills laughs and walks into the restroom while Hatter stands there looking at me.

"You look great," he says. "You really do."

"Thank you, Logan," I say, then give him a big hug that lasts a minute longer than it should.

"Call me later if you get lonely," he whispers.

"Okay," I say. Don't do this!

When I get back to the table, my date doesn't look happy.

"What the hell was that all about?" he asks.

"What the hell was what all about?" I don't even try not to sound like a smart-ass.

"You go to the restroom to meet other dudes?" He points a meaty finger at me. "You are here with me. I'm buying this meal."

"What the hell are you talking about?" I ask.

"I'm talking about you standing over there in plain sight flirting with those two guys and then hugging up on the short one," he says, a little too loud. People start looking.

"Hey, buddy," I say in a low voice. "Not that I owe you any explanation, but those guys are my friends. People I've worked with for years, so why don't you pipe down?"

"You don't tell me to pipe down!" he practically shouts.

"I'll tell you whatever I damned well please," I say, keeping my voice low. "You don't own me just because you take me out and buy me a piece of fucking fried chicken, got it?" I'm pretty sure I could instigate a brawl with this idiot and he would get mad and leave me here, and then I could catch a ride home with Hatt and Wills. I'm sure Chloe would understand. A manager appears at the table.

"Is everything okay here?" the nervous fellow asks. He looks down at Garlen's arms. Garlen says nothing, so I tell the manager that everything is fine as far as I'm concerned and he hurries away.

"Tell you what," he says quietly. "Why don't you call me when you lose fifty pounds?" He tosses his menu down on the table and stands up.

"I'll tell you what," I say, getting up as well. I have to concentrate real hard on keeping my voice low. "Why don't you not call me when you've got some hair on that lumpy ass overwaxed dome and find some pants that cover your ankles?" He looks surprised by that, but looks down at his shoes. "That's right," I say. "A little on the short side, asshole." I don't remember the last time I was this mad.

He glances up toward the bar where Logan Hatter and Drew Wills are craning their necks to look back at him. How fucking embarrassing!

"I assume you can find your own way home."

"You bet your rock-hard nipples I can," I say, turning to walk toward the bar.

I take a seat between Logan and Drew and proceed to drown my problems with enormous amounts of cold beer.

9

⬦⬦

Saturday I wake up and congratulate myself for not going home with Logan Hatter again, even though I really wanted to. I crawl out of bed, swear off drinking forever, and fix a pot of coffee. I take some aspirin while the coffee brews, then pour a cup and head out on the back porch.

Spring is in the air and this lifts my spirits quite a bit. I take a deep breath and relish the warmth. Buster Loo joins me outside and, after some elaborate little-dog stretching, he hops into the yard and makes a few laps in the warm sun. An hour later, I take him for a walk during which he prances around all over the place, which makes me think he appreciates the temperature being over fifty degrees as much as I do.

When I get back home, I call Jalena to see what she's up to today. Turns out she's ditched the diner, opting instead to spend the morning on the Gator with Ethan Allen riding around the farm. I know better than to call Lilly before noon and I certainly don't want to discuss last night's date with Chloe, so I go get Gramma Jones's garden book, pour a fresh cup of coffee, and head back out onto the porch. A gentle breeze ruffles the pages and I can smell that a few of my neighbors have built fires despite the slightly warmer temps. I relax into my lounger and, for some odd reason, feel happy and hopeful. *Don't question it. Just enjoy it,* I think. I look down at the book on the table and think that maybe, just maybe, it's already bringing me good luck.

I flip through the first section again and take a minute to study the bloom chart, trying to commit it to long-term memory. The pages in the second section are just as worn as the first. Some are dirtier than others, and it makes my heart ache when I think about my grandmother studying this book before going to work in her beloved flower beds. I look out at the yard, picturing her on her hands and knees, humming like she always did when she worked. I can't help but think she would be so proud of me if she knew I was sitting here with her garden book, planning a restoration.

In the design section, I recognize several flower bed patterns from the front and back yards. I look at each page, making mental notes of certain arrangements, and then find myself looking at the final section of the book, which is all about trees and shrubs. That's where I find the first Post-it note.

It's a tattered little square, black ink on faded blue paper. On it is my mother's name and a date, June 22, the day she passed away. It's stuck next to a picture of a lavender Queen's crepe myrtle. On the opposite page, I find the same kind of note, only this one has my dad's name and another date, June 25. This note is stuck next to a picture of a white crepe myrtle. I look out into the yard and see a pair of crepe myrtles skirted by vibrant buttercups. Those two trees have just started to bud and, try as I may, I can't remember what color they are when they're in full bloom. I look back down at the book and feel sure that one will be purple and one will be white.

I flip the page and see a note with my grandfather's name on it. It's stuck next to a picture of a pin oak tree. I pick up the book, walk out into the yard, and look up at the giant pin oak that shades the back-left side of the house. It's centered with the back bedroom window, Gramma's bedroom window, which was the one that she had shared with my grandfather. Around the bottom is another flower bed. In there I see an old stepping stone that I've never paid much attention to until today. I lean down, brush the dirt off, and see the inscription, an old Irish blessing.

I look up at the tree. Am I Irish? Was Gramma's family Irish? Or Papa Jones? Jones doesn't sound Irish at all. I wonder what my grandmother's maiden name was. I can't believe I never asked. I put down the stone and pick up the book.

With each page I turn, I find another note stuck beside another picture. I walk around the yard, identifying trees and shrubs planted for my grandmother's two sisters, her brother, and her parents. I discover a group of gardenias planted in memory of grandfather's brothers and his parents. Then I find a star magnolia next to the words "Baby Jones." I look at the date and do the math. My dad would've been two years old when this tree was planted. I've never heard anything about my grandmother having another baby. I've never seen or noticed a grave anywhere near where my whole entire family is now resting in peace in the graveyard behind the church. My eyes sting with tears as I realize she must've had a miscarriage. I stand and wonder if this Baby Jones would've been a boy or a girl. I wonder if Gramma Jones had been far enough along to know. Back then, I don't think they knew what they were having until it arrived. I stare at the star magnolia. I would've had either an aunt or an uncle and possibly some cousins like everyone else I know seems to have in droves.

At the end of the tree section, I find a sticky note that has no name—only a date and a hand-drawn heart. It's stuck next to a weeping willow, not in the backyard but outside the fence and on the far side of the house. I look down at the heart. Did Gramma Jones have a boyfriend? Is that why the tree isn't inside the fence? I look at the date. She planted it on December 29, three and half years after my parents passed away. I walk around to the side of the house and look up at the weeping willow. I hate that tree. I've thought several times about chopping it down because it's a nightmare to mow around. I look back down at the book. Who in the world did she plant that pesky thing for?

I walk back into the house and sit down at the dining table. I turn the page and, tucked into the very back of the book, I find a folded piece of light green stationery. I take it out but don't unfold it. I want to read it, but I'm not sure I want to know what it says. It could be a romantic personal note, meant only for my grandmother's eyes. Or it could be a recipe for tea cakes. I unfold the paper and then quickly fold it back again. What right do I have to do this? What if it's none of my business? What if she had a boyfriend who wrote her dirty letters and this was her favorite one? I put the note back where I found it and close the book. Then I go into the living room and put all of her books back into the box, garden book and all. I take the box to the extra bedroom, her old bedroom, and put it on the bed. I shut the door behind me and go plop down on the sofa. Gramma Jones was the only family I had for a good long while, and realizing how little I know about who she was apart from her role as my grandmother is both embarrassing and depressing. How did I live with her all those years and never know she planted trees in memory of people she loved and lost? No wonder she always took such good care of her yard. Of course, she didn't lose anyone after I moved in with her. Or I should say that she didn't lose anyone that I knew of. I wonder if she ever tried to tell me. Surely I would remember. Maybe she knew that one day, I would get to a point in my life where I would pick up that old book of hers and then figure it out for myself.

10

✧◇✧

Monday morning, I get to school a few minutes late and Chloe is not pleased. She doesn't mention the date, so I assume she heard it was a disaster and needs no further comment from me. I want to ask her why in the world she thought it would be a good idea to set me up with a shitbag like Garlen Blake, but she's already on the edge and I don't want to start an argument. She asks me where Lilly is and I tell her that I haven't talked to her.

"She really needs to tell us what's going on so we won't be worried about her!" Chloe barks.

"I'm sure she's fine; she's a grown woman," I say, and that earns me a nasty look. What the hell is going on here? I wonder. I ask where Stacey is and she says, "Ms. Dewberry arrived at work on time and already has her assignments for the day." She pushes a stack of file folders toward me. "Here's yours."

"I'm in the gym today?" I ask.

"Yes," she snaps. "Is that a problem? I only have one teacher out in A and B Halls. I have two coaches out, so you'll have a busy day."

Very few times in my life has Chloe ever made me mad, but her attitude is really starting to piss me off.

"Is this about the date?" I ask. "Because that guy was a real douche bag."

"No, this is about your job. Right now, it's my job to tell you what yours is."

I walk out before I say something I'll regret and decide that Lilly and I need to have an in-depth discussion about Chloe's newfound anger sometime in the not-so-distant future.

When I get to the gym, I'm still pissed. I stomp down the side of the basketball court, turn into the hallway where the coaches' offices are, and run right into Cameron Becker's gigantic boobs.

"Dammit," I say, taking a step back. "You need to watch where you're going."

"Or maybe you need to watch where you're going," she says, scowling down at me.

I think about fist-whipping her fake tits until one pops out onto the gym floor, but then Chloe would fire me for sure and I don't need that, so instead I say, "I'm supposed to be in the gym, Ms. Becker! I'm not in here on cock-watch."

"Wouldn't do you any good if you were," she retorts, and I resist a powerful urge to slap the crap out of her.

"I've been on cock-watch in here," I tell her. "We all have." Her smirk turns to a frown, so I add, "But you can just keep thinking you're special."

"I can't help it if I have your job, Ms. Jones," she hisses. "And let's not forget that you're the one who left. I don't know what's going on in your life and I really don't care, but I love my job and have no intention of leaving."

"Great," I say. "Well, good luck with the art fair. It's a lot of work, but I'm sure you can handle it."

"What art fair?" she says with a snort. "I'm not doing any art fair. That is so ten years ago."

"Your phony melons are so ten years ago," I say as the bell for first period rings.

"What?" she says, and I'm actually glad she didn't hear me, because that wasn't my best comeback ever.

"Nothing."

"Have a good day subbing," she says, and turns to walk away.

"Bitch!" I say, but she's already gone. I hear sniggering and turn to see Coach Hatter, Coach Spears, and Coach O'Bryan huddled at the gym lounge door.

"Cat fight! Cat fight!" Hatter says, laughing. He walks over and puts his arm around me. "She doesn't know what she's getting herself into messing with you." He smiles. "Somebody better warn her."

"I thought y'all were about to roll!" Coach Spears says. "My money was on you, Jones."

"I was looking forward to breaking that one up," Coach O'Bryan quips.

"I'd kick her ass all over this gym!" I say, and they start laughing.

"I don't know if you would or not." We all turn to see Coach Wills looming in the door of his office. "Cameron can handle herself."

I look at Hatt, who whispers, "Relapse. I'll explain later."

"Jeez, Wills," Coach O'Bryan says. "Give it up, man. She dumped you." Okay, so I see that news broke. I feel sorry for Drew Wills because I know how it feels to have people whispering behind your back.

"Shut your mouth, O!" Wills says, walking past us. I glance at Hatter, thankful neither of them mentioned my stud-muffin date. The other coaches go their separate ways, and Hatter hangs back a minute until they're out of earshot.

"She's driving him crazy," he says. "I'll tell you all about it later." He looks at the folder in my hand. "Hey, which lunch do you have?" I look down at my schedule.

"I don't have one because I'm covering P.E. classes all day!"

"Man, that sucks," he says.

"Tell me about it," I say, getting pissed at Chloe all over again. How dare she be so mean after practically forcing me to go on two absolutely horrific dates. I look at Hatter, who is shaking his head.

"You want me to bring you some lunch?"

"I brought my own, but thanks," I tell him.

"Okay, well, I gotta run. Hope your day isn't too bad." He stands there looking like he might say something else, but he doesn't.

"Thanks," I say. He nods and walks away.

After seven straight hours of rowdy freshmen and boisterous sophomores dropping their cell phones out of their gym shorts, picking them up and texting, and then sticking them back in their sweaty underwear, I go home, beat beyond belief.

"Buster Loo," I tell my little dog when I get there, "this ain't the life for me." I grab a beer from the fridge and sit down at the kitchen table, telling myself not to cry. Buster Loo looks at me, expectantly. "No walk today, boy, I'm sorry. You'll have to make good use of your trusty doggy door." He takes off and returns a minute later with one of his chew toys, and I play fetch with him in the living room. After a while, he gets tired of our game and disappears behind the love seat. I take another beer with me to the bathtub where I run a hot bubble bath. I get in and relax for a while, soaking, drinking, and trying to convince myself that I can go back to school tomorrow and live through another day of substitute hell. I get out of the tub, put on some old pajamas, and look at my phone. I have a text from Lilly.

"Home?" it says.

"Yes," I send back.

"OK 4me 2come by?"

"Of course," I send back, wondering if it's really that hard to type an extra three or four letters or if Lilly just enjoys coded texting that much.

Thirty minutes later, I'm wrapped in a fuzzy blanket on the couch with Buster Loo by my side and his favorite toy, Mr. Wishbone, tucked in between us. Buster Loo starts to growl when Lilly pulls into the drive and when she rings the doorbell a minute later, he rocket launches himself off the sofa, sending Mr. Wishbone flying as he makes haste to the front door. I get up, open the door, and see Lilly standing on my front porch, looking like hell.

"Get in here!" I say. "What's going on?" A million things run through my mind as I pray that nothing has happened to her brother, her parents, or Dax. She starts squalling as soon as she steps in the house. Buster Loo retrieves Mr. Wishbone and promptly takes the toy over to where Lilly is standing. I tell her to sit down, then put my blanket around her because, even though the weather has taken a turn for the worse, she's wearing a skimpy short-sleeve shirt. Buster Loo jumps onto the couch and places Mr. Wishbone on her knee. Then he hops onto her lap, stretches his little chi-weenie body out, and places his paws on her shoulder like he's try-ing to give her a hug. She pulls him up close and he speed licks the tears off her cheeks.

"Aw, Buster Loo," she says, "you're such a sweetie pie."

I go into the kitchen and put on some coffee. After taking two coffee cups out of the cabinet, I grab a bottle of Irish cream and pour a generous serving into each one. "I'll be right there!" I call out. Her answer is a few more sniffles.

Lilly is and always has been an emotional basket case who cries at the drop of a hat, so I try to convince myself that everything is fine and she's just overreacting. Her easy life hasn't made her tough, but the look on her face has me fearing the worst.

I pour hot coffee into the cups and go sit beside her on the couch. When I hand one to her, she's shaking so bad that she spills coffee on her pants. I take the cup from her and set it on the coffee table. She starts sobbing again, so I go to the bathroom and bring back a cold wet rag. She puts it over her eyes and takes a deep breath.

"Lilly," I say when she calms down a bit, "I'm kind of freakin' out about what's going on."

"I'm sorry," she says between sniffles. "It's Dax."

"Oh my God, is he okay? What happened?" Panic washes over me. I set my coffee cup down, too.

"He's fine. At least he is right now," she says. She starts digging in the pocket of her jeans and pulls out a crumpled piece of paper. She smoothes it out and hands it to me. At the top, it says *Department of the Army*.

"Read it," she says, tears streaming.

"'Individual Ready Reserve'?" I say, looking at her. "What is that?"

"Just read it."

As I read the letter, addressed to Sergeant Dax Dorsett of the 82nd Airborne Division, my stomach knots up and I start to feel nauseated.

"What does this mean?" I ask, even though I think I already know.

"They called him back," she says. "He's going to Afghanistan."

"What? When? I thought that mess was almost over."

"Apparently it's not over for him," she says, and starts crying again. "He has two weeks to get everything squared away before he leaves for six weeks of training and after that, he leaves for good." She looks at me. "Two weeks! He has to leave in two weeks."

"Oh, Lilly," I say, and then pause because I have no idea what to say. "How can they do that? Hasn't he been out of the army for over a year?"

"When you enlist, you sign up for four years of active duty and four years of Ready Reserve. They called him back. They can do that. I don't know why they picked him." She pauses to catch her breath. "I guess we're just really lucky." Lilly picks up her coffee cup and takes a sip. Buster Loo is a nervous wreck. He grabs Mr. Wishbone and runs behind the love seat.

"The letter came yesterday along with his orders," she says. "I begged him to try to get out of it, but he just kept saying it was his job and he had to go. We got into a fight because I—you know what? I don't even want to talk about it right now."

"Oh Lord," I say. "I cannot believe this. Did you call your brother? What did he say?"

"I called him yesterday and he said that after his twelve years in the army, nothing surprises him anymore. He told me that a soldier gets called out of Ready Reserve when a unit scheduled for deployment has spots that have to be filled and that's just how it works."

"Oh."

"I'm going home with Dax this weekend," she says, looking miserable. "We're not in a fight anymore. He wants me to meet his family before he leaves." She nods toward the letter. "Which is great, under these circumstances, you know? But he asked me to go, so what was I going to say?"

"Nothing you can say but yes." I look at her. "You haven't met his family yet?"

"No, and he acts funny about it when I mention meeting them. And every time he goes to see them, he always has some excuse why I shouldn't go. Either his mother isn't feeling well or he has to help his dad. It's always something. He's met my family. He even met Luke at Christmas." She takes another sip of coffee. "So finally after all this time, I get to meet his family."

"So he's taking you down this weekend?" I say.

"Yep. We're going on Friday and coming back Sunday, and then he flies out of Memphis the next weekend," she says. "Sunday after next. Can you believe that?"

"I can't!" I say. "How can this happen so fast?"

"I don't know," she says, and stops. "He explained it, but I don't even remember what he said. My mind has just kind of shut down on me." She sighs and wipes her eyes. "You know Luke has been deployed six times, but we expect that, you know, because that's his job. It's part of his life. It's part of our life. It's his career." She looks at me. "This was just such a shock to me. So unexpected."

"I can't even imagine, Lilly," I say, hugging her again. "Look, we'll have a going away party for him here at my house. When did you say y'all will be back from—where does he live again?"

"The Delta. He said we're coming back here Sunday afternoon."

"So, we'll have a party next Saturday night, unless you want to be alone with him."

"I'm taking a few days off next week to be alone with him. It's going to use up all of my sick days, but I don't care and I don't care what Chloe says, either. And I think he would appreciate a party. You know how he is."

I think about Dax. Handsome, fun-loving Dax. Love of Lilly's life Dax. I say a silent prayer for his safety.

"I just can't believe it," she says, petting Buster Loo who has just reappeared sans Mr. Wishbone. He hops back into her lap. "I cannot believe this is happening."

I want to ask how long he's going to be gone, but I don't want to set her off again. I know her brother used to be gone for a year with two weeks off, during which he always came home to Bugtussle and stayed with their parents.

"We'll get through this," I tell her. "We will. So, you haven't told Chloe?"

"No, I'm going to call her on my way home," she says.

"Why don't you call her from here or when you get home?" I tell her. "You don't need to be driving and squalling."

"You're right. I'll call her when I get home."

11

◇◇◇

When I get to the conference room on Tuesday, Chloe isn't there. I go to her office where I find her sitting at her desk, a bleak look on her face.

"What's wrong?" I ask nervously.

"I can't believe Dax has been recalled to active duty," she says, and I wonder how she always has the right words for everything. I mean, does she Google this stuff or does she just know?

"He'll be fine," I say. "He's been deployed twice before. He's a soldier. He'll be fine." I sound like a babbling fool.

"Lilly isn't fine," she says quietly.

"No, but she will be because she has us," I say, looking at her. "We'll take care of her."

"J.J. really hates that he's leaving," she says. "He thinks a lot of Dax."

"Everyone thinks a lot of Dax," I say. "He's a great guy. Hey!" I say, trying to cheer her up. "We're going to give him a going away party next Saturday. Y'all should come."

"We'll be there," she says, and puts her hand on her stomach. "This just makes me feel so sick."

"It makes me feel sick, too, Chloe, but we should be thankful for good and brave people like him who don't mind stepping up to the plate to defend the freedom of this great country." There! Now that was good.

"You sound like a politician," she says without cracking a smile.

"I'm thinking of running for office," I say. "Ace Jones for president." She doesn't smile at that, either. Instead, she asks me if I mind covering P.E. again today.

"Not at all. Whatever I need to do." This is my life. The seventh ring of hell.

"Coach Keeley is the only one out, so it'll only be four periods."

"Oh, okay." Or maybe just the fifth ring.

Wednesday, I'm back in A Hall with Stacey Dewberry, who is rocking a purple one-piece outfit trimmed with gold and rhinestone embellishments.

"Ace—I mean Ms. Jones," she says when I walk into the lounge. "I'm so happy to see you! I've missed you!"

"Uh, thank you, Ms. Dewberry," I say, hoping no one can overhear this conversation. I wonder if I should tell her I missed her, too, but I just can't get those words to come out of my mouth.

"So who are you today?" she asks.

"I'm Ms. George." Another day of solid freshmen.

"Cool!" she says. "I'm Mrs. DePew, right next door!" While she has the gifted class.

"Lucky you!" I say, thinking I might call in sick tomorrow. Surely Chloe would understand.

After the most horrible three hours of my life, during which I continuously curse my decision to take this job while trying not to curse all of these wild-ass, lunatic ninth graders who are all too happy to discover a substitute instead of their regular teacher, I take off to the teachers' lounge for a moment of silence. And that's where I'm sitting with my head on the table when Freddie Dublin walks in. He hums while he rummages through the fridge, no doubt looking for his Vitaminwater.

"Bad day, Ms. Jones?" he asks, closing the fridge.

"That would be one way to put it, Mr. Dublin."

"Sit up, sweetheart," he says, and I do. He steps behind me and begins to massage my neck and shoulders, and it's all I can do not to hang my mouth open and drool. "So much tension here, Ms. Jones. You're so stressed out."

"Oh, that feels so nice," I moan while he continues to work marvelous magic with his hands. "You are so good at this."

"Lots of practice," he says, moving his fingers around my head. I put my hands on the table so I don't fall out on the floor from sheer pleasure. I believe a good massage could cure me of most anything.

"Better?" he says a minute later, taking a seat next to me.

"Yes," I say. "I'm glad you stopped, because I was about to tell you that I love you."

"I get that a lot," he says with a wink. Freddie is wearing a starched white shirt, perfectly cuffed at the elbows and a fantastic pair of khakis. Simple ensemble, but on him it looks divine. "So, I hear Ms. Lane's young boyfriend is leaving her."

"He's leaving all of us," I say. "But she's definitely the most upset about it."

"I saw him at a football game last year," he says, shaking his head. "He's gorgeous."

"Yeah, he's pretty good-looking."

"Who's pretty good-looking?" Stacey asks as she sprays her way out of the restroom.

"Dax Dorsett," I say. "Lilly Lane's boyfriend."

"Don't know him," she says.

"Yes, you know him. He's that handsome cop who comes to the ball games," Freddie says. Stacey just stands there in her purple jumpsuit and stares at him.

Freddie seems to be enjoying the awkward moment a little too much, so, in an effort to move things along, I say, "Yes, he's been called back to active duty and we're having a going away party next weekend and both of you are invited."

"Really!" they say at the same time, but they use two totally different tones of the same word.

"Really," I say. I grab the Post-it notes on the table and a pen. "Here's my address," I say, giving them each a Post-it. "Next Saturday. Probably around seven p.m."

"Dress?" Freddie says.

"Oh no, you can't wear a dress," Stacey says, looking really nervous.

"The dress," I say, eyeballing Stacey, "will be casual."

"I love casual," Freddie says. He looks at Stacey and then at me. "May I bring a plus one?"

"Sure," I say, then narrow my eyes. "Anyone I know?"

"I'll let you know," he says with a wicked grin.

"You better not bring that hoochie-hocker, Cameron Becker," Stacey says.

"Hoochie-hocker?" I say. I can't help it; that cracks me up.

"I wouldn't dream of it," Freddie tells her, then flashes that radiant smile. *Oh Lord,* I think. What have I just done? The bell rings to signal the end of break, and I fight the cluster-fucked hallway back to Ms. George's room where I spend the remainder of the day fantasizing about slamming my head in the file drawer of Ms. George's metal desk until I've decapitated myself.

Thursday, I run two red lights and almost sideswipe a dump truck, but I get to school on time. Stacey has already been dispatched and Chloe is sitting in her office, looking pallid.

"I think you need to go to the doctor, Chloe," I say. She looks up at me, and I notice dark circles under her eyes. "You haven't been yourself lately and I'm starting to worry."

"I'm fine," she says. "But can you do me one small favor?"

Oh hellz bellz! Am I back in freshman hell, or does she have me another hot date lined up for this weekend? "Sure," I say.

"Would you join Lilly and me at my house for dinner tonight?"

"Absolutely," I say, secretly relieved. "What's up?"

"Oh, nothing. You know, I just got everything all moved into my brand-new kitchen and would like to have my girlfriends over for a nice meal." She smiles. "That's all." I want to press her for a more honest explanation, because it's never just "Oh, nothing" or "That's all" with Chloe. But she looks tired and beat down, so I take my folders, tell her to have a nice day, and head off for another day in the fiery pits.

I call Lilly on the way home and make some bad jokes about

Chloe filleting us with a steak knife, but she's not in the mood for my foolishness, so I let her go. When I get home, I shuck off my gut-gripping "teacher" clothes and slip into something comfy. After taking Buster Loo for a nice walk at the park, I refill his water bowl and then hang out with him until it's time to freshen up and head to Chloe's.

I'm excited about seeing the place; I haven't been there since the day after she bought it because she didn't want anyone to see it while it was "under construction." Lilly and I have both mentioned hosting a housewarming party because it's the first house that Chloe has officially owned all by herself, but so far, she's not been too keen on that idea.

12

<>

s I pull into the drive at 505 Skyline Cove, I admire the lush landscaping and freshly painted columns. I park in front of the house, walk up the wide stone steps, and ring the doorbell. Chloe opens the door and when I step inside, I'm overwhelmed by the glorious décor. I follow her through the living room, past a study, and into the kitchen, all of which could put any home in any magazine anywhere in the country to complete shame. Money sure makes for a good-looking life.

"Chloe, this place is unbelievable," I say.

"Oh, it's nothing." She dismisses my comment with a small wave. "It's just home."

Just home my ass! I think as the doorbell rings. Lilly is equally impressed with Chloe's amazing spread, and we ohh and ahh like kids at Christmas when she takes us out back to the massive deck overlooking the lake.

"Chloe, this is resort-style living at its finest," I say, and Lilly quickly agrees. We follow her back inside to the kitchen where some wonderful aromas are wafting from the stainless-steel double oven. Lilly runs a hand over the granite countertop, then raises her eyebrows at me.

"Quite lovely," she says while Chloe fixes three glasses of iced tea. I just stand there and nod.

Chloe politely turns down our offers to help as she slides a pan out of the upper oven, which I see is full of those little appetizers you can buy only at Sam's Club. She uses a fancy-looking spatula to scoop those lovely looking things onto a fancy-schmancy serving dish. Just as we finish those, a timer goes off, and Chloe reaches into the lower oven and pulls out a pan of crab-stuffed shrimp.

"Oh my stars!" I say, inadvertently channeling my inner Stacey Dewberry. "Those are beautiful!" The next pan is full of potatoes, and then comes a beautiful loaf of artisanal bread. I make a joke about her oven being like a clown car, but no one laughs except for me. Chloe goes to the fridge and brings back a bowl of corn relish and a stick of butter riding in style in one of those little dishes made especially for sticks of butter. She refills our drinks while we fix our plates, and then Lilly and I sit down at the kitchen table, which has a very nice view of the lake. Chloe joins us a minute later, and we make awkward small talk while everyone tries to be nice and carefully avoids certain topics of conversation.

"Did you make this?" I ask, taking another bite of the shrimp. "It's delicious."

"Of course not," she says. "Renaldo did."

"Who is Renaldo?" I ask.

"Her butler," Lilly says.

"He's not a butler," Chloe insists. "He just drives up from Oxford twice a week to help out. He prepares and freezes dishes. I had to have a little help during the remodeling."

"Well, you can tell Renaldo that this is the best crab-stuffed shrimp I've ever had," I say, thinking about how differently she and I define "a little help."

She tries to make more small talk, then stops, obviously frustrated.

"I'm sorry for being so snappy and short these past few weeks," Chloe says. "Y'all know that's not like me at all."

"It's fine," I say.

"No problem," Lilly chimes in. We continue eating.

"I'm pregnant," Chloe says. I stop sipping my tea and put down the glass. Lilly starts coughing and making choking noises. "Are you okay?" Chloe asks her.

"Yes," Lilly says. "The bread. It was the bread. I just—" She stops. "I'm sorry. Did you just say you were pregnant?"

"Yes."

"Yes, you're pregnant?" I ask.

"Yes, I'm pregnant. I'm having a baby."

"How do you know, exactly—uh, for sure?" I say.

"I went to the doctor yesterday," she says. "I couldn't say anything at school—that's why I asked you both to come here tonight."

"Okay, well . . ." I don't know what to say.

"Congratulations," Lilly says, but it sounds more like a question.

"Yeah," I say. "Congratulations."

The three of us sit there for a long, awkward minute. I look down at my plate and feel like I might pass out from the stress hovering around the table.

"Lilly, I'm so sorry to tell you this right now because I know you have so much going on."

"Chloe, this is a really big deal! It doesn't matter what I've got going on when you have news like this!"

"You both have to promise not to tell a soul. If anyone at school finds out, I'll lose my job and be humiliated."

Lilly and I exchange an anxious look.

"Technically, that would be illegal," Lilly says.

"Lilly," Chloe says, "you know better than anybody how easy it is to fall prey to the small-town system of warped moral justice."

"That's right," I say, waving a finger at Lilly. "Violate the Code of Socially Acceptable Sins in Bugtussle, Mississippi, and you're out the damned door. Crack a goat or your married coworker and we'll all turn a blind eye as long as the coworker is of the opposite sex and the goat is not related to you." They both stare at me while I giggle.

"So, is J.J. excited?" Lilly asks, and the comic relief I worked so hard to perpetrate evaporates in the silence that follows. Chloe doesn't acknowledge Lilly's question.

"Chloe, you have told him, haven't you?" I ask.

"No."

"Okay," Lilly says, pushing back her plate.

"Do you have anything here to drink?" I ask.

"There is some wine in the fridge. I opened it last night, then remembered I shouldn't drink, so it's full."

I go into the kitchen and get the wine, grab two glasses, and return to find Lilly and Chloe staring at each other in silence.

"Can I get you anything, Chloe?" I ask. "More tea? Some water?" A box of diapers and wipes?

"No, thank you."

I return to my seat and pour Lilly and myself a glass of white moscato. No one says a word. I pick up my wineglass.

"I don't want to tell him," Chloe says finally.

"Well, you know he's going to find out eventually, right?" I ask, and Lilly gives me a stern shut-your-mouth look.

"Why in the world would you not want to tell him?" Lilly asks sweetly. "He's going to be so happy."

"I want him to propose and then I want to get married and then I want to tell him."

I pick up my wineglass and chugalug. Normally, I'm not much of a wine drinker, but this stuff is pretty refreshing. Lilly pours me another and then refills her own. "Okay," Lilly says.

"Okay," I say.

And more silence.

"I don't want him to ask me to marry him because I'm pregnant," Chloe says. "I don't want us to have to get married. I want him to marry me because he wants to and because he loves me, not because he has to."

"Chloe, he does love you," I say. "He's always been crazy about you. Even when you were married to that shithead Richard Stacks."

"Oh, please, let's not talk about him."

"We're not going to talk about him!" Lilly says, giving me the evil eye. I give her my best okay-then-well-you-say-something look. She continues. "I think we can all agree that it would be best to tell J.J., right?" She looks at me and I nod.

"I can't do that," she says. "I just can't. And I can't believe this has happened to me. I'm on the pill and I never forget to take it."

"I do not doubt that at all," I say.

"What are we going to do?" Chloe asks.

"We?" I exchange another look with Lilly. We pick up our wineglasses and then I pour the next round. "This wine is fabulous," I say. "Where on earth did you get it?"

"Ethan Allen gets it for me," Chloe says. She looks at Lilly and then at me, her expectation obvious.

"Well, we are going to find a way to get J.J. to propose before you have to tell him that you're pregnant," I say with great conviction even though I'm only guessing.

"No!" she says.

"Chloe, you have to be realistic about this. We're all adults here." Lilly looks at me. "Well, almost."

"Thank you," I say.

"Anyway," Lilly continues, "J.J. needs to know. He would want to know, and he might get upset if you don't tell him."

"It is his baby, right?" I ask, and Lilly kicks me under the table.

"Of course," Chloe says, taking offense. "Who else would it belong to?"

"Sorry," I say. "That was so stupid."

"Yes, it was," Lilly agrees. "Do you want us to talk to him, maybe try to drop some hints?" Lilly ventures. I shake my head in disagreement because J. J. Jackson does not entertain foolishness in any shape, form, or fashion.

"Please don't do that," Chloe says. "Let's just give it a few weeks."

"A few weeks?" Lilly says. "How far along are you?"

"Almost six weeks. My due date is November 15, so I should have at least another month before I start showing."

"But y'all have talked about getting married, right?" I ask.

"No."

"Not even after you bought this big nice house?"

"No."

"Has moving in together been discussed?" Lilly asks.

"No."

I look at Lilly and she shrugs. She picks up the bottle and fills each of our glasses half full, emptying it.

"You have to tell him, Chloe," I say. "You have to. He has a right to know."

"I am not telling him," she says stubbornly. "Maybe he'll just up and decide to propose."

"Maybe so," I say, realizing that there will be no reasoning with her tonight.

"Maybe," Lilly says, obviously sensing the same.

On the drive home, I call Lilly and we discuss ways to drop some hints to the sheriff that he needs to propose to his damsel in distress.

13

◇◇

Friday, Stacey Dewberry is hell-bent on the two of us going barhopping, and after the sixteenth time I tell her I can't, she finally stops asking. Lilly texts me just before noon and says they're pulling into the driveway at Dax's parents' house and she's about to have a panic attack because they live in a tiny farmhouse and she's wearing a three-hundred-dollar pair of heels. She's not worried about getting them dirty—she's worried about looking ostentatious. I send her a few messages, trying to encourage her, but then her texts stop abruptly so I spend the next few hours worrying about how that's going.

When the bell rings at the end of the day, I walk into the teachers' lounge to get a Diet Mountain Dew. Freddie Dublin is stretched out on the couch with his shoes off. I compliment his wide-striped green and navy blue socks.

"Big plans for the weekend?" he asks as I drop quarters into the drink machine.

"Not hardly," I say. "You?"

"Going to Memphis and seeing a show at the Orpheum."

"That is so cool, Freddie!" I say because it is. "What are you going to see?"

"*Memphis*. It's based on a true story."

"Sounds great. Have a blast." I turn to leave and run right into Stacey Dewberry who, in her haste to get into the lounge, almost knocks me down with the door. I step out of her way.

"Ace—I mean Ms. Jones—I am so sorry about that," she says, hustling past me to the drink machine. "Gotta go! Gotta go!" she chants, and she forcibly inserts her coins into the machine.

"What's your hurry, sunshine?" Freddie asks, still lying back with his feet crossed at the ankles.

"My nerves are shot to holy Hades and I can't drive that bus today without a can of medication." She pulls a Dr Pepper out of the dispenser and holds it up for us to see. "Gotta run, peeps." And run she does. I look at Freddie, who is humming and smiling as he piddles with his phone.

"She drives a bus?" I ask him.

"Obviously," he says, without looking up.

"Who in their right mind—"

"Now, Ms. Jones," Freddie says with a smile. "Surely you don't presume the curious Ms. Dewberry to be in her right mind?"

I freeze, thinking that anything I say can and will be used against me in a court of frenzied gossip and twisted hearsay.

"Enjoy the show!" I say, and then get the "holy Hades" out of there before he has a chance to say anything else. In the safety of the hallway, I take a sip of my semi-cold drink and decide that even though Mr. Freddie Dublin is one of the coolest cats I've met in a while, I will not be entrapped by his trickery and charm. Then I think about Stacey Dewberry behind the wheel of a school bus, and that makes me laugh out loud. How in the world does she do that and sub? No wonder she drinks so much Dr Pepper.

I spend Saturday morning helping Jalena hang rods, blinds, and curtains while discussing the pros and cons of a wall mural. After we unpack what seems like ten thousand boxes of dishes and silverware, she asks me if I could do some flamingos instead of marsh grass.

"Not, like, real-lookin' flamingos," she says. "I want them to be cartoonish. Cartoonish, but not childish. Like they're just about to say something funny and might use ugly words when they do."

"Got it," I say. "I can do that." I grab a pencil and sketch a few flamingos that could possibly be cussing or telling dirty jokes.

"That's perfect," she says. "How long will it take for you to do that?"

"Couple of hours," I say with a shrug. "Depends on how many you want and how pink you want them to be."

"I think I want three," she says. "Like two hanging out on one side of the wall and one on the other."

"Okay," I say. "I'll make the one by itself a little bigger. Like it's a bit closer to you."

"That sounds good," she says as she walks over to the wall. "So, two here. One over there, and could you add some water and the sun in the middle? Maybe some clouds? Like the flamingos are framing a sunset. Kind of blend them into a nice scene."

"That's actually a great idea," I tell her. "I could do this today, you know."

"Really?"

"Sure. No time like the present. Unless, of course, you have another truckload of dishes coming in that needs to be unboxed."

"I think I have enough plates and glasses to do me for a day or two," she says with a giggle. "You wanna go pick up some paint?"

"Do I?" I say, laughing. "Do I?"

"Do you need some kind of special paint for this?" she asks, and I assure her that I don't. We ride to Walmart where I grab four different shades of pink craft paint along with several other colors and a can of glaze. I go find Jalena and see that she's picked up a bag of chicken strips, some jojo potatoes, and a package of frosted sugar cookies. On the way back to the diner, we stop by my house, where I run inside and grab my paint brushes. When we get back to the diner, she fixes us drinks and we eat lunch on paper plates at the bar. After asking her one last time if she's absolutely sure that she wants to do this and assuring her it will not hurt my feelings if she doesn't, I start sketching on the back wall of Jalena's diner. She stands and watches me for a few minutes, and I don't know if she's curious about what I'm doing or worried about me making a mess.

"And if you hate it, it will only take a minute to cover this wall with primer and repaint it, okay?"

"I'm not worried, Ace!" she says, but she keeps standing there. I turn around and look at her. "Okay, I've got to get this menu typed up, so I'll go get started on that." She disappears into the kitchen and returns a minute later with an old FM radio that she sets on the bar and fools with until she finds a station. Then she starts pecking away on her lavender laptop. I line up my colors, pick up my paint brushes, and get to work.

"Okay, are you ready to see greatness?" I ask when I finish the first flamingo. "Close your eyes and turn around." Jalena turns around on her bar stool with her eyes shut. "Okay, look!" I say.

"Wow!" she says when she opens her eyes. "I love it!"

"Thanks!" I tell her. I like it, too. "So you want two more?"

"Abso-freakin'-lootley!"

And so we both get back to work. After I finish the other two flamingos, I get started on the sunset, which is quick and easy work, and then paint some blue-green water and a white seashore. I stand up straight, back and knees cracking, and give the mural a thorough inspection. After a few touch-ups, I sit down on the floor and lean back against the wall to rest my aching back. Then I literally watch the paint dry. When it does, I get up and start on the glaze, which makes the whole scene look soft and faded like an old postcard.

"Voilà!" I say, and Jalena turns around on her bar stool again.

"Double wow!" Jalena says. "I love it! Talented!" She opens her mouth to say something, then stops.

"What?"

She gives me a funny look.

"What is it?" I ask. "If something is wrong, just say so and I'll fix it. This has to be perfect, so no holding back."

"It's not that." She nods toward the wall. "I love it. It's perfect."

"Well, what is it then?"

"I don't even want to bring it up."

"Bring what up?"

"Just never mind. I'm sorry."

"Don't just never mind me, sister. What were you going to say?"

"I was just wondering how you don't miss having your own art gallery," she blurts. "This"—she points to the wall—"is amazing. I'm sorry. I don't want to upset you by bringing up the past. I just don't see how you can not do this for a living."

"It doesn't upset me to talk about the art gallery," I say, trying not to think too hard about it. "It's over. I gave it my best shot and it wasn't for me." I shrug.

"You don't miss it?"

"Hell to the niz-oh," I say, and that's the honest truth. "I mean, I love to paint, but I hated being in there by myself all the time. I'm a social bird, sister, and I can't function without my flock."

"Yeah, and speaking of flocks," she says, eyeing me, "how are things going over at the schoolhouse?"

"Oh, it's terrible," I say with a laugh. "Worse than I ever imagined, but it's okay. It's fine." I pause. "Okay, I'm lying. It's not fine at all. It actually sucks rotten donkey balls, but whatever. It's a means to an end."

"The end of what little sanity you have left," she says, laughing. "I don't see how you do it. Hell, I don't see how anybody does it."

"Teaching isn't as bad as you think." I look at her and she doesn't look convinced. "It's actually nice when you have your own classroom and your own desk and all of your stuff put together just like you want it. It's really cool." She looks skeptical. "Don't get me wrong here. I'm not trying to convince you that subbing isn't the absolute rock-bottom hottest freakin' part of hell. Because it is."

"I just hope it's worth it," she says.

"Me, too," I tell her. "It would suck for real to go through all this crap for nothing."

"So you're pretty sure you're going to get your old job back?"

"I don't know," I say with a sigh. "Honestly, it's not looking good right now. I mean, that hussy Cameron Becker doesn't have any idea what she's doing, but she's made it abundantly clear that she has no plans to vacate my classroom and she's even threatened to get a lawyer."

"Why can't they just add some more classes and have two art teachers?"

"They could if they had enough students to fill up the classes, but Chloe has already told me that barely enough students have registered for the class next year to justify having one art teacher on the payroll, let alone two. That's the problem with electives. The students have to elect to enroll in your class. Chloe says she's had to coax students into taking the entrance exam and she's never had to do that before."

"See? You're irreplaceable."

"Not hardly," I say with a snort. "I take my classes on awesome field trips to the Brooks Museum of Art in Memphis." I smile at Jalena. "Fifteen bucks each to ride a charter bus, lunch at the Hard Rock Cafe afterward, and bingo! Everyone loves your class."

"I'm sure there's more to it than that."

"Well, of course, that's what I like to think, but probably not."

"So what are you going to do if Ms. Becker manages to hang on to your job for another year?" Jalena asks, and I'm tempted to tell her to hold off on the hard questions because she's killing my mood. I look at my flamingos and frown. Dammit! I was so happy two minutes ago.

"Hey, do you like your new flamingos or what?" I ask. Jalena takes the hint and lets it go.

"I love my new flamingos. So are you finished?"

"I have to glaze it again," I say. "But that won't take too long."

"Okay, well, while you do that, I'm going to go print off this menu and see how it looks on paper," she says.

I inspect my artwork one final time, then glaze the wall from top to bottom and right to left. I walk back to Ethan Allen's office where Jalena is sitting at the desk, examining one of her menu sheets.

"Come check out the finished product," I say. She follows me down the hall to the diner and then brags on the mural until I finally have to tell her to lay off. I think she might be overembellishing the compliments because she's worried that she hurt my feelings by grilling me about what I'm going to do if Cameron Becker doesn't give up the art class and move her sassy ass on to some other place. But the mural does look exceptional, if I do say so myself.

"Okay, now come check out my finished product, which isn't quite so glamorous," she says, and I follow her back down the hallway to the office where she plops into the desk chair. "These things are ugly!" She points at the copies on the desk. "They're too plain. I didn't realize how dull they were until I slid 'em into the menu cover and . . . Look at this." She hands me the menu. "Blah blah blah. Boring!"

"It looks very professional," I say.

"Professional is boring."

"Maybe a little, yes."

"Can you put something cool on here before I have to take them to the printer? Liven 'em up for me?"

"Sure," I say. "I can draw a mean penis."

"Yeah, I hear you've drawn a lot of that around here," she says with a cunning smile.

"Ethan Allen needs to stop telling lies about my lust life. You want a penis on here or not?"

"What's your deal with always trying to draw a penis on something?"

"You said to liven it up and that would surely do it," I tell her. "I stay true to the cause of artistic integrity." Jalena rolls her eyes and laughs. "Okay, seriously, you want an alligator on here or some little food baskets or what?"

"I don't care," she says, still giggling. "You've been here every step of the way since the first wall went up, so I think you have a feel for this place as well as I do. Just do your thing." She stops talking and waves a finger at me. "Not your b.s. artistic integrity thing, but your unperverted creative thing."

"Okay," I say with a sigh. "Unperverted. Got it." I smile, thinking this part of helping Jalena is so much more fun than sweeping up Sheetrock dust. "Print me off some extras for doodling purposes, please, ma'am."

"How many?"

"Three or four."

"No problemo, mi amiga." She starts tapping on her laptop again and the printer starts humming. I ask for a sheet of paper and a pen. "You don't have to start right now," she says.

"I'm not," I say, and then ask her a few questions about this and that on the menu because, even though she has complete faith in my ability to create something unperverted that she'll like, I still want to make sure I have a clear idea of what she has in mind. I make a bunch of notes and then decide to surprise her with a little picture of her daddy's marina at Frog Bayou on the back of the last page. I think she'd like that.

"Do you want me to do it by hand or on the computer? I can do it either way." She considers that for a minute, tapping her ink pen against her temple.

"If it's all the same to you, let's skip the computer," she says finally. "I don't want it to look too commercial. I ain't openin' a Red Lobster here." She starts laughing and so do I. "Everything I serve will be homemade, so it would be awesome if the menu had that feel to it, too."

"Sounds good to me."

"It's all about that personal touch, you know? There's a certain quality in that."

"I couldn't possibly agree with you more." I scribble a few more notes. "When do you need these by?"

"Anytime this week," she says, and I get up to go. "Wait a minute! I'm not letting you do this unless you let me pay you."

"Okay," I say. "Why don't you have Ethan Allen order me a bottle of that white moscato he gets for Chloe?"

"Done," she says. "Lifetime supply."

"Yeah, you better check with him first on that," I tell her.

"Nah," she says. "All I have to do is say the magic word."

"Please?"

"No. Shrimp-n-grits."

"Magic words, then," I say, teasing.

"It's hyphenated where I come from." She stands up to give me a big hug. I think about how great it is that I had something to do with two good-hearted folks like Jalena and Ethan Allen finding each other, even if I was just as surprised as the next guy when the sparks started to fly. Maybe their happiness shouldn't be so depressing to me after all. It's a success story that wouldn't have happened otherwise, so maybe I'll start patting myself on the back instead. I need to have some reason to pat myself on the back. Might as well be that. That and those bomb-ass flamingos I just put up on that wall.

When I step outside, the cool wind catches me off guard and I wish I'd brought a jacket. I crank up my car and turn the heat on full blast.

Out on the highway, I get trapped behind a left-lane cruiser who just can't seem to make it past an old grandpa-looking car in the right lane. I stay in the left lane because, after all, it is the one designated for passing. I can see that the person driving the car in front of me is a woman who is fooling with her cell phone, and I hope for her sake that she's looking at a damned directional device or else I'm going to get pissed. More pissed than I already am, that is, after driving fifty-five miles per hour for three miles on a highway where the speed limit is sixty-five.

Unable to stand it another minute, I start flashing my headlights, pointing to the right lane, and yelling, "Get over, asshole! Move it!" I don't know if she sees me acting a fool or if maybe she drops her beloved phone on the floor and goes crazy, but she runs her tiny little car off the road and into the median strip. I hit my brakes and so does the grandpa-car in the right lane. When I pass him, I see that the driver really is a little old grandpa guy. I pass him and the idiot lady whose car still has two wheels in the grass, and then I get back in the right lane, where people with good sense like to drive.

I glance in the rearview mirror and see that the left-lane cruiser has whipped her tin-can car back onto the road. She's coming up fast. In the left lane, of course. Grandpa is quite a piece behind us now, and I'm relieved that he's far removed from the commotion that I know is about to begin. When the idiot lady gets up beside me, she slows down and rides there for a minute. I try not to look over, but I can't help myself. I turn my head and see her over there, waving her arms and screaming. She's pointing with her right hand and still has her cell phone in her left, so I can only assume she's driving with her knees. I shake my head and sigh, wishing I was the kind of girl who could leave an idiot to her idiotic ways, but I've tried that and it's just not my style. I look back at her and smile.

"Pull over!" I yell while I honk my horn and wave my middle finger in the air. "Pull that dumbass-looking car over and let's do this!" I stop flipping her off and start pointing to the upcoming exit. "Right up here!" I wonder why I'm yelling, because I know she can't hear me. Oh wait, perhaps it's because I'm in the midst of the worst road-rage episode I've had in several months. "Pull over!" I yell again. Even though she can't hear me, I'm confident she's getting the message.

Apparently, she doesn't want to pull over and discuss this face-to-face because, even though I'm driving seventy-five miles per hour, she speeds away like a hybrid bat out of foreign-car hell. Yet thirty seconds ago, she was driving fifty-five. I check the rearview and see Grandpa puttering along miles behind. I feel sorry for him and his entire generation because they have to share the road with people like that dipshit, who's up there in the median strip again and people like me who want to beat the shit out of people like her.

It's a truly unfortunate situation for the more-mature drivers on the road. I turn on my signal and exit off the highway. Jeez Lou-eeze, I'm so mad I could bend an iron skillet. And I feel so stupid for letting myself get so mad. Like Gramma Jones always used to say, "Never argue with an idiot."

14

◇◇

By the time I get home, it's pouring down rain. I run inside the house where I find Buster Loo nestled into my fuzzy blanket on the couch.

"My thoughts exactly, Buster Loo. Give me just a minute and I'll be right there." He cocks his head sideways, then tucks his snout back under the covers. "I wouldn't leave my warm spot, either," I tell him.

After a hot shower, I put on some fuzzy britches, even fuzzier socks, and a sweatshirt that I wish were a bit fuzzier. I head to the couch and snuggle up with Buster Loo, who is reluctant to share his warm spot. While flipping through channels, I see a soup commercial and decide that's just what I need for supper.

When I get off the couch, Buster Loo rolls onto his back and looks at me like, "How could you do this to me?" I go into the kitchen and dig through my cabinets, trying to figure out if I have enough ingredients to make something tasty. I find a red bell pep-per in the fridge, look over my canned goods again, and decide on corn chowder. I pull out the Crock-Pot from under the cabinet and turn to see Buster Loo sitting by the stove.

"Want me to turn that on and warm it up in here?" His re-sponse is to wave his paws up and down, his signature trick, and I decide he's more concerned about a potential scrap than the tem-perature in the kitchen because he has yet to take his eyes off the cans on the counter. I give him a little-dog biscuit, wash my hands, and set about chopping and mixing. When I'm finished, I pour my concoction into the Crock-Pot, fix myself a cup of hot cocoa, and return to the sofa. Two hours later, I enjoy not one but two bowls of hot soupy goodness along with a hearty chunk of French bread, and it's so good that I don't even mind I'm dining alone on a Satur-day night. It's peaceful. And I need all of that I can get.

I think about Stacey Dewberry and wonder if she took that hair of hers out partying tonight. Then I wonder if she really enjoys barhopping or if she just does it because she doesn't have anything better to do. I rinse my bowl, slide the soup pot into the fridge, and fix a cup of hot tea. I head back to the couch, where I end up falling asleep while watching *Saturday Night Live*.

Sunday, I sleep late and the cold drizzle has me feeling de-pressed again. I'd love to get out and get started with my new gar-dening hobby, but this weather refuses to cooperate. I piddle around the house, wash some clothes, have a bowl of soup for lunch and then take a long afternoon nap. When I get up, I wander into the guest room where I sit down on the bed and stare at Gramma Jones's box of books. Would she want me pilfering through her things? Would she mind? It's not like she had time to dispose of anything she didn't want me to see. I pick up the garden book, flip to the back, and take out the note. Holding the folded piece of paper in my hand makes me feel weird, like a dirty Russian spy, so when my phone starts ringing in the living room, I put the note back where I found it, lay the book on the dresser, and close the guest room door behind me.

I don't get to the phone in time and the call goes to voice mail. I look at the missed call list. "Lilly Lane." *Oh Lord,* I think as I press the button to call her back. She never calls. When she answers, she's such a sniveling mess that I can hardly understand a word she's saying.

"Can I just come over?" she asks finally.

"Of course, I made some corn chowder yesterday," I tell her. "You want me to fix you a bowl?" She snuffles and sniffs and mumbles something about Dax doing paperwork at the sheriff's office. She doesn't answer the soup question, so I decide to start a pot of coffee.

I'm standing on the back porch when she comes through the gate. It's still raining, but instead of rushing to get out of the dampness, she takes her time walking to the back porch. She's wearing tennis shoes, jeans, and a Delta State sweatshirt that looks three sizes too big. I try to remember the last time I saw her in a pair of shoes like that.

"New shoes?" I ask.

"Yeah," she says with a sniff.

I hold open the door and pat her on the back as she walks into the kitchen.

She goes straight to the couch and wraps herself in my fuzzy blanket. I stop by the kitchen and fix two nonalcoholic cups of coffee. I take those into the living room and find her hugging Buster Loo, who is, yet again, licking the tears off her cheeks.

"I may have to borrow Buster Loo when Dax leaves," she says.

"He can help you through some hard times, that's for sure," I say. "Maybe we could have him certified as a service dog and get him one of those little vests to wear around. Then we could take him in Walmart and stuff." My weak attempt at humor doesn't even draw a smile. "So what's with the outfit?"

"Oh my God, I just had the worst weekend of my life and now I feel like a spoiled, foolish brat."

"But you aren't a spoiled, foolish brat."

"Yeah, I've never thought of myself that way, either, until my little trip to the other side of the state."

"What happened?"

"Oh, it was downright horrid," she says. "Dax's mother took one look at me and—" She stops, sighs, and shakes her head. She takes a sip of coffee and then continues. "All I wanted was for them to see how much I care for Dax. They didn't have to like me. I mean, I wanted them to, but more than anything I wanted them to be happy Dax has someone who loves him as much as I do and they just—" She stops again.

"Were they mean to you?" I ask, thinking I'd get in my car right now and make haste to the Delta where I would promptly punch somebody right in the face.

"Oh no," she says. "Not at all. I could just tell that I was stressing his mother out just by being there because I think she felt like, I don't know, that I needed more accommodating than what they were able to provide, which is ridiculous. Her name is May and I called her Mrs. Dorsett and she insisted on being called May and she just kept going on and on about how simple her house was. I kept telling her how much I loved it, which I did—it was charming and so real—but I think all I did was stress her out more." She takes another sip of coffee. "Then his sisters showed up. Oh boy, that was a blast. Two sisters. Both older than him but younger than me and they were both wearing Mossy Oak from head to toe." She shakes her head. "They tried to be nice, but there was not a conversational level that we could connect on. I didn't fit in and I made everyone uncomfortable. It was so horrible. And his dad, oh his dad was just—" She looks at me. "I don't even know how to explain his father to you other than to say that he's more of a no-nonsense guy than J. J. Jackson and he had grease under his fingernails. You know the kind that never washes off? And he didn't mince his words. Everything he said was direct and to the point." She looks down at her cup. "Like when I thought I would score some points for being a schoolteacher and then he asked me what I taught and I told him I taught French and then he asked me why schools today waste so much time and money trying to teach kids to speak another language. Yeah, that was awkward."

"Oh my goodness. What did you say?"

"I stumbled and mumbled for a minute and then finally said something about the Department of Education requiring certain classes for graduation and that sometimes students' schedules didn't allow them to take the more-mainstream electives—I don't even know. Everyone just stared at me every time I opened my mouth and they really stared at my shoes. I mean, as if everything wasn't bad enough already, everything I took to wear was all wrong." She shrugs. "I didn't know what to expect and Dax didn't do a very good job of explaining that situation. I think he was embarrassed because his family doesn't have much. It kills me to think he might think that bothers me. And then he acted so damned weird all weekend." She crinkles her brow and sighs.

"Lilly, I'm so sorry." I move over to sit by her and put my arm around her. Buster Loo is back on tear patrol.

"And just when I thought it couldn't get any worse, we went to this tiny little mom-and-pop restaurant where everybody knew everybody and I didn't know a soul. Got to meet his old high school sweetie there. That was nice."

"The one you ran off from his house last year?"

"Yeah, she was there with her pink Mossy Oak hat, and Dax's sisters just talked and talked to her. Apparently they'd all just been turkey hunting together or some shit—I don't know. It was obvious that she belonged at that table with his family and I did not. And everyone at the restaurant stared at me the whole time I was in there. Like they'd never in their whole life seen anybody from out of town. I guess not many people wear heels in their little country steak house." She smirks. "It was awful, all those people staring, and then his damned redneck sisters—"

"Well, it doesn't matter what anyone thinks except for Dax, and he thinks you're great." I point to her sweatshirt. "Obviously you found a way to get a little more casual."

"I had to before I went crazy! I got up Saturday morning and drove into town. I'm telling you, Bugtussle looks like a major metropolitan area compared to that place. Anyway, I bought some tennis shoes at a little corner store. I wore my one pair of jeans and this old sweatshirt for the rest of the weekend."

"So it was better after you dressed down a little?"

"Not even a little bit."

An hour later, I talk her into some soup and we chat about school, but I can tell she's not in the mood to be distracted from her misery. We discuss Chloe and her baby situation, and I try to lift her spirits by joking about ways to drop some hints to J.J. She's not interested in that, either. Finally, her phone beeps and it's Dax. She thanks me for keeping her company, pulls on her new tennis shoes, and runs out the door. I take a shower and get into bed, not wanting to go to sleep because I know my next conscious thought will be, It's time to get up and go to school.

◇◇

15

Monday morning I somehow miraculously get to school on time and as soon as I get to my assigned classroom, I start thinking I'd rather go lie in the parking lot and be run over by incoming traffic than be in this classroom all day, but I want my job back, so I've got to stay with it. My ass isn't getting any smaller and my pants aren't getting any bigger, but all I can do is sit there and fantasize about chocolate-covered doughnuts. And speaking of eating, I've figured out that everyone in A Hall and B Hall has either first or second lunch, so I give up on getting to sit at a table with Lilly and Coach Hatter ever again.

After three miserable hours, I'm off fourth period and decide to skip the trip to the lunchroom since I don't have any students to escort up and down the hallway like maniacal kindergartners. I turn off the lights and get my peanut butter and jelly sandwich out of my bag along with a warm bottle of water. Two minutes later, there's a knock on the door and Stacey Dewberry comes in with a bag from the Red Rooster Drive-In.

"Great minds think alike," she says, waving the bag at me. "Need a break from that lunchroom grub."

"Did you get to leave school to get that?" I ask her, eyeing the brown paper bag with envy. Today Stacey is dressed somewhat normally in khaki-colored jeans and a loose white button-up. You might not know she had an addiction to 1980s fashion if she hadn't tight-rolled her pants over a pair of slouched white bobby socks— and if you somehow managed to miss that mile-high hair.

"Oh no, I picked this up on the way in this morning," she says, squeezing into one of the student desks. "Care if I join you?"

"Not at all," I say. "I thought the Red Rooster didn't open until ten thirty."

"They just started serving breakfast," she says, unwrapping a tasty-looking cheeseburger. "I joined their emailing list so I could stay fresh on what's up. You get a free order of pickle-ohs when you do. Totally worth it."

"I do like pickle-ohs," I tell her.

"Rock and roll," Stacey says.

"Yeah," I look down at my sandwich. "Rock and roll."

"You know, I wish I didn't feel the way I do about some of these kids," she says. "Makes me kind of sad, because there's a few that I really and truly don't like at all."

"Sometimes it's hard to love them all like we need to," I tell her. "I never knew how hard it was to be a substitute teacher. I mean, I've always been good with the bad kids because I could find a way to relate to them, to reach them somehow. But with subbing, it's in and out of this class and in and out of that class and that makes it almost impossible to form any kind of connection and it's frustrating because they all seem like bad kids when they're not. I mean, there're a few bad kids who will be bad, no matter what, but—" I stop because I can see I'm losing my audience. "I know what you mean, Stacey," I say. "Sometimes I feel bad like that, too."

"You know who I've made a connection with?"

"Who's that?"

"Hadley Bennett," she says. "She does her own thing kind of like I do," she says. "I don't think she has the best circumstances at home, but she doesn't let it get her down and doesn't use it as an excuse to act a fool."

"I had her in art class last year. She's very talented and so level-headed."

Stacey nods in agreement. "I have so much respect for kids like her who have no choice but to figure it all out on their own and then they get it right." And look at me, still trying to figure it out at the ripe old age of thirty-two. Jeez. Who's the idiot now?

"She thinks I'm cool because I don't conform to the way all the other teachers dress." She looks at me in my black pants, black flats, and pale blue sweater. "No offense."

"None taken," I say, and smile. I'd never thought of Stacey Dewberry as a nonconformist, but that's exactly what she is. "It takes a lot of confidence to veer away from the mainstream, especially when you're in high school."

"That it does," she says, and it occurs to me that Stacey Dewberry is fairly brave herself for being so faithful to her hot rollers, 'fro pick, and helmet-head hair spray. "Hadley also appreciates eighties rock, which brings me to my next point." She starts digging around in her multipurpose book bag. Or maybe it's a purse. I'm not sure. "Where did I put those things?" A second later, she comes up with a white envelope.

"What's that?"

"A surprise!" She opens the envelope and pulls out two tickets. "I don't know when your birthday is, but I've already got you a present. Would you like to see Def Leppard and Poison this Friday in Memphis?"

"Seriously?"

"Totally seriously!" she says, getting excited. "Would you like to go?"

"I would love to go!" I say. "But Stacey, these are third-row tickets. How much did they cost? I'm not going unless I pay for mine."

"No way, Jose," she says. "I won these tickets fair and square by calling in to the *Big Nasty Radio Show* on 102.1 last week."

"Stacey, you're too freakin' cool for your own good!" I tell her.

"You can just keep that ticket if you really want to go," she says.

"Of course I want to go, but I have to pay you for this."

We go back and forth for a few minutes, arguing about the value of a free concert ticket. I finally agree to take the ticket after she agrees to let me cover the cost of gas, parking, dinner, and drinks. She insists we go in her car and I don't argue much on that one.

The rest of the day doesn't suck as bad because I'm so excited about going to a concert with Stacey Dewberry. I find myself wondering if she might tease my hair for me. It has a lot of natural wave, so I think it would really curl up, especially with the help of a professional hot-roller like Stacey Dewberry.

During seventh period, I look up and see five students with their cell phones out, texting under their desktops like I can't see what they're doing. *Who cares?* I think. Sure, they're only teenagers, but their drama is just as important to them right now as mine is to me, and as long as they get their work done and stay quiet, I can turn a blind eye. Let them think they're fooling the poor ol' substitute teacher who has no idea what's going on in the world, let alone the classroom. As long as they aren't back there watching porn, I don't care.

16

<><><><><><><><><><><><><><><><><><><><><><><><><><><><><><><><><><><><>

Tuesday is better because I only have to cover one class for half the day. I eat lunch in the cafeteria with Stacey and she yaps the whole time about the upcoming concert.

After lunch, I retire to a study room in the library where I work on some cutesy little illustrations for Jalena's menu and very much enjoy the three consecutive hours of uninterrupted silence. By the time the bell rings at the end of the day, I'm finished with the menus and quite pleased with my whimsical illustrations. I call Jalena when I leave school and she's still at the diner, so I take the menus by there to see what she thinks. She shows me around her new office, which has a stylish white desk, a hot pink office chair, and two cushy floral chairs on the opposite side. I brag on how cool it all looks and then take a seat in one of the chairs.

"Oh, these are poppin'," she says when she looks at the menus. "This is exactly what I wanted! You are so talented." She flips the last sheet over and smiles when she sees the drawing of her dad's marina at Frog Bayou. "Oh wow," she says quietly. "This is too perfect." She looks up at me. "Thank you, Ace."

"Thanks for asking me," I say. "I enjoyed it." I nod toward the menus, which she's carefully placing in a bright yellow folder. "Those and the mural."

"About that," she says in a tone that makes me nervous. "Almost everyone who walks in here has either comments or questions."

"Really?" I say, feeling anxious. "So, like, good comments and questions or—"

"Of course, good comments and questions!" She looks at me like I'm crazy. "That mural is turning out to be quite the conversation piece, and I think you need to have some business cards made up for me to keep at the register when I open this place up next month."

"You think?" I ask, relieved and a tad bit excited.

"Yes, I think!" she says. "The guy who came in to do my trim work absolutely loved it and asked if you painted for hire. He said that people are always asking him if he knows someone who does specialty painting. And before he came in, one of the guys putting down the flooring asked if he could have your number. He's building a new house and his wife is driving him crazy because she wants him to glaze the walls. He said he didn't know anything about glazing walls and didn't want to mess with it. He asked if I thought you'd be interested." She looks at me. "Are you?"

I sit for a moment and fantasize about spending my days painting murals and glazing walls instead of explaining to ill-mannered high school students that I have no idea where their regular teacher is and do not know why he or she had to take the day off. "Of course," I tell her. "I could do it after school." *Remember, the grass is not always greener,* I think.

"You might rustle up enough business to do it full-time."

"I've given up dreaming the impossible dream," I tell her.

"This has nothing to do with dreaming impossible dreams," she says. "It has to do with your purpose in life." She holds up the menus. "Clearly, God has given you a gift."

"I do not doubt that at all and I very much appreciate it, but having a gift doesn't necessarily mean that you have to try to squeeze a dollar out of it. I tried that, remember?"

"Your gift is an arrow that points you in a certain direction."

"Jalena, I don't think—"

"Let me ask you a question," she says. "Do you think Ethan Allen and I were meant to be together?"

"Of course," I say. "A blind person can see that."

"Now think about how many losers I dated before I met him."

I consider that for a second. "Point taken," I tell her.

Thursday, I decide to go ahead and pick up everything I need for Dax's going away party, and since Lilly loves going to Walmart, I invite her to come along. She perks up a little on the ride over, but not much.

We chat about this and that while I load the shopping cart up with chips, dips, and sweet stuff. She tells me Dax is really fond of spinach dip, so I pick up the ingredients for that along with a loaf of Hawaiian bread. We're standing by the hot dogs, discussing how many packs to buy, when a deep voice says, "Hello, ladies." We turn to see Sheriff J. J. Jackson, in uniform. I point at Lilly.

"Sheriff, this lady is trying to steal some wieners, but I was ada-mantly advising against such behavior." J.J. looks at me without even a hint of a smile. Lilly is equally stone-faced. "C'mon." I play punch her in the arm. "If you confess, he might go easy on you." Lilly is not in a joking mood. The sheriff pats Lilly on the shoulder and looks at me like I've lost all of my marbles.

"We're gonna miss Dorsett, Lilly. But don't worry, he'll be back before you know it."

Lilly just stares at the sheriff and nods. Then I remember Chloe's predicament.

"So," I say, smiling up at the handsome sheriff, "how long have you and Chloe been dating now?"

"Yeah," Lilly says. "Has it been a year already?"

The sheriff looks nervous. "Not sure, why? Do we have an anni-versary coming up?" He glances around. "Y'all better tell me if I do."

"I don't think it's been quite a year yet," I say, and he looks ma-jorly relieved.

"I think it's been about ten months," Lilly says.

"That Chloe is a real catch if you ask me," I say.

"Yeah," J.J. says, "she's a good one, no doubt about it."

"And so pretty," Lilly adds.

"That, too," he says, looking at us with suspicious eyes.

"And so nice," I say.

"She is a keeper," Lilly says, and I make a mental note to brag on her later for coming up with that one.

"Definitely a keeper," I say. "One to keep around for a while."

The sheriff looks from me to Lilly, then back at me.

"Have you girls been drinking?"

"No!" I say. "We just left school thirty minutes ago. I mean, I could use a drink and I'll probably have one later, but not now. No. I quit drinking and driving years ago."

"Years ago," Lilly echoes.

"Okay," he says, looking at us like we're a couple of bozos. "Guess we'll see y'all Saturday night, then." He nods toward the hot dogs. "Don't spend too much time here. I think it's messing with your heads."

"Thank you, sir."

"Yes, thank you," Lilly says as he turns to go.

"Epic fail," I whisper, and turn back to the wieners.

17

<><><><><><><><><><><><><><><><><><><><><><><><><><><><><><><><><><>

Friday, even the loudest, most idiotic little asshole can't put a bend in my stride, but that certainly doesn't stop each and every one of them from trying. It should be against the law for a teacher to take off from school on Friday because substitute hell is at its very hottest at the end of the week. What these maniacs fail to realize is that I'm just as ready for the week to be over as they are, if not more so.

During third period, I look out at twenty-five students, a good solid fifteen of whom are acting like they just snorted a line of crack cocaine. I think for a moment about how surprised they would be if they managed to push me over the edge. I wouldn't tuck tail and run—which is what I think they're going for—I would go stark-raving nuts and give them an earful of the cold hard truth. And the truth would hurt. At least it would hurt their feelings. And it would most certainly set me free from a substantial amount of annoying racket. But I can't do that because there're always a few, usually the ones with the absolute worst behavior, who would run home to Mommy and Daddy—who would never dream of hurting little precious's feelings—and whine about the mean ol' substitute who grew weary of their intolerable brattiness and told them something they didn't want to hear. Then Mommy would call Mr. Byer and cuss him like a dog and I'd get called before the board and fired. Then Chloe would run over me with her office chair and it would be one big huge mess, all because I snapped and screamed something like, *Shut the fuck up!* to a rowdy bunch of devotees to chaos. Of course, I would never say anything like that in a classroom, but I certainly enjoy entertaining that fantasy.

At lunchtime, I sit down with Stacey Dewberry in the noisy cafeteria where we finalize our plans for the night. She's acting peculiar—even more so than usual—and I get the distinct feeling that she's hiding something. I hope it's not that she's back with Joe Red and he'll be joining us at the concert tonight.

After lunch, I tough out two more hours in maniac central and just when I'm certain the day couldn't get worse, Chloe comes over the intercom and summons me to her office during afternoon break. Lilly is already there when I walk in and as soon as I see her, I know we're in trouble. Sure enough, Chloe hammers us about what we said to J.J. in the hot dog aisle of Walmart yesterday. We each make a legitimate effort to change the subject, but Chloe is determined to have this conversation.

"You told him I was a keeper?" she says to Lilly. "How could you do that?"

"I thought it was good," Lilly says, looking at me. "You said it was good."

"I thought it was genius," I say.

"Do not say another word to him about me, got it?" she says, and her face is flush red.

"Okay, calm down, Chloe," I tell her. "You're going to have a heart attack." I look at Lilly. "I'm sorry. We're sorry."

"We're very sorry," Lilly chimes in. "Won't happen again. We promise."

She glares at us until the bell rings.

"Have a nice rest of the day," I say. Her response is a cold stare.

"Shit," Lilly whispers after we walk out the door. "This is going to be a long nine months."

"Seven," I remind her. "Because she's already—" I stop talking because we meet Mr. Byer in the hallway.

"Hello, hello, hello, ladies," he says. "How are we today? Glad it's Friday, I presume? I know I am." He does that funny little giggle of his and flashes that shy smile.

"Yes, sir," I say. "So happy it's Friday!"

"Well, I hope you both enjoy your weekend to the fullest," he says.

"He is so nice," I say, and turn to Lilly, who has stopped dead in her tracks.

"When this weekend is over, he'll be gone, Ace. When this weekend is over, Dax will be—"

"Lilly, you can't think about that right now," I tell her. "Just put it out of your mind. You only have two more classes and then you can go home and see him."

"I can't," she says, and her eyes fill up with tears. "I can't stay here. I've got to go. It's our last weekend together. Oh God! What am I going to do when he leaves?"

"Oh my goodness." I hurry back to Chloe's office and tell her that Lilly's having a breakdown in the hallway. "I don't know if that medicine she's taking is helping or hurting," I tell her. "She's a mess."

"I've thought the same thing," she says, and I'm relieved to hear kindness in her voice.

Chloe follows me to where Lilly is slumped in one of the chairs just outside the narrow office hallway. Chloe stops and knocks on Mrs. Marshall's door.

"Mrs. Marshall, are you in?" she calls.

"Yes, Mrs. Stacks. What can I do for you?" Mrs. Marshall steps out into the hallway, sees Lilly, and says, "Oh no! Is she okay?"

"She's just upset and needs to go home," Chloe says to Mrs. Marshall. "Would you mind finding someone to cover her last two classes?"

"Of course," Mrs. Marshall says. She steps back into her office.

"Lilly," I say, "c'mon, get up. Let's get you out of here."

"Remind me what class you're in today," Chloe says to me.

"Mr. Bridgeton," I say as the tardy bell rings.

"Walk Lilly out to her car and I'll go down and stay in his classroom until you get back."

"Is everything okay out here?" Mr. Byer says, sticking his head out of his office. He sees Lilly and his eyebrows crunch up with concern.

"Everything is fine, Mr. Byer," Chloe says. "Lilly isn't feeling well, so she's going to leave early."

"Is there anything I can do?" he asks. "Do I need to run down and cover her class?" I can't help but think about how lucky this school is to have such a genuinely nice person in charge of things.

"Mrs. Marshall is taking care of it," Chloe says, "but thank you so much."

I look at Lilly and she looks downright pitiful.

"How embarrassing," she says, standing up and smoothing her skirt. "I'm so sorry for making a scene, Chloe." She wipes her cheeks.

"Not a problem, Lilly. Just go sit in my office while Ace runs down to get your purse. I have to get to Mr. Bridgeton's classroom."

"Thank you."

"C'mon," I say, and walk with her to Chloe's office where she sits down and puts her hands over her face. "You'll be fine, Lilly. Just sit tight and I'll be right back." She doesn't say anything, so I take off to D Hall.

I hear a major ruckus going on in Lilly's classroom before I even knock on the door. When I walk in, I see that Mrs. Marshall has recruited none other than Cameron Becker to cover Lilly's class this period. Great.

"Where's Ms. Lane?" one student yells above the roar. "I saw her right before break."

"Ms. Lane isn't feeling well," I say.

"I'm not feeling well, either, so can I leave, too?" a loudmouth in the back of the class hollers. The students roar with laughter and start talking even louder.

"Be quiet, please," Ms. Becker says. "Everyone needs to take a seat."

The students ignore her. I walk over to the cabinet where Lilly keeps her stuff, open the door, and reach in to get her purse. I turn around and look at Cameron Becker, who is failing miserably to get control of the situation.

"Quiet, students, please," she says again. "Stop talking! Right now!" She claps her hands, but no one pays her any attention. The expression on Cameron's face brings back terrible memories from my first year teaching, but then I remember what a hussy she's been each and every time we've spoken. I look at the door and tell myself to walk out. Leave her to it. But I don't because I can't. I stand by the cabinet, listening as the noise level rises to a dull roar. I know what I should do, but I don't want to do it. I look at Cameron Becker and, despite my best effort to be a hard-ass, I feel sorry for the girl. She asks them to sit down and stop talking for a third time. When not a single student bothers to acknowledge her, I unleash the fury that only five years of teaching, a wrecked dream, and a few weeks of permanent substitute teaching can put in a woman.

"Hey!" I yell. "I don't believe anyone in this room is deaf! Ms. Becker has asked you nicely to stop talking and since y'all obviously don't respond to kindness, let me put it to you like this: Get yourself in a seat! Face the front! Shut your mouth! And get out something to do!" I look at Ms. Becker. "Do you have any idea what they're supposed to be doing?" She points to the board. "As you all can see, today's assignment is on the board, so get on it! Right now! And when you finish that, you can find something else to work on quietly, or"—I glance down at Lilly's desk—"Ms. Becker will provide you with a sheet of verbs to conjugate in French. Any questions?" No one says a word. I pick up the stack of dreaded worksheets and make a show of handing them to Ms. Becker. "Write down who you have to give these worksheets to so Lilly will know who gets a zero in the grade book should someone decide not to turn it back in." I point to the intercom button. "Ms. Becker," I tell her, "Mr. Byer is in his office if you need him. I'll let him know you might be buzz-ing him."

"Ms. Jones, I assure you that we will be on our best behavior from here on out," a student says from somewhere in the middle of the classroom.

"Thank you so much," I say with a sweet smile as I search out the would-be diplomat. An entire week of boisterous students plus this especially god-awful day has worn my nerves down to a raw nub, so I'm not in the mood to be patronized. "But I'm still telling Mr. Byer to be on alert for a buzz from Ms. Becker." He picks up his pencil and gets to work.

"Thank you," Cameron Becker says, looking relieved.

"No problem." I take a step closer to her and whisper, "You've got to put the fear of God in them right off the bat and then make sure they've got plenty of relevant work to keep them busy. That's the secret. They're just normal teenagers; they're not bad kids, but you have to let them know up front that you are in control. Not them." *You can do that when you're a "real" teacher,* I think, feeling miserable. She smiles and I am amazed at how beautiful she is. "Have a good weekend, Ms. Becker."

"You, too, Ms. Jones. Thanks again."

"Don't mention it." I walk out of Lilly's classroom, close the door behind me, and stand there for a minute to make sure the students don't go crazy again. Fortunately, they don't. I feel bad for snapping on them, but that situation had to be dealt with or the next step would've been to call in the Mississippi National Guard. Kids get so carried away when their normal teacher doesn't show up, and if the pandemonium isn't reined in immediately, the mob mentality takes over and it's all downhill from there. I walk down the hallway and wonder whose mommy will be the first to call Mr. Byer and report my failure to pussyfoot around an out-of-control situation. Substitute teachers can't talk to students that way. Probably that really loud kid in the back who started yelling about wanting to go home.

When I finally get back to my assigned classroom, Chloe is sitting at Mr. Bridgeton's desk like a prison warden and there is a sentence on the board that reads, "I will not talk in class unless I raise my hand and am recognized by the person in charge of maintaining order within the four walls of this classroom." When I walk in, some of the students look up, obviously relieved to see the sub coming to replace the guidance counselor. It's sixth period, so I'm sure their friends had given them a heads-up on Mr. Bridgeton's absence. I smile when I think about how shocked and disappointed they must've been when Chloe walked into the classroom instead of "the sub."

"Lilly's on her way home," I whisper to Chloe.

"Great," she says, and a few students start to whisper. She turns on them and says, "Don't make me make your sentences longer again." Silence. She smiles at me. "See you tomorrow night."

"See you then," I say.

When she's safely out of the classroom, one brave student raises his hand.

"Yes?" I say.

"Do we really have to write this sentence a thousand times?"

I suppress a smile while I look back at the clock. We have twenty minutes until the bell.

"Would you guys rather do today's assignment?" The question

produces a collective nod and sighs of relief all around. It's amazing how easy it is to maintain order as opposed to establishing it.

"Please, ma'am," the student says. I pick up a stack of papers.

"Mr. Bridgeton left you guys a pretty cool assignment," I say, counting out enough for the first row.

"A crossword puzzle!" the student on the receiving end of the first stack says. Then she looks up in horror and regret. "I'm so sorry. Please don't make me write anymore."

"It's Friday," I say. "Who wants to write extra-long sentences on Friday? Raise your hand." Sure enough, one clown raises his hand. "Well, you're more than welcome to do that," I tell him, smiling. "I bet you guys won't test Mrs. Stacks anymore, will ya?" I can tell from their expressions that they won't.

"Can we work in pairs? Mr. Bridgeton lets us work in pairs."

"Only if you can stay quiet," I say. "As you all know, there are classes all around us, so keep it down, please."

Toward the end of the period, the students start turning in their crossword puzzles and whispering amongst themselves. One student raises his hand and says, "Ms. Jones, I'm going to a concert tonight."

"Really?" I reply, thinking nothing of it.

"Yeah, I'm going to see Poison and Def Leppard with my dad."

Holy effin' shit, I want to scream. No! Then I see an opportunity. "Well, as luck would have it," I say with smugness he can't even begin to grasp, "I'm going to that concert, too. With Ms. Dewberry."

Several kids snicker at that. "Seriously?" another student asks. "Don't you think she's a little weird?"

"Not at all." I think about the conversation Stacey and I had earlier in the week. "Ms. Dewberry is a nonconformist, wouldn't you say? Surely you guys can relate to not bending to what everyone expects of you." I look around. "You have to admit that it takes guts to be so unique." Some students nod; some are oblivious; others are texting inside their backpacks. No one takes the conversational bait.

"Where are you sitting?" the guy going with his dad asks.

"What is your name again?"

"Ben," he says. "Ben Evans."

"Third row, Ben Evans," I say, and I'm proud of it because I've never been anywhere close to the third row at a concert. I try to bait them again. "Ms. Dewberry won the tickets by calling in to the *Big Nasty Show*."

"That is so cool!" Ben bellows, and I have to shush him. In a quieter voice, he says, "Maybe we'll see y'all there."

"Maybe so," I say. Maybe not!

"Will y'all be drinking?" the kid sitting in front of Ben wants to know.

"Don't get yourself sent to the office three minutes before the bell," I tell him. "Of course we won't be drinking. We're teachers. Everybody knows teachers don't drink."

"Coach Hatter does!" someone yells from the back of the room. "My sister works at Ethan Allen's, and she says he comes in there all the time drinking those big mugs of beer and eating like a pig!"

"I assure you, it's near beer, and I hear he's quite fond of half-price appetizers," I say, wishing the bell would hurry up and ring. That gets a laugh out of them while they try to act like they know all about beer, near or otherwise.

"I don't see how teachers don't drink," another student says. "Having to put up with us all day."

"Oh, but y'all are great," I say. "It's a privilege to spend our days with you."

"You don't really believe that," she says.

"Actually, I do," I tell her. "I'm not going to stand up here and say it's easy, especially for a sub, but despite how difficult it is at times, teaching school is a very rewarding career. You guys are great." I stop and wonder if I'm trying to convince her or myself. Then I wonder if I really and truly want to get my old job back. I dismiss that thought, chalking it up to a hard week in the trenches. I used to love my job. Or at least I think I liked it. "Let's move this conversation along, please."

"Are you dating anyone?" the girl says as the bell rings. "You and Coach Hatter should go out!"

"Get out of here," I say. "Have a good weekend, everyone, and be safe! Remember: Don't text and walk into oncoming traffic!" I follow them out into the hallway, feeling guilty for being so relieved that the bell finally rang. I don't ever remember feeling so put out by my students back when I had my own classroom. Now I feel that way every single period of every single day.

18

◇◇

Thank the good merciful heavens, Mr. Bridgeton has seventh period off and I am done in every sense of the word. I collect my things, lock the door, and head to the lounge for some refreshment. Walking down the hallway, I think about Lilly and wonder how she's making it. I know Dax is taking her out on a hot date tonight, so I try to stop worrying. Then I think about Chloe keeping J.J. in the dark about her pregnancy and feel terrible for causing her extra grief by running my mouth to him in Walmart yesterday. I think she's crazy for not telling him, but that's not my decision to make. And then there's this job. Oh goodness! This job. I don't know what I was thinking when I signed up to be a permanent substitute teacher. I certainly never expected it to be what, unfortunately for me, it's turned out to be. I shake my head and sigh. All of this crap is like a big tangled ball of string that keeps getting more twisted and knotted by the day. I walk into the lounge and see

Freddie Dublin sitting smack-dab in the center of the room with his feet propped on the table.

"Hey, Freddie," I say.

"You off this period?"

"Thank my lucky stars, yes." I look at him. "And you?"

"Thank your lucky stars, yes," he says. I put my gigant-o-bag on the table and start digging for change. "So, is the party still on for tomorrow night?" he asks.

"It is," I say, turning my attention to the vending machine.

"Can I bring Cameron?"

"Freddie, I don't know about that," I tell him as I drop quarters into the slot. "She and I aren't exactly friends and we don't need any—" I pause, then for lack of a better word, say, "Drama." This draws a wide smile from Freddie Dublin.

"She said y'all had a moment at the beginning of sixth period." He stops talking. I don't say a word. "Ace, she really wants to come. Cameron has no friends here. None. Except for me, of course, and her fans in the athletic department. We both know a girl can't survive on that." I turn around and look at him. He pats the chair to his right. "Come, sit."

"What are you, her popularity agent?" I ask, sitting down beside him.

"No," he says, not acknowledging my humor. "I'm her only friend in this galaxy and she's high maintenance, if you know what I mean. I'm getting tired."

Freddie tells me another sob story about how poor Cameron used to be the ugly duckling and never had any friends and then she turned into a swan and was equally despised by her peers. I watch him as he speaks, looking for the smallest hint of dishonesty.

It's a sad situation. Just not sad enough. Because if Cameron Becker came to that party and tried to hit on Dax, then I would have to beat the shit out of her, and I'm fairly certain that would lead to a hostile work environment on at least seventeen different levels.

"So what do you think?"

"I don't think so, Freddie." I stop short of adding, *I'm sorry.*

"C'mon, Ace," he puts his arm around me and his sweet-smelling cologne casts a wicked spell on my senses. "Consider it a small favor from you to me, which I assure you I will repay at some point when you really need it."

"Freddie," I say, pulling away from him, "you're impossible." With one hand, he starts to rub my back. He smiles and I revel in his aroma and attention.

"Pretty please. You're nice to Dewberry and we both know it's not because the two of you have anything in common." He lowers his voice to a whisper. "Just give a girl a chance to make a friend. That's all I'm asking."

I take a sip of Diet Mountain Dew and consider his request. I know how it feels to be stuck somewhere with no friends and must admit that it sucks. "Okay, Freddie, but under one condition." He moves his hand up to my neck and I close my eyes. "Will you be personally responsible for her?"

"Of course," he says, massaging. "You can count on me."

"Okay," I say, then open my eyes and look at him. "But if she screws up, I promise you that I will make your life at this school a living hell for the rest of this year."

"Oh, feistiness," he says, patting me on the back. "I like it!"

"I'm not joking," I say, and he stops smiling. "If she really wants to come, you can bring her. But she can't flirt with Dax or J.J. or anybody who is there with their wife and/or girlfriend. Women around here will straight punch a girl in the face for gettin' too friendly with their man."

"That's brutal," Freddie says.

"That's the truth," I say. "Which is why it's so important that no one comes to this party and does something stupid or uncalled for." I look at him. "Got it?"

"Got it!" he says, but I'm not sure he does. "Hey, I'm glad you're off this period, Ms. Jones, because there's one more teeny-tiny thing on my mind."

"What's that?"

"About Ms. Stacey Dewberry," he says. "I understand you're going to a concert with her tonight."

"Yes, we're going in her Iroc-Z28," I say, and we both smile.

"Vintage!" he says. "So, is there any way that we could like, I don't know, say, uh . . ."

"Spit it out, Freddie!"

"Makeover!" he practically shouts. "She needs a makeover worse than Joan Rivers needs some slack in her face!"

While I find that very funny, I don't allow him more than a smile. "She's perfectly happy like she is," I say.

"Ace," he says, looking at me, "she is never going to get laid dressing like she does."

"You don't know that."

"Oh, but I do because she told me so in one of our therapy sessions." He smiles a mischievous smile. "She hasn't had any you-know-what since she broke it off with Joey McRedneck—you know, the one who coerced her into moving over here from Ala-freakin'-bama—and, well, according to her, she'd had quite the dry spell before she met him in the beer cooler that hot and fateful morning." He looks at me and I look at my Diet Mountain Dew. "Nobody's hair deserves to be so abused on a daily basis. You can sit there and act like it isn't an aberration, but we both know that shit needs to be tamed." I concentrate very hard on not reacting. "Please, help me devise a plan to get that puff-monster under control and, oh my goodness, those turtleneck sweaters with shoulder pads have got to go." He reaches over and tousles my hair. "You know hot rollers would do amazing things to these luscious tresses, right?"

"You think so?" I can't help it. I don't care what Freddie Dublin thinks of Stacey's hair. I want mine to look just like it when we go out tonight.

"I know so," he says. He puts a finger on his temple and pretends to be thinking really hard. "What if you let Stacey and me fix you up for the concert tonight? We can use you as the bait and then maybe next weekend we can talk her into a real makeover."

"You know what, Freddie? That actually sounds like fun."

"Yippee," he says without a trace of enthusiasm.

"You should go to the concert with us."

"Oh gawd no," he drawls. "I don't do eighties rock. Sorry, honey."

"Are you kidding me? Who doesn't do eighties rock?"

"This one," he says, pointing at his chest. "And everyone else born after December 31, 1989." That stings a little, but I let it pass. He continues. "Okay, so here's what's going to happen: Stacey is going to invite you over to her house an hour earlier than what was previously discussed and you will agree without asking any questions. Then you will need to act supersurprised when you get to her house and see me, okay?"

"What? Why? What are you talking about?"

"I'm talking about making this operation run smoothly," he says. "During morning break, I invited her down to my classroom and basically had the same conversation with her that I just had with you." He winks at me. "Turns out Ms. Dewberry secretly thinks you need a little more spunk in your wardrobe."

"You are a sly devil, Freddie Dublin. Conspiring with the Dewberry."

"The Dewberry. I like that. So we have a deal then?" The bell rings and Freddie jumps up. Before I even have a chance to respond, he says, "Great! I'll see you there! Okay, I've got to get out of here before those buses."

"You aren't worried about getting busted for leaving early?"

"Oh no, I make Mr. Byer more nervous than he already is. He'd never say anything to me." He grins. "Plus I parked in the senior parking today, so no one will see me leave."

"Are you serious?"

"But, of course," he says. "See you in a bit!"

"Okay," I say as he jets out the door. I sit there for a minute, shaking my head. Five minutes later, I'm still thinking about our conversation when the door flies open and Stacey Dewberry hustles into the lounge. While she speed punches coins into the drink machine, she asks if I'd like to do hair and makeup at her house tonight.

"You could come over at four, which is an hour earlier than we talked about at lunch." After wrestling her Dr Pepper from the dispenser, she turns to face me. She's rocking from one foot to the other and I think she's about to make a break for the restroom, but she doesn't. I suppose the movement might be her physical reaction to trying to run a covert op. I decide not to give her a hard time because she's about to board a school bus loaded with rambunctious students and drive them all over the southeastern side of the county, dropping them off one by one. When I say yes, her face glows with triumph. She hustles out of the lounge and I sit there for another minute, nursing my lukewarm Diet Mountain Dew and wondering what in the hell I just got myself into.

19

⟡⟡

"**B**uster Loo!" I say when I get home. "Where's Mama's little chiweenie king?" He comes barreling down the hallway and jumps onto the sofa. We play speedy-dog fetch and then I take him for a walk around the block. I clean up his dog bowls, put out fresh water, and give him a new rawhide bone, which he gets very excited about. I hop in and out of the shower, giddy with anticipation. I walk into my closet, where I carefully select the most flattering but still-comfortable jeans, and I slip on my favorite Minnetonkas and a Ralph Lauren Woman top I picked up off the clearance rack at Dillard's a few weeks ago.

I put Stacey Dewberry's address into the map app on my phone and see that she lives all the way across town. I tell Buster Loo good-bye and he doesn't even acknowledge me because he's too busy with his new piece of rawhide. Fifteen minutes later, I pull up at a small brick house with bright blue shutters and a black Iroc-Z28 sitting in the carport. I park on the curb behind a spotless Prius with out-of-county plates, which I assume belongs to Freddie D.

"Surprise!" Stacey says as I walk in the door.

"Surprise!" Freddie says in his unenthusiastic way.

I make a big show of asking what Freddie is doing at Stacey's while they escort me to the kitchen where a massive workstation has been set up on the table. There are three sets of hot rollers, two curling irons—one with a fat barrel and one much skinnier—a hair dryer, and three different-colored cans of Aqua Net. Next to all of that, I see a massive pile of makeup and an impressive collection of brushes.

I feel like a queen as I sit down to play along and very much enjoy them fussing over my hair. Once the hot rollers are in place, Freddie and Stacey start on my makeup. Ten minutes later, I walk to the mirror and burst out laughing.

"I look like a French whore!"

"But a very comely French whore," Freddie says with a smile. He snaps his fingers. "Stacey! Wardrobe!"

"Wardrobe?" I ask. "I'm wearing what I have on."

Freddie looks at my pale green polo shirt and jeans. "Tsk-tsk-tsk," he says, waving a finger at me. "No, you're not." Stacey comes down the hallway with two bundles of clothes and Freddie helps her spread them out in the living room. "You and Stacey appear to be about the same size, so we're going to put a little pep in your step tonight, sweetheart."

I stare at the various leggings and oversized shirts, thinking how much I like it when Freddie calls me sweetheart, while Stacey runs to the kitchen to fetch herself a Dr Pepper.

"You are going to look so hot," Freddie whispers.

"Wearing that stuff?" I ask, nodding toward the sofa. He looks at me, and my cheeks burn in the light of his intense attention. "Really?" I whisper. His answer is a nod and wink and, at that very moment, I know that I would do almost anything Freddie Dublin asked of me—well, anything except put on that psychedelic geometric-print top I just spied on the love seat. Stacey returns to the living room and they take turns holding up various shapes and styles of shirts.

"Look at this," Stacey exclaims, pulling out a hot pink top embellished with gold sequined stars. "I haven't seen this thing in ten years! This would look great on you!" She looks at Freddie, who gives his nod of approval.

"Okay, I guess I should try it on."

"Let's get you some pants first," Stacey says, rifling through another pile. After vetoing six different pairs of zigzag, floral, and otherwise multicolored stretch pants, they talk me into trying on a pair of zebra print leggings with my oversized pink shirt. I put down the pair of plain black ones that I'd plucked from the pile and take the zebra print hanger from Stacey. Looking at the pants, I remind myself that I did come to party and these do look pretty comfortable. Stacey disappears down the hallway once again.

"I'm going to enjoy looking at you in those," Freddie says, nodding toward the zebra pants. I look at him and can't help but wonder if he's doing all of this so he can snap pictures of me with his fancy little cell phone and use them to blackmail me into leaving town and, consequently, leaving his lovely and well-dressed pal Cameron Becker unbothered by my presence at school. But then I remember that I was nice to her today so maybe that's not the case.

"Okay," Stacey says, bustling back into the living room. "If you're wearing those pants, you have to wear these. It's the only way." She hands me a black pair of what she identifies as slouch boots.

"What size are those?"

"Nine."

"I wear an eight."

Freddie pulls up the left leg of my pants and looks down. "Well, I see you're wearing socks," he says. "You'll be fine."

I walk down the hallway to Stacey's bedroom, close the door, and carefully place the clothes I take off onto the bed. I don't want to wrinkle them in the likely event that I'll look like an idiot in the ensemble I'm about to try on and end up having to take these hot rollers out, flat iron my hair back into submission, tone down my makeup, and go to this concert looking like a normal person. I slip on the shirt, wiggle into the pants, then pull on the boots. "I can't believe I'm doing this," I whisper to myself as I turn to face the mirror.

While I'm thoroughly shocked by my reflection, I don't exactly hate it. The top falls off my shoulder just right and, big bonus! covers my butt cheeks without looking like a maternity shirt or clinging anywhere it shouldn't. It's a miracle! I stand there a minute longer, adjusting to this new image of me, and then decide that, much like a one-night stand, this getup will serve me well tonight. I walk down the hallway, happy the stub-heeled boots are more comfortable than they look, although I'm pretty sure my fuzzy socks have something to do with that.

"Hotness!" Freddie says as I strut across the living room. He smiles and I wonder again if this might be a blackmail stunt. Then I worry that I'm developing a raging crush on him.

I am losing my ever-lovin' mind, I think. That's what's really going on here.

"You look super-freak fantastic," Stacey says, "Now let's get those rollers out."

"And tease those tresses, honey!" Freddie adds.

A few minutes later, Freddie and Stacey are working my hair with picks and, yet again, I feel like a queen. A very oddly dressed queen—one more likely to show up at the Mad Hatter's tea party as opposed to a castle, be it red or white. When they finish, Stacey picks up her gigantic handheld mirror and has to take several steps back before I can finally see all of my hair.

"Wow," I say, thinking again of the Mad Hatter.

"Naturally curly hair really takes to a hot roller," Stacey observes.

"Go check yourself out in the full-length mirror now," Freddie tells me. I do as I'm told. When I close Stacey's bedroom door and take it all in—the clothes, the boots, the makeup, and the hair—I'd be lying if I said I didn't love it. And what I love more than my outrageous appearance is the fact that I feel like a completely different person. I wish I could bottle this feeling and store it on my bathroom shelf where I could pick it up anytime and spritz it all over me like some kind of exotic perfume.

I return to the dining area where Freddie is hard at work on Stacey's makeup. He doesn't ask me to help. I guess he knows I can't be trusted with sky blue eye shadow and liquid eyeliner—perhaps because I was born after December 31, 1979.

Stacey rattles on and on about how great I look while Freddie fine-tunes her hair. As he applies one final coat of hair spray, I can't help but notice how pretty she is. Her eyes remind me of the ocean, bluish green and brimming with tales untold. Freddie goes into the living room and, from the same wardrobe Stacey uses to show up at school looking like a goofball, he rounds up a sexy, hotshot ensemble that makes me fret about my own. Then I remember I have on zebra print leggings and a top laden with sequins and wonder how I could so quickly forget "the new me." Stacey goes back to change, and when she comes down the hallway a few minutes later, she looks like Joan Jett minus the Blackhearts plus a massive wad of spiral-curled hair. Sure enough, Freddie whips out his camera and asks us to pose for some pictures.

"Let me see that," I say when he's done. I motion for him to hand me the phone that he's trying to slip into his pocket.

"My rock stars," he says with a triumphant smile.

"Indeed," I say, smiling at the photos of me and Stacey Dewberry, who looks pretty badass in a leather jacket, camo leggings, and military boots.

"I kind of wish I was going now," Freddie says, and looks like he really means it. "I could don a pair of those stretchy pants and we could be man magnets for real."

Stacey stops fiddling with one of the many zippers on her jacket, looks at Freddie and then at me.

"Okay, time to get this party started!" I say. "Let's rock and roll!"

"The hard livin' mullet havin' men won't know what hit 'em tonight, ladies!" Freddie says with an accentuated drawl. Stacey Dewberry keeps an eye on him as she reapplies her powder pink lip gloss.

I run to the bathroom, double-check myself in the mirror, and, empowered by my new look, think about how funny it would be to go into Walmart dressed up like this. After all, shocking people is one of my favorite pastimes and, at this very present moment, my guns are fully loaded. But knowing my luck, I'd run into Chloe and there I'd be—caught and embarrassed. I go back to the living room and follow Freddie and Stacey out the carport door. Freddie whistles as he runs a finger over the hood of the Iroc-Z28.

"This is one of those rare moments in life when you know you're witnessing something very few people ever get to see with their own two eyes," Freddie says. "Like a volcano erupting or those goats that climb trees in Morocco."

Stacey howls with laughter like she does at every one of Freddie's cracks while I stand there and wonder if I'm going to regret this. Freddie has us pose with the car and hands me the phone to inspect the pictures before I even ask. Finally we say good-bye. He heads to the Prius and we hop in the Iroc-Z28. After I close the passenger side door on Stacey's car, the window tint makes it so dark that it seems like nighttime. Stacey revs the engine and cranks up some Mötley Crüe. I decide then and there that I don't give a flying rat's ass what Freddie does with those pictures; I'm having the time of my life and we're still sitting in the driveway.

Stacey has to swing by the liquor store because I forgot to stop on the way over and when I see her car reflected in the mirrored front glass, I laugh out loud because it's so freakin' awesome. When we get out, I hear whistles and catcalls and turn to see some boys in a mud-covered pickup truck pulling out of the gas station next door to the liquor store. I hustle in behind Stacey, wishing we had either used the drive-thru window or waited until we were well out of town to show ourselves off like this. Then I decide I don't want to go to Walmart after all.

As soon as we walk in, the man behind the register starts chatting with Stacey. I wander up and down the rum aisle, giving her plenty of time to flirt back with her new suitor. I carefully select a bottle of Bacardi Dark, grab a Coke from the cooler, then walk to the next aisle and pick up Stacey's Southern Comfort. At the register, she tries to give me ten dollars, but I remind her of the deal we made and she crams the money into one of her jacket pockets. I pick up our brown paper bag and turn to go, smiling when I hear the man behind the counter ask for Stacey's phone number.

"Look at you!" I say when we're back in the darkness of her car. "Mackin' before we even get out of town."

Stacey sniggers and asks if I thought he was cute. I tell her I thought he was adorable. And he was, in an ugly-baby-with-a-receding-hairline sort of way.

20

◇◇◇

"**I**f we get too hot in the concert, I might take the T-tops out on the way home," she says as she pulls out onto the highway. "Now that the weather's warmin' up, I'll have these babies out all the time! Well, except when I'm going somewhere I have to be seen." She pats her hair, so I do the same and it feels like a ball of springy wire. In my whole life put together up until today, I don't think I've used as much hair spray as I have on my hair right now. "Can't be messin' up Mama's mop!" she says with a cackle.

Stacey talks pretty much the whole ride to Memphis while I alternate swigs of rum and Coke. I point her into a garage next to the FedEx Forum and by the time we find a parking space, I'm so nervous about my outfit that I don't want to get out of the car. I take a few more shots of rum to get my courage back up. Stacey shuts off the engine, then reaches into the backseat and grabs that massive cassette tape storage box. "Be right back," she says, opening her car door. She puts the tapes in the trunk and comes back with a club, which she places on the dashboard.

"I've only got liability insurance and I can't take any chances with my baby," she explains as she digs through her purse. She finally fishes out two plastic flasks. "Here we go!" She hands one to me, then starts fumbling around in her glove box. She pulls out a Ziploc bag containing a tiny funnel. "Here, you go ahead."

I fill my flask with rum, then give the funnel to her.

"Alrighty then," she says, slinging the funnel up and down when she finishes. A wayward drop of Southern Comfort finds its way into my eyeball and the burning is quick and intense. With my one good eye, I locate the Kleenexes in my purse. I jerk one out of the little plastic wrapper and start dabbing under my eyes.

"This should keep me going for a few hours," she says, dropping the bagged funnel back into the console. I take my pressed powder out and flip it open to make sure I haven't smeared all that mascara Freddie globbed on my eyelashes. I look over at Stacey, who is wiggling around in her seat and wonder what in the world she's doing over there. She catches me looking and grins.

"Trying," she grunts, "to get this bottle." I hear clanking noises and glance back to see three bottles roll out from under the driver's seat into the back floorboard. "Already had a few under there, I guess," she says without looking. I take another swig of rum and finish off my Coke. I try to stick my liquor bottle under my seat, but it won't go.

"Hold on! Don't bust it!" she says. "Just set it back there with the others and I'll throw that pillow over 'em." She tosses the weird pillow over the paraphernalia, then wrestles the club into place on her steering wheel.

When I step out of the car a minute later, I feel a little woozy and wish I'd worn flat-heeled shoes. I hobble back to where Stacey is standing behind the car, checking to make sure the trunk is securely closed.

"You okay in those boots?" she asks.

"I'm fine," I lie. My feet have started to sweat, and I'm almost certain I'm going to fall and bust my ass. I follow her over to the elevator, which reeks of piss and stale beer. We ride down and walk out of the garage onto the sidewalk. Stacey speaks to every single person she sees, and by the time we get inside the lobby of the Forum, we're surrounded by middle-aged men, some of whom, I must admit, aren't that bad-looking at all. I spot a few people who appear to be normal and can't help but think how boring they look compared to us. And they aren't having nearly as much fun as Stacey Dewberry.

I feel like a wingman in a dunce cap as she deftly mingles with her horde of admirers. Stacey Dewberry favors a man with a mullet and the bushier, the better. The mild-mullet to mullet-less fellows are quickly dismissed. I think about striking up a conversation with one of the scorned, but they all scurry away, not noticing me or my zebra-print legs. I feel for the short-haired rejects, knowing how much we have in common, and wonder how Stacey commands so much attention. After watching her run that wacked-out game of hers for a few more minutes, I begin to get a bead on it. All of these fellows—young and old but all sporting some variety of bush mullet—are, I believe, attracted to her authenticity. Stacey Dewberry is clearly in her element, and her veracity is drawing men like moths to a flame. *Or maybe it's that hair,* I think, wondering how my own bouffant is holding up.

I notice a pack of younger chicks—no doubt here to take in some "oldies" rock—saunter past Stacey, casting wicked looks her way as if to say, How dare you glean so much attention in our presence! One group in particular walks past two or three times, visibly frustrated that their six-inch heels and peek-a-boo skirts fail to distract the passel of men orbiting the Dewberry. I wonder if the girls are really that interested in guys with hair stringing down their backs or if they're just attention whores. I take in the outfits—unapologetically slutty, yet feeble and cautious in their attempts at eighties fashion. Like me, they don't appear to be sold on their own coolness while Stacey Dewberry is burning down the house with hers. Those poor girls will have dimples on their other cheeks by the time they understand why their duck-faced smirks went unnoticed on this particular night. I mean, I just now figured it out and I've got at least a decade on their taut little asses. I cringe when I realize I'm in that creepy space between young hotness and the wisdom that comes only with age. I wonder why it has to be that way. It doesn't seem like a fair cut at all, especially for those of us stocking up on our very first vials of antiwrinkle cream. I guess the world would be too dangerous a place for susceptible men and certain ladies if we were allowed to be young, hot, and wise.

I think about the flask in my purse and make a decision. Tonight, I'm going to party like a rock star with Stacey Dewberry. But first, I need to get hammered. I motion to Stacey, and she pulls herself away from her fans long enough for us to buy a Coke and duck into the bathroom, where we mix up our poison.

"We can't afford their fifteen-dollar toddies on a substitute teacher salary," she says, giggling as she creeps into a stall. I go into the one next to hers and pour a substantial amount of rum into my

Coke. I want to take off my boots, wrap my feet in paper towels, and toss these ridiculously hot socks into the trash, but that would most likely have unpleasant consequences later on.

Upon exiting the ladies' room, Stacey and I walk into the crowd. Some have dutifully waited for her return, and I step into the mix right beside her. I smile and chat and sip my drink because I am determined to get on Stacey's level and I don't care if I have to get shitfaced drunk to do it. When the music cranks up, everyone goes their separate ways.

Stacey looks at me and says, "Are you ready for this?"

"I am," I say, following her into the arena. I hobble down the aisle, careful to hold on to the railing. All the way down to the front we go, where we have to show our tickets to a security guard pretending to be an usher who points us toward our row. Our seats are right in the middle, so we have to step over, around, and behind twenty people before we get to our designated spot. We get situated just as the band starts up and the crowd, including Stacey, really gets into the groove.

The people around us are singing and head-bopping and gyrating and otherwise getting wound up. I sit down and try to sip my drink, but I get elbowed in the forehead. I turn sideways and try it again, but someone from behind me hits my arm and half of my rum and Coke splashes onto the floor. I turn back to the front, turn up my cup, and power guzzle what little I have left. I stand up too quickly and my head starts to spin, so I sit back down.

"What are you doing?" Stacey shouts at me. "Get up and dance!" I get up and try, but then my left boot hits the spill spot and takes off without warning and the hefty-looking fellow next to me slides an arm around my waist just before I go into a free fall. I look up, see that he's quite handsome, and smile as I proclaim my gratitude for him literally saving my ass. Then some chick on the other side of him starts yelling and hitting him in the back with her fist, so he takes his hands off me and turns back to the stage. They swap places and she starts giving me the evil eye and Stacey, who is still laughing about the mishap, asks me to swap places with her. I worry about an altercation, but the arena goes dark, fireworks blast up from the stage, and I forget about everything, including how hot my feet are inside those damned fuzzy socks and real leather boots. When the band finally takes a break, I get down from my chair and follow Stacey to the restroom, where I see I'm a hot mess.

"Here, sweetie," Stacey says, getting her makeup bag out of her purse. She pats and dabs my face, then whips out a pick and full-sized bottle of hair spray. In a matter of minutes, I'm back in business.

"Stacey," I tell her as she pats down her own face, "I swear, if I've ever had this much fun, I don't remember when."

"Oh, this is only the beginning, sister," she says, spraying what has to be the sixteenth coat of hair spray on her hair. "C'mon, let's go get some Cokes so we can keep getting our drink on!"

Laughing, I follow her out the door and we get in line at the concession stand. We're discussing the band lineup with a few other drunks when I hear someone yell, "Ms. Jones! Ms. Jones! Is that you?" I stiffen up and look at Stacey, who casually glances behind us.

"Don't turn around," she whispers. "I had those two little pricks in class before. They were supposed to be doing a history assignment, but they had their telephones stuck inside their trapper keepers making all kinds of weird racket. They lied and lied about what they were doing, grinning the whole time like little shit-eatin' dogs. Made me so mad! Just a couple of smart-asses!"

"Stacey!" I say, grinning at her. "Did you use profanity?" And the term "trapper keeper"?

"Ms. Jones! It's me, Camden Price! From sixth period! Remember? It's me and Ben Evans! Hey, Ms. Jones, is that you?"

She points to the floor. "This ain't the schoolhouse! Let's get the hell outta here." We duck out of line and find another place to purchase beverages and then head back to our seats where all of our new friends, all of whom are equally hammered, greet us like you might a long lost family member. When Def Leppard hits the stage, the crowd goes wild and so do we. I catch a faint whiff of marijuana but never actually see anyone puffing. I look around and see that the security ushers seem to be more concerned with keeping people from standing on their seats than anything else. I look up at the stage. Two songs, three songs, eight songs. I'm dancing my fat ass off and having the time of my life.

Stacey and I make another quick trip to the restroom, picking up what we swear will be our final drinks of the night. We hustle back down to our friends in row three, and then when Poison comes out, the excitement in the air is more intoxicating than my supercharged rum concoction that Stacey poured a little SoCo into while I wasn't looking. The band starts playing and we all climb back up in our seats. A security guard comes through and makes us get down. Stacey ignores him until he threatens to escort her out of the arena. I want to tap this asshole on the shoulder and say, So it's okay to smoke pot, but standing in the chairs for the last thirty minutes of the concert is a no-go, huh? Great rules, ass-a-paloooza! I think better of it and keep my mouth shut. Stacey gives him a nasty look as she climbs down.

"It's fine," I yell. "At least they're making everyone get down."

"I wanna stand on that seat!" she yells back. Then the band starts the intro to "Every Rose Has Its Thorn" and she forgets all about it. I'm swaying to the music and having so much fun that I don't even mind when some random dude starts slow-humping my leg. The band takes a short break and the crowd has pushed down to where it's almost impossible to move. The guy is still humping my leg. Both bands come back out and do a few songs together, which is almost more that Stacey Dewberry can stand. My frisky new friend starts speed-humping me and when I turn to tell him to lay off, he tries to kiss me. I quickly turn away from his pooched lips and raucous breath and look at Stacey who instructs me to swap places with her again. The horny toad doesn't even open his eyes and immediately starts humping her leg. Stacey taps him on the forehead and when he opens his eyes, he smiles at his new target and promptly goes in for a smooch. Stacey yells at him that his breath smells like hog balls, but he's determined to get some lip action, so they have a little wrestling match that ends when she takes his shoulders and turns him toward the stage. He promptly slinks into the second row and starts humping some unsuspecting girl there.

"Look at him," Stacey shouts at me. "Like the dang Energizer Bunny on erectile dysfunction medication!" She gets back to singing along with the lyrics and I feel pretty special that I'm able to sing along to a few myself. During the grand finale, confetti shoots down from the ceiling, the crowd presses forward even more, and I smell marijuana again. I look around, don't see the smoker, but do spot our pal the humper bunny engaged in a massive make-out session with a chick in row four.

When the lights finally come on, it's a slow crawl up the aisle and out the door, and it is during this hike that I remember how hot my feet are and notice how bad they hurt.

"Are you okay to drive?" I ask when we finally step out into the crisp, cool night air.

"Hell to niz-oh," she says. "How far are we from Beale Street?"

"Just over there," I say, pointing.

"Something's gotta be open," she says. "I'll be fine after I eat."

21

◇◇

Saturday, I wake up with a massive thumping in my head and a greasy feeling in my belly. Buster Loo perches up on my shoulder and starts sniffing around in my hair. He snorts a few times, then backs up and twists his head sideways as if to say, "So, smoking again?"

"No, Buster Loo, it wasn't me," I say, reaching up to pet him. "But I do remember now why I stopped drinking the hard stuff. It'll take me three days to get over this." I roll out of bed, peel off the sheets, and haul them to the laundry room where I stuff them into the washing machine. "Hate that smell," I mumble, closing the door behind me. I drag myself to the shower where I let the shampoo sit in my hair an extra five minutes. When I get out, I still smell smoke and look down and see a hot pink shirt and zebra print leggings. "Jeez," I say, rolling them into a towel and taking the bundle to the laundry room. "Those are definitely next." I've just put on an old long-sleeve T-shirt and my junkiest pair of cutoff sweatpants when I hear the doorbell ring.

"Dang, girl!" Jalena says when I open the front door. "You look like you got run over by a dump truck. You must've had a big time last night."

"Thank you," I say, motioning her inside. "I did have a rather large time. I partied like it was 1989 and I ain't even joking." I ease into the kitchen and paw around in my designated medical cabinet until I find some aspirin.

"I came to help," she says, holding up a large paper sack.

"With what?"

"With whatever you need," she says. "You've spent nearly every Saturday for the past two months working for free at the diner and now I'm here to help you get this place ready for a party."

I glance around my house. "It is ready."

Jalena smiles. "Oh no, it's not." She empties her bag onto the counter and I see all manner of red and white and blue paraphernalia.

"What in the world is all that?" I ask as I pour Sprite into a glass packed with crushed ice and cherries.

"All of this is how you give someone a proper going away party." She smiles. "And I've just had the best idea." Her smile somehow gets wider. "I'm going to host parties. All kinds of parties. Full setup with invitations, decorations, and, of course, the finest catering service. I'm even thinking about taking a cake decorating class. I could do birthdays, showers, and anniversaries, whatever."

"In addition to the restaurant?"

"No, in conjunction with the restaurant!" She starts picking through the decorations. "I've always wanted to be a party planner, and when I was in that store this morning, I wanted to buy every-thing I saw. Then it hit me—I can host parties in the special-occasion room."

"That is a great idea," I say, thinking she obviously likes hard work a lot more than I do.

"So, I'm starting tonight," she says cheerfully. "You just have to help me with the posters."

"Posters?"

"Yes, posters! We have to make some posters! You can outline the letters and I'll color 'em in."

"Okay." She puts a poster board on the table along with a few pencils and some markers. "I have all that stuff, you know," I say.

"Yeah, I know, but I wanted to have some of my own to keep at the diner."

"Fair enough." I take a pencil and sketch out "God Speed" across one poster, "We" and a giant heart on another, and "SGT Dorsett" on the third. Jalena colors in the letters while I work on the heart. "Is that what it's supposed to say?" I ask her.

"Looks good to me," she says. When we finish, we take the posters out and tack them up on the back porch. Then she breaks out streamers, flags, balloons, the works. I tack and tape each and every corner, border, and edge she tells me to and when we're done, I must admit that it looks pretty cool. I also must admit that I'm quite relieved to be finished because my head won't stop thumping.

"This looks great, Jalena," I say. "How much do I owe you for my part of all this?"

"Girl, I'm trying to advertise. Don't be worried about stuff like that." She shoots me a look. "How much do I owe you for letting me use your backyard area to show off my skills? How much do I owe you for all the times you've helped me? Huh?" And then I figure out what really happened. Jalena got the idea to decorate for this party but had no intention of taking any money from me, so while she was looking around the party supply store, she came up with the idea about the party hostess thing. Or maybe she does want to be a party planner.

"Have you really always wanted to do this?" I ask, testing my theory.

"Yes, I have."

"I've never heard you mention it before today. And you're kind of famous for not wanting to cook when you're not at work, remember?"

"I'll be at work," she says simply. "Honestly, it's something I've had on my mind for a while and then when I saw a whole aisle of birthday stuff on clearance this morning, I thought, 'I need every bit of that.'"

"Alrighty then," I say, laughing. So be it. I fix her a sandwich and we eat out on the porch with Buster Loo sitting like a Coke bottle at our feet. When she leaves, I take another dose of aspirin, put on my shades, and take him for a turtle-speed walk around the block. When I get home, I call Stacey Dewberry to make sure she's still alive and she acts like I'm crazy when I ask her if she's hungover.

"Go get yourself a bacon, egg, and cheese biscuit," she says. "Works every time. I've already mowed the yard and washed my car."

"Jeez," I say. "Your car was spotless yesterday."

"Well, it's even more spotless now."

"Are you kidding me?" I ask.

"Ace, seriously, go get yourself a biscuit. And a hash brown or two." I ask her if she's talked to Freddie; I'm worried about him bringing Cameron Becker, because I'm even more not in the mood for drama than usual, thanks to this headache that I'm almost sure is going to last for the rest of my life. She hasn't heard from him.

"You know," she says, "I don't even have his phone number." I realize I don't, either, but he has both of ours. I look out the window and start worrying about those pictures he took of us last night.

I call Lilly, but she doesn't answer. Neither does Chloe. I make my bed, straighten up my house, and take another shower. I get dressed in some decent, but comfortable clothes, then go into the living room where I shut the blinds and close the curtains. I turn down my air conditioner and stretch out on the sofa. Buster Loo comes and curls up beside me. And that's where I am when Jalena and Ethan Allen show up at six o'clock. I roll off the couch, take another dose of aspirin, and help Jalena as she fusses over the final decorations. Ethan Allen is busy tending the grill and slicing open packs of Italian sausage hot dogs. Buster Loo is watching his every move.

"Did you bring your special toppings for those dogs?" I ask Jalena.

"Right over there," she says, pointing to a Crock-Pot on the bar. "I brought that in and plugged it up while you were over there snoring like a lumberjack." She glances at Ethan Allen. "Y'all kill me, leaving all your doors unlocked all the time."

"Nothing to worry about around here," Ethan Allen tells her, and I suspect it's not the first time he's had to tell her that.

Chloe and J.J. show up next, and Chloe can't stop bragging on what an amazing job Jalena has done with the decorations. I stop myself just before I blurt out that Jalena could host her baby shower. I look at J.J., who has joined Ethan Allen next to the grill, and think about how sad it is that he has a baby on the way and doesn't even know it. Serious as he is, I think he would be very excited. *Not my business,* I think as I rearrange forks and napkins.

"So, Chloe," I say when it's just the two of us, "where's your favorite brother-in-law?"

"Who, Tate?" Chloe asks. "Oh, I must've forgotten to mention to him that there was a party." She smiles, and I spend the next few minutes trying to figure out why I'm so disappointed. *Don't get your hopes up, moron!* I think. *There's probably a very good reason he's still single at his age.* I decide to ask Chloe about that later. I'm sure she'll be happy to tell me all about his romantic woes.

More people drift in, a casserole here, a red velvet cake there. By the time Lilly and Dax arrive, my backyard is packed and every available space for a dish is taken. I go into the kitchen and pour my special homemade banana ice cream into the mixer.

Before we start eating, J.J. gets everyone's attention and gives a short and right-to-the-point speech about how lucky we are to have Dax here in this town and how grateful we'll all be upon his safe return. Everyone claps while Lilly stands beside Dax, beaming at the crowd.

"Obviously, she's got her medication leveled out," Chloe whispers.

"Thank goodness," I say. "Can you imagine how bad this would be if she didn't?"

"It would be bad," she whispers. "Very, very bad."

I don't get in line until everyone there has fixed a plate and I'm sorely disappointed when I get to the hot dog table and find that Jalena's Crock-Pot of toppings has been scraped dry. Dammit! I think, picking up the mustard. Stacey Dewberry shows up after everyone has finished eating and entertains us with a glorious story about a cheese ball gone horribly wrong. I assure her that we've got plenty of food and tell her to help herself. Stacey makes a round of the tables, and when it appears she can't pile anything else on her plate, I motion for her to join us on the porch.

"This food looks good," she says. "Down-home country cookin' can't be beat. Is there any tea?" Chloe goes to get her a cup and I point to the empty chair next to me.

"Join us."

Lilly and Dax are snuggled up in the swing. Lilly is sipping some kind of fruity-looking drink, and Dax is working on his second cup of homemade banana ice cream. Chloe is relaxing in one lounger and J.J. is leaning back in the other. Logan Hatter is perched in the chair directly across from me and Stacey is between us. Jalena is inside and Ethan Allen is hanging out with a group of people at the picnic table in the yard. Freddie Dublin and Cameron Becker have yet to show up.

"Stacey almost killed me last night, y'all," I say, picking at a piece of cake on my dessert plate. "I had a big time, but I can't hang with her."

"What'd y'all do and why wasn't I invited?" Logan asks. I look up at him just in time to see him pop a whole cake ball into his mouth.

"We went to a concert," I tell him.

"I'm sorry, Coach Hatter," Stacey says. "I only had two tickets, but you could've ridden up there with us. I didn't know."

"You could've ridden in the back of the Iroc, Hatt," I tell him, and everyone starts laughing. "With the liquor bottles."

"You would've given me Acc's ticket, wouldn't you, sweetie?" Logan Hatter asks, and poor Stacey looks nervous and confused.

"Uh . . . ," she says, then takes a big bite of her hot dog.

"No, she wouldn't have, Logan Hatter!"

"Who did y'all see?" Chloe asks.

"Poison and Def Leppard," I answer because Stacey is still chewing.

"Classic rock," Dax says, and Stacey gives him an odd look.

"Well, how was it?" Lilly asks.

"I almost OD'd on ibuprofen and aspirin today," I say. "Does that give you a good idea of how great it was?" I stand up. "Who needs another drink?"

Logan, Lilly, and J.J. say that they do and Dax asks if he can please have another cup of ice cream.

"I can get you a bigger cup, Dax," I tell him. "And refill it as many times as you want." I glance at Chloe, who is giving me a nervous look.

"What?" I ask.

"I don't need a drink, thank you."

"Well, of course you don't, Mrs. Stacks," Stacey says. "You can't drink while you're pregnant!" I don't know if she's really talking that loud or if I just imagine it, but as soon as she gets to the end of that sentence, it seems as if time comes to a screeching halt. Everyone on the porch stares at Stacey, who is in the process of carefully applying a spoonful of spinach dip to a chunk of Hawaiian bread. I look at Ethan Allen, all the way out in the yard, and even he is staring. Or maybe he just caught a glimpse of everyone's expression and is wondering what's going on.

22

◇◇◇

"What in the world are you talking about, Dewberry?" Logan asks. He starts laughing, then stops. J.J. is looking at Chloe who is staring at Stacey Dewberry like she wants to kill her. I peek at Lilly, who shrugs and shakes her head as if to say, *Don't look at me to say anything.*

"Who told you that?" Chloe asks, giving me an evil look. I shake my head and put up my hands.

"No one," Stacey says, oblivious as she forks a meatball and then a small square of cheese. She looks up at Chloe. "You were sick and ill as a hornet for a while and now you've got the happy, healthy glow of a woman with child. It's unmistakable." Stacey sees the look on Chloe's face and then glances at J.J. "Oh my stars," she mumbles. She puts down the meatball. "Oh no. I can't believe I just did this." J. J. Jackson doesn't say a word, just sits and looks at Chloe. Stacey stands up and picks up her plate. "I'm so sorry, Mrs. Stacks. I really am. Mr.

Sheriff Jackson, I don't know what to say." Stacey is on the verge of tears, but she continues. "I just assumed that if I could figure it out, anybody could." She pauses, then looks like she wants to die. "Oh my goodness, I didn't mean anything by that." No one says a word because, hell, what could any of us say? "Boy, I have fubared this get-together beyond belief," she says, and then quickly walks away.

"Fubared?" Lilly looks at Logan, who shrugs and looks at Dax.

"Let him tell you." She looks at Dax expectantly.

"Fucked up beyond all recognition," Dax whispers.

"Well, it certainly is that," Logan remarks.

"Shut up, Hatter!" I hiss. "Stacey!" I call. "Stacey! Wait!" I look at Chloe. "I swear I didn't say a word to her. You have to believe me." Chloe looks mad as hell and doesn't say a word. She shakes her head and her bottom lip starts to tremble. I watch Stacey toss her plate in the garbage and walk out the gate. I want to go after her but know I can't walk away from Chloe.

Ethan Allen appears on the edge of the porch. "What's going on up here?" he asks. "Everything okay?" I look down at him, shake my head "No," and he says, "Okay, well, I'm going to go over here and, I don't know, just go on over . . . Okay, so I'll talk to y'all later." He makes haste back to the picnic table.

"Chloe," J.J. says, and I bristle at the tone of his voice. "Could I please have a word with you in private?"

"Of course," Chloe says. She stands up, puts on a brave face, and looks at Dax. "I'm so sorry," she says. "I wish you all the best. Thank you so much for your service. I will pray for your safety every night." She looks at me. "I have to go now."

"I'll talk to you tomorrow, son," J.J. says to Dax and, without making eye contact with anyone else, turns to follow Chloe into the house. I look at Lilly, who shakes her head, and we all sit in silence for a minute.

"Well, holy shit," Dax says finally. Ethan Allen walks up and sits down in one of the loungers.

"Where's Jalena?" I ask.

"Talking to Lulu Cadle about a birthday party," he says. "What's going on?"

"For real," Logan Hatter says emphatically. "What is going on?"

I look at Lilly and she stares back at me like a frightened kitten. "I'm not saying a word," she says.

"About what?" Ethan Allen asks.

"Well, it would appear the cat is already out of the bag, sister," Logan says to Lilly, then looks at me with his eyebrows raised.

"What cat and what dang bag?" Ethan Allen practically shouts. I look at him and then at Logan, thinking they're worse than most women about being nosy and gossiping.

"Apparently, Chloe is pregnant," Logan tells him. "According to Stacey Dewberry, anyway. Which isn't really that big of a deal seeing as how they've been together for what? A year now?"

"So what's the problem?" Ethan Allen wants to know.

"The problem appears to be that J.J. wasn't aware of her, uh, condition," Dax observes.

"Well, he's damned sure aware of it now," Logan says. "That's gonna be a weird ride home." He looks at me. "How is it that Stacey Dewberry knows about this and J. J. Jackson doesn't?"

"There's a million-dollar question," Dax says, putting down his ice cream cup and picking up his beer.

"She wanted him to propose first," I say, and the men all look off in different directions.

"Logan, you can't tell anyone at school about this," Lilly says. "Chloe is really concerned that if the wrong people find out about this, they might try to get her fired."

"Pffft," Logan says, waving his hand. "Have you ever known me to hang out with the wrong people? She isn't going to lose her job, but why the hell didn't she just tell him? This was a hell of a way for him to find out. I thought y'all sat around planning for stuff like this your whole life."

"Who exactly is 'y'all'?" Lilly asks, clearly offended.

"Women!" Logan says. "Is this not the kind of thing y'all get together and talk about for days on end? How to break news like this like with a little bitty football or with some little pink baby shoes or something."

"Logan Hatter!" Lilly says. "It is so painfully obvious why you're still single."

"Well, he has a point," Dax says, and Lilly glares at him. "What? I'm just saying J.J. shouldn't have had to find out like this. It was kind of like he was the last one to know."

Lilly's shoulders slump. "I guess you're right." She looks at me. "We failed Chloe on this one."

"We told her to tell him," I remind her. "We told her and told her and then we told her again."

"We tried to drop him a hint," Lilly says. "But that didn't work out very well, either."

"In the hot dog aisle at Walmart," I say, giggling at the thought. "And Chloe crawled all over our asses, so we backed off." Lilly recounts the story, and the guys think it's pretty funny.

"Well, he was going to pop the question anyway as soon as she got things squared away in her new house," Dax says, and Lilly scowls at him. "He didn't want to stress her out even more than she already was with all the renovations and stuff she had going on."

"How do you know that?" Lilly demands.

"He was looking at a jewelry store paper one day when I walked into his office," Dax says, like it's absolutely no big deal whatsoever. "He's already got the ring picked out."

"Why didn't you tell me?"

Dax looks confused. "Why, because—I don't know, Lilly, hell, I didn't know all this was going on. I'm sorry, baby." He puts his arm around her and she leans into him.

"I'm sure everything will work out just fine," I say. "I hope. And Dax, I'm sorry all of this went down tonight."

"Not a problem," he says. "It proved to be quite a distraction, which I very much appreciate." That comment hits me like a ton of bricks. He's going to Afghanistan. While military budget cuts are all over the news, Dax Dorsett is going to a war zone.

"Hey, Ace," Logan says. "If neither one of us is married by the time we're thirty-five, let's have a baby together—you want to?" I look at him and he grins and everyone starts laughing.

"Sure, Hatter," I tell him. "I'd love that. You're so romantic."

"Great," he says, clearly proud of himself for making a funny. "We can start practicing tonight if you want." And everyone laughs even harder. Except me. I just stand there and look at him, shaking my head.

"Hatt, you're too funny for your own good, buddy," Ethan Allen says, reaching over to slap him on the back.

"I have to call Stacey Dewberry," I say.

"She can join us, too, if she wants," Hatter says.

"Hatt," I say, rolling my eyes, "has anyone ever told you to quit while you're behind?"

"Well, that depends on who I'm behind," he says, winking at Ethan Allen. I roll my eyes and walk into the kitchen where I pick up the phone and call Stacey. It doesn't even ring, just goes straight to voice mail. I call her two more times and get the same thing. Finally, I leave her a message, telling her everything is fine and to please call me whenever she can. I put the phone down and think about Freddie Dublin. Thank God he didn't show up tonight.

As it gets closer to midnight, people start drifting toward their cars. Everyone shakes Dax's hand, pats him on the back, and promises to send care packages. As the crowd thins, I find myself sitting way too close to Logan Hatter. He catches me looking at him and winks at me, then slips his arm around my shoulder.

"Don't get your hopes up," I tease, getting up to say good night to the last of the partygoers. Dax and Lilly walk up and tell me they're calling it a night as well. I can't imagine how Lilly must be feeling right now, her expression unreadable as she says good night. Dax thanks me again and again for hosting such a lively get-together and I tell him again and again that it's the very least that I could do. After they leave, I unplug my Christmas lights and turn to see Logan Hatter still sitting on the swing.

"You wanna come in?" I ask. "There's no one left to drive you home."

"Oh dang," he says. "I guess I'm sleeping with you tonight."

"Your game needs some work, Hatter," I tell him with a smile.

"We'll see about that later, sweet-cheeks." He follows me inside, has a seat in the living room, and pats the sofa cushion next to him. "C'mon, Ace, you know you want to come snuggle up over here where it's warm." Despite my better judgment, I get two beers out of the fridge and join him on the couch. And tonight, I decide not to be lonely.

23

<><><><><><><><><><><><><><><><><><><><><><><><><><><><><><><><><><><><><><><>

The next morning, I wake up at the crack of dawn and the first thing I see is a shaft of light drifting in through the curtains shining on Logan Hatter's shockingly white ass. Oh shit! After throwing some covers over that pasty rump, I slide out of bed and creep down the hallway. I startle Buster Loo out of his slumber on the couch, and he jumps up on all four paws and commences with a first-class barking fit. I pick him up and try to pet him out of his guard-dog rage, but he wiggles out of my arms onto the sofa where he sits and stares at me as if to say, "How dare you!" I pick up my phone and think about texting Lilly, but she's got so much going on today that I don't want to saddle her down with tales of my sexcapades with Logan Hatter. Or maybe I just don't want her to know. I'm not sure. I make a pot of coffee and think about that. And I think about Logan Hatter.

I'm almost as tall as he is, but not quite. He's got a pudgy beer belly that I find endearing and a receding hairline, which he keeps covered with a baseball cap. He's a good guy even if he does fancy himself to still be the stud he thought he was at twenty-two. And he chases women accordingly. But he's single, so I guess he's entitled. Maybe Logan Hatter is just what I need right now, an easy no-strings-attached good ole boy. I pull my housecoat tighter around me and think about last night. Sleeping with him is like sitting in front of someone else's fireplace. It's warm and cozy, but regardless of how pleasant it always seems to be, you know you can't sit there forever.

I pour a cup of coffee, feeling tremendously guilty because the last time I had sex, it was with Mason McKenzie, the Ex-Fiancé. I try to come up with an excuse for myself, but I can't. I just did what I wanted to do and that's pretty much it. I think about all the action movies I've seen where the leading man and some hot chick he saves from certain death run for their lives until they end up in a seedy hotel on the edge of town, humping like rabbits. Maybe that can be my excuse: My life is a battlefield where I'm fighting for some peace of mind and I needed some damned relief. I don't know what Hatter's excuse is for firing up our old flame. One thing I've always liked about him is that he doesn't even pretend to need an excuse.

I'm on my second cup of coffee when I hear him lumbering down the hall. Buster Loo jumps off the sofa and darts out the doggie door as if he simply can't tolerate the perpetrator's presence. When Logan rounds the corner, I notice his hair isn't quite as thin as it once was. I want to ask him how that happened, but it might embarrass him, so I just sit there and wonder.

"Good morning, sunshine," I say.

"I can't believe you took advantage of me like that," he says. "I was highly intoxicated. What kind of person are you?" He gives me a peck on the cheek.

"The kind who makes coffee," I say. "Would you like some?"

"Love some." He walks over to the cabinet. "You moved the cups."

"Look in the one next to it," I say, pointing. "I'm a habitual re-arranger."

"That sounds dangerous." He pours a cup of coffee and joins me at the table. As we chat about the party, I realize I'm a little happier than perhaps I should be to have him sitting here with me this morning. Then it hits me. I love Logan Hatter with all my heart and soul. But not in a romantic I-wanna-have-your-babies kind of way. More like in a let's-have-sex-and-then-not-worry-about-it kind of way.

"Can I fix you some breakfast?" I ask, like we're an old married couple.

"I was hoping you'd ask," he says with a grin. "I haven't had one of your world-famous omelets in years." He looks at the pans hanging about my stove. "Need some help?"

"You just keep me up to speed on all the juicy gossip. How about that?"

"That's an arrangement I can live with." He gets up to pour himself another cup of coffee, then goes and settles into my recliner.

"Those boxers are nice," I say, looking at his Pink Panther underpants.

"Thank you. They were a gift."

"From one of your many lovers?"

"No, from my mother," he says.

"I'm going to leave that one alone." When I start frying sausage, Buster Loo somehow finds it in his heart to come back inside and be social. Logan fills me in on all the latest gossip and then we start talking about Cameron Becker dumping Drew Wills. He has the inside scoop on that just like he does everything else, and it's all news to me because the only two people I talk to on a regular basis at school are Stacey and Freddie. I hardly ever see Lilly during the day and while I do see Chloe a lot, she's not much on sharing hearsay. We don't talk about Chloe and J.J.'s situation.

Logan leaves at eight thirty and I retire to bed with Buster Loo who, after being on the receiving end of a full piece of bacon, is totally over his mad spell. I snuggle up under the covers, then roll over and set my alarm for ten thirty because I have somewhere else to be today.

I roll up to the gates of the Waverly Estate at twelve forty-five on the dot. Gloria Peacock is hosting a brunch and quite a few Bugtussle big shots are there to wish Dax well.

Chloe, Lilly, and I found ourselves in Gloria's social circle for the first time about this time last year when we were in the midst of a terrible jam. Gloria Peacock, a woman of great wealth and status in Bugtussle, proved to be quite nimble at the task of quietly clearing metaphorical waters muddied by small-town scandal. Since then, she's treated the three of us like family, which we all appreciate, but I probably value the most.

When the gates open, I drive in and park in the space indicated by a smiling man wearing a royal blue polo shirt and white starched shorts. A few people I know from Bugtussle are arriving at the same time, so we ride together through the splendid expanse of the Waverly Estate on a royal blue golf cart, the rear seat of which is emblazoned with a magnificent peacock in all its feathered glory. Gloria greets us at the door, then shows me to the patio room where I find Gloria's pal, Birdie Ross, sipping on sweet tea and grinning like a possum. I take a seat next to her and casually work my grandmother's garden book into our conversation. I know that Birdie was a dear friend of Gramma Jones, and I'm hoping she can shed some light on things for me so I don't have to go home and read that letter. Because if there's something to be told, I feel like Birdie Ross will tell it. But when I mention the book, she doesn't respond. She picks up her glass and takes a long sip of iced tea. Gloria Peacock joins us and as soon as she takes a seat, Birdie looks at her and says, "Someone found her grandmother's gardening book."

"Oh," Gloria says, looking at me. "Have we now?"

"Yes, ma'am," I say, and start to feel ashamed, like the time I hung all of Gramma Jones's undergarments out on the line just before her lunch guests arrived. I didn't do it on purpose. I didn't know she had company coming. Or maybe I knew and forgot. Yeah, that was probably what happened. I look at Birdie who is looking at Gloria, and I see some form of communication pass between the two of them. Nothing spoken—not even a nod—just a look. Almost indiscernible.

"Perhaps you should come to the garden club meeting this Tuesday night," Birdie says, finally looking at me. "You're interested in gardening, right? That's why you mentioned the book."

"Right," I say. I feel like a child conjuring up lies about the cookie jar.

"We could use some fresh faces," Gloria Peacock says. "And Essie Jones kept quite an extraordinary yard." She and Birdie exchange another look. "I must say I'm pleased with your interest."

"Yes," Birdie says. "Most pleased."

"What's going on, ladies?" Temple Williams asks, stepping into the room to join us.

"Little Ms. Moppet here has dug up her grandmother's gardening book," Birdie says.

"Oh," Temple says, looking at me. "And what did you find in there?" The directness of her question catches me off guard. I think about the letter and my cheeks start to burn.

"It was the buttercups," I say, like an idiot. "I saw the buttercups." I decide to stop talking in an effort to save myself from further humiliation.

"Of course," Temple says. "It's always the buttercups. The early bloomers get us all excited."

"I love springtime," Birdie says, winking at me. "The sunshine, little green sprouts all over my yard. I consider it a time of great awakening." Gloria and Temple nod in agreement. I sit there, pretending to get it.

"Yes," Temple agrees, "because you know something beautiful is stirring just beneath the surface."

"And then when the flowers blossom and bloom, it's the most magical realization of hope," Gloria says. "Miraculous and inspiring."

"A continuous cycle," Birdie adds.

"Makes my soul sing every year," Temple says with a smile.

I want to stand up and scream for them to drop the cryptic veil and tell me what the hell they're talking about because I'm getting frustrated and confused. But, of course, I don't say a word. Perhaps this is part of the game. Part of the initiation into their elite club of hard-earned wisdom and knowledge. For some reason, I start thinking about wrinkle cream.

"You know, some women keep journals," Gloria begins. "But I never have." She looks at Birdie, who nods. "My garden keeps my secrets."

"You can tell a lot about a woman by what she does with her yard," Temple remarks.

"Indeed," Birdie says. "That's why I always plant cockscomb in the same bed with naked ladies." She looks at me. "With the Clitoria ternatea right in between." She lowers her voice to a whisper. "It's a climbing plant."

The three of them have a good laugh at that, and I wonder for a second if Gloria, Birdie, and Temple might have started smoking hash. Grown in their secret-keeping gardens, of course. Or maybe they've jointly invested in some medical marijuana. Or perhaps this is their way of telling me that they have answers to the questions I have yet to ask.

"Come to the garden club this Tuesday," Gloria says. "I think you will find it most helpful as you begin your journey."

"As a gardener," Temple says.

"A book can only get you so far," Birdie adds.

"Sure," I say. "Okay." I try to hide my apprehension about attending a garden club meeting. I mean, I'm not that old. Yet. But the Bugtussle Garden Club is invitation only, so I focus on how honored I should feel right now. "Thank you," I say with as much reverence as I can muster.

"My pleasure," Gloria says.

"So tell me about your boyfriend," Birdie chirps.

"I don't have a boyfriend," I say. I have a private little freak-out moment, wondering if they somehow know about my sleepover with Logan Hatter. Why would that matter?

"You don't?" she says. "Well, today is your lucky day." Oh God! No! I'm so stupid! "I know the nicest guy." No! Not her, too! "His name is Bo Hammond, and I'll just go on and tell you that he is some kind of hot-to-trot, little missy!" Shit! Somebody just shoot me, please! "Especially when he takes his shirt off." Yuck-oh!

"Your yard man takes his shirt off?" Gloria asks.

"But of course, Gloria," Birdie says. "You know I wouldn't have one that didn't." I can't help it. I laugh at that. Birdie picks up her phone.

"You don't have to call him right now!" I say quickly.

"No time like the present," Birdie says, and Gloria Peacock laughs and shakes her head as Birdie scrolls through her contacts list. I sit there while Birdie carries on with her yard man, thinking that sitting in the gyno's office in that awful paper dress isn't half as awkward and uncomfortable as this moment right here.

"Tell him I'm chunky," I whisper, "so he's not surprised."

Birdie disregards my comment with a dismissive wave. She puts the phone on her shoulder. "Friday or Saturday?" she asks.

"Friday, I guess," I say, feeling as if I have no choice. She chats for a few more minutes, cackles a few times, then asks me where I live. With more apprehension than when I slip my bare feet into the cold steel stirrups, I give up my address. "It's a date!" she says proudly after ending the call. "He'll pick you up Friday at seven."

"Can you give me his number in case something comes up?" I ask, getting my wits about me way too late.

"Sure," she says. "I'll text you the contact, but you better not stand him up!"

"Don't worry," I say. I wonder if anyone has ever been flat-out run over by a train without sustaining any broken bones. I mean, anyone besides me. Birdie gets up and goes to refill her tea.

"Do you know what you really need, Ace?" Gloria asks, her voice barely above a whisper.

"No, ma'am," I say, trying to be honest. My nerves are shot to hell and if she suggests another blind date, I'm afraid I might start squalling uncontrollably.

"You need to find a man who will dance with you," she says. "And *you* need to find him." She points at me. "Not her"—she points to Birdie—"or anyone else can find him for you." Gloria leans back in her seat. "And when the time is right, I'm sure you will."

"Thank you," I say, feeling better.

"Are you over here talkin' about me, Gloria?" Birdie asks when she returns to her seat.

"Oh no, Birdie," Gloria says. "Of course not."

Lilly and Dax arrive just after one. Lilly looks smashing in a dark green smock, which I suspect she bought specifically for the purpose of standing next to her soldier. Dax is wearing his army outfit, which I hear several people refer to as "ACUs" and the gravity of what's going on today makes me want to run screaming into the Peacock woods. Everyone is so proud of Dax, proud to speak to him, proud to shake his hand. Several people, including a reporter from the Bugtussle Beacon, snap photos of him and Lilly.

Shortly after they arrive, everyone files into Gloria Peacock's formal dining room and we all sit around a table three miles long. I wish for a minute that I had invited Hatter to come along with me, but maybe it's better that I didn't. When we're all seated, Gloria stands at the head of the table and, after getting everyone's attention, says, "I would like to say a word, please. Dax, would you please stand? Thank you." She smiles at him and continues. "This country has now been at war for a decade, and while we all eagerly await an end, the brave men and women of our military continue to faithfully serve their country. In honor of Sergeant Dax Dorsett, I would like to share this passage from the speech given by former president George Bush in March 2003, which was, as we all know, the beginning: 'My fellow citizens, the dangers to our country and the world will be overcome. We will pass through this time of peril and carry on the work of peace. We will defend our freedom. We will bring freedom to others. And we will prevail. May God bless our country and all who defend her.'" She raises her glass. "To Sergeant Dorsett." Everyone raises their glass to Sergeant Dorsett.

"What a fine young man," Birdie whispers to me. "God bless his good-lookin' soul."

Later that afternoon, I'm sitting at my kitchen table, staring at Gramma Jones's garden book. I have the letter in my hand and, after thinking about it for a good long while, I unfold it and begin to read:

Dearest Essie,

I very much enjoyed spending the past few days with you. Thank you for the happiness you have brought into my life. I look forward to seeing you again soon.

Yours,

M. Emerson

"'Dearest Essie'?" I look down at Buster Loo. "'Yours'? What does he mean, 'yours'?" Buster Loo takes off for his secret hiding place behind the love seat. "Who the hell is M. Emerson? What kind of shady name is that?"

I look at the date, June 28, and think for a minute. This was written in the summer between my freshman and sophomore years of high school, which means that I would've been at basketball camp, because I was always there during the last week of June. No wonder Gramma Jones always made sure I went to basketball camp every year. She was getting her freak on with M. Emerson!

"Oh my goodness," I say, tucking the letter back into the book. "I wish I hadn't read that."

I call Lilly, but she doesn't answer, so I call Stacey Dewberry. I'm so desperate to talk to someone that I spill the whole story as soon as she says hello.

"You should not have read that letter," Stacey tells me.

"Well, I know that now!" I say.

"I mean, it's like you were spying on your granny while she was taking a bath. Know what I mean? Some things your eyes just weren't meant to see."

"Ew, Stacey, that is so gross," I say, "but also very true."

"So do you know the guy?" she asks.

"No, I don't, but I've got to figure out who he is and if he's still around, or if that tree out there was planted for him."

"Have you looked in the phone book?"

"For what?"

"His name, silly!" she says. "Then you'll have his address. My granny used the same phone book for years and yours probably did the same. If you can find the phone book, flip it open to the white pages and see if she drew a circle around anyone in the *E*s. As in Emerson. If she did, that's probably your, I mean, her guy. But now if you think he's fishy, he could have—or could've had—an unlisted number. Which means your granny might've written it in somewhere else on the phone book. If I were you, I'd check inside the front and back covers first. Look for that little box for important numbers. My granny had names and numbers written all over her phone book. That's why she always kept the same one."

"That's brilliant, Stacey," I say, thinking about the old phone book that's still in the top of the pantry in the kitchen. "I'll do that."

"Great. So do you think Mrs. Stacks is going to fire me tomorrow?"

"What? No! Of course not. She adores you, Stacey. You did her a favor."

"It certainly didn't seem that way to me. I haven't left the house all weekend 'cause I'm afraid I'd get pulled over by Sheriff Jackson and arrested for being a blabbermouth."

"All's well that ends well, my friend. No worries. Everything is fine." I'm guessing, but I don't tell her that. Everything has to be fine because what's the alternative? Chloe and J.J. breaking up? I don't see that happening. "She'll thank you tomorrow, just you wait and see."

"So are you sleepin' with that tubby little baseball coach?"

"What?" I say, completely caught off guard. "You mean Hatter?"

"Coach Hatter, yeah, that one," she says. "Y'all seemed to be fairly interested in each other's goods last night." She sniggers.

"Interested in each other's goods?" I pause for a minute, not wanting to lie to her, but also not wanting the Dewberry to tell everyone in A and B Hall that I sacked the Hatt last night.

"Yeah, I was sitting right there while y'all were carrying on. Remember?"

"Oh, we're just friends," I say.

"Friends with benefits?" she asks. I decide to turn the tables on her.

"Well, what about you? How many of your boyfriends from Friday night have you been getting your freak on with?" I ask, teasing. "That's really why you haven't left your house, isn't it? You've had too much company."

"Oh, I've been talking to a few, but nothing serious. I like to be wined and dined before I do the wild thing." And "thing" is pronounced "thang." "Or at least burgered and shaked," she adds, and we both start laughing.

"Stacey Dewberry, you are too much, sister. Too much!"

24

◇◇◇

Monday morning, Stacey is not in the conference room when I get there, and I worry for a second that maybe Chloe did fire her. Chloe asks me to have a seat and I'm about to ask about Stacey, when she holds up her left hand, upon which I see a big, round, and very shiny diamond.

"Chloe!" I say, jumping up to give her a hug. "It's beautiful! Congratulations!" I look around. "But where is Stacey?"

"She came in early because she wanted to apologize for Saturday night, poor thing," Chloe says. "She was so upset, but when I showed her the ring, she got really excited and forgot all about it."

"That dang Stacey Dewberry."

"That dang Stacey Dewberry, indeed."

"Who says loose lips sink ships?" I quip.

"Don't get carried away."

"Sorry."

"You really didn't say anything to her?" Chloe asks. "Didn't let something slip?"

"No!" I say. "Are you crazy? I take serious offense to that!"

"She just figured it out all on her own?"

"Well, obviously she did, Chloe. She's not a total moron—just a good guesser who dresses a little funky."

"I didn't mean—"

"Didn't mean to insinuate that I would share the secrets of a trusted friend with someone I've only known for approximately one month?"

"Sorry."

"It's fine. I guess I would've thought the same thing if I were you." I look at her and she smiles. "So when's the wedding? How and when did he propose? And, most importantly, why didn't you call and tell me? And why weren't y'all at Gloria Peacock's yesterday? I have so many questions!"

"Well, yesterday, J.J. had to work and I wasn't feeling great. I called Mrs. Peacock and let her know."

"Just forgot to call me?"

"I didn't want to wake you," she says. "I didn't know if you and Coach Hatter might be sleeping late. Or not sleeping at all."

"Very funny, Chloe," I say. "Now why didn't you call and tell me about the ring?"

"I didn't get it until last night."

"So you were too busy having sex?"

"Ace Jones!"

"Just kidding!" I say, "but I mean, evidently you have, right?"

"Would you please shut up?"

"If you tell me how he proposed, I'll think about it."

"He came over when he got off work and I was in the den. He got down on one knee and took my hand and asked me to make him the luckiest man in the world."

"Was he in uniform?"

"Yes."

"That is so sexy."

"I'll tell him you said so."

"Please don't."

"So that was that. He told me he'd been planning to ask, just wanted to wait until everything was finished with the house because he was afraid I would get too stressed out."

"Yeah, that's what Dax said."

"How did he know?" I relay the conversation that occurred after she and J.J. left Saturday night and she immediately starts pouting. Then I remind her that J.J. wasn't the only one keeping secrets. "And technically, he wasn't keeping a secret. More like strategic man-planning."

"I guess you're right," she says.

"So how mad was he Saturday night?"

"I think it hurt his feelings more than anything but, of course, he didn't say that."

"What did he say?"

"He just mainly wondered how Stacey Dewberry knew and he didn't. I can't believe she just blurted that out like that."

"I can."

"I had quite a bit of explaining to do, but he was very nice because he's a very nice person."

"So is he excited now?"

"Very much and so am I. Not to mention tremendously re-lieved." She looks at her ring.

"So tell me one more time when our little bundle of joy will ar-rive."

"Due date is November 15."

I do the math. "Y'all made this baby on Valentine's Day, didn't you?"

"You better hush!"

"Well, I'll tell you one thing. That is going to be one good-looking and very serious baby," I say. "And the wedding?"

"The weekend after school is out, which is the weekend after Memorial Day. That gives us a few weeks to plan and I won't have to take off work for the honeymoon. We talked about it and de-cided to have a small ceremony at the house on that Sunday. I was thinking of asking Jalena if she'd cater the reception."

"That would be right up her alley," I say. "So can I please start planning your shower now?"

"No! You don't do that until at least a month before the baby arrives!"

"The wedding shower, Chloe."

"Oh yes." She smiles. "About that. We talked about it last night and we want to keep everything low-key and personal," she says. "If it's okay with you, I'd like to have a small and informal shower around noon on Saturday before the wedding Sunday afternoon."

"Is that proper?" I ask my friend the etiquette queen.

"I'm not concerned with being proper," she says. "Everything was proper and formal the first time, and we all know how that turned out. This time, I'm concerned with being realistic and making everything as convenient as possible, and this will make life easy on my people in Jackson and our other out-of-town guests."

"Got it."

"And don't stress yourself out. I want the weekend to be fun and relaxed. I want everyone to hang out and visit and really enjoy themselves."

"Too easy," I tell her. "But if you change your mind, let me know."

"I won't and I'm going to put together a short list of addresses, which I will print on mailing labels and have to you by the end of the week."

"You don't have to do that," I say.

"I've already got it half done," she says.

"Okay, then." The bell rings and we get up.

"Here," she says, handing me a folder. "Easy day today."

"Well, thank God. And, again, congratulations, Chloe. For the ring and the baby. I'm so happy for you."

"Thank you, Ace."

I meet Freddie in the hallway and stop to speak, but he doesn't acknowledge me, so I turn and keep walking. By the time I get to my assigned classroom, I'm seriously worried about the incriminating photos he took of Stacey and me on Friday night. I don't see him at break and when I sit down with Stacey at lunch, I ask if she's talked to him.

"Oh yeah," she says, unwrapping her sandwich. "He came down to my, uh, Mrs. Mayfield's classroom during first break."

"What did he say?" I ask, feeling a nip of jealousy.

"He just talked for a minute, but he asked me not to say any-thing to anyone about what we discussed." She looks at the bag of barbecue potato chips in her hand.

"But Stacey," I whisper. "I'm not anyone. We're all friends, re-member?" I can tell she wants to spill it, so I continue. "He was sup-posed to bring Cameron to the party, but they never showed up."

"I know."

"But why?" I ask. She doesn't say a word. She doesn't even look up. Then I have a lightbulb moment. "If it's something he doesn't want to talk about, then you should tell me so I won't have to ask him why he wasn't there." She looks up at me. "I won't say a word to anyone. I promise."

"Not even Chloe?"

"Of course not. But why would it matter if I told her?" I really have to know what's going on now.

"He doesn't want anyone to know."

"Know what?" I ask.

"It's personal," she says.

"Not a word. I promise." I'm dying to know what Freddie Dublin told her that she doesn't want to tell me, and then I wonder for a brief second how I got sucked into this ridiculous drama. Oh wait, I know. Mr. Hypnotic Snake Eyes with the Intoxicating Cologne. Right.

"Let's just say that a relationship ended on Saturday, and he didn't feel like going out Saturday night."

"A relationship? With who? Did he get into it with Cameron?"

"No. Not her. Someone very important to him, that's uh, not a female." She starts cramming potato chips into her mouth. "I've said too much. He doesn't want people to know."

"Know what?" I ask her, and she just looks at me. "Ah, Stacey, about that. People already know. It's not exactly a secret."

"I didn't."

"Yes, you did."

"No, I didn't."

"You had to, Stacey! When he did your makeup Friday night, it looked like a freakin' Hollywood professional had done it! You knew!" She shakes her head. "You suspected?"

"Not at all."

"You made that crack about the dress."

"I was joking."

"Stacey, you're a horrible liar."

"I cannot confirm or deny that."

"It's not a problem for anyone either way, so don't worry about it."

"He'll lose his job if you tell Chloe. She's too straight-laced."

"Is that your word or his?"

"His," she says. "Oh my stars! I've said too much again."

"Stacey, you have nothing to worry about, okay? I just wonder why he thinks I can't be trusted." I look at Stacey. And you can? "Is it because I'm friends with Chloe?"

"I've dabbled, okay?"

"Dabbled? In what?" Then I figure it out. "Oh!"

"I told him that one day—in confidence, of course—and now I'm worried that I've said too much for real and we'll both get run out of town and I really need my paycheck this month." She looks desperate. "Promise me you won't tell Chloe."

"Stacey, I won't. Trust me, it's not that big of a deal."

"It most certainly will be that big of a deal if the PTA gets wind of it. You can't wave stuff like that around like a flag for the whole world to see."

"Everyone's personal life should be just that," I say.

"Well, that sounds good and all, but we both know that's not the way it is down here in the Bible Belt."

"Yeah, I know." I sigh because she's got me on that one. "We do have a surplus of the self-righteous down here." I look at her and she looks like she's about to have a panic attack. "Hey, my lips are sealed. You have nothing to worry about and neither does he. Everyone likes Freddie and everyone likes you. Everything is fine. Nothing has changed. And nothing is going to change because we had this conversation."

"Everyone likes me?"

"Everyone with good sense," I say. "And who cares about the others? Not me."

"Don't be jealous," she says.

"Of what?"

"I'm sure Freddie chose me to talk to because I've dabbled."

"Because you've—okay," I say, thinking this conversation has got to end soon. "Of course." And certainly not because you've willingly introduced him to every skeleton in your closet and he could hang your ass out to dry in a fraction of a second.

"He's very upset," Stacey says. "Just don't take it the wrong way if he acts weird for a while."

"Did he tell you to say that?"

"Yes. No. Well, not exactly."

"It's okay. I respect that."

"He said you would."

"Great." Shit! "So what happened?" I ask, unable to get my curiosity in check. "Who broke up with who?"

"I've already said too much," she says. "But I think he got dumped."

"Who in their right mind would dump Freddie freakin' Dublin?"

"Tell me about it," Stacey mumbles. "He's so awesome."

"And so hot."

"You can't say that about him."

"Why not?"

"Because you just can't."

"He's hot. There, I just said it. See? I can."

"He would be hotter with a mullet," she says.

"You should tell him that sometime," I tell her. We both start giggling about that, and then the bell rings and lunchtime is over. I go back to class feeling genuinely sorry about Freddie's personal problems and wishing he trusted me as much as he obviously trusts Stacey.

When I get home Monday afternoon, I can't get into my jogging pants fast enough. After changing, I walk back into the living room to find Buster Loo parked at the front door.

"You wanna go for a walk?" I ask him, and he gets excited. "Buster Loo wanna go for a walk?"

I take him down to the park and while we're walking around the wooded part of the trail, I start thinking about Stacey's advice to look in the phone book. In a way, I feel like I'm stalking my own grandmother, and that doesn't feel right at all. The guilt is starting to get heavy, because if I'd just paid attention or asked her a few simple questions, I wouldn't have to pry into her personal life all these years later without any idea of what she might have wanted to keep private and what she would've wanted to share.

After we get home, Buster Loo heads for his water dish. I fix myself a glass of ice water, sit down at the table, and think about what I should do. After a few minutes, I put my glass in the sink, grab the step stool, and climb up to where I can reach the top cabinet. And there are the phone books, right where they've always been. I pick them up and return to the table. I set aside the larger area phone books and open the small one with Bugtussle printed on the front.

I flip to the *E*s and start scanning. Eaton, Eins, Ensley, and there it is. Emerson. Seven Emersons to be exact. Three with a first name beginning with an *M*. There is no mark to indicate which one might be the *M* who was so happy to spend a few days with my grandmother. I flip to the back of the book. No names or numbers are written there. I turn to the front and find nothing. Gramma Jones must've memorized all the numbers she frequently called.

I get up and take a notepad and pen out of the junk drawer. I jot down the addresses of the three Emersons in Bugtussle whose names begin with the letter *M*. I look down and see that Buster Loo has joined me in the kitchen. He's looking up at me, curious.

"What is it, Buster Loo?" I ask him. "Am I doing something wrong?" His response is to cock his head sideways and blink at me as if to say, "I don't know. Are you?" I look down at the notepad. This must've been how they stalked people in the eighties. I go get my phone and call Stacey Dewberry.

25

◇◇◇

Tuesday I don't have to sub for anyone, so I stay in the conference room and help Chloe work on student records. Hanging out with her is back to being a pleasant experience now that she's sporting that engagement ring.

Tuesday afternoon, I go home and hang out with Buster Loo until it's time to leave for the Bugtussle Garden Club's bi-monthly meeting. I decide it's in my best interest to wear my semiprofessional-looking school clothes; I don't want to err on the side of inappropriate, and black pants tend to blend in anywhere. Maybe Stacey is right. Maybe my wardrobe does need a little more spunk.

I park at city hall and walk across the street to 307 Ford Place, a newly renovated historic building in downtown, now used for meetings and professional get-togethers. I feel nervous and edgy as I walk down the hallway, because the Bugtussle Garden Club is notorious for gossips, rivals, and outright bitchy women. I remind myself that most apples in any basket are good, but unfortunately, I'm not one who can easily ignore the stench of the rotten-spirited. When I walk in, I see Birdie and Gloria sitting at a table to my right and try to ignore the stares and whispers as I make my way over to them.

"Hello, sunshine," Gloria Peacock says. "Glad you could join us."

"Yes," Birdie says. "Good times to come. Speaking of which, have you heard from Bo?"

"Bo?"

"My yard man," she whispers. "That sexy beast! Hot to trot, I tell ya! If I were twenty years younger, I'd be all over that."

"Birdie, please!" Gloria says.

I had actually forgotten about Bo, but I don't mention that to Birdie. Nor do I mention that I'm almost as excited about this date as I would be about having my ribs cracked with a steel club at daybreak tomorrow. I can only imagine what a tool this guy must be because, honestly, who takes his shirt off while doing yard work for elderly—and slightly perverted—ladies? Wait, I know. An over-accommodating man, that's who. And we all know what comes with an overaccommodating man. Venereal diseases, that's what. Due to his proclivity to accommodate the needs of his penis at every opportunity. Jeez. Of course, he could be the kind of guy who always works without a shirt—who knows? But still, what kind of person does that? He must have a nice body. I think about that bald asshole Garlen Blake and wonder if my two previous blind dates have made me so negative or if it's just good old-fashioned common sense kicking in.

A nice-looking older lady steps up to the podium and calls the meeting to order. Today's topic is garden parterre and when she starts talking, I find myself intrigued and eager to get started on my yard instead of bored to death like I thought I would be. She starts a slide show, stopping periodically for open discussion of the designs presented. One lady remarks that non-variegated monkey grass would look better with the ensemble on the screen and another woman—who clearly has a yard full of variegated monkey grass—points out that professional landscapers designed the layout in question.

"And, technically, Abby, it's called Silver Dragon lily turf. Not monkey grass," she adds.

"No one calls it Silver Dragon lily turf, Carol," Abby replies as if she's addressing the stupidest person on the planet. "Everyone calls it monkey grass."

"Not necessarily everyone, Abby."

"How about this, Carol? You go to any nursery anywhere in the southeastern United States and ask for Silver Dragon lily turf and see how many people know what you're talking about."

"Some would, I'm sure," Carol replies sardonically. "I guess it would depend on their level of education." Abby gasps as the garden club ladies start buzzing like bees.

"Actually, a parterre shouldn't contain any grass," says a woman across the room.

"This isn't fifteenth-century France, Libby," quips another lady. "We're discussing modern parterre."

"Moving on," the lady in charge says.

"Who is she?" I nod toward the podium.

"Mary Ellen Vickers," Gloria whispers. "She's been the garden club president for many years. A positively unflappable woman."

"She's very pretty," I whisper.

"Plastic surgery," Birdie whispers. "Face-lift, nose job, the works."

"Shush that, Birdie!" Gloria whispers, then looks at me. "She is a very nice person and does an excellent job." Birdie leans back in her chair, and when Gloria turns her attention back to Mary Ellen, Birdie grabs her chest and mouths the words, "Boob job." I cover my mouth to hide my smile.

After Mary Ellen wraps up the slide show, she invites everyone to the reception area for drinks and snacks. I follow Gloria and Birdie, and we join some fifty other women in a room filled with treats worthy of a first-class wedding reception.

"Dang," I tell Birdie. "Y'all do this twice a month?"

"Oh yes," Birdie says. "We pay ridiculous dues. It's the least they could do, furnishing us with fancy cheese and crackers."

I put down the plate I just picked up and gaze longingly at a pile of sauced-up cocktail weenies. "Maybe I don't need to be in here snacking since I'm just visiting."

"Nonsense," Gloria says, picking up the plate. "Here." She lowers her voice. "Guests always snack. We have some ladies who've been guests for years. Many of whom were originally invited by people who aren't even members themselves anymore."

"They just keep showing up. Like dogs. Gnawing on whatever they can get their hands on," Birdie says, looking around.

"Birdie Ross, you are in rare form tonight," Gloria remarks.

"I didn't get my nap today," she says. "Wouldn't do for someone to piss me off."

Gloria looks at me. "No one has to pay, but you can't be considered for any of the Yard of the Month awards if you don't."

"And you don't get your name on the bronze plaque, either," Birdie adds. "Which must be all some of these folks are concerned with, because their yards look like crap." The two ladies in front of Birdie turn around and look at her. "What?" she snaps. "Y'all both know I'm telling the truth." One smiles. One scowls. They both turn back to the snack buffet. I start to fill my plate, very selectively, and wonder how much the dues are.

"Your grandmother's yard was something of a legend," Gloria says, and I wonder how anyone but Gloria ever wins Yard of the Month, what with her sprawling acres of land populated by free-wheeling peacocks. "She was in a class of her own because no one touched her yard except for her." Oh, so that's how. Some awards for the working class and others available for purchase. "She always ended up with the most coveted accolades and she deserved each and every one she received. Her knowledge of blooming flowers was unmatched. Here at the club, she was considered the final and absolute authority on that." Gloria forks a tiny pickle. "Every January, she did a presentation on seasonal bloom schedules, but no one could ever replicate her success with flowers. Not even the highest paid professional landscapers and, trust me, they tried."

"That Essie was a pistol," Birdie says, "one of those rare people that I felt lucky to know on a personal level. She made life more lovely and not just with that blasted blooming garden of hers."

They know, I think. They know all about her. All about her life. Her private life. The one I never thought to ask about.

"I'm so happy you came tonight," Gloria says.

"Yes," Birdie agrees. "And if you somehow unearth the secret of those lush year-round blooms, I fully expect you to share that with me—pronto!"

"I thought she did a presentation on it," I say.

"She did," Birdie says with a smile. "But no matter what Essie

Jones was involved in, she never told anyone the whole story. She was mysterious like that. She wanted people to figure out things on their own. To think for themselves. She wasn't going to do the thinking for anyone, no sir."

"I understand," I say, thinking of the mystery tree in the backyard and the letter from M. Emerson. I guess she knew one day I'd be standing back there, wondering. I'm dying to ask about him, but I just can't bring myself to do it.

"C'mon, let's grab some punch and sit down," Gloria says. "After that, you should go look at the plaques they've just put up out back. When someone gets Yard of the Month, they put a small star next to your name with the month and year inscribed on it. You should see how many stars Essie has."

"I'd like that," I say.

I call Lilly on the way home, but she doesn't answer. I wonder if maybe I could talk her into coming to these garden club meetings with me now that Dax is gone. It would be a good distraction, and that yard of hers could certainly use some TLC. Her house is adorable, one of the cutest in town, but her shrubs look like something from a horror film. Plus I wouldn't be the only one there under the age of fifty.

Wednesday passes without much excitement. I don't see Stacey all day, and Freddie still isn't speaking to me. I try not to take it personally. The weather is warming up nicely, so after I get home, I spend the afternoon outside with Buster Loo. I pluck a few weeds here and there, but I don't really feel like getting down and dirty because I'm just not in the mood. I go into the house, wash my hands, and sit and stare at the clock on the microwave. Buster Loo is snoozing on the sofa, not at all concerned with my anxiety.

Stacey finally calls and tells me that she's finished with her bus route, has her bus parked, etc., etc. Apparently she doesn't own any kind of GPS, because I have to tell her sixteen times how to get to my house. Then she calls back after she misses the turn at the end of my road and winds up at the park. When she finally pulls into my driveway, I'm standing on the front porch with my notepad and the Bugtussle phone book. She asks if I checked all the other phone books for Emersons and handwritten names and/or numbers and I assure her that I have. I walk around to the driver's side of my car.

"Hey, just ride with me!" she says. "I could put on some good background music. I was thinking of a theme on the way over. Like some Bad Company. Maybe some Metallica if things get hairy."

"I don't think things are going to get hairy," I say. I look at her Iroc, gleaming in the afternoon sun. "But that car is so cool."

"All you have to do is tell me where to go," Stacey says. "And a hillbilly with a spotlight can't see through that tint, so we'd be incognito to the max."

"Would you mind?" I ask.

"If I minded, I wouldn't have volunteered, silly. Get in."

Ten minutes later, I ask her to turn down the music so she can hear me when I tell her where to turn. Then she misses the turn anyway and we end up riding around the Bugtussle Country Club. As we get closer to the golf course, I notice a big plume of smoke coming from somewhere behind the tree line.

"Look at that," I tell Stacey.

"Aw, man, I hope that Emerson man's house isn't on fire." She looks at me. "You wanna go check it out?"

"I can't really tell where it's coming from," I say.

"Well, it looks to me like it's coming from that way," she says, pointing to a narrow county road that splits off to the right. "Do you know where that road goes?"

"Of course, I've lived here all my life."

"You wanna go check it out?"

"Sure," I say. "Why not?"

Stacey takes a quick right and drives down the road a tad bit faster than I expected. I tug on my seat belt and start to wonder if this car has air bags. I'm pretty sure it doesn't. We haven't gotten too far when smoke starts to roll across the road like fog. Then I hear the sirens. When Stacey turns the next curve, we come upon a massive wall of fire.

"Holy shit wads!" Stacey yells as she slams on her brakes. "We gotta get outta here! Which way do I need to go?"

I look around, but I can't really see because the smoke has gotten thicker, it's almost dark, and the tint on the windows isn't helping. All I can see is the glorious orange flame burning the brush on the side of the road.

"There's really nowhere to go!" I tell her. "There's nowhere to turn for another couple of miles." She puts the car in reverse. "What are you doing?"

"I'm turning around right here!" she says, and starts backing up.

"Can you see?"

"No, can you?" She begins what turns into a seventeen-point turn and just as she gets the car sideways across the road, a fire truck rounds the bend. We both scream as it slides to a stop inches from Stacey's front bumper. She puts the car in reverse and guns it.

I hear a loud thump as the back of the Iroc rolls into the ditch. When I look up, I see the firemen glaring down at us like we're the stupidest people alive. Which we obviously are. With Stacey's car backed off in the ditch, the fire truck is able to get past and we both breathe a sigh of relief after they get by. I'm sitting there wondering where Ethan Allen is because I'm certain it'll take a four-wheel drive and a tow cable to get out of this ditch, when Stacey grabs the gear shift and jerks it down in low.

"It's time to go," she says. She reaches for the volume button and Metallica screams, "It's sad but true" as Stacey Dewberry mashes the accelerator to the floor. The Iroc fishtails, spins out, and stalls. Stacey puts the car in reverse and then guns the engine again. I look over and see her spinning that steering wheel around like a woman possessed. She throws it back in low gear, stomps the accelerator, and that Iroc jumps out of the ditch and onto the road with the tires squalling. We're barreling down the road in the opposite direction of the fire when we meet another fire truck. The Angel of Ignorance must've been watching over us that very moment, because I don't know how a fire truck and a late-model sports car ran past each other that fast on a road that narrow without crashing.

When Stacey pulls back out on the road by the golf course, I am truly amazed that I haven't shit all over her black leather bucket seats. As soon as she gets on the main road, I hear another siren. This one is behind us. And it's not a fire truck.

Stacey flips off the stereo and then pulls over to the side of the road. She presses the buttons that roll down both windows.

"What are you doing?" I ask. "That smoke—"

"My tint is illegal," she whispers. A moment later, J. J. Jackson appears on the driver's side of the car. When he leans down and looks in the window, I smile despite myself.

"Ace Jones," he says. "Why am I not surprised to see you in this car?"

"Hello, Sheriff Jackson," I say. "I can explain."

"I bet you can," he says. Stacey is speed-digging through the console and throwing junk everywhere.

"Stacey," I whisper, "don't worry about it."

"Why? Are we going straight to jail?" She looks at me and then at the sheriff.

"Do you want to go to jail?" he asks. "I'll take you if you really want to go."

"Oh God," she says. "That's him. That's the guy. Oh my stars!"

"Stacey Dewberry, is it?" the sheriff says.

"Yes, s-sir," she stutters. "Stacey Lynn Dewberry. Do I need to get out of the car, sir? I'm sorry for my dangerous vehicular maneuvering. I was just trying to save me and my friend here from certain death gettin' burned to a crisp. And while I'm at it, I'd like to apologize for blurting out about your wife, I mean, your girlfriend, no! Your fiancée's condition at the party the other night."

"Ms. Dewberry," J.J. says in the kindest tone I've ever heard him use, "I'd like to thank you clearing that up for us." He winks at me and pats Stacey on the shoulder. "We were having what some might call a failure to communicate. Your outlaw friend over there tried to drop some hints, but she didn't do such a good job. I'm actually glad you did that. Saved me a lot of trouble."

"And also, I can't find my registration."

"I don't need to see your registration," he tells her. "I'll take your word it's in there somewhere." He tips his hat and smiles. "Y'all just keep one thing in mind for me."

"What's that, Sheriff?" Stacey asks.

"Where there's smoke there could be fire." He looks at Stacey, then nods toward me. "Now take her home before she gets you into any more trouble."

"Yes, sir," Stacey says.

"Thanks, J.J.," I say. "See you later."

"Ace Jones, it better be a lot later."

Stacey doesn't say much on the drive home and when she pulls into my driveway, I ask if she's okay. Turns out she's worried about her car. I run up to the porch, open the door, and flip on the floodlights. Then I go unroll my water hose. Buster Loo comes outside to inspect the goings-on and immediately takes up with Stacey. She holds him while I hose down her car. I feel bad about what happened and I'm going to feel worse if her fenders are all scratched up. I think I'm just as relieved as she is to see that there's no major damage. Just one scratch that Stacey tells me she can buff right out with a buffer she scored for a buck at a yard sale. She offers to buff my car for me. I politely decline. I invite her in the house, but she says she has to go home and get ready for school tomorrow.

"It takes me a while to pick out my clothes," she says. "See you tomorrow, Ace. Bye-bye, little doggie." Buster Loo starts whining when she gets in her car and doesn't stop until I take him inside and give him a treat.

Thursday, Freddie finally makes eye contact. I smile but decide not to push my luck. I've had days when I just wanted to be left alone—I guess everyone has—so I try not to worry about it. I finish up another hard day on the job, the only relief being lunch with Stacey Dewberry who is still pumped up about yesterday's adventure into what we now know was a burning field. The rest of the day creeps by at a snail's pace and then the buses take ten minutes longer than usual to leave. When it's finally okay to go, I think about sprinting to my car because I'm so ready to get out of there. But I don't; I'm not much of a runner.

As soon as I walk into the house, I hear a faint buzzing sound coming from the bottom of my gigant-o-bag. It takes me nearly five minutes to dig out my phone. My first thought is Lilly, my second is Logan Hatter, and my third is the dreaded unknown number, which, of course, it is.

"'Hi, this is Bo Hammond,'" I read aloud to Buster Loo. "'We still on for tomorrow night?'"

I think about texting back all kinds of mean stuff in hopes of making him leave me alone, but then I remember that I don't even know this guy. Maybe I should just give him a chance. Ha! Yeah, right! I get worried when I realize I seem to be developing a character trait that I truly despise in others: being overly judgmental—or maybe just mental.

"Hello," I text back, resisting the urge to make any cracks about his being Birdie's yard man because he could very well make ten—if not twenty times—what I make as a permanent substitute teacher. "Yes, thank you."

"Pick you up at seven?"

"Sure."

"Thanks."

"Thank you."

I look down at Buster Loo. "How did I get reduced to this?" I ask my little dog. He twists his head to the side and flops one ear over. Buster Loo starts running around in circles, then makes a beeline for the front door. "Why, yes, Buster Loo," I say. "I'd love to go for a walk."

26

◇◇◇

Friday morning, I walk into the lounge during second period to find Freddie Dublin with his feet propped on the table. His shoes are on the floor next to the couch. His socks are navy blue with tiny white flowers.

"Good morning," he says, like he hasn't been ignoring me all week.

"Good morning," I say as I walk over to the drink machine.

"Sorry I've been snobby this week," he begins. "I don't want you to think—" He stops. I decide to let him off easy.

"No worries, Freddie. You don't have to explain anything to me." I reach and get my Diet Mountain Dew from the dispenser. "You know, I should start stocking these in the fridge like you do your Vitaminwater. It would save me a tub of money." He nods his head, looking at his socks. "I thought you had class this period," I say.

"Some kind of sophomore meeting in the gym," he replies. "Thank God."

"Well, I hope you have a good day," I say.

"You, too."

At lunch, Stacey pesters me about barhopping until I finally give in and agree to go.

"But it'll have to be tomorrow night," I say. "I have a blind date tonight."

She heckles me about that for a minute, then rewards me with a tidbit of gossip: Freddie and his friend are considering reconciliation.

"That's good to hear," I tell her. "I hope that all works out because I've really missed talking to him."

"He's got some family problems, too," Stacey says. "His parents are splitting up and it's getting ugly. Everyone's taking sides. They're fighting over the cats. It's crazy."

"That's terrible," I say, and wonder again how Stacey Dewberry, Mouth of the South, scored the role of number one confidant for Freddie Dublin. I'm embarrassed by how jealous that makes me.

"Do you think your friend Ms. Lane might like to go out with us?" Stacey asks. "Of course, we wouldn't have a chance of talking to any men with her around."

"Why not?" I ask. Not because I don't know, but I want to see how Stacey phrases her response.

"Because she looks like freakin' Bo Derek in that movie *10!* That's why not!"

I smile as I imagine Lilly's blond hair braided in cornrows. "Much like our pal, Freddie," I say, "she's taking some time right now. Which is perfectly normal; I mean, who can blame her? I'll let her go on like this for another week, but then you may have to go with me to her house and manhandle her out the door."

"Are you serious, Ace?"

"About which part?" I ask, laughing.

"The manhandling part," she says, and she's completely serious.

"Oh no, of course not. But we might go see her if she doesn't come around soon. If you want to."

"I'd like that."

Friday night, I'm sitting on the couch in yet another one of my uncomfortable dresses—one of those scratchy numbers made up of ninety-nine percent slimming fabric and one percent dress—when I notice my date is fifteen minutes late. I stare at the clock, trying not to get my hopes up. At thirty minutes after, I go in the bedroom to change into some normal clothes. At eight p.m., my phone buzzes and it's my not-a-date-after-all. He's so sorry, but he had to work late, and his phone battery died and blah blah blah.

"Thank you, Jesus!" I exclaim, quickly texting him back to assure him that's fine by me. He doesn't mention rescheduling and I certainly don't bring it up. "Dodged the bullet tonight!" I tell Buster Loo, who is in the middle of the living room floor doing the worm squirm. "And the shirtless yard man is probably just as relieved as I am." At ten p.m., my phone beeps and it's Logan Hatter. I promptly invite him over. Then I call Pier Six Pizza.

When I wake up Saturday morning, Logan is halfway through making breakfast. He's also made a fantastic mess, which he promises to clean up after we eat. He pours me a cup of superstout coffee and then instructs me to sit down and relax.

"I'm so happy you're back at school, Ace," he says, and I think again about how much I love him. Like I love my UPS guy and my friend Cynthia who cuts my hair. "I missed you while you were gone, and that Cameron Becker may be the smokin' hotness, but I'm getting sick of her. She needs to go."

"She can't help it, Logan," I say. "It's her first year teaching, remember?"

He picks up the coffeepot and sniffs it. "I'm sorry—did I pour you a cup of crazy just now?" He puts the pot back down. "I thought you wanted your job back. I want you to want your job back. She gets on my nerves. She gets on everyone's nerves. She screams at those poor kids all day every day." I watch him place frozen biscuits on a cookie sheet. "How many of these do you want?" he asks.

"Two, please," I say.

"Two for you, six for me." He looks up. "Just kidding." He looks at Buster Loo, who is sitting next to his foot like a Coke bottle. "How many for you, little buddy?" Buster Loo waves his paws up and down in response. "Six for you, too? Great."

"He wishes," I say, and Logan chuckles.

"Yeah, so she screams all day every day and everyone in the hallway is tired of her. Even Mrs. Spencer said something about it, and she hasn't uttered a bad word about anyone since she started teaching there back in the 1800s." I giggle and he continues. "I don't know how she does it, seriously. How does her voice not give out on a daily basis?"

"Logan, that job is kicking her ass," I say. "I feel sorry for her."

"Yeah, you feel sorry for her because you're palling around with her BFF, Freddie Dublin." He puts the biscuits into the oven and turns around. "That guy's hair looks so good. Every day. How does he do that? Is it some kind of gel? If it is, then you need to find out what kind and go buy me some."

"I'll start an investigation immediately."

"Thanks," he says. "There's just something about him."

"There's nothing about him. He's a very nice person."

"Someone's fallen under his spell."

"He's not like that, Logan. I'm telling you. He's not."

"If he's sweet-talked you out of trying to run Cameron Becker off and get your job back, then he is like that, Ace."

"He's very charming and charismatic. Don't hate him because of his pizazz."

"Oh-kay," he says. "Well, if Little Miss Becker fails her last evaluation, that'll be two in a row, and she'll be outta there anyway. Then you'll have to come back."

"Yeah, she really blew that last one."

"She can blow me," he says. "I can't stand that crazy bitch."

I don't know if I've really fallen under Freddie's spell or if I'm just getting soft in my old age, but I feel sorry for Cameron Becker. "Don't call her that," I say. "I think she's trying as hard as she can."

Logan shakes his head. "Well, she needs to try a little harder."

We have a pleasant breakfast after which he cleans up the kitchen as promised. I sit down on the couch and he takes a seat in the recliner and we watch television until well after lunchtime, which is not the normal protocol for a booty-call.

"So, what are you doing tonight?" he asks, and the question actually makes me nervous.

"Well, Stacey has been hounding me for weeks about going out with her," I say, watching his expression carefully. "So I finally agreed to go honky-tonkin' with her."

"Honky-tonkin' with Stacey Dewberry?" He laughs. "Yee haw, girl!"

"Right," I say. "You wanna come?"

"Well, I don't know what I'm doing yet," he says, and his elusiveness bugs me more than it should. "Might see y'all out."

"Maybe," I say. "If you're lucky."

"If I'm lucky, I'll get to come back here tonight." Okay, now I really don't know what's going on. I immediately start to worry that I'm his backup booty—the one he calls if he doesn't find anyone else. I'm too old for this silly shit! Don't ask, don't tell—that is our relationship.

"You're a pretty lucky guy," I say.

"Am I?" He gets up and starts walking down the hallway. Without looking back he says, "I'm just gonna go back here and see how lucky I really am."

Buster Loo makes a run for the doggie door, and I get up and follow Logan Hatter back to my bedroom.

27

~~~~~~

Saturday afternoon, I call Lilly and she actually answers her phone.

"Hey, sister," I say, trying not to get too excited. "How are you?"

"I'm fine," she says. We talk about this and that, but when I bring up Chloe's wedding shower, she gets in a hurry to get off the phone. I wonder for a minute if she might have wanted an engagement ring from Dax before he left. I hadn't thought of that before now. I change the subject so we can stay on the phone a bit longer.

"Okay, wait a minute before you hang up," I say. "I'm going bar-hopping tonight with Stacey and, remember, you said you wanted to go if I went . . . ." I pause, hoping.

"Not tonight, Ace," she says. "I'm not in the mood."

"What are you going to do?" I ask.

"I'm going to sit here on the couch and watch *Love Actually* again."

"I'll come over and watch it with you. I love that movie."

"You don't have to do that," she says. "Besides, Saturday night is the only time Dax has a chance to call, which makes no sense because, I mean, they're in freakin' Nevada. Why can't he just use his cell phone whenever he wants?"

"I have no idea," I say because I don't. "How's he doing?"

"Well, when he called last week, he was sick as a dog and could hardly talk. Then he fell asleep while we were on the phone," she says. I can tell she's about to start crying.

"Are you sure you don't want me to come over? I'd really like to hang out. I'll bring Buster Loo."

"It's okay, Ace," she says. "I wouldn't be good company. I'll call you tomorrow."

"Okay," I say. "I hope you get your phone call."

"Me, too."

I hang up the phone and look down at Buster Loo. "Little fellow, if Auntie Lilly doesn't get to feeling better soon, you may have to go friend-sit for a little-bitty while." He whimpers and looks at me as if he truly understands what I'm saying.

An hour later, I'm standing in my closet, flipping hangers back and forth and getting pissed off because I can't find anything to wear. I still have Stacey's pink shirt and zebra pants, but I think that'd be a little much for a night of mere barhopping. Outfits like that should be reserved only for hard partying.

"I have got to have something in here that I can wear," I say to Buster Loo, who is doing a fine job of looking concerned about my problem. I push all the school clothes to the side and notice a few boxes I must've forgotten to unpack. "Really?" I say. "More boxes? I can't believe I'm still finding crap I haven't put away yet." I open the box and find a bunch of new clothes that I bought on a shopping trip last year with Jalena. "Dang!" I say, suddenly happy to have found the wayward box. "I forgot all about these!"

I empty the contents onto the bed and dig through the pile until I find a denim skirt and a red-checkered top, which I promptly try on. "Shit," I say to my reflection. "I'm not auditioning for *Hee Haw for Fatties*." I take off the shirt. I go through the pile again, this time hanging, folding, and sorting, and eventually I come up with a nice white top. "Perfect!" I say, then start digging through my closet for some shoes because Stacey told me not to wear my moccasins. She claimed it was because someone wearing boots might step on my toe and possibly break it. I think she just doesn't like my moccasins. I call her to see if she has a pair of boots that I can borrow—in case I want to do some toe-stepping of my own.

"Flat-heeled," I say. "Or very low-heeled."

She says she has just the thing and when she shows up at my door thirty minutes later, she hands me a pair of brown cowboy boots with turquoise inlay. She's wearing a very short miniskirt and a hot pink and black checked top that falls off her shoulder, revealing the strap of a glistening pink tank. Her hair looks like it does every day. Only maybe with a little more hair spray.

"Eight and a half," she says, handing me the boots. "You can have 'em if they fit, 'cause they're too small for me."

"These are beautiful!" I look at the bottom of the boot and see the name, Johnny Ringo. "They look really expensive."

"Got 'em at a yard sale in Birmingham for three bucks," she explains. "I love to hit up those community garage sales in the nice parts of town."

"Me, too!" I tell her. "Let's go to some sometime." Neither Lilly nor Chloe would be caught dead at a yard sale.

"Ain't nothin' to it but to do it!"

"I guess not," I say, slipping on a very thin pair of socks. Buster Loo scurries over and starts sniffing Stacey's go-go boots. She picks him up and baby talks him for few minutes, which he loves. Then he jumps down and scowls at me as if to say, "Why don't you treat me like this?" I tell Stacey that Freddie has finally broken his silence and, of course, she already knows this.

"Well, I'm ready if you are. Let's rock and roll, sister," I say.

"Let's go."

We drive to Tupelo and hit up three different bars before she finds one with an "atmosphere" that she digs. I order my fourth beer of the night and she orders her fifth fuzzy navel. We order appetizers and when we finish those, Stacey is ready to socialize. She hits the dance floor, but I claim that I need to stay put so we don't lose our seats at the bar. After she dances a few jigs, she wants to go check out the men in the pool room. I reluctantly leave my bar stool and follow her into the smoke-filled area where I see eight pool tables. Each table has two players. Some tables have fans standing around watching; some don't. I blink against the haze and wonder how I ever smoked, because I can't stand the smell of cigarettes.

She stops to watch a pair of guys start a new game and I stand beside her, wishing I were at home on the sofa. Of the two pool players, the one without the mullet notices us first. He gives Stacey the old once-over and then nods at his friend. The friend looks up at Stacey and smiles. How does she find so many men with mullets?

"Well, hello, Miss Pretty Thang," the mullet man says. I wonder if he's joking, or maybe making fun of her, but then he sidles up beside her and I see that he's genuinely interested. He flirts up a storm while the short-haired friend looks up from time to time to check me out. I smile. He smiles. I'm not interested. I don't think he is, either.

When they finish their game, Mullet Man asks Stacey to dance and she quickly accepts. I sit down on the bench next to the pool table, and Mullet's pal sits next to me.

"Cal," he says, holding out a hand.

"Ace," I say, shaking his hand.

"Two peas in a pod." He nods toward Stacey and Mullet Man on the dance floor.

"I guess," I say. I look at him. He looks at me.

"You need a drink?" he asks.

"No, thank you."

"Yeah, me neither," he says. "You play pool?"

"Not even a little bit."

"Hmm."

We sit and watch as Stacey and Mullet Man dance through three more songs.

"How 'bout some water?" Cal asks. "Or a Coke?"

"I'd actually love a Coke." He gets up and returns what seems like six hours later with two very small glasses of Coke. Two people have just started a pool game on their table.

"Shit," he mumbles. "Lost our table. Guess we won't be playing any more for a while." He looks over at the lounge area. "Wanna go have a seat? Booths are slightly more comfortable."

"That would be great." I like Cal. He's nice. Not pushy at all. I follow him over and sit across from him in a circular booth where we talk about everything from dogs to water skis to funny old movies. Several songs later, Stacey and Mullet Man join us. I scoot around and sit next to Cal.

"Ace, this is Skeeter. Skeeter, Ace," Stacey says. Despite the mullet, Skeeter is almost kind of handsome. Almost, but not quite.

"What are y'all drinkin'?" Skeeter asks. "Let's get another round."

"Coke," Cal says.

"Sissies," Skeeter says with a harmless smile. He looks around for a waitress. "Stacey, you wanna beer?"

"I'd like a fuzzy navel and a shot of Jack Daniel's," she says, smiling at Skeeter.

"I like a lady who likes her whiskey," he says. Skeeter finally flags down a waitress and places his order. "Sure y'all don't want a real drink?" he asks. Cal and I are sure. Skeeter and Cal start talking about someone who just walked in and Stacey elbows me, nodding toward Cal with her eyebrows raised.

"No," I whisper. "Very nice, but no."

Stacey looks disappointed

"Aw, hell, here they come," Cal says.

"And look who they've got with 'em," Skeeter says. "Hellfire." And "fire" comes out "far." This guy could be Stacey's soul mate.

I look up and see two couples coming our way. The person in front raises a hand and yells, "Well, lookie who's here! Ol' Skeet-dog and Cal-e-forn-ya! Y'all scoot over and let us sit down."

I find out two things relatively quickly. Number one, they all work together—the two guys work in a plant with Cal and Skeeter and the girls work in the office. And number two, our four new friends are all sloppy, stinking drunk. I try not to stare at the girls, but I can't help it. One is wearing a skintight gold dress. The other a silky gray tank top and short shorts. Has it warmed up that much outside?

"I'm Angel," the gold-clad girl says after she catches me looking at her. She points to the tits of the girl next to her. "This is Leta." I glance at Stacey and she scoots over right next to me. I scoot over right next to Cal, and four more people stuff themselves into our six-person booth.

"I'm Ace," I say when we're all crammed in there nice and tight. "This is Stacey. Nice to meet y'all," I say. I offer a pleasant smile even though my skank-alert is going off double time.

"So, what do y'all do?" Angel asks.

"We're permanent substitute teachers at Bugtussle High School," Stacey says with an embarrassing amount of pride and authority.

"Y'all are substitute teachers?" Leta sneers.

"Yes," Stacey says, looking down at the table, her conviction gone.

"Oh wow!" Leta says. "I haven't talked to a sub since I was in high school."

"Like you talked to them then," Angel says with a snort. They turn their attention to a girl walking by who's way prettier and somewhat thinner than either of them. They start dogging the girl out and, over the next five minutes, proceed to peel off insults and put-downs about every other female in sight. Stacey glances at me.

"Fuck those dummies," I whisper, and she giggles. "C'mon." I tap Cal on the shoulder. "Would you let us out, please?"

"Sure, sure." He gets up.

As we walk away, I hear Leta say, "Is that your new girlfriend, Cal?" and they start that damned sniggering again. I ignore it and, once again, wish I were at home on the couch. When we're in the restroom, I tell Stacey that I'm ready to go.

"Is it because of those girls?" she asks.

"Yeah," I say. "And all that smoke is killing my eyes."

"Aw, man, I was having so much fun hanging out with Skeeter until that bunch showed up."

"Well, give him your phone number and let's get out of here."

"Do you think they're out there making fun of us like they've been making fun of everyone else in this place?"

"Oh, I'm sure they are, but who cares? They're trash."

"I don't think they think they're trash."

"People who are trash are never aware of it."

"They seem to think they're big shots because they work in an office. Was it just me, or were you getting that vibe, too?"

"Yeah, they're some pretty tacky bitches."

She sighs. "Skeeter probably won't even ask for my number since they showed up." And sure enough, when we get back out there, he doesn't. He's so wrapped up in flirting with Angel and Leta that he doesn't even say good-bye to Stacey.

28

<<<<<<<<<<<<<<<<<<<<<<<<<<<<<<<<<<<<<<<<<<<<<<<<<<<<<<<<<<<<<<<<

"It was nice to meet y'all," Cal says, looking at Skeeter like he's ashamed of him.

"Nice to meet y'all, too," I say.

"Have fun subbing next week," Leta says, and Angel starts sniggering.

"Yeah, we will," I say. "And y'all have fun sucking dick next week." Everyone stops what they're doing and stares at me. "What is it?" I say. "Is that not how you furniture factory secretaries get up the corporate ladder?" I look at Leta and smile. "By getting down on your knees." I glance at Stacey and she stares back with a wide-eyed look of panic. I look at Angel and then at Leta. "I'm sorry. That's just what I've always heard. Was I misinformed?"

"Uh, excuse me," Leta says to the guy next to her. "I need to get up."

"Uh, Ace, we probably need to go on and get—"

"It's fine, Stacey," I tell her as I watch Leta wiggle out of the booth. "Let's just see what she has to say."

"Listen, bitch," Leta says, stepping up into my face. "You ain't got no right dissing me and Angel like that and you won't do it again. I can't help it that you and your friend here are just stupid substitute teachers. Maybe someday you can get yourself a job as a real teacher."

"Uh, but she is a real teacher," Stacey says. Leta ignores her.

"Who are you calling bitch, bitch?" I say, and take a step closer to her. "For your information, I was a 'real' teacher for almost six years, but I quit that job and moved to Florida for a while where I ran my own art gallery. You probably don't even know what that is since you appear to be about as cultured as a cockroach. I have a little something called a bachelor's degree, also known as an education, which I'm fairly sure you're short on, too, since you have almost as much self-esteem as a common prostitute and the grammar skills of a third-year sixth grader." Leta just stares at me, her cranberry-colored lips spread wide. "C'mon back."

"You better watch your mouth when you talk to me."

"I'm sorry," I say. "Did I use too many three-syllable words? I apologize." I glance down to see Cal and the other guys sniggering while Angel glares at me.

"Go to hell!" Leta says finally.

"Oh wow. That's the most original comeback ever. Aren't you a clever one? I bet you don't have to suck dick to keep your job after all." I look at Stacey. "Let's go."

"You don't talk to me like that!" Leta yells. She picks up the drink closest to her and draws back like she's going to toss it on me. I reach over and slap it out of her hand.

"Aw, hell no!" Angel says, and starts squirming out of the booth.

"Ace, uh, can we please go now? I think things are about to get out of hand."

Angel is coming toward me, pointing and cussing. I put my hand on her face and push her back down into the booth.

"Sit," I tell her.

"Don't you treat her like no dog!" Leta screams. Then she hurls her giant purse, which appears to be a fake Gucci, at my head. I step aside and watch the purse slam into a woman on the edge of the dance floor who is none too happy to be hit in the back by a flying bag. I step over and kick the purse back to Leta, who quickly picks it up and draws back again.

"Hit me with that purse again and I'll knock your damned teeth out," the lady shouts at Leta. Angel gets up and takes a swing at me and I push her down by her face again. This time, she misses the booth and slides down on the floor, her wide-spread legs revealing an electric blue thong.

"Who throws a purse?" I ask the lady on the dance floor. She rolls her eyes and turns away. I look around for Stacey Dewberry and see her making a beeline for the door. Angel is cussing and rolling around on the floor. The four men are just sitting in the booth, watching the melee with genuine interest. Well, except for Skeeter, who is leaned over getting an eyeful of Angel's cooter. I look at Leta just in time to see that she's picked up another drink, only this one is full. She draws it back to throw it but instead pours beer down the front of her skimpy tank top. She screams and I start laughing like a hyena and then she throws the glass at me. Her high level of intoxication makes her moves slow and predictable, so instead of trying to deflect the heavy beer mug, I step aside and it collides with the noggin of the lady who was just hit by the purse.

The woman turns around with hell's fury in her eyes, and I point to Leta and say, "You know who did that. She's been talking about your boots all night." The woman makes a charge at Leta, and they tumble into the pool area where they cause one player to sling his beer onto another guy who jumps up and punches him in the face. In a matter of seconds, there's an all-out brawl going on. I watch with great amusement until Stacey Dewberry shows up beside me and says, "If we go to jail, then we're getting fired and you might not care, but I do, so would you please stop rubberneckin' and come on!"

"I don't think rubbernecking is the correct term for what I'm doing."

"Well, I'm outta here!"

I follow her around the thickening crowd and out the door. We get in my car and pull out just as the cops start wheeling into the parking lot.

"Just in time," I say, then glance over at Stacey. "Dang! That was something. Is that what you do every weekend?"

"Uh, no."

"Are you mad? Don't be mad. I'm sorry. I shouldn't have acted like that."

"Dang it, Ace!" she says. "Something like that could get us both fired. We got out of there just in time. I don't like stuff like that. I don't like fighting and all that mess."

"They started it," I say like a child. "I'm not going to stand around and be insulted by human garbage like those two skanks." I shake my head. "Not happening. Sorry. I don't tolerate bitches and bullies. I never will."

We ride in silence for a few miles.

"I didn't know you were such a firecracker," Stacey says, finally loosening up. "When you popped off that dick-sucking comment, I was so shocked that I couldn't do anything but just stand there for a minute." She giggles. "Man, and did you see the look on their faces? I mean, of all the things they thought you might say, I could tell that was not on the list." She shakes her head. "I'm sorry I bailed like I did. I should've stayed beside you."

"No, you were right to want to leave. I mean, it would've been a great time for me to take the high road and walk away, but unfortunately I'm not a frequent traveler on the high road."

"I had no idea you had that kind of spunk in you! Man! Don't mess with Ace Jones!"

"I haven't been myself lately," I tell her. "Except for the occasional bout of road rage."

"Well, welcome back, Rocky Balboa!" she says, and I start laughing. "Hey, you said back there that you had an art gallery in Florida. That sounds pretty cool. What happened to it? I mean, why did you leave?"

"I don't want to talk about it," I say.

"Why not?"

"Because I just don't."

"I'm guessing whatever reason that is might be why you haven't been yourself lately?"

"Yeah," I say. "That's part of it. I'll tell you all about it sometime, I promise. Just not now."

"Okay, well, just so you know, I like what I saw tonight," she says. "I wish I could talk to people like that."

"No, you don't," I tell her. "Because now I'm not one bit better than those idiotic morons because I stooped down to their level."

"You're all right, Ace Jones. I think you just need to ease up on yourself because you are all right."

29

◇◇

Sunday morning, I get up bright and early and take Buster Loo for a walk in the park. When I get home, I see that I've missed a call from Lilly, which is doubly odd seeing as how she's a habitual texter known for sleeping until noon on the weekend.

"You started a barroom brawl? Are you serious?" Lilly asks when I call her back. The sound of her laughing makes me happy. "What was Stacey doing?"

"Running for the door," I tell her. "She thought it was funny later, but while it was all going on, she was trying to get the hell outta there."

"I hate I missed all that," Lilly says.

"Well, it was pretty funny, but I kind of wished I'd missed it, too."

"So are you going out with her again anytime soon?"

"She probably won't ask me after that fiasco!" I say. "And to think I was worried about her doing something crazy."

"It's hard to out-crazy you, Ace Jones."

"Thank you."

Lilly tells me that she talked to Dax and he'll be flying out of Fort Bragg, North Carolina, in four weeks.

"He's not even coming home before he leaves for a freakin' year-long deployment to a war zone?" I ask.

"My thoughts exactly," Lilly tells me. "He said that's why the army gave him a two-week notice before training. So he could say all of his good-byes."

"That is bullshit!"

"Yeah, as it turns out, there's a lot of bullshit involved with this deal."

"So if you want to see him before he leaves, you have to go all the way to Fort Bragg, North Carolina?"

"Yes," she says. "And I wanted to talk to you about that."

"Yes," I say before she even has a chance to ask. "I'll go with you."

"I'll buy your plane ticket."

"Girl, I just got my monthly substitute teacher stipend—I'm loaded!" I say, laughing.

"Please let me buy your ticket, Ace."

"Absolutely not."

"Well, I'm paying for the hotel and all of our meals."

"You can pay for the hotel."

"Fine then, I will. So do you want to come over and let's get our tickets?"

"I'm on my way," I tell her. "I'll bring lunch." I swing by China

Kitchen and pick up our favorite dishes, which we eat at the dainty white table in her canary yellow kitchen. After lunch, I get on her brand-new computer and search travel sites until I find the lowest airfare from Memphis, Tennessee, to Fayetteville, North Carolina.

"I'm happy we're flying with this particular airline, because they don't charge extra for bags and I know you'll be taking your entire wardrobe."

"And my shoes," she says, and she isn't joking. "I tried looking for tickets before you got here, but one of those airlines upped the fare twenty-seven dollars after I picked my seat and that was before they added all of their taxes and mystery fees!" Lilly says. "It was pissing me off."

"That's why those idiots are filing for bankruptcy," I tell her. "Because they're thieves. Thieves never prosper. Well, not for extended periods of time, anyway." Lilly uses her debit card to purchase the tickets and I write her a check for my part.

"If this check doesn't clear my bank within ten business days, then I'm not going."

"Okay, you stubborn ass," she says. "Thanks for doing this. I really appreciate it."

"It's the least I can do, Lilly, and don't worry, I'll stay clear of the room so y'all can get freaky-deaky as much as you want before he leaves." I poke her in the arm. "Just stay off my bed, okay?"

"Right," she says.

"Fort Bragg, here we come!"

Sunday afternoon, I get a text from Hatter asking if I had a good time last night. I pick up the phone, give him a call, and proceed

to tell him all about my barroom adventures with Stacey Dewberry.

"See," I say when I'm finished recapping our misadventure.
"That's why I just stay at home. I don't know how to act, plus I hate
coming home mad and embarrassed and smelling like beer and
cigarette smoke. I'd rather be on my couch watching *Saturday
Night Live*."

"With me, of course," he says.

"Of course." I ask him what he did last night and the vagueness
of his response makes me think he was with another woman. I
know better than to badger him about it because he's one of those
guys who'd nail his own balls to a burning tree before he told on
himself. *It doesn't matter,* I think. *Keep it casual and don't be an idiot.* We're just friends . . . aren't we? My pep talk does me no good.
What the hell is wrong with me? I'm not in love with Logan Hatter.
I don't want to marry Logan Hatter. I don't even want to date him.
So why am I consumed with jealousy and misgivings about what
he did last night? Don't be an idiot! I know that a woman's instincts
are rarely wrong, unless, of course, she's a psycho. Of all the things
I am, I like to think a psycho is one thing I'm not. Or am I? Let
it go!

"Ace?" I hear him say. "Hello? Are you there?"

"Yes, Logan, I'm sorry. I just, uh—hey, my line is beeping so I'll
talk to you tomorrow, okay?"

"Yeah, sure, sweetie. No problem."

No problem, indeed!

Monday, Freddie Dublin is back to his usual self and I'm almost
too eager to bask in his attention. Stacey has told him her version of
what happened on Saturday night, and he's eager to hear the juicy

details. I want to ask him how things are with his romantic situation, but that would give Stacey away, so I just keep my mouth shut, hoping he might bring it up. He doesn't.

The next few days pass by rather quickly and I have an easy day Friday, lounging in the library until lunch, when Chloe summons me to her office.

"Ace, I have a huge favor to ask you."

"Sure, anything. What do you need?"

"As you know, we have Tate here with us now."

"Right. With his fox."

"Yes, of course. Tate and his stuffed fox." She shakes her head and rolls her eyes. "And while the fox appears to be quite content lounging in the corner of the living room, well, Tate just wants to hang around J.J. wherever he is."

"Uh-oh."

"Yeah, so it's a problem that's progressively getting worse. Tate used to call J.J. when he was at my house, but now he just comes on over and sits with us awhile. Sometimes without calling first. And he's so loud and obnoxious. Even you would think so."

"Thank you for that."

"Ace, he's tearing up my nerves so bad I can hardly stand it. I think my hormones are out of control. I want to talk to J.J. but just can't bring myself to say anything about it because what could I say that wouldn't hurt his feelings?"

"J.J. is a practical man with a lot of common sense. I think he could handle the conversation, and I think he'd take care of it pronto. I mean, he may think you enjoy Tate's company."

"Surely he doesn't think that."

"Sometimes you don't realize how nice you are, Chloe. You hide it so well when you're mad. Well, usually."

"Very funny, Ace," she says with a frown. "So are you busy tonight?"

"As a matter of fact, I'm not," I say. Oh please let her set me up on a blind date with Tate Jackson.

"Would you like to go to Memphis and eat with the three of us tonight?" She crinkles her brow and flashes her sweetest puppy dog eyes. "Please, as a personal favor to me?"

Shit! Why can't it be just the two of us? Slow down, crazy train! Chloe mistakes my hesitation for unwillingness.

"You'll have a miserable time and I'm so sorry to ask you. I just need some company." She's still giving me the ol' puppy dog stare. "I'm begging you. I'll be eternally grateful."

"Sure, I'll go."

"Really?" she says. "Thank you. And don't worry, I won't say a word to Logan Hatter. I promise."

"Not that he would care," I say.

"Right, but still."

"So will your brother-in-law-to-be expect sexual favors from his date? Because I'm not going unless he's expecting sexual favors."

"When's the last time you saw him?"

"I don't know. It's been a while. But I remember that he was a senior when I was in the eighth grade and he was the holy grail of hotness back then."

"You realize that's been like twenty years ago?" I shrug and she shakes her head. "He's really not all that attractive now and he wears camouflage all the time when he's not at work."

"I like camouflage," I lie. "What does he do again?"

"He sells something. I don't know what. I don't care. I work very hard not to hear what he's saying. I swear, I look at him sometimes and wonder how in the world he came from the same gene pool as J.J. Then I start worrying that our child will come out acting like Uncle Tater."

"Uncle what was that again?"

"Tater," she says, and throws some backwoods twang on it that cracks me up. "Uncle Tater, gimme summa 'em biscuits-n-gravy!"

"What are you talking about?" I'm really enjoying this conversation.

"I'm talking about Uncle Tater," she says. "That's what everyone in the family under the age of fifteen calls him."

"That just makes me like him more."

"I'm going to assume you're joking about that as well." She starts fiddling with some file folders. "Ace, I owe you big-time for this. Thank you."

"I'm actually looking forward to it," I say. Chloe stares at me and doesn't say a word. "Okay, see you tonight." I walk back to my assigned classroom while thinking about Kevin Jacobs, the big sexy country boy I met in Pelican Cove who gave me the heebie-jeebies every time he came around. Who knows? A good ol' shotgun-totin' boot-wearin' fox-huntin' redneck might be just what I need.

When the bell rings at the end of the day, I go straight to the lounge and purchase myself a lukewarm Diet Mountain Dew. I'm joined by Freddie Dublin who, after the other teachers leave the lounge, wants to talk makeovers.

"I'm going to invite Stacey over tomorrow and not tell her it's a makeover," Freddie says.

"I thought we did my makeover before the concert as an excuse to give her one later." I look at him. "Was that not the plan?"

"Oh, but of course it was, sweetheart," he says with a sly smile. "But I'd like to surprise her just the same. Can you be at my house in the morning at ten a.m.?" I tell him that I can be. Unless I have a late night with Uncle Tater. Ha! Yeah, right. "Okay, great so don't blow my cover, okay?"

"Okay, but I don't see her ever quitting the hot rollers, so I don't think we should expect any long-term results."

"Honey, I never do," he says, looking down at my moccasins. "But I can't let that stop me from trying."

As he sashays out of the lounge, I think for a minute that Freddie Dublin might be an asshole. I look out the window at the buses, wishing they'd get on out of here so I could, too. Then I start fantasizing about the date I sort of have with Tate Jackson tonight. Lilly is going to die when I tell her, because back when we were in the eighth grade, we would get hall passes from our seventh-period classes and sneak off to the gym to watch the high school boys practice. Tate Jackson was one of our many favorite players. We were stalkers even back then.

30

<><><><><><><><><><><><><><><><><><><><><><><><><><><><><><><><><><><><><><><><><>

Friday night, Chloe's white Lexus SUV pulls into the drive at precisely six fifty-five.

"Right on time, Chloe." I check my hair in the living room mirror and hope the slimming fabric in my dress doesn't take a hike up my thighs at any point during the night. Unless of course I find myself alone with Uncle Tater.

I see that J.J. is driving and wonder who will be coming to fetch me. Obviously they're wondering the same thing, because no one gets out of the vehicle. I'm about to save us all some embarrassment and walk out on my own when the rear door flies open and a big fellow with tousled hair gets out of the back.

"How in the hell did they fit him in there?" I ask Buster Loo, who has jumped onto the back of the love seat to have a look. "Little Man, they're going to look like they're hauling moonshine with both of us in the backseat."

Tate looks a little bit like J.J., but no one would ever mistake them for twins. I grab my purse and put on a fresh coat of lip gloss. A second later, the doorbell rings.

I take a deep breath and walk to the door with Buster Loo following close behind. I open the door and check out my date. His checkered button-up polo shirt is rolled up to his elbows and not tucked into his baggy khaki pants. It's the male equivalent of slimming fabric yet so much more comfortable.

"Hello, Tate Jackson," I say, and, just like that, I'm madly in love.

"Hello, Ms. Jones," he says. "You look lovely." I'm about to thank him and return the compliment when Buster Loo makes a break for it. He bounds down the steps and starts running speedy-dog crazy eights at full throttle in the front yard. I step out onto the porch.

"Buster Loo," I shout. "What are you doing? Get back in here." Buster Loo ignores me and keeps on going. I look at Tate. "I'm so sorry."

"No problem," he says, looking out at Buster Loo. "That little dog can move and shake."

I'll show you some moving and shaking, I think. While he's standing there grinning and watching Buster Loo, I notice the crinkly wrinkles around his eyes. He catches me checking him out and winks at me. I look back at my dog and try to ignore the fluttering of my heart. I am in the deepest of deep shit. Chloe is not going to like this!

"Buster Loo!" I say. "Please come here!" Buster Loo runs up to a shrub and, still standing on the sidewalk, tinkles all over one of the blooms. "Buster Loo! Are we serious right now? Get in the house. C'mon!" Buster Loo finally prances up the steps, stopping to sniff Tate's boot. "Don't even think about it, little dog!" I tell him, holding open the screen door. Buster Loo runs inside, gets in his Coke-bottle stance, and starts begging. I look at Tate and say, "He thinks he deserves a treat."

"Well, it was a pretty impressive show," he says, still smiling. Yay! He's not a dog hater! I have to force myself to stop gazing into his navy blue eyes. It's clear to me that Tate Jackson still has what it takes. Twenty years hasn't tarnished his charisma at all, and I'm almost sure he could charm my big-girl black lace panties right down to my skinny-girl ankles.

He opens the car door for me and smiles as he slides in on the other side. I hope and pray that this will not be the only time I get to go out with him. I also hope and pray that the rear bumper of this car doesn't drag the ground when J.J. backs out of my driveway. I'm relieved when it doesn't. I look at him and he looks at me and I start fantasizing about having buck wild sex with Tate Jackson. Crazy Train Alert! Get off it!

Tate jabbers all the way to Memphis. J.J. manages to get a comment in every now and then, but Chloe doesn't say a word. I sit in the backseat and smile because even though I couldn't care less about duck decoys and turkey calls, I don't see how I could be any happier than I am right this very second. Careful, nutso! Slow down! When we get to Memphis, Tate is the perfect gentleman, opening doors and putting his hand on the small of my back. My heart is thumping and I can't remember the last time I had butterflies like this. I start thinking about how happy Chloe would be if he started hanging around with me instead of them all the time. Don't be a nutcase! When we get to the restaurant, there are only two seats available in the waiting area. Chloe motions for me to sit next to her.

"He just asked me to go to the bar," I whisper, and her eyes bug out when I tell her that yes, I do want to go to the bar with him.

He keeps his hand on my hip as we make our way to the bar and I'd be lying if I said I didn't love it.

"So you're a teacher?" Tate says after we get situated.

"Worse," I tell him. "I'm subbing right now."

"No shame in that game," he says. "Chloe tells me you just moved back from Pelican Cove." The bartender delivers our drinks. I take a sip of draft beer and decide to go with a short answer.

"Yes," I say. "I did."

"Beautiful place," he says.

"It is that," I tell him. "But I'm very happy to be home."

"I know what you mean. I've tried living in some of my favorite vacation spots and it didn't work for me, either. Lived in Hilton Head for a while. Moved out to Durango, Colorado, for a few years. But I always came back home. Or as close as I could get."

"Yeah," I say.

"It's just not the same. I mean, you take vacations to get away from your daily routine, but when you live in your vacation spot and it becomes your daily routine, then you get to a point where you want a break from it. Then you realize you have nowhere better to go than where you are and that sucks." He takes a sip of beer. "At least that's how it was for me."

"My experience was actually very similar to that," I tell him.

"I spent the past five years living in Birmingham. You think I've always wanted to live in Birmingham? No. I haven't. But when I got my priorities straight and got my head out of my ass, I knew I wanted to live close to home. And it's a great place to live. I actually really liked it there, but I've got nieces and nephews here." He nods toward the waiting area. "One on the way. I want to live close to my family now. Be here if they need me. Be here for Sunday dinner at Mama's." Be here to drive your future sister-in-law insane! I start to giggle. "What?" he says. "Did I say something funny?"

"I was just thinking about Chloe," I say. And how happy she probably is right now that she's not having to listen to you jabber. "Aren't they going to have a pretty baby?"

"But, of course," Tate says, puffing out his chest. "Coming from this gene pool."

And there ain't a thing wrong with your gene pool, Mr. Uncle Tater, I think. He winks at me again and I just smile. I want to F his brains out.

"Jackson, party of four. Jackson, party of four."

"That's us," he says. He puts his hand on my back as we make our way through the crowded bar, and I'm tickled pink to be one of the Jackson party of four. We meet Chloe and J.J. in the lobby, and then follow a ridiculously attractive hostess to our table. We have a pleasant dinner, with Tate cracking jokes and telling stories about when they were kids. J.J. laughs more than I've ever seen him laugh. Chloe even manages a chuckle or two and I'm mesmerized by every word that comes out of Tate Jackson's mouth.

Tate picks up the entire check for dinner and since I just paid for a fairly pricey plane ticket, I don't make a huge deal of it. Maybe I can do something nice for him sometime. After dinner, Chloe and I go to the restroom where she accuses me of being flirtatious.

"You like him," she says.

"I don't not like him," I say.

"You want to have sex with him!" she whispers. "I can tell!"

"I don't not want to have sex with him."

"Oh my goodness! What have I done?"

"You haven't done anything," I say, listening to some little old ladies talk back and forth between the stalls. "Let's get out of here."

"You had better not have sex with him," she says, staring at me in the mirror.

"But, Chloe, if I did, then maybe he would start hanging out at my house and wouldn't be at yours."

"Ace Jones! You can't be serious!"

"Hey, I'm just trying to help a friend in need." I smile.

"You know what?" she says. "I should've seen this coming, because if you hated the guys I thought were perfect for you, then, of course, you're going to love the one I dislike the most. It makes perfect sense in an Ace Jones sort of way."

"Exactly," I say, holding the door open for her. On the way home, Tate spots a beer store with a drive-thru and asks J.J. to turn in. He does and pulls up so Tate can order from the backseat. He buys a six-pack of Dos Equis, which we drink on the way home. By the time J.J. pulls up in my driveway, I'm tipsy and mellow and don't want the night to end. Tate walks me to the door and when we stop on the porch, I'm dying for a good-night kiss. Instead, I get a hug and a quick peck on the cheek.

"I'd kiss you, but we have an audience," he whispers, smiling. I look up at him as my heart skips about six beats. He smells so good.

"That's okay," I tell him. I want to take him inside and have my way with him, but I know I don't need to do that. "Maybe another time?" he says.

"Maybe," I say. Maybe hell! How about a hellz bellz yes! "Good night, Tate Jackson."

"Good night, Ace Jones."

I walk inside and flop down on the couch, grinning like a goon.

I think about digging a notebook out of my junk drawer and writing "Ace loves Tater" all over it. I take my phone out of my purse and see a late-night text from Logan Hatter. I silence the ringer and go to bed where I have wonderfully sweet dreams about Tate Jackson.

31

I wake up Saturday morning to find it's one of those perfect spring days that makes you want to spend every second of it outdoors. I brew a pot of coffee, pour myself a cup, and take it out to the back porch where I relax in one of my loungers. I make myself stop thinking about Tate Jackson.

"This is the day I've been waiting for," I tell Buster Loo when he hops out the doggie door. He makes a show of yawning and stretching, then takes off into the backyard. When I go back inside for a second cup of coffee, I decide to get Gramma Jones's garden book and study the actual contents instead of analyzing things I find. I go back outside and flip it open to the bloom chart.

"Interesting," I say. I want more than anything to get out and get to work in the yard, but I have to go to Freddie's for the much-anticipated makeover of Stacey Dewberry. I sigh, disappointed that I have to spend the best part of this day inside. I flip to the back of the book and look at the Post-it notes. Don't do this! But I do it anyway. I stare at the picture of the weeping willow. Was that for that pervert M. Emerson? I know I should just let it go and let who-ever that tree was planted for rest in peace, but my curiosity keeps getting the best of me. Maybe this afternoon, I might drive by a few of those addresses from the phone book. Just to see what the places look like. Then a horrible thought comes to mind. What if M. Em-erson was married. Maybe that's why he didn't spell out his first name. Because he didn't want to be caught by his own little paper trail. No! Gramma Jones would never do that. . . . Would she?

My phone buzzes and it's Freddie Dublin asking if I'll be at his house today. I text back a "Yes," save his number to my contacts list, then go inside and get ready.

When I pull into Freddie Dublin's neighborhood, it becomes obvious that he has another source of income, comes from a wealthy family, or spends every last dime of his paycheck on rent. I park on the curb and, as soon as I get out of my car, I hear the loud rumbling of a sports car. I turn around to see Stacey Dewberry pull up behind me. T-tops out and music blaring, she starts waving like a lunatic when she sees me. She's still singing "Girl Don't Go Away Mad" when she gets out of the car. I can't stop staring because, in-stead of standing at attention on top of her head, her hair is pulled up in a loose ponytail. A few strands have flown out here and there, no doubt thanks to the T-tops. She's not wearing any makeup at all. And she's beautiful.

"You look so pretty right now," I say.

"What are you talking about?" she squawks. "I'm a wreck. Fred-die told me to come over all natural, so here I am." She looks around. "I'm just glad I haven't seen anyone I know this morning.

Well, except that carhop who works the breakfast shift at Red Rooster, but she never pays me no never-mind anyway." She stops chattering, tilts her head to the side, and says, "Hey, what are you doing here?"

I don't really know what to say and I'm a little confused as to why Freddie needs to keep everyone in the dark about what's going on all the time. "Freddie invited me," I say. "Remember, the deal we made about the makeovers." She looks slightly disappointed.

"So that's why he told me to come all natural."

"I guess," I say. "But this is going to be tons-o-fun fun. I loved it when you guys did my hair and makeup for me." She looks at me and I swear she's thinking, Yeah, but you needed that. Clearly, she doesn't feel that she needs any type of beauty intervention. "I need to get your clothes back to you sometime."

"You should keep those," she says. "You looked great in them."

While we're standing there, a little red jelly-bean-looking car pulls up and Cameron Becker gets out. At that exact moment, Freddie Dublin appears on his front porch. He's wearing a white T-shirt and cutoff jogging pants. Unlike my cutoff jogging pants, his appear to have been purchased in the short-legged form. Despite the casual outfit, his hair is styled as usual. I glance at Stacey.

"Did you know Cameron Becker was coming?" I whisper.

"I didn't even know you were," she says. I can only assume that Cameron knew that both Stacey and I would be here, because she doesn't seem the least bit surprised to see us.

"Aren't we an on-time bunch?" Freddie says. "Come on in." The three of us follow him into his lovely little home, which looks like it was decorated by a professional. He has cracked-wheat crackers and some kind of weird-looking dip sitting out on the bar.

"Snacks?" he says in his usual unenthusiastic way. I'm not sure what kind of dip it is and I don't want to ask, so I try a little and find that it's very tasty. I pick up a pink Vitaminwater, one of the six different colors available to choose from.

"Let's sit and chat about what we want to do before we get started," Freddie says. I find myself standing face-to-face with Cameron, and we dance back and forth as we try to figure out who steps where so we can get out of each other's way.

"Yes, let's talk first, because I'm kind of nervous about this," Stacey says.

"There's nothing to be nervous about, right, Ace?" Freddie says. "Makeovers are fun."

"So much fun," I tell her. "Remember how good I looked after mine?"

"You did look great," Cameron says. I stop eating wheat crackers and look at her.

"I had to show her the pictures," Freddie says, and I feel so betrayed. For the next few minutes, things feel awkward and forced. Then we start talking about school and, much to my surprise, the conversation flows along smoothly. No one mentions the elephant in the room, and then Cameron and I start talking about what classes we had in college. Turns out we had some of the same teachers at Mississippi State, so we bond over that. Sort of.

Finally, Freddie tells Stacey that it's time to get started, so she goes and sits at the round glass table in the dining room, which is just behind the living room. Cameron doesn't get up, so I don't, either. I watch as Freddie takes the ponytail holder out of Stacey's hair and starts brushing. Then he turns on a hair dryer. It occurs to me that Freddie orchestrated this get-together so he could work on

Stacey's hair while I spend some quality time with Cameron and see that she's not so bad after all, because he certainly hasn't invited either of us to join him in the dining room. I think about the re-mark Logan made about him, and then Lilly's warning rings in my head like a church bell. Am I being had? I wonder. I think about that for a minute and since I don't know if I am or not, I just sit there and keep talking. Cameron Becker is slightly annoying, but a tad bit funny. I almost kind of like her.

As it turns out, she went through the same process to get her teaching license that I did—got a degree and then took a test—which explains why she's having such a difficult year. I know from personal experience how tough the transition can be from carefree college student to gainfully employed high school teacher respon-sible for daily lesson plans and all that business. I remember my first year all too well. Freddie is taking his sweet time working a conditioning treatment into Stacey's hair, so I resort to telling Cam-eron some of the worst experiences from my first year of teaching. She laughs until she starts tearing up.

"I'm so sorry," she says, wiping her eyes. "I've had such a horri-ble time, and it's just so good to know that I'm not the only one who's felt this way." I resist the urge to get up and hug her. Instead, I tell her everything I learned and every horrible mistake that I made in the five years I had the job that she has now. All of my se-crets and all of my tricks—I tell her everything. Who cares if I'm being had? This poor girl needs some help.

"See," she says after I tell her about the art of assigning great projects, which is to be lenient with the guidelines so the students can show off their own personal style and creativity. "I've never even thought about that. That's brilliant!" She tells me that nine hours of education classes didn't prepare her for seven hours a day in the classroom. I tell her that ninety hours probably wouldn't have prepared me for it.

"Some things you can only learn by experience," I say, smiling at her like she's my favorite little pal in the whole wide world.

"Or having someone like you," she says, smiling that big radiant smile of hers.

Someone like me, I think. *Fancy that.*

Freddie finally comes into the living room, followed by Stacey whose hair is tucked into a polka-dot shower cap.

"What are we talking about?" Freddie asks, like he doesn't know.

"School." Cameron beams. "She's been telling me horror stories and making me feel better!"

"Well, tell me some, too," Freddie says. And so I do. The more I talk, the more I remember and within minutes, I have them all in stitches.

"Okay, so who else wants a conditioning treatment?" Freddie asks when I finally can't think of anything else to share.

"Oh, I do! I haven't had one in weeks and I'm overdue," Cameron says.

"How about it, Ace Jones?" He looks at me.

"It will make your hair so silky smooth," Cameron says. "And Freddie gives an amazing head massage." I look at Freddie and he smiles.

"Sure, why not," I say. "What can it hurt? After you, Cameron."

"That's my girl!" he says. Cameron goes to what Freddie is now calling the Conditioning Chair, and I follow Stacey into the kitchen.

"Check this thing out," she says. "His sink has this cool nozzle that looks like the spout, but it comes off." She pulls it off and starts spraying the sink. "How about that?"

"That's, uh, really cool," I say.

Stacey helps herself to another spoonful of dip. "What is this stuff?" she whispers after Freddie turns the dryer on and starts heating up Cameron's hair.

"I don't know. Maybe hummus dip?"

"What's in it?"

"I don't know," I say. "Hummus?"

"Well, alrighty then." She looks at me and giggles. "I'm having the best time ever."

"You know what?" I tell her. "So am I."

We return to the living room where Stacey proceeds to inform me that one of the men she met at the concert is calling every day, wanting to go out. She tries to explain which guy it was and, despite her vivid description of him and his mullet, I simply can't recollect.

"Honestly, though," she says. "I like that Skeeter fellow better than any I've met in a while. We had so much fun dancing that night."

"I don't think he's a nice person," I say.

"That's always the kind I fall for the hardest," she says with a sigh.

"And what kind is that?" Freddie asks, inserting himself into our conversation.

"The not-nice kind," Stacey says.

"Now, Stacey, nobody needs that in their life," he tells her.

"He's right, you know," I say. Since Stacey is an adamant disciple of the Gospel of Freddie, maybe she'll take that to heart and steer clear of the Skeeters and Joe Reds of the world.

"Are you ready?" he asks me. I tell him that I am. "Please," he says, motioning. "To the Conditioning Chair." I take a seat on the cushioned chair and Freddie brushes my hair, then turns on the blow-dryer.

"Where did you get this stuff?" I ask as he massages condi-tioner into my hair. "It smells wonderful."

"My sister is a hairdresser to the rich and not-so-famous in Ocean Springs," he says. "She's always going to some kind of show or convention or something. Anyway, as a result, I have tons of great hair products." He picks up a shower cap with a tiny yellow rubber ducky sewn onto the top. "Yours to keep. I have a whole box."

"Thank you, I love it."

He tucks my hair into the cap and then tells Stacey it's time for a rinse. I sit and talk to Cameron, who's sporting a shower cap with a picture of a tiara, and we start talking about pets. She has a cat that she rescued as a kitten when she was in high school, and my heart melts when she tells me that story. And if Freddie's plan was for me to see that she's a likable person, well, it's safe to say it's working, because any friend of homeless animals is a friend of mine. I tell her about Buster Loo, and when she tells me she'd like to meet him sometime, I believe her.

After we're all rinsed and have our shower caps tucked into the bags of free samples Freddie put together for us, Stacey gets a pro-fessional blow out while I'm left to air dry. I feel majorly left out as Cameron flat irons Stacey's hair while Freddie does her makeup. Unbeknownst to her, he skips the purple, blue, and greens in her makeup bag and sticks with the browns, peaches, and pinks. The finished product is a stark contrast to what we see at school on a daily basis. Stacey's hair is straight and sleek and, without all of that crazy-colored liner and shadow, her sea green eyes seem to glow. Despite our genuine compliments, however, when Stacey inspects her appearance in the mirror on the wall of the living room, she doesn't like what she sees. Moving her head from side to side, she mumbles and grumbles about the lack of color.

"All of that bold color takes away from your natural features, which are quite lovely," Freddie explains. Cameron and I continue to tell her how glamorous she looks, but she's not convinced.

"I guess it looks okay if I was going to buy groceries or something," she says, "but I couldn't go out looking like this." Cameron smiles, Freddie turns around and rolls his eyes, and I stand there and try not to laugh. "My head feels weird," she says.

I can relate. This whole afternoon has felt weird to me, but I enjoyed it nonetheless. We all say good-bye and go our separate ways. On my way home, I call Lilly to see if maybe she wants to go to the movies or out to eat. She's not interested.

"Do you want to go out honky-tonkin' with the Dewberry tonight? I'll go if you go, and I'll even start another fight if it'll make you feel better," I tell her.

"Nah," she says. "I have to wait for my phone call."

"Are you sure? That phone is mobile, you know. You can take it with you. And I'll go out and tear the roof off every redneck hillbilly place in the five surrounding counties if it'll make you feel better."

That gets a laugh out of her. "Not necessary," she says. She asks if Stacey will have to go out by herself if I don't go with her.

"Oh no," I say. "My new friends, Cameron Becker and Freddie Dublin, are going out with her tonight, so I kind of hate to miss it, but I really want to just hang out on the couch." I tell her all about the makeover and how pretty Stacey looked with straight hair and toned-down makeup.

"God bless her," Lilly says. "I can't believe you hung out with freakin' Becker and Dublin today."

"Hey, what if I came to your house tonight with a bag of China Kitchen and a stack of hopelessly romantic comedies? Would you let me in?"

"I'd actually love that. But if Dax calls, I'll have to drop everything and talk to him."

"Of course, Lilly. But I can't be responsible for my behavior if you leave your cream cheese wontons unsupervised."

"I'll keep that in mind," she says. Then she wants to bet me ten bucks Stacey's hair will look just like it always does when she gets to school on Monday.

"Only a fool would take that bet," I tell her. "I'll see you around seven."

"Sounds good. Thank you."

When I get home, Buster Loo goes straight to the front door and stares at his leash.

"Let's go, little buddy," I tell him. The afternoon is breezy and warm, and I very much enjoy our walk around the park. So does Buster Loo. As I'm walking, I remember that I forgot to drive by and check out those Emersons from the phone book. Oh well, maybe tomorrow. I spend the afternoon in the backyard, pulling weeds and piddling around. At first, Buster Loo stays right beside me and sniffs each individual weed that I pluck, but he eventually loses interest and goes to take a nap in the middle of the yard. Even though I don't accomplish anything other than uprooting a shitload of weeds, I very much enjoy the time I spend out there on my knees. This is good, I think, when I go inside to take a shower. Nothing fancy. Nothing complicated. Just plain old happy. Amazing. But I would be a lot happier if Tate Jackson would give me a call.

After I get dressed, I dig through my DVD collection and pull out the silliest, sappiest movies I can find. Then I call China Kitchen and order Lilly's and my favorite dishes. Buster Loo hops in the car with me and, after I pick up dinner, we head over to Lilly's. It's a nice and very relaxing evening and Lilly doesn't even break down squalling after she gets to speak with Dax for only five minutes.

<><><><><><><><><><><><><><><><><><><><><><><><><><><><><><><><><><><><><>

32

Sunday I get up early, take Buster Loo for a walk at the park, and then get ready and go to church. When I leave there, I pick up some fried chicken and take it home where I eat by myself at the picnic table in the backyard. Well, not really by myself. Buster Loo sits beside me on the bench and stares at my chicken like it might fly off.

"Today is the day," I tell Buster Loo when I give him a small piece of meat. "Mama's going to get her garden on today." He sits up on his hind legs and waves his paws. He wants more chicken.

I go inside and change clothes, then go out to the garage and dig around to see what I can find. I know there's a wheelbarrow in there somewhere; I just have to find it. When I do, it's under a pile of junk that takes me thirty minutes to rearrange. Finally, the wheelbarrow is free. And just above the spot I cleaned out, I see the tools—Gramma Jones's tools. They're hanging in nice neat rows on a piece of Peg-Board on the back wall of the shed. It's the same place they've always been; I just forgot they were there. Under the Peg-Board is a set of old cabinets, also in the same spot since I was a kid. I open the cabinet doors and find several pairs of dust-covered gardening gloves. Each pair still has a price tag, and on the price tag, a faded orange sticker.

She must've got them on sale, I think. I also find a foam strip that I assume is to kneel on, a roll of garbage bags, and all shapes and sizes of flowerpots. I need to revive and expand my herb garden, I think. It'll be twice as nice with all these pots. I pick up a pair of gloves, pull off the tag, and slip them on. I select a few of the gardening tools, put them in the wheelbarrow, and head out into the yard.

I'm amazed how much easier getting rid of weeds is with the proper tools. Who knew? I'd always pulled weeds by hand—the hard way. Come to think of it, I've always done everything the hard way. Work smarter, not harder, Gramma used to say. Indeed.

Buster Loo comes up to sniff my pile of weeds, then returns to his spot in the sunshine. I fill up what turns out to be a really gigantic garbage bag and even though my back is screaming in pain, I get every last little weed out of every flower bed in the backyard. I stand up and stretch, then go around to the front yard, where I fill up another huge garbage bag. I walk around the side of the house to where the weeping willow is planted and wonder why Gramma Jones didn't just write the person's name on the Post-it note. Maybe I'm being too nosy. Maybe it's none of my business. Maybe that's why she didn't write a name there. Maybe it's her secret. Maybe she'd like for it to stay that way.

While I'm standing there, something occurs to me that I hadn't thought of before. I need to plant a tree for Gramma Jones. I decide to go to the nursery after school one day next week and get her the perfect tree. I don't know what kind that will be, but I'm sure I'll figure something out when I get there. I pick the weeds from the beds on the side of the house, tie up the overstuffed bag, and drag it to the curb where I flop it over next to the other one.

I gather up the tools and wash them off and then I hose down the wheelbarrow. After putting everything back where I found it inside the garage, I'm surprised by an amazing feeling of accomplishment. I look around the garage and decide that next week, I'm cleaning this place out and transforming it into my own private garden workshop.

With an aching back and a pounding head, I walk around the yard to inspect my work. I didn't realize how bad it looked until I got all of those pesky weeds out. There're a few gaps here and there, along with some overgrown clumps of monkey grass and jumbo bunches of daylilies. I think if I separate that stuff, I can fill in the gaps and probably have monkey grass left over. I decide to do some more research before digging stuff out of the ground and hacking it up. As I walk back around the house, I have another great idea. Everything I have left over, I'll take to Lilly's where I will begin Operation Get Lilly Lane out of the House and into That Atrocious Yard of Hers. I know she'll never be a gardener, but she loves telling people what to do, so she can point and I can dig and that might solve all kinds of problems for both of us. I smile at the thought, then go inside and run myself a steaming-hot bubble bath. I'm proud of myself because today I found something I enjoy that requires nothing more than what I already have here at la casa de Jones.

Later that night, I get a call from a strange number and answer it quickly, hoping it will be Tate Jackson. It's not.

"Hi, Ace," comes the sweet-as-sugar voice on the other end of the line. "This is Cameron. Freddie gave me your number. Is it okay that I called?"

"Of course, Cameron," I say, surprised by an odd feeling of affection for this person who just a few short weeks ago I wanted to run out of town and, thereby, out of my former classroom. "What's up?"

"Do you think it's too late to do an art fair this year?"

My heart jumps for joy. "Almost, but not quite," I tell her. "Since it's the end of the year, the schedule is pretty lax, so we could have it a week later than usual." We? Who the hell is "we"?

"So you wouldn't mind helping?"

"Not at all, Cameron," I tell her. "As a matter of fact, I'd love to." She thanks me about a hundred times and I hang up the phone, strangely happier than I have been in quite some time. *Call me butter, because I'm on a roll,* I think. A downright happy roll! I giggle because I love how corny I am.

33

<><><><><><><><><><><><><><><><><><><><><><><><><><><><><><><><><><><><>

Monday when I get to school, Stacey Dewberry is there in her usual outlandish garb with her hair styled the usual outlandish way. Her eyelids are thoroughly coated with blue shadow.

"You didn't like the new look?" I ask her.

"Well, you know," she says. "It was pretty and all, but incredibly boring. I mean, I'm used to getting up at five a.m. to fix my hair. What would I do with that time if I didn't use it to fix my hair?"

"You have a point," I say.

Chloe comes in, beaming like the morning sun, and gives us today's assignments. I don't know if this job is getting easier or if I'm just getting used to it, but I don't have any suicidal thoughts when Chloe hands me the folder. Maybe it's because I have another half-a-day schedule today. Either way, it's good not to feel so bad.

The bell rings, and Stacey and I get up to go. I'm thinking of heading to the library, when Chloe asks me to come to her office. I don't have a class to cover until third period and since Chloe is back to her usual chipper self, I'm happy to do so. I sit down and she closes the door behind us.

"Am I in trouble?"

"Hardly," she says, sitting down. "I had an interesting visitor in here first thing this morning. She was waiting for me when I got to work."

"And . . ."

"And it was Cameron Becker, who wanted to get approval to do an art fair."

"And . . ."

"And I told her that she had to speak with Principal Byer, but that I didn't think it would be a problem." Chloe is beaming at me now. "She said you agreed to help her with it?"

"I did."

"What has happened to you, Ace Jones?"

"I just feel sorry for the girl. Stacey and I went over to Freddie's on Saturday and she was there." I tell her about the makeover and she gets a kick out of that. "It was a setup—I figured that out right away—but she's not so bad. I mean, she's a little different, but we have a few things in common, believe it or not." I pause. "I don't know—I just feel like I should help her." Chloe has a tear in her eye. A freakin' tear. "Chloe, good word! You're getting as bad as Lilly."

"I can't help it," she says with a sniff. "I'm so proud of you. My Ace Jones is all grown-up."

"Don't jump to such drastic conclusions," I say, resisting the urge to roll my eyes. "Is that all you needed?"

"No, well, there is one more thing." Her expression changes to one of concern.

"What's that?"

"Tate asked for your phone number. Like a hundred times. I told him I'd have to talk to you first." My heart flips and flutters, and I feel like I'm right back in seventh grade.

"Why didn't you call or text me or just go on and give it to him?"

"I wanted to look at you when I asked you," she says. "You have a crush."

"Yes, I do," I say. "A bad one. And it's been a really, really long time since I've had a crush on someone. So long, in fact, that I don't even remember who or when it was." I stop to think. "I guess it was Logan Hatter, although crushing might not be the best way to describe our involvement with each other." That makes her laugh out loud.

"Are you still sleeping with him?"

"No," I say. "And I knew that wasn't going anywhere. I just couldn't help myself there for a week or two. Old Coach Hatter's got it going on in the sack and that's a fact."

"Stop it!" she wails. "Stop talking! Please!"

I giggle. "So give Uncle Tater my phone number already!" I say. "Dang!"

"Okay," she says. "Have you talked to Lilly? She's been kind of out of it since Dax left."

"I went over there Saturday night. She's depressed, but who wouldn't be? Dax called her while I was there and she managed to talk to him without squalling for the first time since he left. Poor thing."

"I expected him to give her a ring before he left."

"Yeah, I think she did, too. But I mean, everything happened so fast. It was like he got that letter and then he was gone."

"Well, yeah."

"And speaking of her being depressed, she's not much help planning a shower. Would it be okay with you if I talked to Jalena about it? She has a special-event room in the diner. . . ." I can't believe I'm suggesting to Chloe Stacks that we have her shower in a diner.

"Of course that would be okay," she says. "I want to keep it small and casual. J.J. and I don't want anything about this wedding to turn into a big hoopla."

"I'm sorry, Chloe. I had it in mind to have it at Lilly's, but she's just so—"

"Ace, the diner is fine. Stop worrying about it."

"Okay, then," I say. "It's a really cool place. I painted some flamingos on the wall and they're pretty awesome if I do say so myself. I mean, there aren't flamingos in the party room. They're in the main part. And the tables and stuff are so cute and the dishes are really adorable."

"Ace, it's fine."

"Maybe we should have it somewhere in Tupelo at one of those fancy restaurants, or I could rent the clubhouse at the golf course." I wished now that I hadn't even suggested the diner. I'm glad I haven't mentioned it to Jalena. What was I thinking?

"Are you listening?" she says, waving at me. "There's nowhere I'd rather have a wedding shower than at Jalena's diner. It's perfect. And I was going to ask her to cater the reception."

"Really? Okay," I say. I'm going to make that special-event room look like the freakin' Taj Mahal of wedding showers. I don't care if

I have to take out a loan on my house. As soon as I get out of Chloe's office, I text Jalena and ask her if I can come by this afternoon and talk about the shower. I'm relieved when she says that I can, and it's all I can think about for the rest of the day.

When I get to the diner, Jalena tells me she's more than happy to help with the shower and delighted to be hosting it at the diner. She flops out a big old catalog, and we start looking for shower invitations.

"So you weren't kidding when you said you wanted to be a party planner?" I say, flipping through the pages.

"Girl, I don't joke too much about serious matters. Here, let me show you what I have in mind. It'll take you all night to look through all of that." She flips to the back of the catalog. "I've been thinking about this since you texted." She finds the page she's looking for and points to a very classy invitation that I think Chloe would love. On the opposite page is a picture of all the cool and fancy trimmings recommended for that particular theme. "What do you think?" Jalena asks. "When I saw this, I thought, 'Now, this looks like Chloe.'"

"It looks like it would cost a fortune."

"If you get it all from this place, it would. But we're just going to order the invitations because I have most of the stuff in that picture already. As a matter of fact, before I even heard from you this morning, I had found a set of those columns for sale online. Ethan Allen just went and picked 'em up for me."

"How do you already have all this stuff?" I ask because I'm sensing a cover-up.

"'Cause I've been shopping flea markets and clearance racks, and going to some estate sales! I've been on the ball. You want to see what I've got?"

"Sure."

I follow her to the storage room where she shows me the props she's collected so far. "I was self-appointed CEO of the prom committee in high school," she says. "I love this kind of thing!"

"This is great," I tell her. "You sure are making this easy for me."

"And that is exactly what my business plan is based on. Easing the pain of hosting an event by eliminating the stress of planning."

"That sounds like a winner to me."

She tells me that she needs to show me something else, so I follow her to her office where she plops down in the hot pink desk chair. I take a cushy seat on the other side of the desk. She opens her laptop and starts pecking away. Her printer starts to hum, and then she hands me a sheet of paper and a pen.

"Mark what you would like for the shower, my dear," she says as I look over the menu. "Don't forget to select what flavor mint you would like and if you'd like candied pecans or traditional peanuts."

"Oh, you're too much," I say.

"I know how to throw a party. I've been telling you that since the first time I met you."

"You've made a believer out of me, my friend," I say, marking boxes next to appetizers. I'm going to be broke as a convict when this is over. "Are you going to make all this?"

"Of course," she says, laughing. I hand her the list and she slips it into a polka-dot file folder. "Now let's talk about a cake for the shower. That's the only thing I can't do. But lucky for you, I've been hanging out at the new cupcake place downtown, you know, doing research for the job." She gives me a very serious look that cracks me up.

"There's a new cupcake place downtown?"

"Don't you read the paper? It was on the front page last week."

"No."

"You need to get out from that rock you're living under." She gets up and gets her purse. "C'mon. You've got to see this place." And so I ride with Jalena to Miss Calico's Cupcakery in downtown Bugtussle.

"Cupcake mania!" I whisper as we stand in the long line.

"You'll see why in just a minute."

Sure enough, ten minutes later, I fall madly in love with a Guinness cupcake. Jalena slices off a sample of her red velvet cupcake and I fall in love all over again.

"Look," she says, unfolding a brochure while I finish off my cupcake. "Miss Calico can do petits fours in six different flavors."

"That would be perfect!" I say. And then, just to be on the safe side, we sample a few more cupcakes. I place my order and tell Jalena that we have to get out of there before I get on my hands and knees and beg Miss Calico for a job.

"She's hiring," Jalena says, getting into her Jeep.

"I could not work in there," I tell her. "I'd wind up on one of those shows where they have to knock out a wall and haul you out with a forklift."

34

<<<<<<<<<<<<<<<<<<<<<<<<<<<<<<<<<<<<<<<<<<<<<<<<<<<<<<<<<<<<

Tuesday is another easy day at school, so during seventh period, I go down to Cameron Becker's room. I give her a thumb stick with all of the files I've created over the years, and then we go over her plans for the art fair. Something seems to be bothering her and when I ask, she tells me that she didn't get the response she was hoping for when she made the announcement to her students.

"I don't think they think I can do it," she says.

"Then you will show them that you can do it."

I give her a good pep talk, but she doesn't look convinced. I walk out of her classroom just before the bell and meet Logan Hatter in the hallway.

"Well, hello, Ms. Jones," he says with a smile. "Are you over here looking for me?"

"No matter where I am or what I'm doing, I'm always looking

for you, Coach Hatter," I tell him. We chat for a minute and when I tell him that I'm helping Cameron with the art fair, he just shakes his head.

"Where's the old fireball that wouldn't rest until she got her job back?" he asks quietly.

"I don't know, Hatter," I tell him. "Burned-out a little maybe."

"Well, you gotta do what you gotta do."

"I guess."

"Hey, since you're having so much free time these days, why don't you come eat lunch with us? All Chloe talks about is getting married, and if Lilly says anything at all, it's about Dax. And then I've got Wills crying on my shoulder all the time because he misses Miss Tits down there so much. I need some humor in my life."

"Maybe I can join y'all tomorrow," I tell him.

"Good deal," he says.

When I leave school, I ride by the nursery where I have a much harder time picking out a tree for Gramma Jones than I thought I would because everything she loved is already out in the yard. The man who owns the place sees me struggling and comes to see if he can help me find something.

"I'm looking for a tree," I tell him. "A special tree to honor a special lady who loved to work in her yard."

"I have just the thing." He walks over to a pretty little tree that I recognize. "This is a star magnolia," he begins. "It's a—"

"I'll take it," I say, cutting him off. "It's perfect." If it'd been a snake, it would've bit me.

He tells me how much it is, and I pull the cash out of my pocket and pay for it. He tells me to wait a minute and goes inside his office. He brings back some newspapers, which he spreads out on the back floorboard of my car.

"To protect your carpet," he explains. He carefully positions the shrub in the backseat.

"Thank you," I say, smiling at the kindly gentleman.

"Thank you for stopping by," he says.

"What a sweetie," I say to myself as I drive my new star magnolia home. I carefully unload the little shrub and take it to the backyard. Buster Loo greets me at the gate and follows me up onto the back porch. I know just where I'm going to plant this new tree, but it's already dark, so I'll have to do it tomorrow.

Wednesday, I meet Cameron Becker in the library after school and help her get everything finalized for the art fair. It's clear that this project means a lot to her and it makes me happy to see how happy she is, sitting there telling me where everything is going to go. Her layout is pretty much the opposite of how I always did it, but who cares? Her plans are pretty cool, so I don't say a word. She tells me her students are starting to get more excited, and I tell her that they're like a roomful of mirrors reflecting her own enthusiasm.

"I forgot to tell you yesterday that you need to get an announcement in the school newsletter next week," I tell her. "Send an e-mail to Mrs. Marshall and she'll make sure it gets on there."

"Okay," she says, scribbling.

"The Peg-Boards are in the gym, so just ask a few of the coaches to help you." I stop and look at her. She looks down, and then I remember. "I guess you, uh, know who to ask about that. You only need two or three, and Hatter will be glad to help. He helps me every year." She doesn't say anything, and the air between us becomes tense and awkward. "Cameron?"

"I'm sorry," she says. "I just—" She looks at me. I decide to be nosy.

"What happened?" I say. "With you and Wills. What was that all about?"

"I guess you heard what I did." She appears to be somewhat ashamed of herself.

"Yeah, it's a small town. Everybody knows everybody's business and it's certainly none of mine. I was just wondering because, well, I like Wills. He's a good guy." She looks up at me. "And I like you. But you don't have to tell me anything. You don't owe me an explanation of any kind." But you certainly owe Drew Wills one.

"I'll tell you," she says. Then we just sit there for a minute.

"Okay . . ."

"I was just trying to figure out where to start."

"We're waiting on the buses to leave, sweetheart. You can start from the beginning."

"Well, I liked Drew as soon as I saw him because I'm fond of the big athletic type. So I started going to the gym and flirting, but I didn't want to be obvious about it and just flirt with him, so I flirted with everybody and while that eventually got me a date with him, it also got me labeled as a hussy." She looks at me.

"I never said that."

"Everyone else did. And remember that day I failed my evaluation, when Stacey Dewberry said I liked pecker?" I suppress a giggle. "It's okay—you can laugh," she says. "Cameron Becker who loves pecker." She mocks Stacey Dewberry's country accent. "I certainly didn't appreciate it at the time, but Freddie thought it was hilarious. I guess it was pretty funny." I laugh a little, but not too much. "Anyway, after we started dating, I fell in love with him so fast because he's so sweet and he's funny and he's kind. No one has ever been so nice to me. So I kept going down to the coaches' office every morning because I wanted to see him and I kept carrying on with everyone because I didn't want to smother him and run him off like I did the only other boyfriend I've ever had in my life. I was so happy to be with him, but I did everything wrong."

"How have you had only one other boyfriend?"

"One serious boyfriend. I've dated my fair share of a-holes and losers, but I'm just, I don't know, kind of defensive. I've never had any real friends and so many people have turned on me, lied to me, and, well, I was scared. I didn't want to overdo it. Then when he popped the question, I just freaked out. I was like, 'I've never been able to maintain a healthy relationship in my life. He'll eventually be like everyone else. He'll use me and then leave me.' It was more than I could stand, so I ran. I grabbed a bottle of his alcohol and ran." She shakes her head. "How's that for tacky? Then the next day, I wanted to talk to him, so I went down to the lounge, but then I freaked out again because I didn't know what to say, so I just talked to everyone else but him. He got up and left and I knew I'd hurt his feelings, but I didn't know what to do." She looks at me. "Needless to say, we don't speak anymore and Freddie is the only friend I have and I know I'm getting on his nerves. I don't know what's wrong with me. I'm like a wrecking ball on relationships. I'm either swinging back and away or flying forward and crashing. I wish I could just level out and be normal."

"I don't think anybody is normal," I say. "At least I hope not."

She giggles a little, then says, "So if you don't mind me asking, why did you move back home? It seems like a dream to live in Florida right next to the ocean."

"Because I'm crazy," I say. Then I decide that maybe she deserves a better explanation. She was having a hard enough time being an inexperienced first-year teacher at a brand-new school and then I showed up wanting her job. So I tell her the truth. "Once upon a time," I say with a smile, "I formulated this idea of what my life needed to be like in order for me to be happy. I clung to that idea and believed in it with all my heart and all my soul, and so it became my biggest dream. I put that dream up on a pedestal, looked up at it every day, and thought, 'If only I could have that, I would be perfectly happy.' Then about this time last year, a bunch of crazy shit happened and I saw my chance to live that dream. Guns blazing, I took that opportunity. I went for it. And within a matter of months, I had exactly what I always wanted. The amazing guy. The amazing house. A super-cool art gallery of my very own. I had it all." I have to stop because I start tearing up. "I'm sorry. But it still hurts a little." I look at her, so pretty and young, and wish I had found out when I was her age that my dream was a sham. I take a deep breath and continue. "Then a terrible thing happened, Cameron. I discovered that I wasn't quite as happy as I always imagined I would be. And that realization was as embarrassing as it was disappointing because I'd given so much power to that one idea. That one dream. So then I gave it every chance I could before I finally gave up and came back home in January." I'm surprised by how liberated I feel after telling her all that. Other than a string of therapists, she's the only one I've told the whole truth about how I really feel. I've told parts and pieces of what happened to Chloe and Lilly, but I didn't want to burden either of them with the whole ugly truth. "So don't think you're the only one who has made terrible mistakes," I tell her. "I wrecked my whole life for a dream that turned out to be all wrong for me. And that's the worst, having to admit to yourself that you were wrong." I look up and see that the buses are gone. "So, how's that for depressing? Do you feel any better now?" She giggles. "See, it's not so bad, is it? You're lucky. You have something that can be fixed."

"Do you really think so?"

"I know so."

"Please don't say anything to him."

"I won't say anything to him, but you know I'm really good friends with Hatter, right?"

"Are y'all still sleeping together?"

"How does everyone know about that?"

"Everyone doesn't. Stacey told Freddie and he told me." So everyone knows.

"Okay, well, no. He's great, but we aren't sleeping together. Anymore. So let me just pass it along that you want to talk to Wills, and we'll see what happens here in a day or two."

She smiles that big beautiful smile of hers and we get back to discussing the art fair. She jots notes in her stylish little notebook, and I decide to talk to Chloe and see if she can offer some suggestions on what Cameron could do to pass that last evaluation. I know it'll be the final nail in the coffin of my old job, but maybe I can think up something else to do with my time. I make a mental note to have some business cards made up to put at Jalena's diner when it opens next month. Who knows, that just might work out for me. I mean it probably won't, but it might.

I go home and take Buster Loo for a walk at the park. While

we're there, I spend a considerable amount of time wondering what I'm going to do now that I'm almost sure I'm about to be unemployed. I'm damned sure not going to sign up for another year of subbing. Even though things have improved considerably now that the semester is almost over, hell will freeze over before I do something like that again. I decide that I don't want to go to summer school because I'm not particularly interested in teaching psychology. Being crazy and teaching about crazy are two totally different things. I think about sending applications in to some other districts, but I don't want to start all over in a new school. I don't even really want to teach anymore, but that's my safety net, so I can't stop my mind from coming up with ways to make it work. I finally decide that I will indeed have some business cards made up. I can design them myself and then ask Jalena which printer she uses. I get a peaceful feeling when I think about painting murals and glazing walls for a living. I stop short of conjuring up a bunch of if/then stipulations. I'm just going to try to see what happens. Like Gramma Jones used to say, it'll all work itself out in the wash.

When Buster Loo and I get back home, I pick up the phone to call Logan Hatter.

"Hey, sexy baby," he says when he picks up. "What can I do for you?"

"Hey, Hatt," I say. "I've got some gossip for you."

"Well, it's about time," he says, laughing. "I was going to cut you off if you didn't start putting out soon."

"You wouldn't dare!"

"Yeah, you're right. I wouldn't."

"So how's Wills?"

"Well, he's still pussy-whipped by that damned old screaming girl and won't even think about looking at anyone else, let alone try to hook up, but other than that I guess he's all right. Why? You interested? Want me to fix you up?"

"Ha-ha. No. And has that damned old screaming girl not let up any these past few days?"

"Come to think of it, she has," he says. "And I saw y'all in the library after school today. What's up with that? What are you doing? Are y'all having an affair?"

"Wow, you're on a roll today, aren't you, Hatt?"

"Always, baby, always. So what's the gossip?"

"Cameron wants to get back with Drew."

"The hell you say."

"She's sorry. She wants him back. She misses him. You know the drill. But she doesn't want to rush things. She's skittish about relationships, so he needs to ease up and be patient with her. That's the story. Can you handle it?"

"I can handle it. I'll call him right now. I mean, this is a little seventh grade, but I loved seventh grade. I was a stud in seventh grade."

"You're a stud now, Hatt, and you know this."

"Yeah, right. I'll holler back."

I don't have any classes at all to cover on Thursday, so I decide to spend the morning putting together a file for Cameron Becker that will help her not only pass her final evaluation but also do exceptionally well. I recruit Chloe to help and while she refuses to show me Cameron's classroom report, because that's confidential, she does offer a few key points for her to consider. Like writing the day's assignment on the board and not forgetting to call roll.

After school, I sit down with Cameron and go over everything.

I look over her lesson plan book and help her map out the rest of the year, which is really easy since the students are working on individual projects for the next week. I suggest she wrap up the year with a short unit on whatever aspect of art she loves the best.

"I love Picasso!" she says.

"Well, there you have it."

"Too easy," she says. "I did a major research paper on him during my senior year, so I have lots of facts." We discuss the best way to translate that to classroom instruction. "I wish you had been my mentor this year," she says. "Mrs. Knight was nice, but we just didn't, I don't know, click." She pauses. "Okay, I'm not telling you the truth about that. She wasn't nice at all. Actually, she was kind of mean to me."

"Mrs. Knight has no business being a mentor," I say. "She only does it because she gets a little extra money. She's one of those psycho-jealous people who doesn't like anyone who's slimmer and/ or prettier than she is." I look at Cameron and smile. "So it could be said that she, um, doesn't like anyone." We giggle and pack our stuff to leave. I don't mention Wills and she doesn't, either. I wonder what the holdup is on that.

When I get home, I walk out onto the back porch and look at the star magnolia that I bought to plant for Gramma Jones. I look out at the star magnolia already in the yard and think about the Post-it note labeled "Baby Jones." I go to the garage and load up my wheelbarrow, then haul my new little tree out to the far corner of the yard. I set it on the ground next to the other one. I dig a hole, sprinkle some fertilizer, and, after wrestling the tree out of its container and tickling the roots like the man at the nursery told me to, I lower it into the ground. I work with it for a minute, making sure it's set straight, then fill in the gaps with potting soil. I water the tree and then go sit on the edge of the porch and look at it. Buster Loo comes to sit beside me.

"Look at that, Buster Loo," I say, but he doesn't. He puts his snout on my leg and rolls his eyes up to look at me, so I pick him up and give him a big chiweenie hug. "It's like it was meant to go there," I tell him. He puts his snout on my shoulder and I sit there, petting my dog and admiring that special little tree.

35

◇◇◇

Friday is a full day of subbing and I don't know if I left my rose-colored glasses home or what, but it's awful. I have lunch with Stacey, who tells me she's also having a worst day ever. She invites me to go out with her tonight and I invite her to go to Ethan Allen's so we can keep it low-key.

"It's a pretty regular crowd," I say.

"I went into that place one time and some big tall fellow behind the bar wouldn't stop looking at me. Kind of freaked me out. I left and never went back."

"Was he wearing a cowboy hat?"

"How did you know?"

"That's Ethan Allen. He was at the party you came to at my house, remember? He was probably staring because he's never seen anything like the full-blown glory of your spectacular hair."

She pats her hair. "Well, not everyone can do this."

"That's true," I tell her. "So what do you say? Give Ethan Allen another chance? He's actually a very nice guy. His girlfriend, Jalena, is also pretty cool. Maybe Lilly will come with us. And I'll invite Freddie and Cameron, too."

"Okay," she says. "But he better keep his eyes to himself."

"He's not like that at all, I promise."

After school, I go down to D Hall to check on Cameron and I run into Lilly in the hallway.

"Hello, sunshine," she says. "What brings you down this way?"

I point to the end of the hallway. "Ms. Becker."

"Chloe is so proud of you for all of that," Lilly whispers. "And so am I. It's really nice. Very not like you."

"Thanks, Lilly," I say, laughing. "I see you're back to your usual self."

"Well, Dax is almost finished with that damned training, so he's calling every night."

"Good. Hey, why don't you come to Ethan Allen's tonight? Stacey is going and I'm going to invite Cameron. I think you would really like her." Lilly looks skeptical. "Or maybe not. I don't know. Just give her a chance."

"Freddie Dublin really did a number on you, didn't he?"

"It wasn't him," I say, and she raises her eyebrows at me. "Okay, it wasn't all him."

"Right," she says.

"So will you go? You can go to Ethan Allen's office if Dax calls while we're there."

"Sure," she says. "Why not?"

"Great," I say. Yee haw! I'll be springing that garden club idea on her soon.

I knock on Cameron Becker's door and walk into my old classroom.

"I love what you've done with the place," I say.

"Come see what these kids are doing for the art fair," she says. "I cannot believe how talented they are! I let them pick what they wanted to paint and, honestly, this is the best work they've done. I'm so proud of them."

"They have so much personality and creativity, but they'll just sit there, pretending not to be on their cell phones until a worthy challenge arises and then presto! They're geniuses!"

"Look at this one." She points to an impressive portrait of a monarch butterfly resting on a magnolia bloom. "Worst kid I've had all year. Couldn't stand her and I'm sure the feeling was mutual. She wouldn't cooperate with me on anything and was about to fail and now look. It's like we're best friends all of a sudden, me and that little smarty-pants."

"She needs to start putting together a portfolio for college."

"I know!" she says. "That's exactly what I told her." I follow Cameron back to her desk where she picks up the file folder. "This has been a real eye-opener," she says. "If I'd had this at the beginning of the year, my life wouldn't have been so horrid for the past eight months. Do you need it back?"

"Nah. Just hang on to it and pass it on if you see someone who needs it."

"Thanks," she says. "So, guess what."

"What?" I say. I don't have to guess because I know. Hatter has already called and told me all about it.

"I have a date tomorrow night."

"Oh really. With who?"

"Oh, some guy named Drew Wills." She giggles.

"Good for you."

"He was so sweet. He called me and was like, 'I wanna slow things down and show you that you can trust me.' I cried like a baby. He came over. We made up. It was great."

"Well, good for you," I say. "So why aren't y'all going out to-night?"

"Oh, his mother's birthday is today and they're having a party. Big family get-together. He invited me to go, but I told him I'd rather not. I'm just not ready for that. I was afraid it would hurt his feelings, but it didn't."

"Well, that is great because tonight you can go out with Lilly and Stacey and me, and we can invite Freddie, speaking of whom, I haven't seen him in a day or two."

"He's on the coast."

"Doing what?"

"Job interviews."

"What? No way."

"Yeah, he doesn't love it here. Wants to be down closer to home and closer to New Orleans. He loves New Orleans. Plus, he has a friend in New Orleans who came up here for a visit and didn't love it either and now he won't come back."

"That's so sad, but I don't want him to leave!"

"I know. Me, either."

"Okay, well, I guess I'll talk to him when he gets back. So I'll see you tonight? Ethan Allen's around nine o'clock?"

"I'll be there."

"Awesome."

I go home, take Buster Loo for a walk, then piddle around in the yard until dark. I dig up and separate some monkey grass, leaving the daylilies to divide in the fall because I read that they might not bloom if divided in the spring and I don't want that. After filling in several gaps, I have enough monkey grass left over to fill up two five-gallon buckets.

"I'll take that to Lilly's tomorrow," I tell Buster Loo. "Plant it around those god-awful shrubs of hers."

I walk around the yard and inspect the flower beds. Even after all that thinning out and rearranging, I still have a few gaps. I decide to go buy more flowers. And while I'm at it, I'll get some flowers for Lilly, too.

I get to Ethan Allen's at five minutes after nine and find Stacey Dewberry sitting at the bar next to Jalena.

"This girl is crazy!" Jalena explains when I join them. "She's been telling me all kinds of stuff."

"I do not doubt that," I say.

Ethan Allen walks up and leans on the bar. Jalena winks at him and says, "And I have hollered laughing when she told me about this weirdo staring at her."

"Didn't know I was creepy until a minute ago," Ethan Allen says. He looks a little embarrassed, so I decide not to pick on him about that. Lilly comes in a few minutes later and then Cameron Becker comes in shortly after that. The two of them turn every head in the place, male and female.

"I feel like everyone is staring at me," Cameron says, taking a seat at the bar.

"Well, it's because they are," Stacey says. She looks at me. "Why do people do that so much around here? Just stare at you. Don't even try to hide it."

"It's worse than this in some other parts of the state, trust me," Lilly says.

I introduce Cameron to Jalena, and it's fairly obvious that Cameron is excited to be hanging out with the girls.

"I don't even remember the last time I had a Girls Night Out," Jalena says. "I guess it was when we were back in Florida and that wasn't Girls Night Out—it was Girls Night In."

"We need to crank that tradition back up," I say.

"Oh, I don't think so," Ethan Allen says. "That wouldn't be good for business."

"Yeah, right," Lilly says. She waves a hand around the crowded bar. "You're just struggling along here, aren't you?"

"What's Girls Night In?" Stacey asks. "That sounds kind of dull."

I explain it, but Stacey doesn't look interested. "I like to belly up to a bar, myself," she says, then turns around on her bar stool and does just that.

We drink and dance and have a large time hanging out and acting silly. Cameron Becker can't turn around without someone hitting on her, so she goes back to her bar stool and stays there. She's soon joined by Lilly, who is equally uninterested in flirting and foolishness. I lose Stacey Dewberry on the dance floor and when I find her later, she's cutting some serious rug with a man sporting a king-sized mullet. When things start to wind down, Ethan Allen joins Jalena and me on the dance floor. Eventually, we all end up back at the bar. Except the mullet man, who Stacey tells us had to go outside and smoke.

"You need a karaoke machine," Stacey says when Ethan Allen pours her a fourth Southern Comfort Special.

"I had one one time," he tells her. "Turns out a lot of people want to sing who can't and it got to where it was running more people off than bringin' them in. Ended up selling it at a yard sale."

"Aw, man," Stacey says. "I could really break it down to some Lynyrd Skynyrd right now."

"We've got 'Sweet Home Alabama' and 'Free Bird' on the juke-box over there," Ethan Allen tells her.

"'Sweet Home Alabama'! That's my song! Because, you know, I'm from Alabama." She looks at me. "Did I ever tell you that I'm madly in love with Kid Rock?"

What? "No, but I can't say I'm surprised."

"Yeah, you know he did a song about 'Sweet Home Alabama.' A song about a song. He's a genius. I love him so much."

"I like that song, too," Cameron says.

"You know, I saw Kid Rock at a concert down in Orange Beach a few years back," Stacey says. "He jumped up on top of his piano and all I could think about was, 'Oh, what I wouldn't give to be a piano with bumper stickers and Kid Rock all over me right now.'" She starts digging in her purse.

I glance over at Jalena, who whispers, "She is great!" I look around and don't see Lilly.

"She's back in the office," Ethan Allen says. "Phone call."

"Good for her."

36

Saturday morning I wake up without a headache because I only drank three beers instead of getting hammered like I usually do. I roll out of bed, take a quick shower, and throw on some old shorts and a T-shirt.

"Buster Loo," I say, and he peeps out from under the covers. "I know this is earlier than we usually get up on Saturday, but come on, I've got us a little adventure planned for today." He jumps out of bed and starts stretching on the rug. Then he rolls over on his back and looks at me. "You can do it, little man. C'mon." I take off down the hallway and that gets him in gear because Buster Loo doesn't care where you're going—if you're going in a hurry, he's ready to move. He passes me in the kitchen and hops out the doggie door. I brew half a pot of coffee and pour it into a big to-go cup. I get Buster Loo's leash and walk out onto the back porch. When he finishes his doggie business, we get in the car and go to the nursery.

"You back for another tree?" the gentleman asks when he sees me poking around his greenhouse.

"No, sir, not today," I tell him. "This morning I'm looking for some flowers." We talk while we walk around his impressive spread of plants and I find myself captivated by his interest in and knowledge of all things green. I tell him that I need flowers to fill in some gaps in a fully matured yard and then some for a bed I'll be starting from scratch. We discuss shade versus sun, annual versus perennial, so forth and so on. He knows just what I need for each project, helps me find the colors I want, then helps me load the containers into the back of my car where I still have the newspaper from earlier in the week.

"I'm giving you a discount for buying so much," he says. "But you'll have to come in and let me find my calculator." I follow him into his office where he sits down behind a big wooden desk covered with papers. He pulls a pen out from under a stack of papers. "I need to get this mess organized," he says. "Where is my receipt book?" It takes him a minute to find it and, in the process, he uncovers an old, dusty nameplate. I stare at the name spelled out on the triangular block of wood.

"Here it is," he says. "Tell me your name again, sweetheart."

"Ace," I say. "Ace Jones." He stops writing and looks at me. I look at the nameplate. MELVIN EMERSON. He puts down his pen and his eyes get cloudy.

"I thought you looked familiar," he says. "You're Essie Jones's granddaughter." It's not a question.

"I am," I say. My chest tightens up as we sit and look at each other for a minute. Finally, he gets up and comes around to where I'm standing on the other side of his desk. He sticks out a hand. "I'm

Melvin Emerson, but everyone calls me M." I shake his hand and I don't know what I want to do more—run out of there screaming or give him a big, sappy hug. "It is so nice to meet you. I thought a lot of Essie. She was very special to me." He keeps shaking my hand.

"Thank you," I say.

"You played basketball when you were in high school. You were good." Again, statements, not questions.

Yeah, and you were snaking my grandma while I was at basketball camp! I think, but don't dare say. Gramma Jones wouldn't be too proud of me for spouting off something like that. "Yes, that's me. But that was a long time ago."

"Oh, it wasn't that long ago at all," he says. "I'm sorry, but you can't pay me a dime for those flowers."

"Oh, no," I protest. "I can't do that. At least let me pay you what they cost."

"Heh, heh, heh, you're just like her. A little on the stubborn side." For some odd reason, I feel like squalling. "Okay," he says. "You can pay me what they cost."

"Thank you," I say. "How much is that?"

"Not a dime," he says, and starts to snicker. "I've had this nursery for thirty-five years, Little Ms. Jones. You bought all perennials, which multiply like crazy. You should see the garden I have out behind my house. If I didn't dig 'em up and sell 'em, they'd take over the whole property."

"Well, I have to pay you something."

"Then pay me another visit sometime and let's talk about your grandmother," he says. "How about that?"

"That's a deal," I say, and we walk out to the car, where he sees Buster Loo.

"Well, look at that little guy," he says. "Let him out and let him run around a minute. It's no fun to be cooped up in the car." I open the door and Buster Loo looks like a rodent-sized gazelle as he leaps from the passenger seat. He barrels over to M. Emerson and starts paw tricking. "Hey there, little feller," he says. "What is this, a wiener dog?"

"He's a chiweenie, actually," I say. "Part dachshund and—"

"Part Chihuahua," he says, finishing my sentence. "You're a pretty little thing, I tell you that."

I stand there, watching M. Emerson pet Buster Loo, and I feel as if my heart is about to burst. I go over and kneel down to pick him up and Buster Loo completely ignores me.

"Thank you for the flowers," I say.

"Thank you for coming by here today," he says.

After I scoop Buster Loo up and put him back in the car, I walk back to where Mr. M. Emerson is standing and give him a big hug. I'm surprised by how thin he is and I wonder how old he is.

"Have you figured out her secret yet?" he asks. My face burns with embarrassment. There's no way he could know I know about the letter. He continues. "The secret to having the most beautiful flower beds in Bugtussle?"

I breathe a sigh of relief. "No," I tell him. "I haven't."

"Barnyard," he says with an adorable grin. "Essie put barnyard in her beds, but she never would tell anyone."

"Barnyard?"

Mr. Emerson points to the cow pasture to the left of his nursery. "Barnyard," he says again.

I start laughing and can't stop. Mr. Emerson gets tickled, too.

"Can you imagine what those snooty old ladies up at the garden club would think if they knew that?" he says, still chuckling. "They would die."

"Well, I'm glad I used gloves last time I pulled weeds," I tell him, and he starts laughing again.

"Oh, Ace Jones, you're just like your grandmother," he says. "Please come back here and see me real soon."

"I'll be hanging out here all the time now, Mr. Emerson."

"I'd like that," he says. "And please, call me M."

As soon as I pull out onto the highway, I start squalling and I'm not even sure why. Buster Loo gets upset because I'm upset, so I get myself under control and try to keep my composure for the rest of the trip home. When we get there, Buster Loo hops out of the car and makes a beeline for the gate. I open it for him, then go back to the car and unload the flowers I got for my yard. I load a few things from the garage into my car, then go inside and grab a Diet Mountain Dew from the fridge. I walk back outside and look at the flower beds. "Barnyard," I say. "I cannot wait to tell Birdie Ross about the barnyard." I run back inside and grab my phone, then get in the car and drive over to Lilly's. When I pull up in her driveway, I dig my eyedrops out of the console and, after putting a few drops in my eyes, I rub some of the liquid around my eyes so they won't look red and puffy. I walk around the back door and when Lilly opens it, I see that she's been crying, too.

Basket cases, I think. *We're all just a bunch of fucking basket cases.*

"What are you doing?" she asks. She has a tissue in her hand.

"Get dressed and come outside," I say. "I need you to tell me where you want these flowers."

"What flowers?" she sniffles.

"Your flowers."

Between my ten gallons of monkey grass and the free flowers from Mr. M. Emerson, Lilly—who actually gets down and digs in the dirt with me—and I transform the area around her house from something pitiful and scary to something pleasantly pretty.

"I have another surprise for you," I tell her before getting up and walking back to my car. I pop the trunk and get out a hedge trimmer along with a ten-ton bright orange power cord.

"What in the hell do you plan on doing with that thing besides getting electrocuted to death?"

"Plug me up and stand back," I tell her.

"Don't worry," she says. "I'll stand way back. Should I go ahead and call 911 or wait for you to actually cut into something vital?"

"Go ahead and give 'em fair warning," I tell her, and laugh my evil, wicked, crazy laugh that always cracks her up. "Just kidding," I say. I crank up the hedge trimmer and look over to where she's standing, looking at me like I'm deranged. "Steer clear, my dear, and observe a professional at work." Unbeknownst to her, I did a practice round at my house the other day, so I know exactly how to operate the hedge trimmer. At least I think I do. After ten minutes of trimming and retrimming, I shut the machine off and stand back to survey my progress.

"That looks so much better," she says.

"Everything looks better after a good trim," I say. "Shrubs, bushes, the muff."

"You just get crazier every day, don't you?" she says, laughing.

"I try. Now, here, help me move this cord, and I'm going to carve a serpent out of those hedges over there."

"Are you sure you can do that?"

"No, but I'd like to try." She gives me a wary look that makes me laugh. "Maybe later?" She shakes her head. "No? Okay, then." I finish trimming Lilly's shrubs and hedges, then help her bag up the trimmings in one of my superbig garbage bags.

"Wow, Ace, this looks great." She looks at me. "How much do I owe you for those flowers?"

"Well, the flowers were free."

"How did you get the flowers for free? Did you steal them or are you sacking the flower salesman?"

"Actually, I think Gramma Jones was sacking the flower salesman."

Lilly's jaw drops at that. "Are you kidding me?"

"Nope," I say. "His name is M. Emerson. He owns the nursery. He and Gramma Jones were, uh, friends."

"I have to hear all about this."

"I can't talk about it today. Maybe tomorrow."

"Tomorrow then," she says. "What are you doing tonight?"

"Sitting on the damned couch. Drinking beer and eating pizza topped with aspirin and ibuprofen. I can hardly move."

"You should sit on my couch and do that. The least you can do is let me buy you some pizza."

"Can we watch *Saturday Night Live*?"

"Absolutely! I'll make us some blue coconut margaritas!"

"You know I don't drink that shit!" I say, laughing. "I'll go home, get a shower, and then BYO—some of my own beer."

"Okay, let me know when you're on your way back and I'll call in the pizza."

"Okay."

I go home and kick my shoes off at the back door. I go inside, take a long, hot shower, and throw on some clean cutoff jogging pants and an old T-shirt. Then I grab Buster Loo and head back over to Lilly's where I hang out for the rest of the night and wonder why Tate Jackson hasn't called me yet.

◇◇

37

Another week passes during which I do not hear from Tate Jackson, and I think every single day about quitting my job as a permanent substitute teacher. On Friday, I go to Chloe's office during my off period and tell her that we need to talk.

"What's going on?" she says when I sit down.

"First of all, it's the end of the year, so why am I having to work so much? Where are all of these teachers going? What's the deal?"

"There have been a lot of meetings at the county office this week," she says. "Everyone should be back next week and you can go back to getting paid to sit in the teachers' lounge and gossip with Stacey Dewberry." She smiles.

"Thank you," I say, smiling back. "That's just what I wanted to hear."

"I can't believe you hung in here this long, Ace. Honestly, I didn't think you'd last two weeks as a sub. And a little birdie told me that the board was pleased that Cameron is hosting the art fair, and I have a feeling that she's going to do great on her evaluation next week."

"Don't forget Stacey Dewberry," I say. "She's more popular than I am now."

"And that," she says, laughing. "You've really done a great job with everything and I am very impressed and I very much appreciate it."

"I am pretty awesome," I say.

"Yeah, you're so awesome that we've had a lot of parents calling in bragging on what a nice sub you are."

"Really?"

"Of course not! Rest assured, we have had some calls about you, but I took it upon myself to deal with those."

"Bring me up here next time you get a call about me," I tell her. "I'd be more than happy to talk to some of these kids' parents."

"I know you would," she says. "This is why I handle it. Some of the parents don't have good sense."

"Complaints my ass," I whisper. "I've got some complaints for them!"

"Okay, so the pain is almost over and you've survived. You only have two weeks left."

"How's the wedding planning?"

"Great," she says. "Everything is in order. Jalena is decorating and catering, and I can hardly wait."

"That's fantastic," I say. Technically, our conversation has come to a close, but I just keep standing there.

"Got something else on your mind?"

"I haven't heard from your favorite soon-to-be brother-in-law."

"Oh Lord," she says. "I've been meaning to tell you—"

"Wait, let me guess. He's dating a twenty-year-old bean pole."

"No! Nothing like that," she says. "He's been out of town on business. He's kind of a workaholic."

"You think he's screwing anybody while he's gone?"

"Ace, really?" she says. "What else?"

"Your shower is all taken care of. I think you'll be most pleased."

"Jalena Flores is an amazing woman," Chloe says. "She's made this whole wedding-planning thing so easy for me. I was expecting to be more stressed out."

Jalena and her business model. "She's got a plan and it appears to work." The bell rings and she stands up.

"Oh, Ace, did you get that e-mail about the bridesmaids' dresses?" I tell her that I did. "So what did you think?"

"Well, as for me personally, I would've preferred some kind of sea foam green silk dress with, like, some lace on the chest and maybe some mauve-colored puffy sleeves that would, of course, have to be sewn on by hand." She starts laughing. "But a nice chocolate and white polka-dot sundress from Macy's isn't so bad."

"Do you like the dresses? I mean, I loved the polka-dots. And I didn't want it to be too formal or too boring, and I thought maybe the dress would be something you could wear again."

"I love it," I say as we step out of the office and into the bustling commons area. "And they actually had my size, which was a huge relief. I've already ordered it and the shoes you recommended."

"Good deal."

"So when do we find out if we're having a boy or a girl?"

"At my next visit," she says, looking around nervously.

"So what are you hoping for? And don't say, 'Just a healthy baby and we don't care either way,' because I know you want a healthy baby. Everybody wants a healthy baby."

"I'd like to have a girl," she says, her voice barely above a whisper.

"Maybe you'll have triplets!" I say, just to get her wound up.

"Ace Jones, you better shut your mouth!"

I go back to my classroom and try to think positive, but by the time the bell rings at the end of the day, I'm just barely hanging on to what's left of my sanity. I go down to D Hall, stop and chat with Lilly for a minute, then peek in on Cameron.

"How's it going?" I ask her.

"Great, but I have a few questions. Could you come in for a second?"

"Sure." I glance out the window at the buses in the parking lot. "Is it just me or does it take them longer to leave on Friday?" I ask Cameron.

"I don't think it's just you."

I think I'll talk to Stacey Dewberry about that. See if she can pass out some Dr Pepper to all the other drivers and maybe speed things up a little bit.

When I get home Friday afternoon, I'm exhausted. I call Pier Six as soon as I get there and then munch on pizza off and on for the rest of the night.

On Saturday, I get up early and go outside to plant all of my new flowers. Saturday afternoon, Stacey calls and says she's going out with Cameron and Freddie. I decide to pass because I'm exhausted. Lilly comes over and we talk about the who/when/where of our trip to North Carolina next weekend.

"Have you started packing yet?" she asks me.

"No, but I've been putting a lot of thought into what I plan to take with me." She laughs because she knows better.

On Tuesday, Lilly goes to the garden club meeting with me, not because she wants to, but because I guilt-trip her into it. Gloria and Birdie are most pleased to see her and she actually ends up enjoying herself. During the "snack time," I tell Birdie about the barnyard and she almost busts a gut laughing.

"She never would tell me," Birdie says. "I pestered her all the time. Boy howdy, I'd love to get up at that podium and give a presentation on that," she says, snickering. "Wouldn't you just love to see the look on some of these ol' coots' faces?" She pokes me in the arm. "You could help me."

"What are y'all laughing about?" Gloria asks.

"Oh, nothing," Birdie says, and picks up her punch cup.

On the way back to her house, Lilly and I rehash our travel plans. She's all packed up and ready. I'm not sure where my suitcase is, but I don't tell her that.

On Wednesday, I help Coach Hatter, Coach Wills, Coach Keeley and Cameron Becker get everything set up for the art fair. When I tell Cameron I'm going to be out of town, she freaks out— just like I knew she would—but I assure her she can and will do an excellent job. Hatter and Wills agree to hang around for the event in case she needs some emotional support.

Thursday, I have a full day of subbing and wonder if Chloe was just kidding about this week being easier. Must be more meetings at the county office. Thursday night is a mad dash to pack. Jalena has agreed to dog-sit for me while we're in North Carolina, so I pack Buster Loo's travel bag, too. It's after midnight when I finally get everything together.

I get up early Friday morning, take Buster Loo to Jalena's, then head to school, where I have yet another full day of subbing. I don't see Lilly all day and we text back and forth, ironing out our plans for the afternoon. Our plane leaves at five thirty, so we pretty much have to dash out the door as soon as the bell rings. Chloe meets us in the foyer and tells us to have a safe trip. I follow Lilly to her house after school, and when I see how much luggage she has crammed into her car, I suggest that I get my two carry-on-sized bags and ride with her, because our plane would be long gone by the time we moved all her crap into my car.

38

<><><><><><><><><><><><><><><><><><><><><><><><><><><><><><><><><><><><><><>

When we get to the airport, I run to get a luggage cart onto which we load Lilly's two gigantic suitcases, a carry-on, and two purse-sized bags.

"I'll check my carry-on and then carry one of these bags for you," I tell her as we hustle across the walkway to the terminal. "You're the reason airlines started charging extra for baggage—you realize that, right?"

"Ace, I have to have my stuff," she says.

As we stand in line to check our bags, I look at the time on my phone. We have thirty minutes until our plane starts boarding.

"Why didn't we leave school early?" I ask her.

"You said we'd have plenty of time," she says.

"Never listen to me about how to get somewhere on time, Lilly," I say. "You of all people should know better than that."

We check in, get our boarding passes, and the lady behind the counter smiles and says, "You ladies might want to hurry."

Instead of screaming, *No shit, lady!* I smile and say, "Yes, ma'am. We will." Lilly and I hustle toward the security checkpoint.

Even though I spent an hour studying the "what not to pack in a carry-on," the wicked bitch on the other side of the scanner unzips my suitcase and starts pawing around in it.

"Try not to sling anything out if you can help it," I tell her.

"If you didn't have nonpermissible items in your suitcase, I wouldn't be doing this," she snaps.

"Really, because it looks like you're enjoying it."

"I assure you I am not."

"You know what, I believe you because you don't look like the kind of person who enjoys much of anything," I say. If I had six hours instead of sixteen minutes to get to my gate, I still wouldn't be in the mood for this crap.

"Ace, just shut up and let her do her job."

"Lilly, I'm trying to have a pleasant conversation."

The TSA woman finally finds what she's looking for—an orange Fossil bag with my makeup in it. She digs around in there until she pulls out a tube of ChapStick. She looks at me like I just got picked up for slinging drugs in the bathroom of an elementary school. "Not permitted. What would you like for me to do with this?"

"How about handing it to me and letting me stick it in my pocket?"

"Ace, my God, shut up." Lilly looks at the TSA officer. "Just throw it away. We'll buy another tube."

"I'm not speaking to you, ma'am, so could you please step aside if you've been cleared?"

Lilly looks at me. "I'm so sorry. Ace, say whatever you want."

"What's the problem with the ChapStick? I read online where it's permitted."

"It's not permitted."

"It was the last time I flew."

"Where was that?"

"Pensacola to Key West."

"I didn't hear you say Memphis."

"That's because I didn't say Memphis," I say. "I flew from Pensacola to Key West and back with that same damned tube of Chap-Stick."

"Don't use profanity with me or I'll have you detained."

"Detained? What am I? A terrorist?"

"Are you?"

I lean over my suitcase and whisper, "Do I look like a fucking terrorist?" I point to the tube in her hand. "That's fucking Chap-Stick! Why don't you just give it back to me?" I really don't care about the ChapStick; I just want to antagonize her as much as she's antagonizing me.

"It's not permitted and I'm issuing you a final warning on the language."

I reach out and touch my suitcase.

"Do not touch the bag, ma'am."

I touch it again. "Oops," I say. "I didn't mean to do that."

"Do not touch this bag!" she roars.

I touch the bag again. "That was an accident." I look at her and smile. "I'm so sorry."

"Security!" she yells, and everyone stops what they're doing and stares at me.

"Security!" I yell. "I'm being harassed!"

Security officers swarm around me and one orders me to step inside the small office area.

"What's the problem here?" the man behind the desk asks the TSA officer.

"She's harassing me, and I feel that I'm being discriminated against because of my intelligence level," I say.

The man looks at me. "What?"

"This woman attempted to engage me in idiotic conversation and I'm psychologically incapable of reacting in a positive way to such foolishness and we had an altercation after she threatened to throw away my ChapStick."

"ChapStick is not permitted!" the TSA officer roars.

"This is ridiculous," the security officer says. He looks at the TSA officer. "Throw that in the trash."

"I wouldn't do that if I were you," I say. "You better check your own Web site first."

"Would you both step over here, please?" he says.

The security officer taps on his computer, turns the screen around, and looks at the TSA officer. "Looks to me like you need to familiarize yourself with the updated list."

"But you said—" she stammers.

"No buts. Give her back the ChapStick!"

She hands me the tube and I smile. "Who wins? I win?"

"Ma'am, collect your things and get to your gate!"

"Yes, sir!"

I walk over to my suitcase, which she promptly zips up.

"Can I touch it now?" I ask.

"Yes."

"Are you sure?"

She stares at me. I pop open the ChapStick and make a show of rubbing it all over my lips.

"I know you liked touching my panties," I say.

She turns and stomps away. I look back at the security officer who jerks a thumb toward the gate departure area.

"Move it!"

"Yes, sir," I say, and slip my ChapStick into my pocket.

It's pouring when we touch down in Fayetteville, North Carolina. Lilly rents a car and then asks me to drive to the hotel. She's texting Dax and not saying much.

When we get to the hotel, she says, "I was hoping I'd get to see him tonight, but I'm not gonna get to."

"Why not?"

"Who knows? His commanding officer told them they would have some time tonight, but apparently someone changed their mind and no one will be allowed to see their families until tomorrow."

"That sucks," I say.

"It all does," she replies. "I'm going to take a shower."

Saturday, we drive to Fort Bragg, and I pull in to the Visitor Center where I go in and get a pass. I also get a map and I don't know if I was holding it upside down or sideways or what, but we spend the next thirty minutes on a scenic ride around the post. Finally, we find Dax's barracks and I sit in the car while she walks up to see him. They come down a few minutes later and I hardly recognize him. He's wearing ACUs and looks taller and skinnier than last time I saw him.

"Thank y'all so much for coming," he says. He appears to be nervous and in a hurry.

"He's got a few hours, so he's going to ride back to the hotel with us," Lilly says.

Awkward!

When we get back to the hotel, I tell them I'm walking a few blocks down to the mall where I plan to get a much-needed pedicure and see a movie. Neither protests and I kind of wish I hadn't come, but Lilly didn't want to come alone and who can blame her? I make myself scarce all afternoon and get pretty bored walking around the mall, but I don't care. This is as close as I've ever come to doing something for my country. Lilly sends me a text and tells me Dax has to head back to Fort Bragg, so I hustle to the hotel and do the driving. Lilly doesn't want any supper, but she does accept my offer to stop by the liquor store for a bottle of wine, which we drink out of disposable coffee cups when we get back to the room.

When I get up on Sunday, Lilly is not only awake, but dressed and ready.

"I couldn't sleep," she says.

We pack up, check out of the hotel, and drive to Fort Bragg. After taking three wrong turns and driving down a one-way street the wrong way, I finally get to the correct parking lot. While she fusses with her hair, I look around at all the cars and people. We get out and walk toward an old theater where Dax is waiting at the bottom of the steps. He hugs Lilly, then hugs me, and we stand there and talk about silly stuff for a while—like the fact that I can't follow directions highlighted on a map.

"I have to go in there for a minute," Dax says. "Y'all wanna come in and sit with me?"

"Of course we do," Lilly says. We follow him inside and sit down in chairs that look like movie theater seats, only they're made of wood. We listen to two men give short speeches; then everyone claps and we're dismissed. I didn't hear a word of either speech because I couldn't stop looking around and thinking about all of these people, all of these families.

We walk back outside and stand around for a few more minutes. I gawk at the buses and try not to stare at the people milling around. I see little kids, big kids, and teenagers. Moms, dads, and grandparents who are easily identifiable thanks to their personalized patriotic shirts. Girlfriends, boyfriends, just friends. I spot a small group of soldiers off to the side, talking and carrying on. I guess their loved ones have already come and gone. Or maybe, like Dax's parents, their loved ones didn't have the money to make the trip. I take a step away from Dax and Lilly as the crowd draws in close to the buses.

Dax unzips his backpack and pulls something out. It's a small gift-wrapped box with a bow that's all mushed up. Dax fiddles with the ribbon for a second, then hands the box to Lilly. My heart pounds as she pulls the wrapping paper off, piece by piece. I'm fully expecting to see him drop to one knee and I want to turn away because I can't handle the stress of watching. When Lilly opens it, she hugs him and then kisses him and I'm dying to know what's in there. She gives the box back to Dax and turns around. She picks up her hair. He takes the necklace from the box and fastens it around Lilly's neck. My heart feels as if it's about to explode as I stand there and wonder if Lilly thought it was an engagement ring, too.

Somehow, everyone knows it's time for the soldiers to get on the buses. I go over and give Dax a hug, stealing a quick glance at the pendant on Lilly's new necklace. It's a blue circle with two silver A's side by side. Dax sees me looking at it. He points to a patch stuck on the right arm of his uniform.

"That's my unit," he says. "I asked her not to take if off until I get home."

"That is so sweet, Dax," I tell him, and give him one more hug. "We all love you so much. Take care of yourself and hurry home."

I turn around and almost trip over a stroller. I apologize to a lovely young lady who can't be more than twenty-five. She's wearing red high heels. Standing beside her is a man, dressed just like Dax, who is holding a baby. The back of the baby's shirt says DADDY'S LITTLE SOLDIER. He's saying good-bye. I walk away from them and go back to the theater. I find the restroom, which smells just like my old elementary school, and lock myself inside a stall where I squall for the next few minutes. *Get it together!* I think. Not a soul out there was crying and carrying on like this. I get eyedrops out of my purse, apply a fresh coat of powder and lip gloss, and go back outside just in time to see the convoy of buses pull out of the parking lot. People stop waving. Up until this very moment, I didn't fully understand how much is required, not just of the men and women in uniform, but of the people left standing on the grass. I hold my breath until I get my emotions back under control. I see a woman wearing a shirt that says HOME OF THE FREE BECAUSE OF THE BRAVE. I look around and wish so many people didn't have to be so brave. Especially those little ones. I look for Lilly but don't see her. Everyone starts walking toward the parking lot. I finally spot her and walk over to where she is.

"Where did you go?" she asks.

"To the restroom," I tell her. "I'm sorry. I was having a melt-down."

"Yeah, these things are hard if you're not used to it."

"How in the hell does someone get used to it?" I ask, watching a mom load three kids into a Tahoe.

"It's just a part of life in the military," she says. "Certainly not the most pleasant part."

"No shit," I say. "I don't see how people do it. Every person in the country should have to see this at least once."

"People don't have to see it to appreciate it."

"Not just appreciate," I say, "but understand. Really understand. Like I do now."

When we get in the car, Lilly is quiet. She's sniffling when we drive out past the gates. By the time we get to the airport, she's squalling like a baby. I pull over in a bus parking lot and pat her on the back until she calms down.

"I'm sorry," she says. "I wasn't going to cry. I promised him I wasn't going to cry."

"Lilly, that's ridiculous. I squalled my eyes out in a stinkin' 1970s-model bathroom stall and I'm just here for moral support. It's okay."

She stops crying and starts wiping her eyes. I drive around to the rental car booth, and we make our way inside the airport. Lilly and I come within an inch of getting arrested at the security check after she tells the rude woman picking through her purse to just throw the whole fucking bag away and stop talking to her and my ChapStick finally ends up in a TSA trash can.

39

When I get up on Monday, I wish I'd listened to Lilly and taken the day off. I'm thirty minutes late and Chloe tells me that she's sorry, but I've got a full day of subbing today. I go to the lounge and I'm power guzzling Diet Mountain Dew when Freddie Dublin walks in.

"Oh my," he says. "Did we sleep late and do our hair in the car?"

"Ha-ha, Freddie," I say. "You're a funny guy."

"How's your friend?"

"Lilly? I'm sure she's doing much better than me because she had the good sense to take the day off." I look at him. "Are you leaving us?"

"Ah, I haven't heard back from them yet, but my grandfather is head of the school board, so I'm sure I'll get the job." He doesn't look happy.

"Lucky you." Now I wish I had gone out with them last Saturday night.

"Not hardly," he snorts. "It's my mother's father, and he's one of these people with an extraordinarily oppressive personality. That's why I came all the way up here. To show him that I didn't need his heavy hand to help me get a job. I think he had a lot to do with my parents' splitting up."

"Why go back down there, then?"

"Well, my mom—" He stops talking and sighs. "She needs me. Dad ended up with the cats. She never liked the damned cats anyway, so I don't know why she cared or put up such a fight about it, but nonetheless, I can't leave her down there all alone with her father trying to tell her what she should do every second of every day. It's a mess. My dad always protected her from her father, but I guess a person can only take so much. My mom is weak. I can't blame my dad for having an affair, but I also can't leave my mother to her own devices."

"I'm so sorry, Freddie."

"And then there's Jarrett," he says with a sigh. "He lives in New Orleans. Like everything else in my life these past few months, that's gone to shit, too." He looks at me. "I really don't have a choice. I have to go home and try to, I don't know, put my world back together with the pieces I have left. I didn't realize how bad things had gotten until I went home last week. But, on the bright side, Jarrett agreed to have dinner and we're talking again, so all is not completely lost."

I walk over and give him a hug. "I'm going to miss you so much." I revel in his fragrance. "This place won't be the same."

He looks around the lounge. "I'm sure it will be." He smiles. "You'll have to come down and visit. We're right across the bay from the Beau Rivage."

"We have to go out before you leave."

"Well, I'm leaving this Friday, so I don't know if I'll have time, but seriously, you guys will have to drive down and visit. It's an easy drive." Dang! That happened fast. Or maybe it didn't.

"Do you need some help packing up?"

"Oh no. My dear sweet mother has already made arrangements with a moving company. All I have to do is pack my clothes."

The bell rings, but we just stand there.

"Here we go," he says with a sigh. "Another day, another dollar."

"Right."

When I get home Monday night, I get a call from Birdie Ross.

"You busy tomorrow night?"

"Nothing planned," I say. Please don't let this be about a blind date.

"Why don't you and Lilly come over to my house. I'll make you supper."

"Okay," I say, wondering what she has up her sleeve.

"There're some things I need to tell you," Birdie says. "And Lilly."

"Will Mrs. Peacock be there?"

"No, she's out of town at the very present moment. Gone to see one of her grandsons graduate. Can you be here by six?"

"Sure," I say. "Thank you."

I call Lilly and she doesn't answer. I send her a text and tell her that we've been invited to Birdie Ross's house for dinner tomorrow night. Two hours later, she sends back an "OK."

Tuesday, I don't have to cover any classes and Stacey Dewberry doesn't, either, so we hang out in the library. I ask her about throwing Freddie a going away party. She says she's already suggested that and he's not interested.

"He's kind of depressed," she says.

"Yeah, I gathered."

Stacey and I go to Freddie's classroom seventh period, but he's not there. We find him in the lounge, with his feet propped up on the table. His socks are brown with white polka dots. We talk him into going out to eat in Memphis on Thursday night before he leaves on Friday.

When I get home from school, I take Buster Loo for a walk, then take a shower and get dressed. I go get Lilly and we drive over to Birdie Ross's house.

She lives in a ranch-style home on the edge of town, and her yard is thick with blooming trees and flowers. When we pull up, she walks out her front door and greets us on her flagstone sidewalk.

"Hope you girls are hungry!" she says.

"I stay that way," I say.

"I can see that," Birdie says, and starts laughing.

"Ouch," I whisper to Lilly, who starts laughing, too.

Lilly and I sit down at Birdie's large oak table, and she serves us chicken potpie with homemade bread.

"Oh, this is so good," Lilly says, helping herself to another slice of bread.

"Thanks," Birdie barks. "I don't cook like this much anymore."

"Well, call us anytime you do," I say. Birdie smiles as we continue to brag on her chicken potpie.

When we finish, she instructs us to take our glasses and go to the living room. Her couches are worn and comfortable. I look around at all the pictures of her kids and grandkids and imagine many happy times have been had in this room over the years.

40

◇◇

"**I** know you want to know who she planted that tree for, and since you met M., well, you know he's not dead. So there's something I think I need to share, but I can't tell you the who without telling you the why."

"Okay," I say. Lilly takes a sip of her tea.

"I really can't believe that, between the two of you, you haven't figured this one out." I look at Lilly and she looks at me. I shrug.

"I've been doing most of the detective work myself," I say.

"Well, you know Essie was one of my very best friends. We went to school together, went to the same church, and got married around the same time. And we had kids the same age." Birdie looks at me and shakes her head. "I can't even imagine what she went through after Jake passed. He was such a fine boy." *Don't cry,* I tell myself. *Don't do it!* "Essie loved her family and her life as much as a woman could, and when Jake moved to Nashville, it damned near killed her, but not for long because then you were born." She points to me and I can feel my nose stinging. *Don't do it!* "Oh, you were the light of her world, but I don't have to tell you that, now do I?" I shake my head and look at the floor. "When her son moved back home, she couldn't have been more excited if she'd won the lottery because, in her eyes, she had, because not only was her son coming home, but that little fireball Gracie was coming, too!"

"Gracie?" Lilly asks.

"That's what Essie called her when she was a little bitty thing, but she stopped when she moved down here because—"

"I wanted to be called Ace because that's what Daddy always called me."

"So after the accident, a part of her went away and—" Birdie stops to get a tissue. "A part of all of us went away."

Lilly starts sniffling and Birdie hands her a tissue. *Do. Not. Cry!* I bite my lip and look up at Birdie who is blowing her nose. *Don't do it!*

"I remember both of y'all at the hospital," Birdie says, and her voice cracks. "Y'all did such a good job of being big girls that day." She pulls open the drawer of the end table, pulls out a piece of paper, and starts fanning herself. "Oh God," she says. "This is why it's taken so long, because I knew it would be so hard." Tears are welling up in my eyes and I reach for a tissue. Birdie looks at Lilly. "Lilly, do you remember your grandfather being there that day?" she asks.

"Yes, he rode with us to the hospital that morning."

"And he held Gramma's hand when they told her," I say, feeling sick. "I try real hard not to think about it that much."

"It's okay to hurt sometimes," Birdie says. "It's a part of life. Not my favorite part, but what will be will be." She dabs at her nose. "We were all good friends and, Lilly, your grandma had gone on, what, a year or two before?"

"Two years," Lilly says. "She'd been gone for two years, and I was so mad at the world until—" She stops and looks at the ceiling. "Until that day when I realized how much I had to be thankful for." She looks at me. "I'm sorry. I don't think I ever told you that."

I pat her on the back and she scoots over next to me on the couch.

"Well, when you gals started back to school that year, Essie and Eddie Lane went out on a few dates."

"What?" I say, and look at Lilly. "Did you know that?"

"No," she says, smiling. "Did you?"

"Of course not."

Birdie giggles. "That's the thing about teenagers—they think they're the only ones who can sneak around."

"Why wouldn't they have told us?" Lilly asks.

"They were just going on friendly dates—at first anyway—and y'all were both so busy with school, Ace playing ball and Lilly cheerleading. Did you not ever notice they always sat together at the ball games?"

"Well, now that I think about it," I say.

"Yeah, things heated up rather quickly for them."

"Ew!" Lilly says, and I just start laughing.

"See, now that's why they didn't tell you," Birdie says matter-of-factly.

"Point made," I say, still giggling. I look at Lilly, who just shakes her head and smiles.

"Anyway, as you girls started having more and more of a social

life, they started seeing more and more of each other and things got
a little hot and heavy."

"Hot and heavy?" Lilly asks. "What does that mean?"

"Do we even want to know?" I say, feeling sure I don't.

"They fell in love," Birdie says, and we both gasp. She gets up
and walks over to the bookshelves built into the far wall of her
living room. She pulls out a few boxes, then pulls out a few more.

"Now where in the shit—," she says, opening another box.
"Here we go!" She brings a large envelope over and puts it on the
coffee table.

"Your grandmother asked me to keep these many, many years
ago." Birdie opens the envelope and pulls out a stack of cards and
photographs and a navy blue picture folder. She opens it and turns
it around for us to see.

Lilly and I gasp again when we see my grandmother in a ruffled
red dancing dress and her grandfather in a tuxedo, standing in a
semi-embrace and smiling like the world was their oyster.

"They went on a cruise?" I say. "When did they do that?"

"Oh, c'mon girls," Birdie teases. "Think a minute."

"Spring break," Lilly says. "We were always gone during spring
break."

Birdie shows us several more pictures, and we laugh and talk
and have ourselves a big time looking at our grandparents having
so much fun.

"Look at this!" Lilly exclaims. "They went everywhere together!"

"Hey, I have a picture of her here," I say, holding up one of her
with the Smoky Mountains in the background.

"I have one of Papaw there, too," Lilly says. "They went together?"

We look at Birdie. "A bunch of us went together," Birdie says. She flips over another picture. "Look here—this was my boyfriend at the time. We went up there and hiked and went white water rafting. It was great fun."

"Where did y'all stay?" Lilly asks.

"We rented cabins," Birdie says. "Oh, here's another one of the cruise. They loved that."

"So, did they, uh . . . ," Lilly asks, and I give her a don't-go-there look.

"Have sex?" Birdie chirps. "Well, of course they did and lots of it."

"Oh gross!" Lilly exclaims.

"Too much information," I say.

"And y'all wonder why they didn't tell you," Birdie chides. "You young-uns, always thinking life ends at a certain age." Birdie looks at the pictures. "I remember when I was eighteen, I thought thirty was old. Then at thirty, I thought forty-five was ancient. Then I turned fifty and realized that I was just getting started." She looks back down at the picture of her and her boyfriend. "We're all just kids. Kids with wrinkles."

"What happened to your boyfriend?" Lilly asks.

"I married him," she said proudly. "He was my fifth husband. Passed away five years ago."

"Fifth?" Lilly asks.

"Oh, my romantic life is another story for another day," she says, picking up the stack of cards.

"Well, I would love to hear all about it," I say, and Lilly nods in agreement.

"Me, too!"

"We'll put that on our list of things to do, but right now, let's talk about this." She picks up a stack of cards and looks at me. "These are from Eddie to your grandmother. Some of them are from M."

"Who's M.?" Lilly asks, like she's offended.

"M. kept Essie company after Eddie passed away," Birdie says. "That was almost more than she could stand. M. was the only person who could make her laugh in the months after that." She looks at me. "But they weren't romantic for a long, long time."

"So the tree in the yard was for Eddie?"

"What tree?" Lilly asks, and I explain that to her.

"Why didn't you just ask me? I would've recognized the date."

"I just, I don't know, didn't get around to it," I say.

"It broke my heart when Essie passed, but a part of me thought, 'Thank you, God, that she doesn't have to lose anyone else.'" Birdie picks up another few cards and looks at Lilly. "And these are from Essie to your grandfather." She looks back and forth between us. "Your mother gave them to me to keep with the rest. She knew about their romance, knew that y'all didn't know, and wanted to keep everything together for a day like today."

"The keeper," I say, smiling at Birdie.

"The keeper," she says. "Would y'all like to have these?"

Lilly is crying again and I'm tearing up and we both just sit there like knots on a log.

"Should we take them?" I ask. "It kind of feels like it might be too personal."

"Might do you both some good," Birdie says. "There was a reason you dug your grandmother's old gardening book out of the attic," she tells me. "That tells me you're ready for these to be yours now." She sighs. "You were so young when your grandmother lost your grandfather. It took a long time for her to decide she could love another man. Unlike me. It only takes me a minute," she says, and Lilly and I start giggling. "Essie was a nervous wreck when she realized she was falling for Eddie. I told her, 'Essie, you don't have to open your heart just yet, but you might want to open your mind to the possibility you could fall in love again.'" Birdie looks at me. "And do you know what she told me?"

"What?" I say, dabbing my eyes.

"She said, 'Birdie, I'll think about opening my mind a little more if you'll think about opening your legs a little less.'" And Lilly and I get hysterical.

"So that's where you get that sassy mouth from," Lilly says with a laugh.

"Your gramma was a wise woman. A strong and wise woman." She stands up. "Okay, girls, party's over. I've got a poker game to get to." She hands a few cards and pictures to Lilly and a few cards and pictures to me.

"Poker? Are you serious?"

"Yes, down at the nursing home. I go down there every Thursday night and flirt with all the men that play." She shoos us toward the front door.

"Life don't stop till they drop you in the dirt, girls." She gives each of us a big hug. "I expect to see you both at the next garden club meeting," she says. Lilly and I assure her that we will be there. We say our good-byes, take our stuff, and head out to the car. When we get on the road, Lilly and I gag and laugh about the fact that our grandparents had sex with each other. On a cruise ship, no less. I drop her off, happy to see her so happy, and hopeful the next twelve months pass by quickly for her.

Riding home, I think about my grandmother. I thought she was perfect, always so nice and so pleasant. She never looked depressed and she never complained about what she didn't have. She never spoke ill of anyone; she was just a continuous fount of kindness and patience. She was a survivor. And she never gave up on love.

I think about her at my age, what her life was like. She started every morning with a hot cup of coffee and a smile. She had a wise saying for literally every situation. I think about the box in the attic. The box of photo albums. Photo albums that she always wanted to sit down and look at with me but never did because I was always too busy and never had time. Now I know I have to look at that box. And I'll just have to guess what she would've told me about the pictures inside.

When I get home, I go up in the attic and pull down the box of photo albums. I look at the pictures of her and my grandpa when they were young, my daddy as a boy, her backyard when it was nothing but a few patches of grass and an old wooden fence.

Her garden was her story that she pampered and pruned and made beautiful. Her pictures are her past, people whom she loved and cherished. I look through the next album and see pictures from my parents' wedding day, pictures of me as a baby. Pictures from Christmas, Thanksgiving, birthdays. I feel a wave of guilt for leaving these stories in the attic so long, collecting dust. I decide to stop letting it all hurt me and start embracing the love that I had and being thankful for the time that I had it. I take the pictures from the cruise and decide to go buy some frames because they should be on display, along with several others.

I decide to start living like Gramma. Being careful, pampering and pruning, caring deeply so my life can be beautiful like hers was. I go back upstairs and bring down one more box—the one I packed all of her jewelry in. Scarves, pins, and long beaded necklaces. A pair of old sunglasses.

I walk into her bedroom and put the box on the dresser. I slip on a long set of pearls, then pick up a scarf. I wrap it around my head just like she always used to do when she was going out to buy groceries. I pick up her pins, looking at each one before placing it back in the box. I slip on her sunglasses and smile at myself in the mirror. I'm proud of how much I look like her. I think about her, my mom, and my dad, and say a little prayer for them to help me get to where I need to be in this life.

◇◇

41

I spend Saturday morning running around all over town picking up Chloe's shower gifts from all the places she's registered. I call Jalena to see how she's doing, and she tells me that she had everything ready last night. I rush home, apologize to Buster Loo for not taking him on a walk, get ready as fast as I can and head over to Jalena's. Lilly and Stacey are already there. Cameron pulls in behind me, and they help me get the presents from my car to the party room, which Jalena has made look like a wedding shower wonderland.

"This is amazing," I say when I walk in.

"I know. I said the same thing," Lilly says.

Soon, the place is packed and Chloe arrives looking like an angel in a flowing cream-colored dress. Jalena has to bring in extra chairs, but we eventually get everyone a seat. Chloe opens what seems like a thousand wonderful gifts and Jalena unveils the appetizer buffet that is out of this world. I step over and help place spoons.

"Everything but hot wings," I whisper to Jalena, and she giggles.

Jalena and I stay busy keeping the buffet stocked, and I see her run out of several things I wanted to try.

"Aw, man," I tell her on one of our trips back to the kitchen. "I really wanted some of those pinwheels."

"I've got a few samples saved for us," she says with a smile. "Plus one of each of the petits fours."

"Yee haw!" I say.

When the shower is over and people start drifting out, several folks want to see Jalena's diner, so she takes them in there and shows them around, kitchen and everything. The flamingos turn out to be a hot topic of conversation, and several people tell me that they'd like for me to do a mural in their homes. A few take my number and tell me they'll be in touch.

When we're alone in the diner, Jalena narrows her eyes and says, "Did I not tell you that you were going to need some business cards? I have a diner to run here, and I won't have time to be stopping everything I'm doing to say, 'Well, that nut Ace Jones did that, but she won't have a business card made, so here's her telephone number.'"

"You know, I had actually decided to do just that. I was going to ask you which printer you use."

"Good."

"Can I just say that I think you're going to have a very successful place here because you are one bossy boss woman."

"I take that as a compliment," she says and disappears into the kitchen.

"Hey, Chloe," I say when I walk back into the party room, "would you like for us to start loading up your vehicle?"

"Oh no," she says. "J.J.'s nieces are about to get started on that."

We stand around and chitchat for a while longer and I go back three times to get some more of Jalena's pineapple cheese dip. We pester Chloe about a bachelorette party until she snaps at us and we finally hush.

"Chloe, ever the party animal," Lilly whispers, and I start giggling.

"Are y'all talking about me?" Chloe asks, coming up between us and putting an arm around each of our shoulders.

"Not us," I say.

"Never," Lilly says.

Later that afternoon, after everything has been cleaned up and put away, I sit down with Jalena and, while we're snacking on the samples she saved for us, talk about how well everything went.

"I don't like showers," I tell her, "but this one was great."

"It's because it was for someone you care about."

"Maybe that's it."

"People sure are nice around here," she says. "You used to tell me all kinds of stories about people from Bugtussle, Mississippi, and I have yet to meet anyone like those you used to talk about."

"Yeah, things have changed. They're not so bad."

"I don't think the people have changed. I think you have."

"Maybe so," I say, getting depressed because all of this wisdom is making me feel old.

When I get home, Lilly is sitting in my driveway.

"What are you doing?" I ask.

"Will you go with me to the pet store?"

"For what? Are you buying a bird?"

"No," she says. She looks like she wants to say something else, but she doesn't.

"Okay, what's up? What's going on?"

"I have a kitten."

"A what?"

"A kitten."

"What in the world are you doing with a kitten? Where did you get it? And where is it right now?"

"Well, I was really missing Dax the other day and I had to get out of the house, so I went and got a cherry limeade and was just riding around on some back roads when I passed a sign that said, 'Kittens in need of love. Free to a good home.' And I thought, 'I have a good home,' so I stopped and got one. Okay, I'm lying. I got two. Because there were only two left and they were playing and stuff and I didn't want to separate them. So, yeah, I have two kittens. One is solid gray and the other is black-and-white."

"Have you fed them?"

"Oh yeah, the people were really nice. They packed up a little care package and gave me everything the kittens would need for the first few days."

"Yeah, I bet they were really nice," I say, and I'm being sarcastic. I can't believe Lilly stopped at a stranger's house and picked up two kittens.

"They were." She starts digging around in her purse. "I have this list. Will you go with me?"

"Of course." I poke her in the arm. "So can Uncle Buster Loo cat-sit sometime?"

"Well, I'll have to have some references first. I can't leave my sweet little kitties with just anyone."

"Let me go inside and get him. He would be so upset if I went to the pet store without him." I go in and get his leash and take my dog to the pet store and help Lilly stock up on supplies for her new cats, what's-its-name and what's-its name. When we get back to her house, I ease Buster Loo into the cat introduction. One paws at his wagging tail and the other rolls around near his front paws. Buster Loo just stands there, looking stressed out. Then he flops down on his side and starts playing with the kittens.

"Okay, he can kitten-sit," Lilly says.

"I still can't believe you brought these home with you," I tell her.

"I love them," she says. "They make me laugh and they're sweet."

42

◇◇

Sunday afternoon, the wedding goes off without a hitch, and it's a beautiful and wonderful ceremony. Tate walks me down the aisle and I can't help myself from thinking, What if this were us? We have pictures made immediately afterward and the photographer is bossy and impatient. In all the hustle and bustle, I haven't been able to say more than two words to Tate. He's been very nice but seems distracted. As we wait our turn for pictures, I ask him how he's doing.

"Oh, I'm fine," he says. "I've been meaning to call you." *Of course you have,* I think. I believe him because I want to. "And I'm nervous about making this goddamned toast."

I don't have time to reply because the photographer starts barking at us and we have to step up and smile for the camera. After the cutting of the cake, the dancing of the first dance, and the toasting of the toast, of which I think Tate does a stellar job, Chloe says that she has to get away from the crowd for a minute. I follow her down to a sitting area by the lake where we're soon joined by Lilly, Stacey, and Cameron. Jalena shows up a minute later with a bottle of champagne, a handful of plastic wine cups, and a bottle of water for Chloe. She pops the top and I hold the cups while she pours. We all sit back and relax, sipping and chatting and watching the lake change color as the sky gets darker.

"What a lovely evening," Cameron says. "Chloe, you looked like a dream up there."

"Thank you, Cameron," she says.

"I tell y'all what," Stacey says. "Chloe did look like a dream, but this girdle I decided to wear is a nightmare."

"Go take it off," Lilly says. "Get comfy."

"I might later," Stacey says. "I spotted a good-looking man in line at the punch bowl, so I'll just tough it out in case I see him again."

"So where are y'all going on your honeymoon?" Jalena asks.

"J.J. won't tell me," Chloe says. She narrows her eyes. "Do y'all know?"

"Like he would tell us anything he didn't want you to know," Lilly says with a snort.

"That is true," I say.

"Okay, so I have an announcement," Stacey says. "I'm going to summer school. Roll Tide."

"Summer school?" I say. "So they took your classes?"

"Yes, they did," Stacey says. "I'm moving to Tuscaloosa. Gonna graduate in August. My counselor over there is so nice. I have to take two online classes instead of one, but that's okay because I'll still be getting paid and my counselor introduced me to a financial person and I'm getting a big grant. Gonna be able to pay my car off again for like the tenth time."

"Stacey, that is great! Why didn't you tell us?"

"Well, all of this was going on and I didn't want to take any of Chloe's thunder away. But I'm pretty excited."

Chloe gets up to hug her. "Congratulations, Stacey. I'll do everything I can to make sure you have a job here next year." She looks at me. "What am I going to do about subs in A and B Hall?"

"Hell if I know," I say.

"Have you heard from Dax?" Chloe asks Lilly.

"Yes, they're getting settled into their FOB or something like that. He claims that he's fine and that he's not in imminent danger. I try to believe him."

"He'll be home before you know it," I tell her.

"I can't wait."

"So," I say, turning to Chloe, "what are we going to name this baby?"

"Oh, I can't even think about that right now," Chloe says.

"Yeah, Ace, let her enjoy her shotgun wedding for a minute," Lilly says. "Dang!"

"Thank you for that, Lilly," Chloe says, getting up. "Girls, I need a hug."

We get up and take turns hugging Chloe, the most beautiful bride I've even seen.

Cameron and Stacey start bragging on Jalena's catering skills, and Chloe reaches out and takes my hand and then Lilly's. "Y'all are the best friends a girl could ask for," she says. "I love you both so much." I hear a rustle in the bushes and turn to see J. J. Jackson coming down the hill. "J.J.?" Chloe says. "Why didn't you just come down the steps?"

"Your aunt Clareen is camped out up there, and I had to find a way around that, if you know what I mean." He wipes his face with the back of his hand. "She's always kissing me and she slobbers." Chloe starts giggling.

"Sorry."

"Hey, that ring looks good on your hand there, Sheriff Jackson," I say.

"Yeah," he says, looking at it. "I think so, too."

"J.J.," someone yells. "Is that you?"

We all look up to see Chloe's aunt Clareen teetering at the top of the steps. "How did you get down there?"

"I think Aunt Clareen has a crush on you," Lilly says.

"I need to get back up there," Chloe says. She looks at J.J. "I just needed a minute."

"Who doesn't?" he says, glancing up at Aunt Clareen. "Oh yeah, and Ace," he says, glancing my way, "Tate is looking for you."

Lilly, Stacey, and Jalena start making all kinds of racket about that, and I smooth my skirt and say, "Well, who am I to keep the gentleman waiting?"

I find Tate leaning on the outdoor bar, which is made of stone and facing the lake. He's talking big-game hunting with the bartender when I ease up and order a beer. As the bartender works the keg, Tate Jackson and I make small talk.

"So what about that aunt Clareen," I ask, nodding toward J.J. who has just been approached by the silver-haired little lady. We watch as she elbows her way in between J.J. and Chloe.

"Oh, she's a hot one," he says. "Looks like the type to wear cheetah print underwear."

The bartender has a hearty laugh at that while I stand there and smile. I try to bat my lashes like Lilly always used to do.

"I brought my boat up," he says, like I know all about his boat. "You wanna ride up to Pickwick with me tomorrow?"

"I'd love to," I say. And just like that, I have a date that I'm actually looking forward to. We wander away from the crowd, talking about nothing in particular, but it's the most interesting conversation I've ever had in my life. When the band starts to play, he looks at me and smiles. He puts down his cup and takes mine from my hand.

"Ace Jones, would you like to dance?"

"I would love to." Do I dare to dream again?

After two songs, the music stops and I'm sorely disappointed that I have to step away from Tate Jackson. Chloe appears on the bandstand with a microphone.

"Can I have all the single ladies over here, please?" she says sweetly. "It's time to toss the bouquet!"

"You better go," Tate says, and I roll my eyes. "C'mon, be a sport." He pats me on the butt and I almost pass out.

"Okay, okay!" I say, thinking I should probably get away from him before I start humping his leg. I join the crowd of single ladies where Lilly is standing, looking like she wants to die, and Stacey Dewberry is hunched over like a lineman waiting for the snap.

"I hate this part," Lilly whispers.

"Oh, it's not so bad," I say. "Just pay attention and don't let it hit you in the face."

"You probably want to catch it, don't you?" she says with a coy smile.

"Hey, shut up," I tell her.

"Ready?" Chloe says, and turns around. "Three . . . Two . . . One . . ."

Chloe launches that bouquet of red roses over her head, and it flies through the air as gracefully as if it had butterfly wings. And then it begins to come down closer, closer, and closer. I see Stacey reaching for it, but the bouquet soars just out of her reach. It's coming right for me! Roses facing upward, the ideal position for a perfect catch. I put my hands up and my heart begins to pound. That bouquet is almost . . . almost . . . almost in my hand. I'm already planning my wedding to Tate Jackson when Aunt Clareen lunges in front of me, a streak of silver, and latches onto those flowers like a leech.

"I got it!" she yells. "I got it!" And then she trips and tumbles down on the deck. As she rolls around with her legs in the air, which I can't help but think she does on purpose, I see that she is indeed wearing cheetah print panties. Now what are the chances of that?

"Safe!" Stacey Dewberry shouts, extending both of her arms like an umpire. And then we all rush to make sure Aunt Clareen is okay. Thank goodness and not surprisingly, she is. When the ruckus is over, I walk back to where Tate is standing. He's holding two fresh drinks.

"Intercepted," he says with a smile. He hands me a beer.

"That it was," I tell him. "Thank you."

"I was right about the underwear."

"That you were," I say. "Makes me wonder how you knew."

"Oh, you don't wanna know that," he says. "But I will say that those cheetah print granny panties are almost the sexiest thing I've seen all night." He drapes his arm around my shoulder and my cheeks starts to burn. "Almost."

"And who is this fine young man?" I hear someone say. I turn to see Gloria and Birdie, both dressed to the nines and wearing wide-brimmed hats. Birdie isn't conspicuous in her assessment of Tate Jackson.

"This is J.J.'s older brother, Tate," I say, trying hard to stop blushing.

"Oh, I remember you," Gloria says with a smile. "It's been years. How are you?"

"Looks to me like he's just fine," Birdie says, and then commandeers the conversation, peppering Tate with questions until he's summoned by the groomsmen who, no doubt, have some mischief planned for the bride and groom.

"I see you've found a man who likes to dance," Gloria says.

"It seems that I might have," I tell her.

"I'd be on that feller like white on rice," Birdie says, checking out his backside as he walks away.

"Or something like that," Gloria says.

"Definitely something like that," I say. Who knows? I just might have to go buy myself some cheetah print granny panties.

ACKNOWLEDGMENTS

◇◇

Many thanks to Danielle Perez, Heidi Richter, Susanna Einstein, and Molly Reece.

Special thanks to Brandon, whose patience seriously knows no bounds. Thanks also to Wanda and Barry Raines and to Brent Raines. Very special thanks to Mandi Harris, Molly Crow Wren, Sandy Jackson, Melisa George DePew, Jenny Miller Little, Edgar Serrano, Michael Raines, and Aaron Raines. Thanks also to Tina Houston, Amy Gahagan Moore, Frances Yates, Mary Jo Smith, and Rhonda Lauderdale Goodwin.

A great big thanks to Cat Blanco of the Book Exchange in Marietta, Georgia; SIBA (Southern Independent Booksellers); Kathy Patrick and the Pulpwood Queens of Jefferson, Texas; the BB Queens and Lemuria Books of Jackson, Mississippi; Emily Gatlin of Reed's Gum Tree Books in Tupelo, Mississippi; Lyn Roberts of Square Books in Oxford, Mississippi; Everyone at Thacker Mountain Radio; Tom Warner of Litchfield Books in Pawleys Island, South Carolina; B. Bronson Tabler of Tabler Law in Tupelo; Scott Thompson and the Ole Miss Alumni Association; Sue Ellen Babb of Eaton, Babb, & Smith; Brant Sappington of the *Banner-Independent/Daily Corinthian*; Sam and Karen Grisham of the *Prentiss County Progress*; Cyrus Webb of *Conversations LIVE!*; Stephanie Bell Flynt of *Midday Mississippi*; and Karen Brown of *Mississippi Edition*.

Thanks to Mary Kay Andrews for sitting at a table next to me at the Mistletoe Market in Marietta, Georgia. That was a great day! Thanks also to Janis Owens and Michael Morris for the kind and encouraging words. And thanks to Jennifer Ingram Gillman for always being so nice.

Stephanie McAfee was born in Mississippi, and she now lives in Florida with her husband, young son, and chiweenie dog.

CONNECT ONLINE

www.stephanie-mcafee.com
www.facebook.com/booksbystephanie
www.twitter.com/stephaniemcafee

Read on for an excerpt from the book that first
introduced Ace Jones!

DIARY OF A MAD FAT GIRL

Available now from New American Library

A ll of my bags are packed and I'm ready to go. If I had some white shoe polish, I'd do like we did in the nineties and scribble "Panama City Beach or BUST" on my back windshield.

Spring break is finally here, and for the next week I'm a free woman. No students to teach, no projects to grade, no paintbrushes to wash, and, best of all, no bitchy Catherine Hilliard riding my ass like a fat lady on a Rascal.

I'm sick of her and I'm tired of my job and I need a vacation worse than Nancy Grace needs a chill pill. I wish we were leaving tonight. I squeeze a lime into my beer and head out the back door with Señor Buster Loo Bluefeather hot on my heels. While Buster Loo does speedy-dog crazy eights around my flower beds, I flip on the multicolored Christmas lights, settle into my overstuffed lounger, and start daydreaming about white sandy beaches, piña coladas, and hot men in their twenties.

My phone dings and in the two seconds it takes me to look at the caller ID, I wish a thousand times it was a text from Mason McKenzie.

I wouldn't give Mason McKenzie the time of day, and he knows I wouldn't give him the time of day, so it's ridiculous for me to wish that he would text me, but I still do. Every day.

Of course, it's not a text from him; it's one from my best bud, Lilly Lane.

Call me. I will never understand the logic of sending a text message that says *call me.* Lilly Lane is one of those cellular addicts who could carry on a full-fledged six-hour conversation via text message. Sometimes her messages are so encrypted with abbreviations that I just pick up the phone and call her, which pisses her off. She's like, "I'm texting you. Why are you calling me? If I wanted to talk to you I would've texted you and told you to call me."

Oh, so I'm the idiot? Right.

Then I'll say something like, "Hey, heifer, save it for someone who cares and tell me what the hell that last message was supposed to mean. I'm not Robert Langdon. I can't decode symbols, and if you don't want me to call you, then send me some crap I can read."

But I can read this particular text, so I prop my feet up on the lounger and give her a call.

"Ace," she says, and it sounds like she's been running, but she's not a runner. "I'm not gonna be able to go to Florida."

"What are you talking about?" I'm confused because spending spring break in Panama City Beach is one of our most sacred and beloved traditions.

"I can't go." She pauses. "I'm sorry."

"Sorry?" I yell into the phone. "Are you freakin' kidding me?

We're supposed to leave in the morning, Lilly! Like nine hours from *right now*! What the hell do you mean you can't go?"

Silence. And then it dawns on me.

For the past five months, Lilly has been seeing someone on the sly whom she will only call the Gentleman, and she's more tight-lipped about him than she was about the time she got a hot dog stuck in her cooter. I think he might be a gross old man with tons of money. I thought about making a list of all the gross old men with money in Bugtussle, Mississippi, and doing some investigating, but I'm not much of a list maker so I probably won't do that.

Lilly, however, is a habitual list maker, and I don't mean the kind of list you take to the grocery store. She can go on a date with some dude and by the time they get to wherever they're going, she's got a list a mile long of everything she thinks is wrong with him.

I know this because she keeps me updated with a continuous stream of text messages. Not because I ask for them. I don't.

After the date is over, she documents the potential suitor's faults on a piece or twelve of loose-leaf paper that she then files in an al-phabetized four-inch binder. I mean, God forbid she should forget one small thing about a guy nice enough to take her goofy ass out to dinner and a movie.

Some poor fellows hang around long enough to have their list read to them, and the truly unfortunate get shown the actual note-book. Imagine a man looking at a hot pink polka-dot binder stuffed with more than ten years' worth of documentation on Mr. Wrong.

The Gentleman, however, does not have a list. As far as I can tell, he has only an itinerary. Since the commencement of her su-persecret affair, Lilly has been to New York City, Los Angeles, and Chicago. In the past five months. *Five months*. And she returns from these escapades with truckloads of fancy shopping bags stuffed with extravagant gifts.

I guess she may have finally found her Mr. Right, although I have serious doubts about how right a man can be who requires such secrecy concerning his identity.

Further adding to the mystery of this surreptitious affair is that new BMW convertible she started driving about two months ago. I mean, she has some serious cash stacked up from her days as a lingerie model, but I don't think she'd blow every last dime of it on an automobile. Maybe the Gentleman is a rich man in a midlife crisis. The car is red.

Whoever he is, I hate his guts because I'm relatively certain he's the reason my vacation plans are now in ruins.

"Oh," I say, "I get it. It's him. The Gentleman's got bigger plans for you, Lilly? A little trip down to the Redneck Riviera doesn't quite measure up to your new travel standards? I can't buy you six pairs of Manolos and three Gucci purses so I'm out now?"

"Ace, please don't do this to me. Just get someone else to go."

"Don't do this to *you*?" I yell and feel my face getting hot. "How about you don't do this to *me*? And who the hell am I gonna get who can pack up and be ready on such short notice? I'm the only person I know who is that spontaneous."

"You could ask Chloe," she peeps.

"Oh, yeah, that's a great idea. I mean, Chloe can't go to the mailbox without being watched, so I'm sure her *adoring* husband would just love it if she took off on a trip to the beach, where she might actually get to relax and enjoy herself. Why can't I come up with ideas that brilliant?"

Chloe is married to Richard Stacks the Fourth, a prominent pillar in the Bugtussle community who puts a ridiculous amount of effort into his let-me-get-that-door-for-you-my-sweet-beloved-wife-because-I'm-a-perfect-husband persona. In private, however, he talks to Chloe like she's a shit-eating dog. It's been almost six years since that midnight phone call when Chloe quietly confided the details of her first verbal beat-down. She'd only been married a few months and asked me what I thought she should do. I told her to pack her crap and come to my house. She wouldn't. I told her to go in the bedroom and superglue his lips together. She wouldn't do that, either. I was about to ask her why she called me if she wasn't going to heed my stellar advice, when it dawned on me that what she needed was for me to clarify who the bad guy was and that it wasn't her. Soon afterward, Richard had an affair with a skanky-ass local woman who, upon discovering that she was not his only mistress, told everyone in town that he was a gruesome nymphomaniac with a weird, tiny penis. His other concubines obviously didn't mind sharing, and rumors of his sexual deviance became standard fodder for the rumor mill.

Chloe refuses to acknowledge his infidelity, shrouds herself in ignorance, and stands by in silence as he flaunts his gentlemanly manners in public. She won't entertain even the slightest suggestion of divorce and ignores me when I say he should be killed. I've offered to do just that on several occasions and come up with some good places to hide the body, but she is determined to make her marriage work because she thinks he can change. I think the only thing that can change a man like that is a bullet to the skull. Just like that Dixie Chicks song about Earl.

Silence on the line.

"Well," I say.

"Well," she says, "I think you should go on down to Florida and try to patch things up with Mason. You could stop by Pelican Cove on your way to Panama City and y'all could have lunch or something, and maybe work things out. When I was at the bar the other day, Ethan Allen told me he isn't seeing anybody and, honestly, Ace, I think he's just waiting on you to come back."

"Is that what you think?" I ask, heavy on the sarcasm. "How could you even bring that up right now? What the hell is wrong with you?" I pause. "But, hey. I do appreciate you sitting up at the bar and hashing out my personal business with Ethan Allen."

"Ace, I'm sorry but you're the only person who doesn't see what a big mistake you made when you packed up and left Mason in one of your famous fits of rage! No one else will say anything to you because they know you'll go ape-shit crazy—"

"Just stop right there," I interrupt. My face is on fire. "You have got to be out of your damn mind. I mean, first you text me and tell me to call you, which is stupid as shit by the way; then you tell me you're ditching our trip, a trip we take every year and you *know* how much it means to me; *then* you suggest I take along our poor little friend who can't go to the grocery store without being interrogated; and after *all of that*, you have the balls to start babbling about how I need to patch things up with Mason. Seriously, Lilly?" I take a deep breath. "Is that what you really think, or is this you worming your way out of our trip because your Gentleman came calling?"

She doesn't say anything.

"You have to admit it's a pretty convenient thing to bring up now."

Silence still.

"You're gonna ditch me the night before we leave?" I ask, making a legitimate effort to be calm. "Really?"

"I'm sorry. It's not what you think. I have to be somewhere."

"You have to be somewhere?" The sarcasm oozes like lava. "Where exactly do you have to be, Lilly?"

"Paris." She sounds like a baby frog trying to find its first croak.

"Really, I thought you quit modeling because you found the lifestyle too exhausting and unfulfilling, and that's why you came home and started teaching school. Am I right about that?"

"You know I'm not modeling."

"Just trying to be a better French teacher?"

"Ace, please—"

"Spring break in Paris," I say with the sarcasm full throttle. "Well, don't that just take the cake? I'm so happy for you and your Gentleman friend. Or should I say your Gentleman financier." I put a little French twist on the last syllable. For effect.

"You are so cruel," she whispers.

"Oh, yeah, I'm definitely the bitch in this relationship." I pause. "Tell me who it is, Lilly. Who is this Gentleman whose plans for you are so much more important than the plans you made with me?"

"You know I can't tell you who he is."

"Why not? I really wanna know."

"Ace, stop, please. I can't."

"Right. Of course you can't. I mean, why would you? It's not like you can trust me. It's not like we're best friends, good ol' BFFs forever, right, Lilly?"

"Ace," she says, and I can tell she's about to start her stupid squalling like she always does when she needs people to come around to her way of thinking.

"Okay, well. Hey! Thanks for waiting until Friday afternoon to let me know. Have a great trip and I'll talk to you later—" I pause. "Or maybe not."

She starts mumbling a string of apologies and I push the red button on my phone with enough pressure to drive a nail through wood. Sorry means as much to me as that dog turd Buster Loo just dropped in that dwarf yaupon holly.